THE PURE

THE PURE

JAKE SIMONS

Polygon

First published in Great Britain in 2012
by Polygon, an imprint of Birlinn Ltd

Birlinn Ltd
West Newington House
10 Newington Road
Edinburgh
EH9 1QS

www.polygonbooks.co.uk

ISBN   978 1 84697 226 3
eBook ISBN 978 0 85790 170 5

British Library Cataloguing-in-Publication Data
A catalogue record for this book is available on request from the British Library.

Typeset by IDSUK (Data Connection) Ltd
Printed and bound by ScandBook AB

Behold, the guardian of Israel neither slumbers nor sleeps.
Psalms 121:4

1

Uzi – that was his name now, Uzi – had been living quietly in London for three months. He had no strong feelings about it. It was just a place. As grimy, as vicious, as glittering as any other city. The main thing was, it wasn't Israel. It wasn't home. That was why he came. His old self – the man who was part of a band of brothers – had become nothing but a distant memory. And he could barely even remember the man who had once had a wife, a child. Now he was alone, renting a dive in a poor part of North London. An ugly flat – he felt he deserved ugliness. And it was a good place for business.

It was Saturday night, and he needed to forget everything. The voice in his head, for once, didn't complain. He got on a bus, and as it fumed through the traffic, the sun began to die. The evening was humid, gripping the passengers with suffocating fingers. He didn't get a seat, didn't want one. Automatically he became invisible, became alert, turning his back to the staircase, watching the other passengers. There: three teenagers, stoned, on the back seat. A man standing three paces away, carrying a backpack, with callouses on the knuckles of his right hand – a fighter. Behind him a pair of pickpockets, though tonight they weren't on the job. All these things he saw, he couldn't ignore them. And there was more. He could tell you the make and model of the mobile devices that everyone on the bus was carrying. He could tell you which passengers were suffering from ill health, and what their complaints might be. He could tell you their nationalities, their temperaments, their heights and weights; he could tell you which ones had noticed him. He could tell you which of these people, under pressure, would buckle, and who would hold out till the end. None of this was psychic. It was his training.

Darkness fell, and the crawling traffic groaned. When he arrived in Camden, hunger was making him light-headed and he couldn't stop thinking about sex. He didn't want to eat in a proper restaurant. There was a stall he knew that sold falafel, but he didn't want a falafel. He wanted something English. He had studied English culture – and American culture, Canadian culture, Persian culture, Russian culture, and the rest – he knew what people ate. He remembered a café that looked pretty cheap. A greasy spoon. He ate bacon and eggs, with chips and a slice of bread. £2.99 all in. He went back into the street and lit a cigarette.

He hung around for a while, smoking, feeling like some sort of ghost. He regularly went to clubs round here, ones filled with teenagers, places where he, as a forty-year-old man, would never fit in. Somehow it was easier around young people; at least he had a reason to be an outsider. On the streets, it was more complicated.

He moved to check his weapon, but there was no gun there. Just an empty space. Of course. He smiled bitterly to himself; he just couldn't get used to this. He shrugged, flicked his cigarette into the gutter. Then he entered the Underworld.

The music was loud, it lodged itself in the ribcage. He pushed his way to the bar. The place was busy, groups of teenagers – children, really. Back home, everything would be shrouded in a thick fug, like teargas. He liked it that way, felt less exposed. But in England smoking had been banned.

At the bar he quickly drank two beers and a shot of vodka. Then, grabbing a bottle of Heineken by the neck, he pushed his way into the crowd. He needed a release. A group of teenagers were in the middle of the dance floor, grinding. In the corner, the pushers. Nearer at hand some older revellers, professionals who, he thought, worked in the finance sector, their hands describing arabesques in the air. And several feet away was a large group of people of all nationalities, foreign students perhaps, bopping around self-consciously. He had a sudden sense of dread, as if something terrible was about to happen. What could he do? He danced.

Someone jostled him from behind, but he could tell from the nature of the contact that it was accidental. A new song started playing, with a repetitive high-pitched shriek. There – six paces away – a girl he recognised. Short and slim, with a dead-straight fringe that brushed her eyelashes. Hungarian, he thought. They had spoken drunkenly a few nights ago, but he couldn't remember her name. She had thrown herself at him then, and he had rejected her. But tonight, in the whirling coloured light, she looked like a different person. She was dancing woodenly, self-consciously, and there was something compelling about that. He caught her eye and she looked away, then recognised him and smiled. He moved closer and danced to the rhythm in his ribcage.

'Hi,' he said, his voice fighting with the music. She shrugged, and he put his mouth close to her ear.

'Hi,' he repeated.

'Hi,' she shouted back, and giggled.

'What's your name?' he yelled. 'I can't remember. Sorry.' The girl said something he didn't understand. He bent his head low and she repeated it into his ear; she did not flinch as he rested his hand in the small of her back.

'Mariska.'

'What?'

'Mary.'

Uzi smiled and moved away. She held his gaze, then looked down coyly. He understood – and was surprised – that there were no hard feelings. Last time they met the chemistry had been there, but she was simply too young, too innocent, too pathetic. It had all been too easy; she had been absurdly impressed by his world-weariness, his stories – all lies – about being a Russian presidential bodyguard. There had been no thrill of the chase.

He thought back to the stories he had told her last time, trying to remember the details. Russian presidential bodyguard – yes, that's right. But for how many years? Eight? Ten? Had he admitted to having a son? Had he told her his age? He was getting sloppy. But it was instinctive, this lying. Even now that he had left his old life behind, he found it hard to tell the truth. His training had left an indelible mark, had changed him irreversibly. It had been designed to. For weeks on end they had assigned him a false identity, sent him out into the streets, then arrested and interrogated him, violently; then immediately assigned him another false identity and released him on to the streets again, only to pick him up and interrogate him once more; and then there would be another identity, and another, all day, for days at a time, until he had become used to maintaining a cover story, and withstanding torture for it. Until he had almost forgotten who he really was. Until his true identity had become irrelevant.

Mary, he recalled, was studying English in the mornings, working in a Hungarian café in Soho in the afternoons. She had been heading to some sort of music festival, he couldn't remember which one. She was nothing but a child, really. They existed in different worlds.

A new song was playing now, something with a thudding bassline, blow after blow to the heart. Again he felt that something bad was going to happen, but he shrugged it off. A mist grew in his abdomen, rising to his chest, intensifying, and suddenly he wanted this girl. Fuck the consequences. He began to dance like a beast in a mating ritual. A few of the other students glanced at them, then turned away. Mary smiled in the blue-and-pink light and he found himself smiling back, feeling physical pain at her innocence. It was like looking into a mirror and seeing everything he was not.

He was sweating. As one song bled into another and the dance floor became more and more crowded, they became separated from Mary's friends, who were now dancing in a knot twenty-five paces away. Uzi was jostled – again, he thought, by accident. He bent low to speak to her.

'How was the festival?'

She looked at him, wide-eyed, and smiled. Now their bodies were touching.

'You remember.'

'Of course I remember.'

'Festival was very nice.'

'Good.'

'Your name – it was Tommy?'

'That's right, Tommy.'

'From Russia?'

'That's right. Tomislav.'

She laughed, and suddenly, in the flashes of coloured light, she looked powerful, like a goddess. Uzi felt sick. For a while they continued to dance, and he felt the blood rush into his neck and drain again.

'Shall we get a drink?' she shouted. He nodded. She took his hand and led him from the dance floor. The lamb leading the wolf, he thought, the rabbit leading the huntsman.

The air was close and humid as they left the club and stepped into the blackness of the night. Mary was tottering slightly, holding on to his arm, and he was supporting her, his hand straying on to her hip. He was drunk; nothing concerned him any more. Sweat had plastered his hair to his forehead. One-handed, he lit a cigarette and the girl laughed at something. She had her phone out – it had cartoon stickers on it – and she was trying to send a text. Under the orange light from the streetlamps, she looked different. Her hair wasn't as good as it had looked in the club, she had a few spots on her cheeks, and she wasn't slim at all. She was bordering on plump, and that inflamed him. She was visceral. She waited while he finished his cigarette, then they got into a cab.

'Give the driver your address,' he said. 'We're going to your place.' On the way he started to kiss her, which she accepted unhesitatingly, and then he began to knead her breast, pushing himself against her thigh, smelling her. She made not a sound, accepting everything, instigating nothing. He no longer cared where he was, or what he was doing, or to whom. It was just him, the taxi, and a girl; nobody to see or hear him.

By the time they arrived at her house, a long, grey dawn was beginning to break, fat with moisture. Uzi paid the driver and followed her to the door. He didn't know where they were, he hadn't been paying attention. He felt intoxicated, reckless. She fumbled with her keys in the lock.

'I have night-blindness,' she said, 'sorry.' Unusual phrase, he thought. In a strange way, it moved him. And then they were in, through a brief catacomb of hallways. She was shushing him; he had his hand on her hip, he wouldn't take it off. His other hand was straying unconsciously to the empty space where his weapon used to be.

She led him into a studio flat, incredibly neat, with a faint smell of plastic, like a toyshop. She offered him a drink but already he was on her. He pushed her to her knees, pressed her face into his crotch. He had a feeling like clouds of insects were being released from his brain, and he gasped and looked up at the ceiling. She made no sound, just knelt there, face in his crotch, not moving. Her phone was still in her hand. He pulled off his shirt and fell awkwardly on the floor, pulling her on top of him. The bed seemed untouchable, so neat, he couldn't do it. He rolled over, trapping her beneath his body. He wanted her to moan, to make a sound, to respond to him. But she did not; she simply accepted him, whatever he did, and it made him want to fuck her desperately. One of her hands slid over his shoulder, and she did not flinch when she felt the cyst on the bridge of the muscle. He clawed off his jeans but before he could penetrate her he came, and they lay side-by-side on the floor, the white mess strung over them both. For a while there was silence as the dawn began to hum outside.

He thought about a battle from the Lebanon campaign. His unit had been staging a counter-attack. As they advanced he had felt so strong, part of a single massive being made up of air support, artillery, tanks, infantry units. Invincible. Together they had gone forward, firing like madmen, scattering the enemy, reducing them to the occasional flash of machine-gunfire here, a cluster of isolated silhouettes there, a solitary truck trying to turn back. But then – suddenly – at a certain indefinable moment, the tables had turned. He had looked around and found that he was alone. His comrades, his air support, were nowhere to be seen; his artillery was nothing but a distant thudding. And all around him swarmed the enemy. The flashes of machine-gunfire had become unified, coordinated, and figures with RPGs were materialising everywhere. He had stumbled backwards, firing as he retreated, ducking to protect his head, his eyes, his jaw, as bullets whined past him, kicked up the ground beneath his feet. On his own, disorientated, dislocated from his system of support. No comrades, no back-up, no security. This was how he felt now, with a girl he didn't know, in a flat somewhere in London.

'Let's get into bed,' she said quietly.

'I'm fine here.'

He looked at her, this woman from another world, this person he did not know, her breasts splayed and her pubic hair a dark tangle against his leg. He wondered who her parents were, if she had siblings. He wondered how her life would end. Her fringe was at all angles, she looked ridiculous. Her hand was cupped over his belly, and like this she fell asleep.

When her breath was deep and rasping, Uzi got silently to his feet. He felt sorry. He went into the bathroom and washed among the unfamiliar toiletries, all covered in Hungarian script. The toyshop smell was stronger in here, perhaps it was shampoo or something. For a long time he looked at himself in the mirror, his grizzled, worry-furrowed face with its sandpaper smudge on his cheeks and neck. He examined the cyst on his shoulder. Outside, cars went past. Israel felt a million miles away. The alcohol lay hot and heavy in his belly and his mouth was dry. He tiptoed back into the bedroom. The girl had turned on to her front, hugging herself like a child. She must have been quite drunk, to fall asleep like that. She was lying in front of the door. He thought of moving her into the bed, but he didn't want to wake her. He gathered his sweaty clothes together, dressed and nudged the door open. She sighed and rolled over, but didn't wake up. He kissed her gently, incongruously. Then he slipped out the door, through the catacombs and into the street.

The morning was humid and he did not feel as if he was entering fresh air. Already he was out of breath. He took a cigarette out of his pocket but he didn't light it. His fists were clenched. He still had a feeling of dread, and almost turned back to check that the girl was still alive. His vision became blurred; he could feel tears on his cheeks. Then his inner ear began to itch, and he knew the voice was coming.

'Good morning, Uzi. How are you today?' it said – as always – in Hebrew. He thought it had a sarcastic tone. He thought it knew what he had just been doing, thinking, feeling. But he couldn't be sure.

'Leave me alone,' he replied. 'Just leave me alone for today, all right?'

The voice fell silent. It could be respectful like that.

The sky was swollen and dark with humidity. Uzi pulled out his phone – no missed calls, no texts, and the time was 07:23. How stupid he had been to think it was possible to forget. London. Another day. He saw a bus stop and walked to it. Rain began to fall.

2

When Uzi awoke later that day, it was 2.30 p.m. and his body was covered in bars of sunshine. His ears were still ringing from the music in the club, and he had a hangover. There had been no nightmares – a pleasant surprise. He fumbled on the floor beside the bed, found his cigarettes. He smoked one, screwed it into the porcupine of butts in the ashtray. Then he turned on to his side and tried to go back to sleep. But his ear began to itch again.

'Uzi, we need to talk.'

'I told you, leave me alone,' he mumbled into his pillow. 'I haven't got the strength to talk to you today.'

There was a pause while the voice considered.

'OK. I'll give you a break. For today. Believe in yourself.'

The Kol was always saying that. The itch in his ear gradually receded and he breathed a sigh of relief. Many people had these kind of voices, he knew they did. But for him, he thought, it was different. He only ever had one voice, and he called it the Kol, meaning 'the voice' in Hebrew. Always it was female, very calm, almost hypnotic, with a metallic edge. Occasionally the voice sounded older, usually when things got serious. Sometimes it would leave him alone for days on end, leave him to his own devices. Other times it would be with him all day, nagging from his left ear like a fishwife. Often it made him crazy. And it always tried to make him talk back.

But the Kol had promised to leave him alone for today, and he was going to make the most of it. He pressed his head into the pillow as deeply as he could and allowed his mind to drift. It didn't take long for sleep to close in on him. That was

9

when the nightmare came. He should have known it. Brussels, gleaming diplomatic Brussels. His hand stretching out before him like a pale trident. The cold slap of his palm against the girl's sternum as he shoved her with all his strength. Her face, stretched by a languid terror as she fell in slow motion backwards into the road. Her hair flicking in ropes and tendrils against the night sky as her head hit the windscreen of an oncoming Mercedes; the snarl of acceleration, the flinging body, the black bonnet. The single cry. His first kill for the Office.

At 3.30 p.m. he awoke again, and this time he got up. Music was playing somewhere, he could hear it coming through the floorboards. He took a strawberry mousse from the fridge, peeled the lid and spooned it into his mouth. Then he turned on his two televisions; they had to be used together, as one had no picture and the other had no sound. He parted the curtains and looked out into the summer's afternoon, scratching his woolly head. A group of children were clustered around a smashed bus stop, kicking a lump of concrete. He closed the curtains again, lit another cigarette. Compulsively, he placed his foot against a leg of the coffee table and nudged it, feeling the weight; heavy, too heavy for a regular table. There was no sign it had been tampered with. His 'slick' was secure.

In the bathroom, he unscrewed the showerhead and rattled it over the sink, then scraped at it a few times with a spoon. He'd read that dirty showers contain dangerous levels of mycobacterium avium, which if inhaled can rot the lungs. When satisfied, he dropped his cigarette butt sizzling in the toilet and had a cold shower. Snail-like, he slipped back into the shell of his clothes, shaking the moisture from his head.

It was hot in the flat. Something about the quality of the heat made him think back to the summers of his youth. That summer when, at the age of fourteen, he had won the national junior shooting prize, scoring 197 out of 200 with an old Shtutser rifle. His parents told everyone about it; he had been the envy of the entire Gededei Noar Ivri, the Battalion of Hebrew Youth. The beginning of an illustrious career, he thought bitterly.

The kill, the Brussels night, appeared in his mind; he blocked it out. He thought about the Hungarian girl. He had a headache. In the kitchen he swallowed an aspirin without water, then, finding the capsule still sharp in his oesophagus, filled a glass and drank. It was as if a furnace was raging inside him, and the water was turning to steam. He refilled the glass and took a key from a drawer. He was ravenous, his soul was hungry. Leaving the glass forgotten on the counter, he left the kitchen, unlocked the spare bedroom and entered.

The room was filled with an unmoving, fragrant cloud, and the windows were blacked out. He could hear the hum of his small machines. As his eyes adjusted to the gloom, a dozen wooden structures were revealed, like balsa wood wardrobes, their walls made of white sheets pinned up with thumbtacks. Concertina pipes looped lazily on to the ground and out the window. Carefully, he opened one of the boxes and dazzling light spilled out, blanching his face. He reached inside.

The plants, set amongst reflective silver sheeting, were full and supple. He inspected the leaves closely, pinching and twisting them in his fingers: the white hairs had begun to turn reddish brown, almost ready to be harvested. Their roots were threaded into a bed of pebbles, through which a mechanical pump sent bursts of chemical solution. Hydroponic cultivation. Complicated but more efficient, and no soil needed. He spent a few minutes going from box to box like a zookeeper, checking the temperature and humidity gauges, then the extractor fans and pumps. He got some chemicals from the bathroom and replenished the plastic reservoir in the corner of the room, checking that the timer was running properly. Finally he opened the airing cupboard in the corner, took out some drying trays, divided a pile of desiccated buds into eighths, and bagged them up. Casting a final eye over everything, he left the room and locked the door behind him.

He put on some aftershave, jeans and a linen jacket, turned off the televisions and went out, carrying his crop in a rucksack. Pickings would be rich tonight. One deal, one thousand pounds. But first there was the matter of that bastard Avner. He checked his phone and there was a text waiting, the first for days. It said: c u 4 ok? Reluctantly, he replied: ok.

3

When Uzi arrived at the café in Primrose Hill, Avner Golan was waiting for him, sitting at a table in the corner, nursing a latte in a glass. Uzi hated the sight of a latte in a glass. Whoever thought of a latte in a glass should be shot. He was feeling jumpy. It was dangerous to arrive at a meeting point when your contact was already there. On operations, if you arrived and your contact was there waiting, you cancelled the meeting. It was forbidden even to go to the bathroom and leave your contact at the table, for who knows what they could be doing in your absence? But he fought his instinct. This was Avner, he reminded himself, just Avner. Granted, a bastard through and through, but one of the few people that could, to some extent, be trusted.

Uzi knew that under his arms and in the centre of his back were ovals of darkness. He didn't care. He gave Avner a cursory comrade's embrace and sat down, taking out a packet of cigarettes.

'Ah, my brother. You're still wearing your old clothes,' said Avner – for some reason he was speaking in French – taking the corner of Uzi's jacket in his fingers. 'Paranoid as ever.'

Uzi snatched his jacket away. Sewn into the corners were little lead weights, making it possible to swing it open with a twist of the body and draw your weapon in a single movement. They had both perfected the movement years ago in training: swing draw, swing draw, swing draw. (The famous 'Israeli draw', where the sidearm was snatched from the holster with an empty cartridge and racked at the same time, was slower. For the Office, it had to be quick: swing draw.)

'This jacket suits me fine,' said Uzi, replying also in French. 'You're the one who won't speak on the phone. Who always wants to meet in four eyes.'

'Meet in four eyes? You're still using the jargon, my brother. It's over for you now, don't you get it? You've quit. Now you've got to let it go.'

'A man can't let go of himself. You know that.'

'A man can, Adam. A man can let go of his old self.'

'Uzi. Call me Uzi.'

'You're embarrassed to use the name your mother gave you?'

'Fuck you.'

'We can't play those games any more, I'm telling you. This is real life.'

There was a pause as they both, instinctively, scanned the room, with practised casualness.

'You look well, Avner.'

'I am well. Wish I could say the same about you.'

'You could,' said Uzi testily.

'Your French is as good as ever.'

'Yeah, thanks.'

'I thought French would be nice for today. A creative language.'

Uzi shrugged and fingered his cigarette packet. Avner's iPhone bleeped.

'Why can't you stop using these children's toys?' said Uzi. 'With you it's always Apple this, Apple that. Always the latest one.'

'I've ordered you a double espresso,' said Avner.

'Do you have a light?'

'This is England, remember?'

'Shit.'

Uzi, riled and hot, put away his cigarettes. The waitress arrived with his coffee. She was surly, beautiful, with a pencil in her hair. Uzi imagined her in an army uniform; she glanced at him and looked away. He stirred a sugar cube in, drank it in a single draught. It burned his tongue and he liked that. Steadied, he turned back to his companion.

Avner Golan had the air and physique of a paratrooper. His prominent nose and teeth, coupled with his rather narrow face, gave him a deceptive air of friendliness. He and Uzi had joined the Office in the same cohort; fifteen people were recruited every three years, if enough good candidates could be found (for each of the fifteen, five thousand had been rejected). Seven of their contemporaries had failed the final tests for one reason or another; two had been assigned to the Shiklut department, as audio intel analysts; two, Uzi and Avner, had become Katsas, operational in the field; and rumour had it that Golding, the most religious of the group, had become a Kidon – an assassin.

'We're brothers, Adam,' said Avner. 'You should come and work with me. I'm running a business now.'

'You're no longer shovelling shit for London Station?'

'Sure, I'm still doing that. But the money stinks, and I've got debts. So on the side I have a legitimate business.'

'Legitimate,' Uzi repeated sardonically. 'Sure. You've been a bastard ever since I've known you.'

'What about you? Are you still making money how I think you're making money?' asked Avner.

'Very little changes,' said Uzi, 'even when everything's different.'

'You're small fry, Adam. You've become small fry.'

'That's all I want right now. Small money. Nothing big.'

'I'll get some off you before you leave,' said Avner.

'Thirty pounds for an eighth.'

'Bullshit.' Avner dug with a long-handled spoon into the bottom of the glass and slipped some froth between his lips. 'You wouldn't ask me for money, brother.'

Uzi shrugged.

'No wonder you've still got the jacket weights,' said Avner, dismissively. 'I'm being serious. Come and work for me.'

'I already have a day job,' said Uzi.

'As what?'

'Protection operative.'

'Security guard?'

'Protection operative.'

'What's behind the front?' said Avner suspiciously.

'I told you, it's a day job. Just a day job.'

'Bullshit. Who do you guard?'

'Schools, synagogues,' said Uzi wearily. 'You know the sort of thing.'

'Like I said, security guard.'

'Like I said, protection operative.'

'Life in the fast lane.' Avner snorted, finished his coffee, and sat back. 'I don't like to see you in a mess, Adam.'

'I don't like to see you at all,' said Uzi, eating a sugar cube.

'You're like a horse,' said Avner, 'the way you eat sugar. It's like a horse.'

They fell silent. Uzi picked up his coffee cup, saw that it was empty, put it down again. He was still feeling jumpy, he needed a cigarette. Come on, Avner, he thought, enough with the small talk. But Avner wasn't ready. Not yet.

'How's that girl?' said Uzi for something to say.

'She does the job,' Avner replied. 'What about you? Getting much action?'

'Not really,' said Uzi.

'I should set you up. I know lots of girls.'

'Matchmaker, matchmaker.'

'That waitress, for example. Don't tell me you didn't notice her,' said Avner. 'She's got a reputation. She'll suck your cock. All you've got to do is walk up to her and put it in her mouth.'

'Fuck you, Avner,' said Uzi, 'you just want me to get it bitten off. I'm going outside for a smoke. Stay here if you want.'

He got up from his chair and left the café, ignoring Avner's remarks. Once in the street he felt a desperate anger arise from nowhere. Whatever Avner was going to say, why didn't he just come out and say it? All this beating about the bush. Uzi fumbled with his cigarettes. He was enraged, he needed to let fly. What a load of shit. It was always the same with Avner. He had known that meeting him would be a mistake. But in a perverse way, he thirsted for the anger, the resentments, the hatred. They reminded him of home.

He smoked the cigarette as his temper smouldered. His ear began to itch again, and he passed his hand over his face in frustration.

'Uzi.'

'What do you want? You said you would leave me alone today,' he mumbled, trying not to look as if he was talking to himself.

'I think we should discuss Avner Golan.' It was the older voice this time. He hadn't heard the Kol sounding so old in a while.

'Look, I can handle this myself, OK? I'm not a baby. I don't need you.'

'I'm your friend, Uzi.'

'I don't need you. Not today.'

The voice paused, thinking. 'OK,' it said at last.

'Too fucking right.'

'Believe in yourself.'

'Yeah, whatever.'

Uzi shook his head as if to rid it of all remnants of the Kol. Through the window of the café, Avner could be seen chatting to the waitress, making movements with his hands as if he was describing a watermelon. A group of teenagers walked past, looking ridiculous in impossibly tight jeans, asymmetric haircuts, Ray-Bans. They were children. Everyone in England was a child. Nobody knew what real life was about. He finished his cigarette and, fortified, went back into the café. Avner dismissed the waitress charmingly and turned back to him.

'Better?' said Avner.

Uzi shrugged. 'No worse.'

'I haven't ordered you another espresso.'

'I didn't expect you to.'

This time, Uzi let the silence hang.

'Right,' said Avner at last, 'let's get down to some *tachless*.'

The Hebrew word clashed with the French and Uzi glanced around the café.

'Relax,' said Avner in Hebrew, 'just take it easy. That's no normal waitress. We're safe here. If anyone followed you here, they're not listening to what we're saying now.'

'You're trying to fuck with my head.'

'Here's the deal,' said Avner, dismissing Uzi's anxiety with a sweeping motion of his hands. 'The way I see it, we're in the same boat.'

'Really? How do you figure that?'

'You've always been a head-in-the-clouds bastard, the only idealist I've ever met in the Office. Me, I'm like everyone else, just in it for the money. That's why we always worked together so well. But right now, we've both been screwed by the powers that be. That's all that matters.'

Uzi scowled. 'I quit because of the corruption. You were demoted because you crossed the wrong guy. That doesn't put us in the same boat.'

'Details, details,' said Avner cheerfully. 'The point is, you and I can make money together. And at the same time, do some good.'

'Do some good?'

'I have a proposal for you.'

Uzi found himself already needing another cigarette. Avner picked up the signs; he waved the waitress over and ordered Uzi another espresso. They were silent until the coffee arrived. Then, as Uzi sipped, Avner spoke again. 'Fact is, they fucked me. They demoted me to Bodel – a courier, for fuck's sake – the sort of job that goes to someone fresh out of the army. Me, a Katsa, with all my experience. I'm a laughing stock. It's humiliating.'

'You can't complain,' said Uzi. 'Using the Office's surveillance equipment to blackmail the Johns on the Tel Baruch beach? You played the fucking fool.'

'How was I to know the guy was a Shabak officer?'

'That's not the point.'

'No, my brother, *that's* not the point. You want to know the point? This is the point. I'm going to cut loose from the Office, but I've got a chance to make some big money first. Forty million dollars, my brother. Forty million. And I want you in on it. Sixty-forty.'

'I'm listening.'

'There's an election coming up in the homeland.'

'Yeah.'

'I have friends in the opposition party. They want me to help . . . facilitate their victory.'

'You have friends on the political left?'

'Left-wing, right-wing, it's all the same to me. Corrupt bastards, to a man. It's a travesty, the state of our country. I just network, you know? I network.' Avner smiled.

Uzi raised his eyebrows. 'Go on.'

'Like I said, they're offering us forty million dollars. We split it sixty-forty. My job will be to set everything up. I'll do all the work. All you have to do is talk to WikiLeaks.'

'About what?'

'Operation Cinnamon.'

'No way.'

'Hear me out. If Operation Cinnamon hit the news, the prime minister would be impeached quicker than Richard Nixon. The right-wingers get voted out, the left-wingers get voted in. We get our forty million dollars. Game over.'

Uzi shook his head. 'You actually thought I would agree to this? You fucking idiot, Avner. Do I look suicidal to you?'

Avner laid a hand on his arm. 'Listen to me. The PM used the Office – used you – for his own ends. I know you're burning up about it, and with good reason. Now is the time to redress the balance. You want to change the course of history? You want to stand up for peace? You want to get stinking fucking rich? Then this is how.'

'Stand up for peace?' said Uzi. 'Leaking top secret information is standing up for peace?'

'Getting rid of this government is standing up for peace. It would be to you, anyway. Helping the peaceniks. Isn't that what you want these days? With your left-wing principles?'

'I'm not about politics. I'm no left-winger. I'm just a soldier who knows that when the PM uses the secret services to kill his opponents, it's time to get the hell out. I'm not a fucking crusader or anything. I don't give a shit about the government.'

Avner winced. 'You need to look at the bigger picture,' he said. 'Do you want the government to bomb Iran?'

'What do you think? Of course I don't want them to bomb Iran.'

'Well, then. The attack plans are already drawn up, my brother.'

'What?'

'I'm telling you. Operation Desert Rain. A daredevil air strike to destroy Iran's supposed nuclear materials – pinpoint and covert, not enough to spark a war. Or so the PM hopes. The voters will love it. A trumped-up target, a nighttime bombing raid, and there you have it: an election winner for our friends in the government.'

'But there is no credible Iranian threat.'

'We both know it. The Iranian nuclear programme is nothing but a paper tiger. The Americans fucked it with that cyber attack last winter – it'll be years before Iran even thinks about turning their uranium into yellowcake. But that doesn't matter to our beloved government, especially when an election is approaching.'

'Fuck. You're sure of your source?'

'Cast iron. This is big time, my brother. The dogs of war are barking.'

'You sound like you care, Avner.'

'Like I said, I'm in it for the money. But you care, my brother. I know you do.'

'So?'

'So if you leak Operation Cinnamon, the world will learn about this little scheme too. There will be a scandal. Operation Desert Rain will be aborted. Those GBU-28s will stay sitting in the warehouse for a few more years, rather than being dropped on Iran this year. And it will all be down to you. Plus, you'll be a rich man. Did I mention that?'

Uzi passed a hand across his face and drained his coffee. 'The Office would kill me.'

'They wouldn't.'

'Why not?'

'You'll do what I'm going to do. You'll take the fucking money and run.'

'They'll find me.'

'They won't. I'll fix it so they won't. I still have access to the Office mainframe, don't forget. I still have horses in the system. You have horses too, come to that.'

'My horses are all burned. Or turned. They had to disown me to keep their careers.'

'Rubbish. Rothem is still working for you. And Moskovitz.'

'Don't give me that.'

'Come on, my brother. You're still alive, free, in England. You think that happened by magic? You think the Office has gone soft? No, that's because of your horses.'

'Maybe,' said Uzi. 'But if I spoke to WikiLeaks I'd be screwed, horses or no horses. The Office would go crazy. They'd find me, and that'd be it. Game over. Vanunu would be nothing compared to me.'

'My horses are strong, Adam. They would protect us both.'

'Who have you got?'

'Never mind who I've got.'

'You're not going to ask me to trust you, surely.'

'Come on. We've got enough field experience. We know what we're doing. We could just disappear. Start again. That's what you want to do anyway, right? You're only forty, you're a young man. Your whole life is ahead of you.'

Uzi blew out his cheeks. 'Even if you had ROM himself as a horse, I'd be fucked. The PM would fuck me personally.'

Avner leaned closer. 'You're no stranger to risk,' he said. 'You're not someone who is afraid to stand up for what he knows is right. You have the power to change the course of history. How can you possibly refuse?'

There was a pause.

'You've got it all worked out, haven't you?' said Uzi.

'Of course,' grinned Avner. 'Ever the professional. It's all set up with WikiLeaks. As soon as you're ready, I'll schedule the meeting. When it's all in the can and ready to go, we sign the letter and take the first flight out. By the time the story breaks, we'll be drinking fine wine in Paris. With completely new identities.'

'Paris?'

'Or wherever you like. If you prefer, we can go our separate ways, no questions asked.'

'Passports?'

'I've taken care of it. Canadian.'

'Top passports?'

'Of course.'

'When do we get paid?'

'As soon as you speak to WikiLeaks.'

'Cash?'

'Deposits into bank accounts in Liechtenstein. We watch the money go in. Then we give WikiLeaks the go-ahead to break the story.'

'I wouldn't want to go to Paris. I'd just lie low in London. Carry on with business.'

'Suit yourself. Your funeral.'

'And if I'm out?'

Avner pushed his empty coffee glass aside and placed his palms in parallel on the table. 'Look, Adam. This is what I'm trying to tell you. We're in the same boat. You got fucked after Operation Cinnamon, and I got fucked trying to make some extra money. You're sitting outside synagogues with a finger up your arse during the day, and selling cannabis to lowlifes by night. I was an A-grade Katsa and now I'm living like a ghost. What have either of us got to lose? We have the power to bring the whole rotten house down. You can be a real fucking hero – you can clean up Israeli politics. Me? Well, I can get rich.'

'Strange sort of hero, in exile the rest of my life. Looking over my shoulder the rest of my life.'

'Let's give this a name. We're professionals, after all. Operation Regime Change. You like that? I think it has a nice, ironic ring.'

'Operation Regime Change,' Uzi repeated doubtfully.

'Think about it. Let me know if you're in.'

Abruptly, as if late for an appointment, Avner got to his feet, put a hand on Uzi's shoulder, and left the café. Uzi sat there for some minutes, feeling black with rage. He hated Avner, the Office, everything. He left the café and stalked off down the street.

4

The weather was impossibly humid and a horrid lethargy lay upon everything. His temper smouldering, Uzi made his way towards Camden, keen to put as much distance as possible between himself and Avner. He could feel a coldness shining from his eyes. Whoever caught his gaze looked away, and that was a good thing. He planted his feet one after the other on to the steaming pavement, like a robot, like a monster, and it felt as if he wasn't moving at all. The streets were quiet and stiflingly hot, the temperature was boiling his blood. He'd had enough of feeling expendable, like a pawn, an attack dog, it was making him feel sick. For years he had been steeped in darkness, in a world of shadows where anything was allowed, where the only morality to be answered to was the security of Israel, and the humiliation of her foes. Where the only thing that mattered was that there was always a battle to be fought. He had given the Office everything – his body, his mind, his friends, his marriage even – only to find out that what they wanted from him, what they really wanted from him, was his soul. And now that he had fled, he was left wondering if they hadn't already taken that too.

When he arrived in Camden he was sweating horribly and needed a drink. By this time his anger was waning, leaving him feeling resigned, drained, soiled. He bought a few cans of lager and found a quiet spot by the canal, amongst the bushes, where he smoked a spliff and watched the water move lazily by.

Gradually, the world seemed a better place to be. Then he lay on his back in the sun-bleached grass and looked up into the greyish, boiling atmosphere. For the first time in months, he found himself thinking about Noam. How old must he be now? He couldn't remember. Couldn't even remember, how about that. Still, it was understandable. The boy was his in name alone; they had no connection really, no relationship to speak of. He wondered if his hair was still blond, or if it had grown darker over time. He wondered if he was still at school. For a while he tried to recall at what age children leave school. Sixteen? Eighteen? Something like that. He wondered if the boy had a new father. He had been away a long time.

He sucked deeply on the spliff and allowed the fragrant smoke to filter into the very bottom of his lungs. Then he held his breath, feeling his head grow dizzy and his legs become lighter than air. He was alone, profoundly so, and he felt it. Parents? Dead. Wife? Estranged. Siblings? Roi didn't count. He had double crossed his own brother on his father's will. The bastard. Uzi knew his life was bleak, he was utterly alone in the world. If he weren't stoned, he'd probably be crying. On the other hand, if he weren't stoned, he'd never be thinking this way. Who gives a fuck, he thought to himself. Who gives a fucking fuck. And he smiled.

It hadn't always been like this. Uzi's dope habit was unremarkable at first, when he was in the regular army. Most people did it. Even when he was selected for the Navy commandos, the occasional dalliance was not out of the question, after a difficult operation or a long tour of duty. But to the Office, dope was unacceptable. He wasn't a heavy user at that time, was surprised that they were so concerned about it. But it could be used against him, they said; lawbreaking compromises operatives. In the end, he had to admit it made sense. The organisation could ill afford any embarrassments, especially since the year before, when a pair of rookies had been spotted by a member of the public planting a dummy bomb under a car in a Tel Aviv suburb; the alarm was raised, and the Office's training methods ended up all over the press. Not, he had to admit, good for the image of the organisation. So he agreed, and for the first six months he kept his word. Not, of course, that it matters any more.

Uzi was halfway through his spliff when he heard someone approaching along the towpath. He sat up sharply and his head swam. Before he could get to his feet, a figure emerged into view, dark against the sun. A woman, good-looking in an old-fashioned way, like an actress from an old film, dressed in tight-fitting chinos and an open-necked black shirt. She saw the spliff in his fingers and slowed down. His feet blocked the path.

'Walking by yourself?' said Uzi.

'I have friends,' replied the woman guardedly. 'Can I get by?'

A sassy voice, low and unhurried, with an accent that Uzi instantly placed as East Coast American. There was something in the way she phrased the question that made him think he could make her stay. He lay back in the desiccated grass and nodded to the space beside him.

'Join me for a few drags. I could use the company, and I'm too stoned to try anything on.'

'But I don't know you.' She didn't move to walk on as she said this, and Uzi knew then that she was his.

'I don't know you either,' he said. 'Who cares?'

'You going to charge me for this?'

'You should be charging me.'

'You are stoned, aren't you?' said the woman, smiling slightly and resting her head on one side. Her mahogany hair fell over one shoulder; her eyes were the colour of coffee.

'Save me from myself,' said Uzi. 'This is some strong shit. Or you can carry on and meet your friends. I don't care either way.'

The woman shrugged and sat down, and Uzi passed her the spliff. She felt familiar somehow, in a way he couldn't place.

This was reckless, Uzi knew that, but he didn't care. Death, that's all anything could bring, and so what? Anyway, as Avner had reminded him, he wasn't on operations any more. He took a drag and passed the spliff to his new companion, smoke threading between his fingers and disappearing into the greyness of the atmosphere.

'Thanks,' she said, propping herself up on her elbow and drawing heavily, professionally, on the spliff. She adjusted her position, and Uzi noticed a diamond-encrusted watch on her wrist, a Versace handbag in the dirt beside her. He was surprised that such a woman would be sitting here beside him in the grass like a teenager. But his head was too fogged to make sense of it. 'Just what I needed,' she said suddenly. 'Hits the spot.' She inhaled again, deeply, then passed the spliff back. 'You got any to sell?'

Uzi shook his head. His mouth was numb and he couldn't be bothered.

'Where you from?' said the woman.

Uzi was about to say Russia, or France, or Canada, but he didn't have it in him any more.

'Israel,' he said.

'Oh?' the woman replied, coughing into an almost-closed fist. Uzi thought he saw a strange expression flit across her face, one that he couldn't define; but it may have been his paranoia, he may even have imagined it. 'I was there only a month ago,' said the woman. 'Whereabouts?'

'Tel Aviv,' Uzi replied shortly. 'What were you doing there?'

'Visiting family.'

'You have family in Israel?'

'Sort of. You know, not close family.'

'You're Jewish?'

'Half Jewish.'

'The right half or the wrong half?'

'I hate that question. The wrong half.'

There was a pause, and Uzi became aware of the background noise, the constant ebb and flow of the traffic that he only noticed when stoned. The occasional call of a bird. Without any reason, he smiled. This woman was obviously from a rich family, or married to a rich husband. And she wanted to rebel.

'They call me Daniel,' he said dreamily.

'That makes me the lion,' said the woman. 'I'm Eve. This is some good shit. How did you come by it?'

'Here and there,' Uzi replied, 'you know how it is.'

'What do they call this stuff now? It's new, isn't it? Stronger.'

'Fuck knows. I smoke it, I don't make love to it.'

There was a pause.

'Come on,' said Eve again, 'tell me where you get it. Or do you grow your own?'

'Just smoke if you're going to smoke,' said Uzi.

She snorted and pulled on the spliff with her mouth, closing her eyes as if she were in a hot bath.

'I just love this shit,' she said, half to herself. 'I want to buy shiploads of it. I want to go to sleep with it every night.'

'Look,' said Uzi, raising himself on his elbow and glaring at the woman, suddenly disproportionately angry, 'are you police?'

'Do I fucking look like it?' Eve replied.

'Then smoke and be happy,' said Uzi. 'I don't like the way you're talking. You're asking too many questions.'

'Take it easy,' said the woman. 'I'm only asking.'

For a while they smoked in silence. Uzi was stoned, and he didn't give a shit. He was ready to die, and he didn't give a shit.

'I think you're the dealer,' said Eve suddenly. 'I think you're selling this stuff.'

Uzi finished the spliff and tossed the butt into the canal. Then he sat up slowly and tried to get his bearings. For a moment he couldn't remember where he was. He had the idea that he was on operations somewhere, Moscow perhaps, or Beirut. Then it came back to him and he checked his watch. Twenty to seven.

'Look, I've got to go,' he said.

His companion made no reply. The world tilted slightly as Uzi got to his feet, but he steadied himself and lumbered off along the towpath.

5

'You did well,' said the Kol – the younger voice again – out of nowhere. 'You did well with that woman.' There hadn't been an itch. Why hadn't there been an itch?

'How many times do I have to tell you?' said Uzi. 'You're supposed to be leaving me alone.'

'Believe,' the Kol said.

'I don't want to hear from you again today, OK? I'm serious. The whole day.'

'Believe in yourself.'

Back on the street, the weather was no cooler and more people were about. A smell was in the air, a bonfire perhaps, or a barbecue. Uzi thought people were looking at him strangely, avoiding him. Exhaust from buses swirled hot around his ankles as he made his way down the High Street in the direction of Inverness Street Market. When the sun broke through the broiling clouds the glare was unbearable, and before Uzi knew it he had bought a pair of sunglasses from a street vendor for £8.99. Camden was dimmer now, and he liked it that way. He was in a smiley haze, enjoying this new dusk. He was being careless, he knew that, and if there was trouble tonight he would only have himself to blame. Selling a rucksack of stash while stoned: this was the behaviour of an amateur. But, according to Squeal, these people were safe. Squeal was the only person Uzi knew in England who he wasn't trying actively to avoid. At least, not usually. They had met the day after Uzi arrived. Uzi had knocked on his door and asked to borrow an egg. Nothing unusual there, of course, one neighbour borrowing an egg from another. Uzi also wanted to get the gossip on the residents of the block. He couldn't afford trouble on his doorstep; for the first time in his life he didn't have a safe house to go to.

Squeal was an albino Ghanaian, extremely thin and rather short, top-heavy with a mass of vanilla dreadlocks hanging down his back. He wore sunglasses to protect his eyes, and his wiry frame, together with his unusual way of moving, made him look like a stringed puppet. His voice was soft and lisping, and at first one would never have associated him with the nickname. However, upon getting to know him the reason for his nickname became obvious.

'Eggs?' said Squeal, folding his arms and unfolding them again. 'What the fuck. You taking the piss?'

'I've just moved in,' Uzi replied. 'I need some eggs. One egg, even. One egg.'

Squeal looked bemused.

'I know you've just moved in,' he said. 'I know every fucking person that moves into this block. And out of it. Every fucking last man Jack. What's your name?'

'Tomislav. You can call me Tommy.'

'You're not fucking Polish, are you?'

'Russian.' Uzi paused and sniffed the air. 'Dope?'

Squeal began to close the door, muttering something unintelligible. Uzi wedged his arm into the open doorway.

'Fuck off,' said Squeal, 'or I'll call the police.'

'Don't worry,' said Uzi. 'Look, I just want an egg. One egg. That's all.'

Squeal stopped pressing the door and looked closely at him. 'Hang on a minute,' he said, breaking into a hesitant grin. 'You've got the munchies, haven't you? You're stoned, aren't you? Aren't you?'

Despite himself, Uzi smiled broadly. Then he heard Squeal laugh for the first time. He sounded like a puppy.

'Come in, dude,' said Squeal. 'Make yourself at home, yeah? The eggs are on me.'

Uzi stepped through the door into the gloom. 'I'm making shakshuka, he said. 'I need shakshuka. You ever had shakshuka?'

By the time Uzi arrived at Inverness street market, the stalls were closed and the road was bald and barren. Detritus lined the gutters. He ambled at a diagonal across the cobbles, shaking his head to clear it. It was hot and his trainers were sticking to the pavement. The stash in his bag felt unnaturally heavy, the way it always did before a drop. The bars and restaurants were empty yet pristine, all primed for an influx of customers later in the evening. He removed his sunglasses, tried to pull himself together. Over the years he had been part of countless high-pressure, 'no zero' operations where the outcome could be nothing but decisive. Yet now he felt nervous. His life wasn't threatened, this was a straightforward sale, and he was nervous. To steady himself he lit a cigarette, but could only manage half of it because he was keen to get to the meeting. Dropping it into the gutter, he headed for the Blue Peacock café.

A girl in an apron approached him as he entered. She was very pretty, and he smiled at her. He thought she reminded him of a woman he could have known long ago, but he wasn't sure. She spoke with a Polish accent and in a moment of hazy generosity he considered buying her a drink, buying her a house, proposing to her. He pulled himself together again and asked in Russian if Andrzej was there. She asked him if he was Tomislav Kasheyev. He nodded and she gave him another sort of look, as if he might be a policeman. He ordered a Scotch. Then she showed him upstairs to the back room.

There seemed to be no air and for a moment Uzi thought he would pass out. He was dehydrated. He turned to ask for some water, but the girl had disappeared. He drank his Scotch. The room was square and gloaming, with blacked-out windows and red drapes lining the walls. Incongruous music was playing in the background – Metallica. Three men sat around a table, their

32

amber beer glasses clustered around a candle in the middle. Two were leaning back casually, and one – Squeal's contact, Andrzej – sat hunched forward, his arms folded into his stomach. Little could be seen of them on account of the shadows; the room was lit only by candles. They looked up, scrutinising Uzi carefully. Then they beckoned him over and he took a seat among them.

'Special delivery,' he said in Russian.

'Wonderful,' said Andrzej, in the same language but with a strong Polish accent. 'What excellent service. Wonderful.'

'Party, is it?' said Uzi, not letting go of his rucksack. 'Birthday party?'

'Yes,' Andrzej said, 'for one of my girlfriends.' They all laughed and drank.

Uzi lit a cigarette and nobody said anything. One Metallica song ended and another began. Then Andrzej lit up in the same way, blowing a jet of smoke over Uzi's shoulder. They all laughed. Sidelong, Uzi sized them up. Well dressed, but in a try-hard sort of way. Small-time. Unsure of themselves. But he knew that amateurs could be more dangerous than professionals; these men could be volatile. They were in a jovial mood, but they clearly had something to prove.

'So, Tomislav, my friend,' said Andrzej with a smile. 'Let's see the goods.'

'Put the money on the table,' said Uzi.

'Open the bag,' said Andrzej.

Uzi reached into his rucksack and pulled out a spliff. Then he tossed it on to the table and sat back.

'Why the hurry?' he said. 'Have a puff. Free sample.'

This seemed to slacken the atmosphere. Andrzej rested his cigarette on the edge of the table and lit the spliff. The Poles handed it around.

'I'm not going to lie to you, Tomislav,' said Andrzej, 'this is some good shit you got here. Some good, good shit.' Evidently, he was the only one who ever spoke.

'Yes,' said Uzi, 'you're going to have a great party.'

The men eyed him warily as Andrzej produced a thick envelope. Upon seeing it, Uzi removed the stash from his bag and put it on the table, without letting go. He felt strangely relieved to have emptied the rucksack. Andrzej moved to take the stash, but Uzi held fast.

'Not until I've counted the money,' he said. 'I'm sure you understand.'

Andrzej pursed his lips and made a generous gesture with the spliff, leaving loops of smoke in the air. Then he dragged on it and exhaled exaggeratedly. The other men laughed. Uzi opened the envelope. It took him a long time with one hand. What an amateur, he thought, what a fucking amateur. Lost my edge.

'Come now, don't be so wary,' said Andrzej in flowery Russian. 'You are amongst friends here, Tomislav.'

Uzi took his hand away from the stash and counted the money quickly. His head was fuzzy and he had to start again. When he looked up, Andrzej was cradling his stash.

'This is only nine hundred,' said Uzi. 'We agreed a thousand.'

'A hundred here, a hundred there,' said Andrzej casually. 'We are aiming for a long-term relationship. There's no need to be petty. Next time we'll pay you more. When we have full confidence.'

His companions laughed.

'We agreed a grand,' said Uzi, knowing that this was a test of his gullibility; if he gave in now, they'd rip him off for ever. 'A grand or no deal.'

'You should be grateful for the money,' said Andrzej. 'One thousand is too much. As you know, you could buy a herd of cows for this on the steppe. Maybe two herds.'

The Poles laughed again.

'Don't fuck with me,' Uzi said. 'I've got a business to run.'

'It's only a hundred pounds.'

'I don't care. Don't fuck with me.'

'Don't be a prick, Tomislav Kasheyev.'

'Fuck your mother.'

'What?'

With a single movement, Uzi snatched the stash and got to his feet, backing towards the door. The men rose too. One of them spat. Uzi threw the money down and pushed his way into the restaurant. It was busier now, and he almost collided with the waitress as he dashed into the street. His heart was beating and he couldn't escape the feeling that he needed another spliff. Part of him was relishing the adrenaline. It had been a long time.

As soon as he turned a corner the Poles were there. They had taken the back exit and doubled back. Bastards, he thought. He had given them back their money, but that was not enough. They walked towards him, illuminated by the bloody sun which was beginning to die behind the houses.

'Tomislav,' called Andrzej, smiling, 'there was no need to be impolite.'

Uzi felt the old coldness spreading through his body, shining out of his eyes, and suddenly he was hyper-alert. They couldn't allow him to insult them, just as he couldn't allow them to rip him off. He stepped into the middle of the road, drawing them out where he could see them. In his mind's eye he saw, from fifteen years before, the mock street with the wooden men that would pop out to be shot; his training was kicking in, and that meant danger. There were no snipers on the roofs, of course there weren't, why would there be? It felt strange being unarmed, not even a knife. Reckless. No backup, of course not. The streets were strangely deserted. He was ready to die. His shirt was sticking to his body and his eyes tracked the men like an animal. They fanned out, Andrzej walking straight towards him and the others taking the flanks. The way they walked, so brazenly, it was clear they were amateurs. But he was outnumbered, slowed by the dope, and he'd lost his edge. A hundred yards away, some passers-by stopped, staring.

'Don't be stupid, my friend,' called Andrzej. 'Why are you being stupid?'

Uzi glanced to his left and then bolted to his right, heading for a gap between two cars. One of the men tried to grab at him. Uzi gripped the man's wrist and landed a heavy punch on his temple.

They scuffled as the man went down, and in the process Uzi felt a swipe across his leg. He kicked the Pole hard against a parked car; the man crumpled and something fell from his hand. Uzi turned to run, but it was already too late. He was boxed in: Andrzej on one side, his second accomplice on the other. And both held butterfly knives.

'You're being stupid, my Russian friend,' said Andrzej smiling. 'Take a look at your leg.' Uzi looked down. His trousers were flapping open and a bloody wound gaped in his thigh. 'See? Business is business.'

Uzi did not feel any pain, but the sight of his own blood enraged him. This was stupid, to get cut for the sake of a hundred pounds, to get cut by such amateurs. But still his rage was channelled, kept in check, in the old way. Andrzej's companion looked away and in that instant Uzi sprang at him, twisting his knife hand away and butting him in the face, his Krav Maga training returning seamlessly to him. The man recoiled and bucked in an unexpected way, breaking free. Then he lunged and Uzi was just able to sidestep, spinning the man into the wall. But his knife caught his shoulder, and another gash appeared. This one Uzi felt. A sharp pain, like a paper cut. And now he felt the pain in his leg as well.

'Your life is about to end here, far from home,' said Andrzej. 'Ask yourself if it is worth it. For two herds of cows in Russia.' The other man stood panting, holding his knife at throat height. And now the other was picking himself up painfully from the ground. 'Give me the bag or we will take it from your fingers when you're bleeding in the gutter like a pig.'

Suddenly, from between two parked cars, a figure stepped into view. A woman: elegant and slightly aloof, like an actress from an old film, too striking to be a woman in the street. She looked at Uzi, nodded, then focused on the Russians.

'OK,' she said slowly, 'that's enough.' She slipped her hand into her Versace bag and a pistol glinted. Uzi recognised it at once; an American-made Taurus .22 snub-nosed revolver, two-inch barrel, nine-shot cylinder, optimal penetrating power. Just the weapon for a woman: compact and powerful. And she held it comfortably, like a professional. 'Put the weapons down,' said Eve. 'Then fuck off. I'm only telling you once.' It was only then that Uzi noticed a gang of five men standing in the shadows behind her.

An odd expression came over Andrzej's face, somewhere between admiration and fear. For a moment he caught Uzi's eye, giving him a glance that penetrated to his soul. After what seemed like an age he dropped his knife to the ground and slipped off into the darkness, followed by his accomplices. Eve pursued them at a slow pace, holding the pistol, shepherding them away; her men followed too, in the shadows. Uzi saw his chance – he only had a split second – and bolted. He didn't think Eve would follow him; he didn't care who she was or what she wanted. Death was close now, and some ancient instinct was driving him on. He ran hard, veering around corners, as police sirens began to wail in the distance.

6

Fifteen years ago, when the Office first approached Uzi – or Adam, as he was known then – it had come at the right time. His parents had been dead for exactly a year, and the storm that ripped through his life thereafter had abated, leaving behind a landscape of desolation. Everything was ruined in him; everything had collapsed in the split second it took the bomber on bus 23 to pull the cord on his suicide vest.

The phone call had been like an aircraft crashing into the ocean. The voice was soft, telling him only the basic details, and instantly he had known. He had gone under. The voice had sounded like the surf. His breath had been knocked noiselessly out of him and he found himself sitting on the floor, the telephone dangling on its wire before his face. He was a member of Shayetet 13, Israel's most elite naval commando unit; renowned for their psychological resilience, they could function under levels of combat stress and fear that would have been debilitating to any other soldiers. The training had lasted twenty months. But it hadn't prepared him for this. Over the next year he learned to adapt, to function in a state of devastation, perhaps more effectively than before. But he would never again come to the surface.

When he was growing up, in a nondescript suburb of Tel Aviv where the summers were unbearably hot and the winters made a mockery of the sun-baked apartment blocks, the ocean was always present. He would go there most days with the kids from his class; they would have barbecues, eye up girls, play guitar, tumble in the waves, and on Friday evenings, on a spit of rock with hundreds of others, they would play drums, a great tribal pulse. Somehow his parents were in everything: the rocks, the sky, the ocean. His father, a squat, grizzled Special Forces officer, with battle scars from '67, and half deaf from the bombs of '73, had taught him to swim and to fish; they had played beach football and drunk beer together into the evenings. His mother; well, his mother. A painter who painted the seascape.

It was like being told you will never see the ocean again.

He had gone back to Atlit – the secret naval commando base on a fortified island in the Mediterranean – the following morning. But his commanding officer had turned him away, forced him to take a week's compassionate leave, to see a Navy psychiatrist. It was during this time, as the days and nights blurred in endless cycles of numb insomnia, that two men from his unit – two of his friends, his brothers – were killed during a kidnap operation on the coast of Lebanon, their blood mingling with the shingle and the surf.

Nehama had stayed by his side throughout. She had loved his parents, and buried her own grief as best she could in order to support him through his. That, perhaps, was where the trap-door opened. While she encased herself in rock for his sake, he sank to the ocean bed, and there would never be any way back. Over the months a distance grew between them; they slept spooned in opposite directions, they could no longer hold each other's gaze. Their expressions of love became occasional and hollow. He no longer turned to her, the girl he had loved since childhood. He was still submerged, still drowning, and when she reached out to him, through her stone walls, through the water, the distance was simply too great.

So when, a year on, Uzi's – Adam's – commanding officer took him aside and ordered him to report to the Shalishut military base on the outskirts of Ramat Gan and not to mention it to anybody, including Nehama, Adam knew intuitively that this was the change he needed. That Nehama needed. He shut his M-4 in a secure locker – it was too cumbersome, and he had his Glock – and, uncomfortable in the early summer humidity, with heat raging through him, caught two buses and arrived at Shalishut in good time.

He was met by a young soldier who showed him to a nondescript door in the bowels of the base. Before knocking, the soldier asked Adam for his sidearm; Adam refused, but the soldier was adamant, so in the end Adam drew the weapon and handed it over, butt first. He always felt nervous unarmed, but it was a military base, after all. The soldier knocked, and opened the door for Adam as if he were important. Then he left, closing the door behind him.

In the room Adam saluted reflexively, only to be surprised by a middle-aged man in civilian dress: open-necked shirt, polyester trousers, something of the kibbutznik about him. Another man was sitting silently in the corner, peering over his spectacles, taking notes.

'Welcome, Colonel,' said the first man.

'Thank you, sir,' Adam replied.

'I am sorry about your parents.'

'It has been a year, sir.'

'A year is not very long.'

'It will be longer.'

The man smiled and gestured for Adam to sit down. 'I can see from your file that you have been promoted quickly, Colonel. You are serving your country well. Would you say that is correct?'

'Shayetet 13 is not a holiday camp, sir,' said Adam, suddenly rather irritated.

'Of course,' said the man, 'but I am going to tell you how you can serve your country better. Would you be open to suggestions?'

'Who are you?'

'My name is Yigal.'

'From where? NID? Shabak?'

Yigal waved away his questions like smoke. 'So, would you be open to suggestions?'

'I might, sir,' said Adam.

'What about Nehama?'

'Nehama, my wife?'

'Who else?'

'What about my wife?'

'Would she be open to suggestions?'

'What kind of suggestions?'

Yigal sighed.

'Try to relax, Colonel,' he said slowly, as if to a child. 'Do you want a coffee? Cigarette perhaps?'

Adam shook his head, although he wanted both. There was a pause. He thought about getting up, walking out, but he didn't. The man in the corner was writing in pencil, the scratching was loud in the room.

'The computer picked out your name,' said Yigal. 'Your profile fits our criteria. You were selected out of fifteen thousand possible candidates.' He looked up as if gauging the impact of this on his interviewee, then continued. 'Our primary objective is to defend Jews all over the world. We're like a family, and we think you might fit in. Of course, if you are interested, this would only be the beginning. You would need to go through our tests and so on. Not many people succeed.'

'Of course,' said Adam, failing to keep the customary irony out of his voice.

Yigal looked up sharply, then continued. 'Training would be in Israel, but you wouldn't be able to live at home. You would be given leave to see your family every three weeks. If – if – you pass all the tests and complete the training, you may have to work abroad. Your family would not accompany you. You would see them every other month.'

'For how long?'

'A weekend, sometimes longer.'

'The pay?'

'A little more than you presently receive.'

'How much more?'

'A little more, Colonel.'

More scratching from the man in the corner.

'So tell me,' said Yigal, placing a pen carefully, in parallel, on the desk. 'Based on what I've told you so far, are you interested?'

'Based on what you have told me so far? I might be, sir.'

'Good.'

Suddenly shouts could be heard, men's voices, outside the room. Adam looked from Yigal to the man in the corner; their eyes were fixed on the door behind him. As he turned, following their gaze, the door burst open and he was knocked from his chair to the floor. Everything went into slow motion. He saw it all in exquisite detail, a moving tableau. Maybe this was his time; if it was, he didn't care. Shots rang out and he caught a glimpse of Yigal, half-standing, shuddering as several bullets hit him in the chest. Three masked figures were whirling like dancers, their sub-machine guns flashing. Adam turned to see the man in the corner being shot in the chest as well, and slumping over. A slim figure in a black ski mask, fragile hands – woman's hands – aimed a weapon at Adam. He rolled to the side and scrabbled to his knees, groping for his Glock. The holster was empty. The woman kicked Adam hard against the wall. He had no chance. His head struck concrete and he was dazed. As quickly as they had appeared, the attackers were gone.

The room swam, then came into focus. Adam clambered to his feet and, shouting for a medic, ran over to Yigal. The man was half-standing, supporting himself on the desk, small flowers of blood peppering his chest.

'Yigal,' said Adam, 'sit down. Apply pressure.'

Yigal stood upright and looked Adam full in the face. 'Close the door and take a seat, Colonel.' His voice was strong.

'You've been injured, Yigal, listen to me. You're in shock.'

Without a word, Yigal removed his shirt. Underneath he had a pale blue T-shirt, completely unmarked. 'Close the door and take a seat,' he repeated.

Adam looked over at the man in the corner. He too was removing his bloodied shirt, and picking up his notepad and pencil. Dumbstruck, Adam shut the door and sat down.

'I'm going to ask you some questions,' said Yigal. 'How many assailants were there?'

'Is this a joke?'

'How many men were there?'

Adam pressed the heels of his hands over his eyes. He couldn't remember. It was all a blur; he had to think. He was sweating, and adrenaline was rushing through him.

'I want your answer,' barked Yigal. 'How many men? What were they wearing? What weapons were they using? How many shots did each man fire? Did they say anything to each other? Come on, come on. OK, write it on the pad. You have sixty seconds while I make myself a coffee.'

He left the room via a side door while the man in the corner continued to take notes, glancing up inscrutably from time to time. Adam clenched his fists on the table, imagined himself floating back to the scene, watching it playing out again, in slow motion, before him. Two men, one woman, black ski masks, combat fatigues. One in a black flak jacket. Two with micro Uzis. One with an M-16. Impossible to say how many shots were fired, their weapons were set to semi-automatic; come to think of it, each assailant shot two bursts, one at Yigal and one at the man in the corner. Had they said anything to each other? Had they? Adam put down the pen and looked up into space, reliving the experience vividly, ignoring his throbbing head. From the next room came the sound of a coffee machine. He'd have to be quick. The attackers had certainly shouted something, but what? What was it? He relaxed his mind. Yes . . . It was coming back. The word was 'deception'.

Yigal came back into the room preceded by the smell of coffee, and looked at Adam's sheet of paper. His face moved not a muscle. He stuck a cigarette between his lips and lit it with a Zippo.

'Deception,' he said blowing smoke from his nose. 'Are you sure?'

'Yes,' said Adam, 'I'm sure.'

'A woman? One was a woman? Are you crazy?'

'That's what I saw.'

'Maybe you were mistaken.'

'No mistake.'

Yigal passed the sheet of paper to the man in the corner, who read it carefully and nodded.

'Congratulations, Colonel,' said Yigal suddenly, 'you've passed the first stage. Now you must make a serious decision. From now on, there's no backing out. This is hard and dangerous work, mostly abroad. Think about that. If you're not interested, say so and we'll never contact you again. If you are interested – seriously interested – come tomorrow to the address on this card. 0800 hours. Do not be late. After each round of tests we'll call you with the results. If you've passed, we'll give you the details of the next round. If you fail, that's it. You have one chance only. OK?'

'One question,' said Adam as he rose to leave, 'which organisation are you from?'

Yigal gave him a stony glare and sucked on his cigarette.

'0800 hours,' he said, 'if you're serious.'

With that he left the room, followed by his colleague. Adam was given back his Glock and escorted off the Shalishut complex, into the blazing sunshine. It was only when he was sitting on the bus on the way back to his base at Atlit, shielding his eyes from the glare of the sun, that he noticed that the hair on the back of his head was clogged with scabbing blood.

7

After what seemed like an age – a painful age – Uzi heaved himself in through the door of his flat. The pain from the knife wounds was sharp and unremitting. Even now, dizzy and trembling from the loss of blood, barely able to think, he was cursing himself for his foolishness. The humiliation was worse than the injury. He staggered into the sitting room, leaving half-footprints of blood on the carpet, and felt the weight of the table. It was heavy. His slick was secure. He lay down heavily on the sofa.

'Uzi,' said the Kol.

'I – I'm OK.'

'You know there is nothing I can do.'

'I don't expect anything. What could I expect from a voice in my head, right?'

'Are you losing blood?'

'I'm going to call a Sayan.'

'You can't.'

'What else can I do? Go to hospital and answer all those questions? Bleed to death like a chicken? Now get out of my head – I'm starting to go crazy.'

'Don't forget who you are, Uzi.'

'Yeah. And don't worry, I'll believe.'

'I'm with you. Believe.'

Clenching his teeth against the pinch of the makeshift tourniquets he had tied around his arm and leg, Uzi picked up the phone and dialled a London number. It was midnight. The phone rang for a long time before somebody picked it up.

'Hello?' came a bleary male voice.

'Roger Cooper calling for John Jackson,' slurred Uzi. There was a pause. A woman could be heard sleepily asking questions. Then, finally, the answer:

'There is nobody by that name here.' The line went dead.

Following procedure, from memory Uzi dialled another number, a mobile number, and waited while it rang.

'What do you want me to do?' came the same voice.

'Waxman. Are you alone?' said Uzi.

'Nobody can hear me.'

'Good. I'm going to text you an address. Get here fast. Bring type O-negative blood.'

'How much?'

'As much as you have.'

'In the ambulance?'

'Yes.'

'It'll take half an hour.'

'Twenty minutes.' Uzi hung up. Wincing in pain but not making a sound, he sent the text to Waxman. Then he made his way into the kitchen, stirred several spoonfuls of sugar into a glass of water and forced it down. His main priority until Waxman arrived was to remain conscious. He sat at the kitchen table, resting his head in his hands.

As the sugar entered his bloodstream and his dizziness subsided, an old mixture of fear and rage began to spread through him. He was going to give Squeal hell. What was he playing at? He'd sworn it would be nothing but a safe, straightforward sale. Or was he setting a trap? And then there would be the matter of the . . . the . . . His mind trailed off. There was a sudden jerk as his head slid from his palms towards the table and snapped upwards again. He was going down. There wasn't much time. Dried blood had stiffened his jacket and trouser leg; the tourniquet was stemming the flow, but it wasn't perfect. Waxman would be here soon. He just needed to hold on.

He got to his feet and stumbled into the sitting room. Waxman was a reliable Sayan, and a good doctor, but tended to get nervous when working with the Office. If Uzi passed out and was unable to open the front door, Waxman couldn't be relied on to break in. In fact, he may not even be able – physically – to break in. Uzi put the door on the snib, left it ajar, and lowered himself to the carpet beside the table, the slick.

He shouldn't be contacting Sayanim, and he knew it. If the Office found out, they may lose their patience. But he had no choice. He could still remember the phone numbers and contact protocols for dozens of Sayanim; it was the last resource he could draw on in an emergency. They were many and varied: doctors, estate agents, interior designers, bankers, lawyers, businessmen, IT technicians, local council workers, even refuse collectors. All Jewish. They made the work of the Office possible. Whether you needed a car, a room, a shop, a business, a stash of money – or medical attention – one phone call to a Sayan was usually all it took. No questions asked. On many occasions they were used to provide an 'element of comfort' for operatives. But Uzi wasn't an operative now. He was an outcast. The room had begun to seem hazy and distant. He slumped back on his elbows, waiting for help to arrive.

It had been a strange thing, this journey from life as a respected naval commando to losing blood on the floor of a dilapidated flat in north London. Fifteen years was all it had taken. In that time the Office had plucked him from his world, taken his life force and spat him out. To begin with, he had been different. He had seen action countless times, knew the horrors of combat, but he had still believed that the State of Israel was in the hands of the righteous. He had trusted his superior officers, and the politicians above them. Mistakes happened from time to time, of course they did; this, after all, was war. But ultimately there had been no doubt in his mind. He was still under the influence of that heady mixture of idealism and testosterone, a blue-and-white ego. This was the exoskeleton that had remained in place even as his insides collapsed after his parents died; this was what had enabled his friends and comrades to feel like they still knew him. This was all he had had to cling to, and it was this that the Office tapped into and channelled, sucked out of him, until he became – almost – as cold-hearted and reptilian as the rest of them. Until he could take no more.

It was the special treatment, more than anything else, that seduced him. He had attended the next stage of the tests. How could he not have done? Already he was feeling special – one in fifteen thousand. The building itself, the Hadar Dafna office block on King Saul Boulevard in Tel Aviv, was nondescript. A building-within-a-building: metal detectors, glass walls, desks, elevators. But from the moment the very first tests began, the very first medical examinations, the atmosphere was like nothing he had experienced before. Normally there would be hundreds of soldiers filing past one desk after another, getting measured, injected, examined. This time there was only him. He alone had to make his way along a corridor, going from one room to the next. In each room was a doctor, or a physiotherapist, or an optician, and each gave him their exclusive attention. They took their time. They were meticulous, and obviously highly qualified. It was eerily silent; even the traffic could not be heard. He felt unsure of himself, of course. But at the same time he felt like a king.

After the medical he had a three-hour interview with a psychologist, answering endless questions. Would you regard killing for your country as something negative? Do you believe freedom is important? Is there anything more important? What is the worst thing your parents ever did to you? Do you think revenge is justified? On a scale of one to ten, how honest are you with your wife? Do you have any Arab friends? Have you ever had a homosexual impulse? Do you trust your instincts? Do you have any regrets about anything you have done in the military? Do you think there are some orders that should not be followed? Do you sleep well at night? How do you feel about targeted assassinations? How often do you exercise? Can you remember the last time you fired your weapon in combat? How did it feel? What wouldn't you sacrifice for your country? Do you respect Islam? Do you eat pork? Bacon?

Do you? It was the attention to detail that sucked him in. He was special – treated like a precious commodity.

It was through the Office that he had discovered Nehama's news. That's when he knew it was over for him and his wife, and just starting for him and the Office. Yigal had told him casually in the car on the way to his induction weekend. He had passed all the preliminary tests, had met with a contact twice a week for four months. He had attended weekend examinations at the Country Club where he had to mingle with other candidates for hours, maintaining a cover identity and trying to expose theirs. He had followed people through the streets of Tel Aviv, had been arrested and withstood interrogation. He had been stripped, blindfolded and doused with cold water again and again, but he had never abandoned his cover story. Finally the phone call had come: you're in. Friday, 0630 hours. A car will pick you up. Bring clothes for different occasions, to last you until Monday night. Then the line went dead.

So he found himself being driven through the city towards an undisclosed location in an anonymous white Mercedes. Dawn was breaking outside. Yigal was sitting in the passenger seat; Adam was in the back. The driver of the car was the psychologist, the note taker. Nobody spoke. Then, after about twenty minutes, with the pinkness still visible in the sky, Yigal broke the silence.

'Mazal tov, my friend.'

'For what?'

'What do you think?'

'Making it through the tests?'

'Yes, of course. You're in. But you could still fail the training, don't forget.'

'That would be a shame.'

'Wouldn't it? Anyway, mazal tov. I can see you're going to be a great father.'

'Excuse me?'

'Mazal tov again.' Yigal turned his face away, looking out at the road.

'You seem to know something I don't,' said Adam.

'Not any more,' said Yigal over his shoulder.

Adam tried to dismiss the information as just another part of the training, just another mind game. But as the car sped through the city, something deep inside him began to twist. Nehama had polycystic ovaries. The chances of her being able to conceive a child were slim. Surely she wouldn't have kept the information from him?

He took out his phone, brought up her number, almost pressed 'call'. But he hesitated; biting his lip, he sent her a text instead. He was surprised when the answer came immediately: 'Talk when you get back.'

Adam's emotions went in all directions at once. But he'd been pursuing this goal for months single-mindedly; he'd got through the recruitment process, and he wasn't going to let anything stop him now. The car reached their destination. As he opened the door and stepped out on to the sun-faded gravel, he drew on all of his training to marshal his thoughts and feelings. He raised his face to the new sun, allowing it to tighten his skin. Suddenly his mind felt taut, clear, locked down. Ready for anything.

'Daniel? Daniel?'

Uzi opened his eyes. For a few moments, a haze of glittering sparks moved across his field of vision. He blinked, and they gradually cleared.

'Waxman?' said Uzi.

'Don't try to move, Daniel. You've lost a lot of blood.'

'Where am I?'

'In H2.'

'H2?'

'Hatzola Ambulance 2.'

'Where are we?'

'I just transferred you here for treatment. We're parked outside your flat.'

'How the hell did you carry me down two flights of stairs?'

'It wasn't easy.'

'Fuck.' Uzi felt woozy and the pain from his wounds was almost unbearable. But, to his relief, it was no longer a critical sort of pain. Instinctively he felt that his core had been stabilised, that he was not going to lose his life. Not yet.

'Nice ambulance,' he said, mustering a sardonic smile. He was lying on a narrow bed; all around him was medical equipment.

'This thing cost eighty thousand pounds,' said Waxman.

'A private ambulance for the community. Rich Jews, eh?'

'Generous Jews. Hatzola's a charity, Adam.'

'That's what I meant.' Uzi saw Waxman glance nervously at his watch. He looked jittery, as usual. That's what the Office did to its Sayanim. 'Will you do something for me?'

'Of course.'

'In my pocket there should still be a packet of cigarettes. Light me a cigarette.'

A look of alarm passed across Waxman's face. 'A cigarette?'

'What, you can't hear properly? Yes, a cigarette. A cigarette,' said Uzi.

Waxman, unsure of himself, complied.

Uzi inhaled deeply, coughed, and blew a jet of smoke vertically towards the ceiling of the vehicle.

'I'll open the door,' mumbled Waxman.

'Don't touch the fucking door,' said Uzi. 'You could get us both killed.'

The man paled and Uzi broke into a grin. 'Relax, my brother, relax,' he said. 'Have a cigarette.'

Waxman declined and stood there, awkwardly, in silence.

'So,' said Uzi, wincing, 'tell me how it is.'

'Daniel: you're a lucky man,' said Waxman, relieved at the opportunity to slip back into his doctor's role. 'Both times the blade missed your arteries. You've lost blood but I'm giving you a transfusion. I've sewn up the wounds. I could have done with a hospital, but needs must.'

Uzi traced a tube from his arm upwards to a bag of blood. 'How long before I can get off this thing?'

'Half an hour minimum.'

'Twenty minutes. I have my cigarettes.'

Waxman shuffled his feet. 'I would lose my position if I let a patient smoke in an ambulance.'

'So what? We'd take you and your family straight to Israel. That's where you should be anyway.'

'Perhaps. But my children are at school, my wife and I have our careers . . .'

'But I was never here, right?'

'That's right.'

'So.'

Uzi sucked the last embers of life from his cigarette. 'Pass me an ashtray, will you?'

Waxman looked around and offered Uzi a cardboard kidney dish. Uzi stubbed out and for a while lay there in silence. Waxman sat on a fold-out chair.

'So have you been working much for us lately?' Uzi asked.

'A little. I did something last month, I think it was.'

'Serious?'

'No.'

They fell silent again until the bag of blood emptied. Then Waxman removed the needle and helped Uzi to his feet. Uzi felt strange, light-headed but strong. Waxman pressed a bottle of pain-killers and a bundle of fresh dressings into his hand. 'I'll remove the stitches in three weeks' time.'

'I'll do it myself,' Uzi replied as he stepped out of the ambulance into the breaking dawn. 'Let's hope I don't call on you again.'

Waxman smiled for the first time, openly relieved to have completed his mission.

Suddenly, Uzi was overcome with a sense of recklessness. Fuck them, he thought. A gnat biting an elephant. Fuck them. 'You've done a great job,' he said casually. 'How does fifty thousand sound?'

Waxman gulped. 'I've never been paid before . . . I'd donate it to charity. Well, most of it.'

'Good. Who's your contact at London Station?'

'Arik.'

'Well, speak to Arik and he'll transfer the funds. You know the communication protocol?'

'Yes, but I'm supposed to use it only in an emergency.'

'Use it now. Tell Arik I authorised it.'

'OK.'

'And Waxman?'

'Yes, Daniel?'

'Don't spend it all at once.' With that, Uzi slammed the ambulance door and made his way back to his apartment.

8

The painkillers had a limited effect, and Uzi knew he would be unable to sleep, so he decided not to try. Through a crack in the curtains he watched until Waxman's ambulance disappeared down the road. In the bathroom he scraped out the inside of the showerhead with a spoon and washed as best he could, without getting the bandages wet. Then he rolled himself a spliff and sat in front of his two televisions. The softening hand of marijuana caressed his injuries, led him to a pleasing remove from the world. He almost didn't notice when his ear began to itch.

'That was cheeky,' said the Kol, 'that thing with Waxman.' The voice was as cool and unemotional as ever.

'Can't we get back into our routine?' he mumbled. 'You were supposed to only come out at night.'

'I am the Kol. I can come out whenever I please.'

'You're a heartless bitch, you know that?' said Uzi.

The Kol fell silent. Uzi squinted at the screen through the fragrant smoke. The heat of the day was beginning to fall into his apartment; he opened the window and sat down. Slowly but surely, his eyelids became leaden and his mind gently wandered. The picture of Ram Shalev – the one which had been on the front page of all the newspapers after he was killed by Operation Cinnamon – appeared his mind. Smiling in his garden with his two children, his wife. The trees behind, the vivid blue sky, the button-down shirt. Uzi tried not to hold on to the image. He knew it would only make things worse. Eventually it passed, and for a while images of the ambulance appeared, pleasant images, as if it had been a comfortable place to be. As if it were a womb.

Then, memories of a kill sprang up, his second kill for the Office. Beirut, 2007. Lebanon was being rebuilt in the aftermath of the Israeli bombardment. A network of new roads and bridges was being constructed throughout the capital; Adam was posing as a building contractor, bribing local construction workers to build plastic cases into the infrastructure as they worked. Airtight plastic cases containing little Israeli-made bombs that could remain in a serviceable state for years, even decades, buried in bridges and motorways, to be detonated remotely at the push of a button. They would give Israel a great advantage if there was another war. But it was dangerous work. Not only was there a good chance that one of the construction workers would be caught in the act, but it was difficult to trust them. They were being paid handsomely, of course, but the operation had been put together in haste, and Adam hadn't had time to build up a solid connection with these men; as a result their relationship was always poisoned by suspicion.

One in particular – Walid Khaled, a wiry old labourer with the eyes of a beaten dog – had been spotted one night photographing the bridge with his mobile phone. No chances could be taken. A kill request was sent to Israel and the prime minister approved it within hours; an emergency closed-doors court case had ruled that the action was unavoidable. The only snag was that all the Kidonim – assassination units – were tied up elsewhere in the world. Adam would have to carry it out himself, despite his lack of expertise. The danger was too great; if Khaled reported him to the authorities, or, if he was clever enough, sold the information, the Office's mission would be compromised and Adam would almost certainly be dead. There was a chance that Khaled was innocent, of course. But Adam had no choice.

This was no time for a signature hit. The Office's usual brand of audacious, broad daylight attack – a devastating volley of dum-dum bullets in a public place, followed by a single shot to the temple – was out of the question. The operation was in a delicate enough state as it was. So Adam armed himself with a newspaper and a bottle of vodka, and arranged a meeting with Khaled.

He wasted no time. As soon as the labourer drove up in his dust-covered jalopy, Adam slid into the car and forced a Desflurane ether mask over the man's face. Khaled struggled, but had been taken by surprise. His fingernails scratched Adam's cheek; that was all. Adam drove north along the coast, with Khaled slumped in the back, until he found a stretch of secluded cliffs overlooking the Mediterranean. He hauled the unconscious labourer into the driver's seat, rolled the newspaper into a funnel – it was the Lebanese *Daily Star*, the ink rubbed off on his fingers, for some reason he remembered that – and poured half a bottle of vodka through the funnel and down the man's throat. Vodka, which he knew Khaled drank in secret. Vodka, which burns easily. He poured the rest of the bottle over the front seats, threw in a match and watched it go up. When the fire was raging, he pushed the car over the cliff. Then, after a long hike to the nearest town, he took the train back to Beirut.

It was this kill that floated back into his mind as he dozed; the rough scuff of the newspaper against his fingers, the lolling face of the labourer, vodka darkening his shirt like sweat; the vast, black Mediterranean sky and the indigo ocean, the flap of the flames as they burst into life in the car; the heat; the long, slow-motion tumble of the vehicle on to the rocks; the surf below. The feeling of it. The voice in the back of his mind – which he didn't allow himself to hear – asking whether there couldn't have been another way.

He was awoken by a loud buzzing.

'Tommy? It's Squeal. Open up, I can smell you're there. I'll huff, and I'll puff . . .'

Uzi yanked the door open.

'Just coming to see you, my man. To see how you're doing. You flush now? Sale went well?'

Uzi gripped Squeal by the biceps and brought him into the flat, his milk-coloured dreadlocks rasping as he looked around in bewilderment.

'Hey man, what gives? What gives?'

'What gives?' Uzi repeated, shoving Squeal down on the sofa. 'This is what gives.' He showed him the bandages on his arm, his leg. 'Your friend Andrzej did this. I thought you said he was safe.'

'What? Tommy, no way. You're kidding me.'

'Do I look like I'm fucking kidding you?'

'Shit, man, shit,' said Squeal. 'What happened?'

'That bastard tried to screw me. I was outnumbered. Butterfly knives.'

'Jesus, man. Jesus. Do you think he'll come after me?'

'I couldn't give a fuck.'

'Andrzej's been jumpy recently,' said Squeal. 'I know he's been jumpy. I should have warned you.'

'Why has he been jumpy?'

'He's had a few run-ins with the Russians, you know? Liberty.'

'Liberty?'

'Yeah, Liberty. That American bird.'

Uzi showed no sign that Squeal had got his attention. He started rolling a spliff, keeping his voice casual.

'American bird?' he asked.

'You've heard of her, yeah? American woman running a Russian gang. New on the scene, as far as I know. She's big time. Not just dope and E: crack, smack, the lot. Cross her and she'll fuck you good and proper.'

'An American woman running a Russian gang?' said Uzi, pretending to be one step behind, lighting the spliff.

'Straight up,' Squeal replied. 'Apparently she's got a way with them. Ruthless as fuck. Like I said, new on the scene. And you know what it's like with Russians and Poles.' He mimed a mushroom cloud with his hands and squealed.

Uzi passed the spliff across and closed his eyes. The pain had been dulled into a jangling throb, pulsating through his nervous system at a regular pace. Squeal smoked until half the joint was gone. Uzi didn't have the energy to ask for it back. Finally, leaving the remaining half smouldering in the ashtray, Squeal disappeared into the kitchen and came back with two strawberry mousses, two plates.

'Not now, Squeal. Not now. I've been cut,' said Uzi, shielding his eyes from the sight of the mousses.

'Don't be a pussy, Tommy. Come on. Pudding wars.' Squeal peeled back the lids of both tubs and upended them on the plates. They stood there, two pink, quivering sandcastles.

'I'm not doing it,' said Uzi.

'You are,' said Squeal. He placed the mousses side by side on the table and crouched over one of them, his mouth slightly open, poised an inch from the slippery surface. He looked at Uzi expectantly. Reluctantly Uzi assumed the same position above his mousse.

'On three,' said Squeal. He thumped his hand on the table three times and both men slurped loudly. The puddings vanished, as if by magic.

'Ha,' said Squeal, his mouth full, 'there's still some of yours left.'

Uzi looked at his plate, feeling slightly nauseous. He was right. 'Fuck.'

'That's another point to me, then,' crowed Squeal, displaying his own clean plate. 'You're only two ahead now.'

'I told you, I'm not well. I've been cut, for fuck's sake. By your friend.'

'No excuses.' Squeal's burst of energy subsided and he slumped back on the sofa.

Uzi's head drooped forwards, and once again he was standing on the edge of a cliff outside Beirut, watching a fireball consume a car below, the wind stripping him of his thoughts.

9

'Fuck, man. What happened to you?' said Avner, in French, as Uzi opened the door of his apartment.

'I haven't got the strength,' Uzi replied in Hebrew. 'Let's just speak our own language like normal people, OK?'

'Whatever you say,' Avner said, in Hebrew this time. 'So who did you piss off?'

Uzi shut the door, double-locked it, then, limping slightly, went into the kitchen.

'You've got an infestation,' said Avner, accepting a coffee and nodding to the worktop where a line of ants stretched to the window. 'What are they, crabs? Pubic crabs?'

Without a word, Uzi took a cloth and swept the insects to their deaths. With the movement he winced slightly.

'Looks bad,' said Avner, 'your shoulder.'

'I got Waxman to patch it up.'

'Waxman the Sayan?'

'Waxman the Sayan.'

'With the ambulance?'

'With the ambulance.'

'You cheeky bastard,' said Avner, 'you'd better be careful. The Office will have your balls.' Avner's phone rang. He allowed it to ring until it went silent.

'Have you heard of Liberty?' said Uzi.

'Liberty?'

'Liberty. American woman running a Russian drugs gang. You should know. You were stationed in London for long enough.'

'Ah yes, Liberty. I remember now.'

'I thought you might. What is she, CIA?'

'Used to be. Her name is Eve Klugman. Served as a covert operations officer in Iraq and Afghanistan, then resigned when she had a child. A year later her husband and baby were killed in a traffic accident. She spun out, married a Russian drug dealer based in London. Then he was killed, too, and she took over his gang.'

'I ran into her last night,' said Uzi.

'She can be pretty brutal. She's got a reputation.'

'Can you get me her file? From the Office?'

'I can't do that any more than you can, Adam. You know that.'

'Stop bullshitting me. What about all these horses you keep talking about? You're in London Station. Get me the file.'

'Horses can only do so much. Why do you want to know, anyway? Did she do this to you?'

'Don't be stupid. It was some Poles, small-time. Only three of them.'

'You're losing your touch, Adam.'

'The knife only needs to get through once.'

'It's never got through before. And you got cut twice.'

There was a pause. Uzi wondered when Avner was going to mention Operation Regime Change. But he said nothing.

'I need your help,' Uzi said.

'I knew this was coming.'

'I can't just sit back and do nothing. It would kill my business.'

'So this was about business?'

'I've got to do something to show them I'm not someone they can fuck with. Otherwise they'll all be at it. I'll be dead by the end of the year.'

'Why don't you just give it all up? Come and work for me.'

'It's got to be proper, hard revenge. A real deterrent. This can't happen again.'

'I could use a man like you.'

'I don't want to work for you.'

'You need to get a stable job, Adam. Something to give you some structure. Leave all this low-level stuff behind.'

'I told you, I have a day job. I'm a protection operative.'

'That's too similar to the Office. Psychologically speaking.'

'What are you, a fucking therapist?'

'Come on.' Avner turned his attention to his coffee.

'Look, will you help me or not?' said Uzi after a time.

'You haven't told me what you're going to do yet.'

Without a word, Uzi went back into the sitting room, beckoning Avner to follow him. There he drew the curtains. He was sweating, the back of his neck was itching horribly and the cyst on his shoulder was aching.

'Right,' he said, and then couldn't think of what to say. So he crouched on the floor and started prising the top layer of wood from the coffee table.

'Don't tell me,' said Avner. 'Don't tell me you're still building slicks.'

'Aren't you?' Uzi replied, not looking up.

'It is a slick,' said Avner. 'I don't believe it. You're actually still doing this stuff.'

The panel came away and Uzi put it aside. In the table was a hollow cavity filled with canvas-wrapped objects.

'I can't watch this,' said Avner. 'You've got to move on, Adam. Seriously, I can't watch.' But he didn't turn away.

With precise movements Uzi uncovered the first object. A 9mm Beretta 92F, steel through and through, the trademark weapon of the Office. Next was a 9mm Glock 17, the type he used to carry in Shayetet 13, light and tough. These were followed by several magazines of bullets.

'Just like the old days,' said Avner. He reached into the slick and pulled out a small rucksack. 'You've got all the kit, haven't you? You've got the lot.'

Uzi sat on the sofa, a sidearm in each hand, a half-smile playing across his lips. He watched as Avner reached into the bag, drawing out object after object. A matchbox filled with putty for taking impressions of keys. False number plates. Various listening devices. Miniature cameras. A dagger.

'It's all here,' said Avner, shaking his head. 'I don't believe what I'm seeing.'

Uzi offered him the Glock.

'The Beretta,' said Avner, 'give me the Beretta.' Uzi obliged and Avner aimed it into space, chuckling. Then he stood there, weighing it in his hands like a gold bar. 'I can't remember the last time I held one of these. I wonder what happened to mine?'

'You probably sold it,' said Uzi drily.

Avner looked him square in the face. 'Look, I'm not going to kill anybody, if that's what you're thinking.'

'Nobody gets killed,' Uzi replied. 'I'm not stupid. Like I said, I'm talking about a deterrent.'

Avner sat next to him on the sofa. For a moment both men were silent, looking at the weapons in their hands, lost in the memories they evoked.

'Have you thought about our conversation?' said Avner suddenly.

'What conversation?'

'Operation Regime Change. Are you going to do it?'

'I haven't decided. I've been too busy getting knifed.'

'It's important, Adam.'

'Why are we talking about this all of a sudden?' said Uzi, suddenly annoyed. 'All you can think about is one thing.'

'Look, Adam. I'll make you an offer.'

'Let's hear it.'

'I'll do you a favour if you do me a favour. What you need to do is agree to Operation Regime Change.'

'Anything else?' said Uzi, sarcastically.

'Nothing more than that. You do that and I'll help you out with your Polish problem.'

'Are you serious?'

'What?'

'I help change the course of history and you help me sort out a couple of Poles?'

'That's it.'

'You're something else, Avner.'

'There's a lot of money in it for you.'

'Money,' said Uzi, rolling the word in his mouth. 'Money.'

He lit a cigarette and tossed the pack to his companion. 'OK,' he said at length, 'what have I got to lose? I'm fucked as it is, right?'

'Right,' said Avner, a little too quickly. 'So we've got a deal?'

'We've almost got a deal,' Uzi said. 'But what you're asking for is big. So I'm going to ask you to do a few more things for me.'

'What?'

'First, get me the file on Liberty.' Uzi watched for Avner's response, and read from his face that he could do it.

'Second?' said Avner, examining a fingernail.

'Second, we go fifty-fifty. Not sixty-forty.'

Avner smiled tensely. 'Anything else?'

'Yeah, one more thing. Stop calling me fucking Adam. It's Uzi, get it? From now on, you call me Uzi. You agree to all of that, and we've got a deal.'

10

London was copper in the evening light as Uzi left his apartment and stepped into the street. Avner was waiting for him in a white van, his elbow on the open window like a side of meat. Already Uzi was sweating. He was wearing a new jacket, into which that afternoon he had sewn new weights. He was carrying a small rucksack.

'You're early,' said Uzi.

'Can't wait to get going,' Avner replied. 'It's been a long time.'

'You've changed your tune. Yesterday you were complaining like an old woman.'

Avner started the engine and started to reverse around a corner and down a narrow alleyway.

'It's true. We should have prepared better,' he said, adjusting the steering wheel by increments and craning over his shoulder. 'We haven't done enough surveillance, we haven't got good enough intelligence. We haven't even got a backup plan.'

'Relax,' said Uzi. 'We won't need a backup plan. This is child's play. It couldn't get any easier.'

'The knife only needs to get through once. Twice in your case.'

'Fuck you.'

Uzi lit two cigarettes and passed one to his companion. 'Look,' he said. 'We can't afford to wait until everything is perfect. I've got to do this now. Also, they won't be expecting it.'

'Why not?'

'I got Waxman to make enquiries about a murder there. Posing as CID.'

'You're kidding.'

'Straight up. They think I'm dead.'

'And Waxman did that for you?'

'He didn't do it for me. He did it for his country.'

Avner laughed. 'You're a cunning bastard, Adam, you know that?'

'Uzi.'

'Ah, sorry. Uzi.'

'I got Waxman to tell them the bar is under surveillance and anything out of the ordinary would be noted. So they won't run. We'll get them tonight.'

Avner was still chuckling as he parked the van in the shadows of the alleyway.

Uzi jumped down and fitted false number plates on to the van. Then Avner gunned the engine, routed his iPod through the van's sound system and turned it up. Immediately Uzi recognised Hadag Nahash, the most famous – and left-wing – hip-hop band in Israel. People from the Office were into Subliminal, the right-ist rapper famous for 'The Light From Zion'. To listen to Hadag Nahash was tantamount to treachery. Uzi got into the van and turned the aggressive beat up louder. Avner drove to the end of the alleyway and turned on to the road. Uzi's ear began to itch and he thought the Kol was going to make an appearance. But then the itch faded. He hadn't heard from the voice in a while. Long may it continue, he thought. Nodding their heads to the rhythm, they set off in the direction of Camden.

When they arrived, Avner killed the music and parked the van in the shadows behind the Blue Peacock. The air was thick with exhaust and heat, and a cloud of birds was circling overhead. The sun was almost dead.

'Right,' said Avner, 'let's do it.' He took from his pocket a small moisturiser tub and opened the lid to reveal a transparent, glue-like substance.

'No,' said Uzi, 'no way. I'm not using that stuff.'

'What are you talking about?' said Avner, dipping his finger-tips in the tub.

'It irritates my skin, you know that. Itches like fuck.'

'So you're going to put fingerprints everywhere?'

'I'll wear gloves or something.'

'Gloves in a bar? In the middle of summer?'

'I'll worry about that.'

'You brought some gloves?'

'You were going to bring some.'

'I brought this stuff instead. I forgot about your delicate skin.'

'Give me that,' growled Uzi, and began to apply the substance. For a few minutes they sat there in silence, hands in the air, waiting for their fingertips to dry.

Uzi got out of the van and listened for a moment. The dull throb of a bassline coming from the bar. Traffic. The whine of a distant motorbike. Nothing out of place.

Several square windows were set into the back wall of the building, and a fire escape zigzagged up to the roof. Uzi, limping slightly, climbed the fire escape until he was level with a first-floor window. The music obscured everything, no other sounds could be heard from the building. The window was blacked out, as he remembered it. His fingers were already beginning to itch. He rummaged in his rucksack for a tiny camera on adhesive pads, which he stuck to the glass. Then he returned to the van.

On Avner's iPhone nothing could be seen but blackness, the opaque glass of the window. He pressed some buttons and the camera focused on the room. Gradually a scene emerged from the haze, in green monotone, but distinguishable nevertheless. Andrzej could be seen in his usual place at the table, and his two comrades lounged on sofas. Girls were moving around with drinks, smoking joints.

'That's the target?' said Avner.

Uzi nodded. Suddenly he almost felt sorry for them, these small-time gangsters from Poland. But business was business. He put on a baseball cap and a pair of wire-rimmed glasses. Then, looking at his reflection in the rear-view mirror, he peeled a moustache and goatee beard from a piece of waxed paper and fixed them both to his face. Without a word, both men got out of the van.

The Blue Peacock was noisy and filling up with people. Uzi's disguise was thin but effective; he wasn't recognised. They made their way to the bar and ordered two pints of Staropramen. Then, at a table in the corner, they sat, drinking, waiting. Uzi scratched his fingers against his jeans. 'I'm desperate for a cigarette,' he said. 'This fucking country.'

'You should thank them,' Avner replied, 'they're saving you from yourself.'

They drank.

'Come on, come on,' said Uzi, his casual body language contrasting with the urgency in his voice. 'What are they waiting for?'

'Relax,' said Avner. 'You really have lost your touch, haven't you?' He took out his iPhone. 'It's OK, our friends aren't going anywhere.'

Uzi gazed out onto the dance floor and, without warning, an image of a kill – his third, for the Office at least – flashed into his mind. It had been a simple one. A Hamas lynchpin on an arms-buying mission had made an unforeseen detour and ended up staying in the same hotel as Adam, in Paris. The opportunity was too good to miss. Adam's original mission was put on hold. The kill order was given. Again, looking out at the dance floor, he felt the weight of the rifle in his hands. Again he saw, through his coin of glass, the man who was going to die, walking on the Pont de la Concorde, smiling, talking in a way that would be familiar to his mother, his friends. The cross-hairs touched his face. Now. And the living man became a corpse. This was Adam's sorcery, the sorcery of the Office. How easy it was to make a ghost.

'Drink up,' said Avner, 'it's almost time.'

A barmaid turned up the music. That was what they had been waiting for: cover. Avner was watching Uzi keenly, his face illuminated from below by the light of the iPhone. He passed it over. There was Andrzej on the screen, there were his two sidekicks, sitting around the table. Andrzej was waving the girls away; the men were getting down to business.

From his inside pocket Avner took out what looked like a phial of eye drops, and with a quick movement squeezed two squirts into each of their half-full pint glasses. There was a slight fizz; the beer settled. They got to their feet and made their way across the bar. The girls who had been in the room, who had appeared on Avner's iPhone, emerged and crossed to the dance floor. In the next moment, while everyone was looking the other way, Uzi and Avner slipped up the stairs.

The corridor was narrow, forcing them to go up single file. There was a stifling smell of beer and marijuana. Uzi followed Avner, holding his pint glass tight and grinding his teeth. His footsteps felt loud in his ears, echoing in the confined space, though the music was loud. They arrived at the door. Avner knocked loudly, and the door opened a fraction. Immediately he snaked his hand into the gap and flung his beer into the man's face. There was a howl. Avner pushed his way into the room, aiming his Beretta. Uzi followed, drawing his Glock and throwing beer across the faces of the two other men who were getting up from the table. They crumpled, also howling now, clawing at their faces as if they were wrapped in flames. Andrzej himself, blinded by the beer, careened across the room like a bull, arms flailing, bellowing; Uzi sidestepped and struck him a heavy blow with the butt of his Glock. He went down awkwardly, making a strange coughing noise. Uzi placed a foot on the back of his head, pushed his burning face into the floor.

Avner rammed a chair under the door handle. Swiftly, Avner and Uzi searched the Poles, taking their knives and lining them up on the table. They gagged them and handcuffed them with plastic cords. Then, gripping Andrzej by the hair, Uzi removed his disguise, peeling off his beard and moustache and tossing his cap and glasses to the floor.

'Remember me?' he said in Russian. 'Oh I forgot, you can't see very well at the moment. Don't worry, you will soon.' Andrzej, behind his gag, gurgled. His skin and eyes were crimson from the acid-laced beer. Uzi struck him a blow across the face and left him to his muffled moaning sounds on the floor. 'I am your Russian master. Nobody fucks with me. I want you to remember that.' Andrzej shook his head feverishly as Uzi turned away, coldness pouring from his eyes, heat raging inside him.

Avner left the room and Uzi jammed the door closed again behind him. Then he turned towards the three Poles, who were slumped against the red drapes like dolls. He raised his gun. Three pairs of bloodshot eyes stared out blindly. 'I have a gun in my hand,' he said, 'and I need some target practice.' One soiled himself, then the other. Not Andrzej, though. Not yet.

From his rucksack, Uzi took several rolls of brown packing tape. This was a technique he had picked up from the Christian militias in Lebanon, but he'd never had to use it. Until now. He started with Andrzej, winding the packing tape around one of his ankles. The man kicked frantically, and Uzi struck him in the groin, wincing with pain from the wound in his shoulder. As Andrzej writhed in pain, Uzi wrapped the packing tape around both of his ankles, binding them together, then around his feet, and up his legs, leaving no gaps, layer upon layer. Andrzej struggled, but it was too late. Uzi carried on, up and up, passing the roll of tape from hand to hand under his body, until he reached his neck. The brown tape covered his chin and mouth. Then his nose, eyes, hair. Uzi peeled back the tape around his nostrils to prevent him from suffocating. All that was left was a man-shaped shining parcel, glistening like wood in the gloom. Uzi stepped back and stared at the other two men. Their faces were shiny and sore from the acid. He picked up another roll of tape.

It took Uzi and Avner some time to get all three 'parcels' out of the window, down the fire escape and into the van. Uzi's injuries made it difficult; it was as if being in the presence of the people who had stabbed him was causing his wounds to smart. The men were arranged in rows in the back of the van. They made no noise. Then Avner gunned the engine and they threaded through the night-time traffic in the direction of the M1.

'A job well done,' said Avner in Russian, still full of adrenaline. He threw back his head and laughed.

'It's not over yet,' said Uzi in the same language. He reached into his rucksack, pulled out a CD and slid it into the machine.

'What's that?' asked Avner as the sound of strident classical music swelled.

'Mily Balakirev,' said Uzi, 'the most Russian of Russian composers.' He turned it up louder. 'A little psychological flourish for our Polish cargo.'

The van, one vehicle among hundreds, thousands, tens of thousands, crept under the dystopian network of uplit flyovers at Staples Corner and pulled into an all-night car wash, music still blasting. Long fluffy cylinders fell softly on the bonnet, climbed over the windscreen and spread tendrils of foam across the van. Uzi and Avner lit cigarettes, breathed ropes of smoke through their noses. On the front and back bumpers, the water covered the false number plates. As a result of contact with the soap the top layer cracked. The fragments slipped, eroded and gradually dissolved, exposing a second set of number plates below, another false identity. The wash cycle finished. Avner steered the van out of the carwash and back on to the road. Uzi looked in the rear-view mirror, all around; nothing untoward could be seen. But he could feel it. He'd felt it all night. They were being watched.

11

Adam stepped out of the white Mercedes and laid eyes for the first time on the prime minister's summer residence. Now he knew for certain what he was dealing with, and this only heightened the tension. There was only one organisation based here. Everybody knew it. Its name was legendary. The massive, whitewashed building, set on a hill and surrounded with every luxury imaginable, was the seat of the most famed and feared intelligence service in the world. And he had just been accepted into it.

In the glaring sunlight, he looked about him. Several identical cars were parking alongside in the formation of a fan, and from each a new recruit emerged, accompanied by their recruiters. They were ushered in past the guards, through metal detectors, past the retina scanners, past more guards, and into the atrium of the Midrasha – the Academy.

The atmosphere was silent, almost sacrosanct. Everything was white: the walls, the ceiling, the stairs. The floor was pale marble. A staircase spiralled upwards, constructed to look as if it were suspended in thin air. A glass wall faced an inner garden full of trees heavy with figs and dates. On either side two long corridors stretched into the distance. On the walls, fully two metres tall, were aerial photographs of the land of Israel. And prominently displayed above the main entrance was the motto of the Academy, embossed in gilt upon stone: 'By way of deception thou shalt make war'.

The new recruits were shown into an airy classroom of butter-coloured stone. They settled into their seats. The initiation process had made them guarded, ready for anything; they dared not speak. Around the edge of the room sat the recruiters, murmuring to each other in confidential tones. Then a hush fell in the room and everyone got to their feet. Adam turned to see a bear-like man prowling to the front as if intent on something immensely practical. Behind him was a smartly dressed woman, in her forties Uzi guessed, with the bearing of someone who has the power to subjugate any level of chaos with ease. The man rested heavily on a lectern and the woman stood behind him, holding a leather folder like a breastplate. Everyone sat down, and Adam felt the aversion he normally felt to synagogue rise within him, then disappear.

'Welcome, recruits,' said the man. 'I am Ezra Oren, the head of the Midrasha. Congratulations to all of you for passing the tests. You are now theoretically members of the organisation we call "the Office". It has a real name, and that is well known. I will speak it once now, and you will never hear it from me, or any other member of the Office again. You are now working for HaMossad leModi'in ule Tafkidim Meyuchadim (the Institute for Intelligence and Special Operations) – the Mossad. Know this, appreciate it – and forget it.'

Adam felt as if all his blood had been drained from his body and replaced with ice, which was then pumped out and replaced with boiling water. He wanted to move, to run, to punch, but he couldn't. The Mossad. He had known, of course; everybody had known. But now it had been declared. And nobody could ever take it away from him.

'You were each chosen above thousands of other candidates,' Oren continued, 'because you have the raw material we need. Now we need to mould you into intelligence operatives. I can promise that not all of you will make it through training. In the past we have had groups in which not a single person qualified. We would rather that than risk having one substandard person in the Office. We are like a family; we rely on each other to survive and to defend Jews around the world. So we don't care about size or quotas. If you want to be part of the best intelligence service in existence – the best family in existence – you need to be the best as well.'

Part of Adam's mind felt detached, ironic. But the rest of his mind – most of him – was drinking it all in as the heat passed through his veins.

'The game you are stepping into is dangerous,' Oren continued. 'From now on, the highest price is no longer your own life. There are many things more valuable than that.' He looked coldly from one recruit to the next. 'You must trust your instructors completely. They are field operatives on sabbatical, not career instructors; afterwards, they will return to the field. They will see you as future partners, future colleagues, not students. That is, apart from myself: I have been in the Office for thirty years, and there are now very few places in Europe that I can still go safely. So I am babysitting you children – for the moment.' He paused, leaned on the lectern again.

'In short, our methods are based on experience, not on theoretical textbooks and regulations,' he went on. 'That's what we are offering you. And on a personal note, I must tell you that the story from my Shabak days – about my bursting a man's eyeball during a mock interrogation in training – is not true.' He straightened up and glanced at the woman behind him, rubbing his chin. His expression was stony, impassive. The woman stepped forward.

'Michal Bar-Tov, head of internal security,' she said with the briefest of nods. 'You have heard what you can expect from us. For this, we expect you to give us your whole life. From now on you must expose everything – I mean everything – to us. New friends can only be made with prior approval. You must bring in your passports and documents, as well as those of your family, to be stored here. When people ask about your new job, tell them you're working for the defence department and can't talk about it. Whatever you do, don't tell them you're working at a bank or a kindergarten. It will only arouse curiosity.' There was a slight ripple of laughter, which she silenced with a glance. 'There will be a lie detector test every three months which you will all be obliged to take.'

'No, you're not obliged,' Oren contradicted her. 'You children have the right to refuse the lie detector. Which gives me the right to shoot you.'

Somebody cleared his throat into the silence.

'Lastly,' said Bar-Tov, 'you must never talk about work over the phone, or at home, or in any other unauthorised situation. Anyone who does this will be severely punished. Don't ask me how I will know. I am the head of internal security. I will know everything.'

She paused and looked around the room, scrutinising every face, every expression, every movement of every eyelid, every shuffle. Adam stole a glance left and right. His fellow recruits looked tough, battle-hardened and wily in their own ways. But none of them dared move, let alone speak.

'Children,' said Oren, drawing himself up to his full height, 'enjoy your last few minutes as blind people. Today we start to open your eyes.'

After that, the morning passed with various inductions. In silence the recruits filed through the technology room, the listening department, the library of passports and documents, the armoury, the recreation area. They would be given training in five areas: intelligence gathering, communications protocol, general military knowledge, covert and secret technology, and undercover operations. And Adam, like the other recruits, was impatient for it all to begin.

He didn't have to wait for long. After a sumptuous lunch in the prime minister's dining room, with menus sourced from the best restaurants in the world – Office operatives would have to be comfortable in such environments, and this would form part of their training – they were ordered to hand in their identity cards and driven in groups of three to downtown Tel Aviv. Adam was once again placed in the charge of Yigal, who was as taciturn on the drive back into the city as he had been on the way out of it. The hottest part of the day had given way to the scorching closeness of the mid-afternoon, when heat seems to rise from everything: the tarmac, the pavement, the cars. Adam began to feel drowsy as the Mercedes hummed gently through the traffic. The psychologist was driving; Adam's eyes rested on the hair on top of his head until it blurred, and he dozed.

But it was thoughts of Nehama, still his Nehama, that prevented him from losing consciousness completely. Had she planned to tell him she was pregnant? Was she intending to leave him? Was she afraid of what he might say, of what he might do? He checked his phone: nothing. The dumb inanimateness of a tool not being used. He turned it off.

Eventually the psychologist parked somewhere in the HaRakevet district, north-west of the LaGuardia Interchange. They got out, and Adam followed him and Yigal through the streets, feeling naked and vulnerable without his ID card. If he were caught there would be trouble, especially given his standing in the military. They reached the Yad Harutzim, a street famous for its cafés and bars. They bought coffees and stood on the corner, in the shade.

At length, Yigal spoke. 'Look over there,' he said, gesturing into the sun. 'See that police officer across the road? Here's your task. Find out his first name and his last name. Find out where he's from. Sit with him in his car and have a drink of water. Then come back.'

'What shall I do if he asks for my ID? I was told to hand it in.'

'Then what do you want me to say? Think of a cover story and stick to it.'

'I'll be arrested.'

'Stick to your cover story. You have seven minutes.'

Adam drained his coffee, crumpled the paper cup and dropped it in the bin. Then he walked as casually as possible across the baking tarmac. The police officer was leaning on his squad car, surveying the street.

He was an imposing figure, almost a full head taller than Adam. For some reason he reminded him of the legendary Golem, the statue that was brought to life by a mystic seventeenth-century Rabbi and oath-bound to protect the Jews. His hand was resting on the butt of his handgun as if he were ready to use it; his sunglasses reflected his badge, his squad car, the street. A rookie, Adam thought. Only a rookie caresses his weapon like that. As he approached, the officer watched him, sensing that he wanted to talk. The man seemed nervy, probably just out of the army. This was not an easy assignment.

'Officer, hello,' said Adam in his best American drawl. 'Do you speak English?'

'A little,' stumbled the officer in a heavy accent, taken off-guard.

'I wanted to ask you a question,' said Adam. 'Can I ask you a question?'

The policeman nodded stiffly.

'I'm a film-maker,' Adam said. 'From America. You know? I make films.'

The officer looked confused. 'Film?'

'Yes, you know. Movies. *Terminator*? *Die Hard*? *Batman*?'

'OK,' said the officer, without breaking a smile. 'So?'

'I'm making a film set in Tel Aviv, and I need a police officer to act in it.'

'Police?'

'Yes, like you. Turn to the side?'

The officer hesitated then offered his profile. And that was when Adam knew he had him.

'Yes, you'd be perfect,' he said. 'What's your name?'

'My name?'

'Yes.'

'Yaakov Riff.'

'From where?'

'Me?'

'Yes, where are you from?'

'Giv'atayim.'

'Do you have a number where I can contact your superior officers to ask their permission, Riff?'

This level of English was beyond the officer, and it took some time for him to understand. The minutes were slipping away, but Adam couldn't take any chances; one wrong move could ruin everything. At length, the officer took out a piece of paper and wrote a number down, leaning on his squad car. Adam decided to go in for the kill.

'We pay one thousand dollars a day,' he said. 'I know it's not much, but we're talking about a small part. How does that sound?'

When, through repetition and gesticulation, the officer understood what Adam was saying, he nodded like a schoolboy. His hand, for the first time, left his sidearm. It was now or never.

'This car,' said Adam, 'you can drive it fast?'

The officer nodded.

'You are good at driving fast?'

Another nod. A small smile now. Adam walked around the car, looking at it from different angles through fingers squared to mimic a camera.

'You want I should get in?' asked the officer. Adam's heart took a leap. He shrugged nonchalantly.

From then on, it was easy. The officer posed. Adam asked to see the perspective from the front seat of the car; the officer welcomed him in. The vehicle smelled so strongly of Magic Tree that Adam's subsequent coughing fit was only partially faked. Either way, it wasn't long before the officer offered him some water. Adam glanced surreptitiously at his watch. Seven minutes exactly. He asked the officer to turn to the side again so he could see his profile against the light. He caught eyes with Yigal across the street, and raised his cup in salute.

People are there to be used, Adam realised. You don't need a gun to make them do what you want. Find the right opening – money, sex, revenge, vanity – and they're yours. No question about it. This was superhuman. All in the name of freedom, democracy, his people. This was special.

12

'I can't wait to fuck the Office,' said Avner, 'those bastards.'

They were sitting in the van, parked in the shadows under a broken streetlight in a Tesco car park.

'Sure, sure, they're all sons of whores,' said Uzi, scratching his fingers, 'but is it really worth it?'

'Worth what?'

'Going into hiding. Spending the rest of our lives on the run.'

'Getting nervous?'

'Who said anything about nervous?'

'Look, Uzi, you've agreed already. If you're going to let me down, just tell me. I can bail out of this operation now.'

'Don't go mad, Avner. Of course I'll do it.'

'Don't even think about it, then.'

'OK, OK. Trust me.'

'I trust you just like you trust me,' said Avner.

They both smiled, and Uzi cleared his throat. The hot night sat heavily around them.

'Do you think we should check on the Poles?' said Uzi. 'They've been quiet for almost an hour.'

'You've gone soft,' said Avner. 'Check on them if you want.'

Uzi snorted and sat back. For a while he looked out of the window into the darkness. Then he got out and went round to the back of the van. Just as he was about to open the door, he heard a voice.

'Uzi.' His ear hadn't itched this time.

'What do you want? I'm busy.'

'It's night-time. We arranged to speak in the night-time.'

'If there's nothing to speak about, we don't need to speak,' said Uzi under his breath, glancing warily around.

'But there is something to speak about. There is a lot to speak about.'

'I'm sure there is. But I'm busy right now, OK? I'm on an operation.'

'You didn't tell me anything about an operation.'

'I don't have to tell you everything. You're not my mother. This is a personal operation, it has nothing to do with you. You're going to drive me crazy, you know that? You're going to drive me crazy.'

There was a silence and Uzi thought the Kol had gone. But then, just as he was reaching out to the door handle, the voice spoke again.

'Believe in yourself, Uzi,' it said calmly.

Uzi shook his head and sighed. Avner's face could be seen watching him quizzically in the wing mirror. Uzi made a gesture that all was well. Then – tentatively – he opened the door of the van.

There were the three men, like felled logs in the half-light. It was as silent as a morgue. His fingers were itching and he cursed. He climbed inside, closed the door and squatted among them, holding a cigarette lighter aloft. A chill came over him despite the heat. He couldn't account for this feeling of dread; in the past, this never would have bothered him. Before doing anything further, he lit a cigarette from the flame of the lighter and inhaled deeply. One of the men coughed and let out a low moan. At least he was alive. The other two did not move.

He stretched out his free hand and rested it lightly on the shiny chest of the man nearest to him. It might have been anybody; they were covered in tape from head to foot, there was nothing individual about them. The chest was rising and falling normally. He removed his hand and shuffled on his haunches over to the third man. His chest seemed still. Uzi flattened his hand on the chest and applied a little pressure. Nothing. The cigarette lighter flickered out, plunging the world into blackness; only the red glow of the cigarette remained. Silence sat tangibly inside the van. Uzi sparked the lighter and looked again. He turned his face to the side and lowered his ear to the man's nose. Nothing – nothing. The lighter went out.

Just as Uzi was about to light it again, there was a crackling, jolting sound and something collided against his face. This was followed by a muffled moan, and a muffled shriek, which was joined by another, lower voice, all the more unnerving for its lack of volume. Uzi was knocked again, and overbalanced on to his back. The parcelled men were bucking and rearing in the darkness all around him, making unearthly noises. He got to his hands and knees and scrabbled on the floor, trying to find his lighter. The van was bouncing on its suspension, creaking. He knew he should call out, but he couldn't. Pride or terror, perhaps both. His eyes opened wide, then wider, he couldn't see a thing. The weird cacophony continued all around him, these alien sounds, the crackling of packing tape, bodies wriggling and jack-knifing like fish.

The door was flung open, the overhead light came on, and there stood Avner, Beretta drawn. With a succession of sharp blows with the butt of his weapon, together with a stream of Russian curses, he subdued the chaos. Then he helped Uzi climb down.

'Look at you,' laughed Avner, closing the door. 'What's happened to you?'

'Fuck you,' Uzi replied, 'just fuck off.'

He got back into the van and put another cigarette between his trembling teeth. He had no lighter. He cursed, beat his fists against the dashboard.

The door opened and Avner climbed in, still chuckling.

'What's so fucking funny?' said Uzi.

'Relax, my friend, relax,' Avner said. 'You've had a hard night.'

Uzi punched the dashboard once more and they fell silent. He lit his cigarette from Avner's lighter, and smoked aggressively. When the cigarette was finished he took some cannabis from his pocket and started to roll a joint.

'Come on,' said Avner, 'we're on an operation. Take it easy.'

'This isn't a fucking operation.' Uzi growled. 'I left the Office, remember? There aren't any more operations.'

'Look, just put the joint down. If you're stoned and something goes wrong, we'll both be fucked. I saw you talking to yourself out there.'

'What's your problem? It's just a spliff.'

'Not when we're on an operation. Not when I'm on your side.'

'But are you on my side? You're still working for the Office, if only as a shit shoveller.'

'What are you talking about? I'm doing you a favour.'

'You call this a favour? This isn't a favour. It's a two-way street. I'm helping you with your political hocus-pocus as well, don't forget. Getting you your money.'

'Whatever. I just don't want a stoner with me on an operation, that's all.'

'Fuck you.'

Uzi lit the spliff and began to smoke. There was a pause. He looked through the windscreen at the supermarket. The last of the customers had left the shop long ago, and inside the staff could be seen moving to and fro, stacking shelves, cleaning floors. Soon it would be time to end this thing and go home for a few hours' sleep. He was feeling mellower now. He looked over at Avner, who was resting his head on the side window.

'Want some?' he said, holding out the spliff.

'Oh fuck it,' said Avner, and took a long drag.

The moon shone and the Tesco staff started to leave.

'Let's do it now,' said Uzi.

'Not yet,' Avner replied. 'It's still too busy.'

The air was close and still. Avner opened the sun roof. There was a pause.

'I think we're being watched,' said Uzi.

'We're not being watched.'

'I can feel it.'

Avner shook his head. 'Already you're getting spy syndrome? You've got to kick the dope habit. You're not the man you used to be.'

'None of us are.'

'But with you it's because of the dope.'

'What are you, a therapist?'

'You've got to give it up, you know. This habit.'

'Whatever.'

There was a pause.

'Do you have any idea where you might go?' said Avner.

'When?'

'After our operation. When we start over.'

'I told you, I'm staying here in London. Otherwise I wouldn't bother building my business. I wouldn't be bothering with these jokers in the back.'

'You can ruin your life if you want. I'm going somewhere nice.'

'You should try Greece. It's cheap over there at the moment.'

'I can't speak Greek,' said Avner.

'You could learn.'

They stopped talking as a car swept past them, headlights sweeping the road, heading for home.

'Funny, isn't it?' said Uzi. 'What we've become.'

'Funny?' said Avner.

'A year ago we were gods. Now look at us. Taking petty revenge on some small-time losers. Funny, eh?'

'Yeah, hilarious.'

They watched the supermarket for a while longer. More staff left. Then it was time. Avner released the handbrake and the van rolled silently out of the shadows towards the bottle bank. They pulled ski masks over their faces, then Uzi used a pair of bolt cutters to open the lid. Avner hauled the three parcels out and laid them out on the tarmac. They were breathing, but otherwise not making a sound.

'Now, children,' said Uzi in Russian, 'your eyes will be feeling better by now. Who wants to see again?' He reached down to the first of the men and pulled away the tape from around his eyes. A pair of pupils flicked from side to side.

'Like Arab women,' said Avner, restoring the gift of sight to the second man. Uzi laughed and did the same to the third. Then he laughed louder to show he was not afraid. There they were: three wrinkled mummies with eyes.

'Now, my Polish children,' he said, 'we are about to start our lesson for today. We're learning not to fuck with Tomislav Kasheyev. Concentrate, children, because you'll have an exam on it later.'

Widening eyes. The occasional scuff against the ground. Uzi was sick to the stomach but he didn't admit it, even to himself. His wounds were hurting. But business was business.

'Get on with it,' said Avner under his breath.

'See behind me?' said Uzi. 'Recycling. They only empty it every two weeks.'

The first two men struggled and made muffled cries as Uzi and Avner hoisted them on to their shoulders and slid them down into the bottle bank. The third was limp, resigned, and sobbing. The bottles clashed and clattered as the men struggled in the dark, panicking.

'Study hard,' said Uzi into the echoing space. 'Don't forget there's an exam coming. Be careful of falling bottles. And remember: next time, don't fuck with Tomislav Kasheyev.'

He slammed the lid and, without looking back, climbed into the van and lit a cigarette. Avner joined him and rolled the vehicle back into the shadows, away from the CCTV. There he prised off the remaining false number plates before revving the engine and driving off into the night.

13

That night, Uzi couldn't sleep. He knew he would be cursed in this way; he'd always suffered from insomnia after operations. The adrenaline. For a long time he lay with his head pressed into the pillow, in a mumbled conversation with the Kol. Then he sat up in front of his computer, scratching his fingertips, smoking spliff after spliff and eating strawberry mousses, watching the flickering screen. Before slamming the lid on the Polish men's tomb he had stuck a disposable camera, the size of a fingernail, to the inner wall with adhesive pads. It was this that transmitted the images he watched on his computer screen all night; grainy images, in greens and blacks, three parcels slumped amongst the jagged fragments of glass, writhing occasionally and lying still again. He felt like a child watching caterpillars in a jar. Several times he had an impulse to go back and release them. But he didn't.

As morning broke, the bottles began to fall. One parcel in particular, which happened to be lying in an unfortunate position, became all but submerged within a single hour. Some of the bottles broke; Uzi couldn't see any blood. He couldn't afford to follow his urge to go back and release them. He knew that the gags would be growing less effective by now, having been soaked in saliva and chewed for hours on end. He knew their ordeal would be over soon.

Sure enough, at around midday the bottle bank was suddenly illuminated. Two minutes later, a policeman in a reflective jacket climbed in and fumbled tentatively through the glass towards those strange, brown mermen, who by now were jerking and flailing madly, hoping to be rescued. Uzi waited until he had seen the policeman pulling away the packing tape from their faces. Then he clicked the red button in the corner of the screen, and when asked 'are you sure?' clicked 'yes'. The picture went black. Several miles away, with a fizzing sound that nobody had noticed, the camera had destroyed itself.

Uzi wasn't worried that the operation would come back to bite him. He had seen the terror in his victims' eyes. He knew there was no way they would dare to retaliate, or get the police involved. They had been humiliated, and the word would soon get around. He was safe. Instead, what haunted him over the next few weeks as he sat in a cramped shed at the entrance to Hasmonean Girls' School in Hendon, equipped with nothing but a two-way radio and a CCTV screen, waiting for his wounds to heal, was – as usual – the Brussels kill, his first for the Office. He had taken life before he joined, of course he had, but only in the midst of combat. That Brussels kill had been his first, as they say, in cold blood. And it haunted him more than any other.

Strangely enough, it wasn't really Uzi – Adam – that had killed the whore, Anne-Marie, that night. Or, at least, he wasn't the only one to blame. She had stumbled across information that would have burned a sensitive operation involving bugs, the UN, illegal arms shipments and Iranian sanctions; Adam could barely remember the details. But it was compromising enough for the Office to sentence her to death, and to order Adam and Avner to carry it out. It was their first operation together, and by that stage they had already become friends, so far as their world allowed. Neither of them could stomach the notion of killing this innocent woman with their bare hands. They were not Kidonim, black ops assassins, but they had been through a rigorous training. They knew countless techniques for squeezing the life out of someone quickly and silently, and disposing of the evidence afterwards. But they had both felt some pity for Anne-Marie in the dealings they had had with her. She was a mother, they knew that, of two small children, and lived a life of drugs-addled squalor which – amazingly enough – hadn't succeeded in extinguishing her sense of humour. This was not an easy task. Not that they questioned the fact she had to be eliminated. There was a bigger picture at work, and they were both convinced that if the Office gave them such an order, it was for the sake of saving many lives. It was for the defence of Israel, for the good of the world. They still thought like that, back then.

It had been Avner's idea to spread the responsibility for the hit. He had been reading about execution systems in America, and was inspired by the fact that electric chairs are hooked up to multiple levers, so nobody knows who is actually responsible for delivering the fatal current. They could kill Anne-Marie, he suggested, by the same principle. Between them, they worked out the details. Through a car dealer Sayan they sourced two identical, unregistered black Mercedes saloons and fitted them with false number plates. When Anne-Marie went to work, as she always did, in the eerie shadows of the Boulevard Adolphe Max, Adam drove up and posed as a client. She knew him anyway; he had used her services once or twice, so there was no distrust. He called her over to his window, beckoning her round the car and into the road. Avner, who had parked half a block behind, gunned his engine and raced towards them; at the last minute, as Anne-Marie bent towards him, Adam shoved her into the path of Avner's Mercedes. His hand like a pale trident. The cold slap of his palm against her sternum. Her terrified face; her hair unwinding into the night. Her head hitting the windscreen. The single cry. And they both sped away.

On the one hand, someone can't be killed by a push. If it hadn't been for Avner hurtling along the road, she would still be alive today. On the other, Avner was simply driving his car; if it hadn't been for Adam, no kill could have taken place either. This was the puzzle they devised for themselves, a conundrum of guilt to prevent their souls from being permanently stained. But not knowing was worse than knowing. It haunted Uzi at the time. More than a decade later, as he sat in a fog of boredom in a cramped shed outside a girls' school in Hendon, it haunted him still.

Preceded by an itch, the Kol spoke up. 'Uzi.'

'It's not night-time.'

'You need to get the Liberty file. Just a reminder.'

'It's still not night-time.'

'I'm not omniscient, you know. I'm just a voice. You need the file, you need to read her information, see her picture.'

The school phone rang. The Kol said, 'Believe,' and the itch faded.

'Yes?' said Uzi, picking up the phone.

'It's me.'

'Hi, Avner.'

'I need you to do this, Uzi.'

'I will do it.'

'When? It's been three weeks.'

'When you've given me the Liberty file, I'll do it.'

'The Liberty file? I've told you, for fuck's sake, I'm working on it. But the election's approaching. We don't have much time.'

'Tell that to your horse at London Station, not me.'

'Just agree to do it.'

'A deal's a deal.'

'This is pissing me off.'

'I should care? We have a deal.'

'Look, I need to arrange the meeting,' said Avner.

'OK, OK.'

'I'll call you tonight.'

'I'm busy tonight.'

'What are you doing that you're so busy?'

'Never mind what I'm doing. I'm busy.'

'Let's arrange the meeting now then.'

'I've told you, not without the Liberty file.'

'Why are you so obsessed with her anyway? What are you planning?'

'Nothing. Look, I've got to go. There's someone here.'

Uzi hung up and blew out his cheeks. He needed a cigarette. He went to the door of the shed and opened it. There stood a girl dangling a schoolbag from her elbow as if she'd never in her life cared about anything.

'You the security guard?' she said rudely.

'No, I'm Mickey Mouse.'

'Israeli?'

'How could you tell?'

'Your accent. I'm Israeli, too,' she said, switching to Hebrew. 'Where are you from in Israel?'

'Tel Aviv.'

'I grew up in Petach Tikva.'

'Small world, kid,' he said impatiently. 'What do you want?'

'You're in a bad mood. Do you need a cigarette or something?'

'How can you tell?'

'All you guys smoke.' She took out a packet of Marlboro Lights, looked over her shoulder and put it back in her pocket.

'Aren't you going to give me one?' asked Uzi.

'I didn't come here to give you a cigarette. I came here to see if you found my phone.'

'You lost it?'

'Obviously.'

'Seems like I'm not the only one in a bad mood,' said Uzi.

She smiled slightly. 'OK, so I need a cigarette too. Can I smoke in here?'

'Are you joking? This is England.'

'I know. I just didn't know whether you cared.' She shifted her schoolbag from one shoulder to the other. 'So nobody handed in a phone?'

'No. Give me a description and I'll tell you if I see it.' Uzi beckoned her into the shed and hunted for a pen.

'It's an iPhone,' she said, 'pink case.'

'Nice,' said Uzi, writing it down. 'You should be more careful, kid.'

'OK, Dad.'

She took the pen and wrote down her name and details in loopy, girlish handwriting. Gal Liberman. On the top of the 'i' she drew a heart.

'Now,' she said, 'I'm going for a smoke over the road. Are you going to stop me?'

'Why should I?'

'Rules.'

'I'm not a teacher. My job is to keep you safe.' He surprised himself with those words, even more so because – somehow – he meant it.

'Can I borrow a lighter, then?'

Uzi rummaged in his pocket and gave her a lighter.

'Oh,' she said, 'naughty boy.'

'What?' He followed her gaze. There, lying on the floor at his feet, was a small bag of cannabis. He stooped to pick it up and waved her out of the room.

'Wait,' she said, 'wait a minute.'

For a moment they stood without speaking. Uzi saw her – really saw her – for the first time. Her skin was pure and childlike; her wiry hair fell like a mane over her shoulders. She seemed frozen in that briefest of moments between childhood and adulthood. A barely ripe fruit. Her top buttons were undone; the schoolbag over her shoulder was pulling the neck of her blouse open. He could see the beginnings of a little swell of breast, and a thin sliver of underwear.

'How old are you?' he said.

'Old enough.'

'To do what?'

'To buy some of that from you.'

'Some of what?' said Uzi, playing for time.

'Oh please,' she said sarcastically. 'That.'

'I'd lose my job.'

'Now that would be a tragedy.'

'I only sell to friends, kid.'

'I'm a friend now. Do this for me. At a good price.'

'It's not going to happen.'

She rolled her eyes in the way that only a teenager can. 'What's your name?' she asked.

'Daniel.'

'OK, Daniel. I know your little secret. If I told people you had drugs in here, you'd lose your job anyway.'

'You're not going to tell anybody.'

'No? What would you do to me, Daniel?' She looked at him levelly and he felt a rush of electricity into his groin. 'What would you do?'

'Don't be stupid,' he said.

'You don't be stupid. All I want is an eighth.'

He paused. 'You tell nobody.'

'How much are you going to charge me?'

'Thirty.'

'I'm a kid, for god's sake.'

'Don't you get pocket money?'

'I'm not paying any more than twenty. Take it or leave it.'

'Do I have a choice?' said Uzi.

'What do you think?'

'You drive a hard bargain, Miss Liberman.'

'Call me Gal,' she said, and laughed.

'Fine, twenty then.'

'And I get to keep your lighter, too.'

'Have the fucking lighter. Anything else?'

'There might be,' she said, shifting her schoolbag from one shoulder to the other. The sliver of underwear widened. 'That depends on you.'

'What do you mean?'

'You're here tomorrow?'

'Sure. All day.'

'I have a free period at eleven. I'll get it from you then.' Oddly, she shook his hand. And she was gone.

14

That evening, Uzi needed to let off steam. He was sick of sitting all day cooped up in a shed, watching parents and students going to and fro like ants, hour after hour. He was sick of raising and lowering the barrier. He was sick of not being able to smoke. He was sick of Avner Golan, for making him agree to this kamikaze project.

He went home, ate some instant noodles, watched a Bruce Lee movie on his two televisions. The Kol was mercifully quiet. He ate a strawberry mousse, then got ready to go out. Before leaving his apartment he almost gave Avner a call to schedule the meeting with WikiLeaks, just to get it over with. But he stopped himself. He wanted that Liberty file first; it was his bargaining chip. He needed to see the file on the woman who had saved his life.

Uzi walked the streets. Autumn had a blustery grip on the world, and leaves stuck to the pavement. He needed some action, any action. In a moment he decided that the time had come to return to Camden, to revisit the crime scene. But this time he was going with his Glock. He'd been steering clear of the place since the stabbing, lying low. But he wanted to carry on with business soon, and he needed to know where he stood. Had his deterrent worked? Hopefully it had sparked off rumours; hopefully other dealers would be scared of him now, would give him a wide birth. Soon he would know.

When he arrived in Camden it was dusk, and he could smell a bonfire burning. He was hungry and bought a piece of desiccated pizza from a dirty stall on the High Street. There was one club, Meteor, just behind the Market, which was frequented by the local pushers. It was labyrinthine, sprawling over three floors, with countless dark niches and corners in which to do deals and have private conversations. It was to Meteor, then, that Uzi went, his Glock strapped under his armpit.

The music was loud and Uzi felt good to be back. The bassline vibrated in his bones. At the bar he ordered a Coke and poured whisky from his hip flask into it. Then he found a table on the balcony, overlooking the dance floor, and sat there drinking, thinking of cigarettes, keeping an eye out for dealers. When he'd drunk half the Coke, he poured in more whisky and carried on. He became lightheaded as the alcohol entered his bloodstream, and the flashing lights of the club made him feel somehow at peace, as if he was sitting deep inside himself, as if he was overlooking Hades. He noticed some activity in the shadows, some transactions taking place, but nobody seemed to have spotted him. It was as if he had become invisible. He drank.

The dry ice machine was turned up high, and clouds of it moved slowly across the dance floor. Through this mist Uzi saw four men making their way up the stairs to the balcony. They seemed polite and inconspicuous, and didn't look even once in his direction; because of this he knew they were coming for him. The mist clung to their legs, slipping away as they climbed the stairs. If he got to his feet, it would inflame the situation. He shifted round in his chair, feeling strangely calm, and folded his arms across his chest so that the fingers of his right hand nestled under his armpit, on his Glock. The Office had taught him how to fall back on his chair, kick the table over and shoot with one movement; he had found the technique easy in training, though he had rarely used it in the field. Ironic. It looked like it might come in useful now he was an exile.

The four men split up and approached him separately, from different angles. Uzi took a cigarette from his packet and put it between his lips. The strange feeling of calmness could not be shaken, and he wondered if it meant he was about to die. He didn't recognise any of the men. They didn't look English. Closely cropped hair, pale skin, rough movements. Polish perhaps.

In seconds, all four were standing around his table. One of them spoke in a thick Eastern European accent, loudly, over the noise of the music.

'Adam Feldman?' he said. His real name. The Office, he thought. It could only be the Office. He tightened his grip on the gun under his armpit.

'Who are you?' he replied.

'Our boss wants to speak to you.'

'Who is he?'

'She.'

'She?'

'She says you know her. From Camden.'

'What is her name?'

'She says you know her name. She is waiting for you.'

'Where?'

'Come this way, please.'

The men did not seem expert, but they certainly were not amateurs. And there were four of them. Uzi had little choice. He got to his feet and followed them through the noise and flashing lights, past the gyrating bodies, through the clouds of dry ice, along corridors, down echoing spiral staircases, and finally out through a fire exit. Outside, the music sounded muffled and atavistic. A fine rain was falling in great, soaking sheets. There, engine snarling, lights off, squatting in the water-sliced shadows, was a sleek, black Maybach 62. The back door was open; through the rain, a woman could be seen sitting on the seat of soft cream leather.

'Liberty,' said Uzi.

'You've been doing your homework,' she said in a languid American purr. 'When we met, I said I was called Eve.'

'I Googled you. You've obviously Googled me, too.'

'You could say that,' she said, a note of seeming warmth in her voice. 'Join me here on the back seat, Adam.'

Uzi paused and weighed up his options. If things turned nasty he didn't stand much of a chance; Liberty was armed last time, and she was likely to be armed now as well, not to mention her men. He could try to talk his way out of it. But why? He had nothing to lose any more.

He made his decision and got into the back of the car, sliding across the seat. Two of the men got in the front. The doors slammed with muffled thuds and Uzi had the sudden sensation of sitting inside a jewellery case. The engine whispered as the car moved off. There was a strong smell of aniseed. Liberty was wearing a white blouse this time, and gold gleamed at her throat and fingers. Her hair was twisted over one shoulder, exposing her caramel neck, and her eyes burnt with a dark fire. Her handbag was resting on her lap.

'I heard what you did to Andrzej and his friends,' she said. 'Everyone's talking about it. Very effective. Original, too. The number plates were a nice touch.'

'I knew we were being watched.'

'I'm impressed.'

'Don't patronise me, Liberty.'

'Relax, Adam. Drink?' she said, gesturing towards a minibar.

'Vodka,' said Uzi. 'Can I smoke?'

'This is England, remember?'

He looked at her sharply.

'OK, OK,' she said, 'if you must. I'll have the car cleaned later.'

Uzi lit the cigarette he had been holding between his teeth, accepted the vodka and sat back. Liberty arranged herself in the seat like a child about to watch a film, looking at him intently. She was holding a whisky tumbler containing a cloudy white liquid, in which was a bright red straw.

'What's that?' he asked, blowing smoke from his nose.

'Pernod and water.'

'I thought I could smell aniseed,' said Uzi. 'Foul. Reminds me of Arak.'

She regarded him levelly and he noticed the smallest of quivers in her lip. Then she laughed gently. 'No accounting for taste.'

'How do you know my real name?' said Uzi.

'Always so blunt,' said Liberty, 'you Israelis.' She took a sip of her Pernod through the straw, looked out of the window, looked back. 'You shouldn't be asking me questions. You should be thanking me.'

'What for?'

She laughed again. 'For saving your life.'

'I don't know who you are, or why you did what you did. But you want something, that's for sure. You're no Good Samaritan.'

'Everybody wants something,' said Liberty, touching him lightly on the arm.

He drank the vodka and placed the empty glass in its holder. 'Enough,' he said. 'Just talk.'

Liberty leaned towards him. 'I know who you are, Adam Feldman,' she said, and sat back again, watching his face. 'Now tell me what you know of me.'

'I don't know anything.'

'Come on, Adam. You're a spy.'

'Not any more.'

'Once a spy, always a spy. It's a curse. You're cursed.'

'I'm less cursed than I was.'

She sighed. 'So you know that people call me Liberty,' she said. 'Do you also know that I'm ex-CIA?'

'What do you want from me?'

'I may be a black horse, but I still have contacts in the intelligence community. I've seen your CIA profile. We're the same, you and I. Both ex-intelligence. Jewish. Both disillusioned with our governments. Both in the substance business, albeit on a different scale. Both out for ourselves now, and only ourselves. Fuck everyone else. Fuck the world. Am I right?'

'You tell me.'

'We've been trained to operate as machines. We've done things that took away our humanity. We know things that could get us killed.'

'What do you want?'

'OK, I'll put my cards on the table. I want you to work with me. I'm running a gang of Russians, getting the goods into the UK, selling it on. I'm making a lot of money. And you know what that means: lots of people wanting a piece of the pie. I can't trust these fucking Russians. I need someone who can speak their language, someone who has experience. Someone who isn't scared of using direct methods where necessary. I want you to be my eyes and ears, to work to protect my interests.'

'I protect my own interests. Nobody else's.'

'We'll have the same interests. I'll pay you well.'

'You Americans think you can buy anything.'

'You might be growing some good shit, but you're not exactly a high-flyer, Adam.'

'Call me Uzi, OK?'

'You're a nothing as Uzi, and you're a nothing as Adam. A double nothing. How much are you making, five hundred a week? Work for me and you'll be living in luxury.'

'I don't give a shit about luxury. I need to keep my head low. If I attract attention to myself, it could be dangerous.'

'Luxury can be discreet. The highest form of luxury always is. Look, I'm only going to say this once. I'll pay all your expenses. I'll deposit four thousand pounds a month into a bank account of your choice. And you'll have protection from those Poles.'

'I don't need your protection.'

'Sure.'

There was a pause. One song stopped, and in the interval before the next one began, rain could be heard pattering on the roof. The Maybach cruised through the waterlogged streets of London, devouring the road. Liberty nodded gently to the music, drinking Pernod through her straw and looking out the window at the rain. Uzi stubbed out his cigarette. Then he poured himself another vodka and drank it.

'What makes you think I'd accept?' he said at last.

'What do you mean?'

'I don't know who the fuck you are. You send four gorillas to pick me up in a club. You want me to work with you, but we've never met, really. It doesn't add up.'

'I have nothing to worry about,' said Liberty. 'I'll be paying you more money than you could possibly get anywhere else. That tends to ensure loyalty. And like I said, I've seen your profile. I think we're the same.'

'You haven't answered the question. What makes you think I'd accept?'

She leaned closer. 'Two reasons. One, you've got nothing to lose. Two, you've got everything to gain.'

'Well, you're wrong,' said Uzi. 'I work for myself, nobody else. I'm surprised your CIA contacts didn't tell you that. And anyway, if my government found out I was working with an ex-CIA operative, they'd fuck me.'

'They wouldn't. You're not working for them any more, remember? And I'm no longer CIA. Anyway, America and Israel are the best of friends.'

'You think?' said Uzi bitterly.

For a moment they stared at each other. At last, Liberty spoke. 'All right, leave it. Would you like another drink?'

'Give me one for the road and drive me back to the club,' said Uzi. 'You've taken up enough of my time tonight.'

Half an hour later he was standing alone, on the rain-washed pavement, his right hand under his arm, fingering the handle of his Glock as he watched the Maybach roar away into the darkness. In his left hand was a business card with nothing but a mobile number printed in black across the middle. He had no intention of calling the number. He put it in his pocket and took shelter under an awning to smoke a cigarette. Then he made his way back into the club.

15

The following morning Uzi awoke, terrified, from a dream that he couldn't remember. His mouth was moistureless and his tongue felt like a slab of wood. For a while he spoke to the Kol, under his breath. As usual, he was told to believe in himself. He smoked a spliff and took two aspirins with a large glass of salted water and lemon, a hangover cure he had picked up in Russia. Then, late for work, he caught the bus to Hendon.

All morning he thought of nothing but Liberty. Her proposal added up perfectly. They were the same, she and him. He knew that he would be an asset to her business, that with his help it would grow. But working with a partner always meant uncertainty, and uncertainty always meant danger, particularly without an organisation to fall back on. And if he was seen to be consorting with an ex-CIA operative, there would be nothing his horses – or what was left of them – could do. The Office was renowned for jealously guarding its assets and intelligence, and would act ruthlessly to protect it. He had seen it happen before. He would be done for. This was what he pondered as he sat in the shed, lifting the barrier occasionally for a teacher or parent or caretaker. But there was another reason not to get involved with Liberty, one that he felt in his gut. The way her proposal added up was just a little too perfect, and the way she had come into his life just a little too contrived. Perhaps it was paranoia; maybe Avner was right, maybe he was suffering from spy syndrome. But it all felt too well planned. Believe in yourself, Uzi, he thought. Don't forget who you are. Believe.

There was a tap at the door of the shed. Through the window he could see the outline of a schoolgirl. He opened the door.

'You've been expecting me,' said Gal.

'I didn't recognise you. What have you done to your hair?'

'Dyed it. Ever heard of that?' She nudged past him and into the shed. He closed the door behind her. Her hair was now raven-black and swept across her forehead. It made her eyes look as vivid as sapphires. Around one of her wrists was a stack of black bracelets. They were new as well. 'Have you found my iPhone?' she said. Again, her shirt was being pulled to the side by her rucksack. Again, the sliver of underwear. Again, the little swell of breast, but now a heart had been drawn on to the skin with felt-tip pen.

'What's that?'

'I'm thinking of getting a tattoo,' said Gal. 'I'm updating myself while my parents are away in Israel.' She pulled her shirt a little lower to reveal more of her breast, fading from bronze to white. Again, the rush of electricity to his groin. She pointed to the felt-tip heart. 'What do you think?'

'Updating yourself?'

'Yeah. You should think about it once in a while.'

He shrugged, waiting for the question that he knew would come.

'So did you bring the stuff?'

'No. I forgot,' he said.

'What do you mean, you forgot? You forgot I saw you with drugs on school premises? Or you forgot to keep your side of the deal?'

'You're full of shit, you know that?' he said.

'I want my stuff.'

'Fine, kid. Fine. I'll bring it tomorrow.'

'Where do you live?'

'Kilburn.'

'OK. Let's drive there after school, OK? Pick up my stuff.'

'I don't have a car.'

'I do.' She gave him a withering look and headed for the door. 'Three thirty.' She sniffed, turned and was gone.

The phone rang. It was Avner. As soon as he heard his voice, Uzi hung up. He needed to think. He checked his two-way radio was working, went across the road and had a cigarette. The nicotine gave him a buzz, calmed him. He smoked another. Then he returned to the shed. When he got there, the phone was ringing again.

'Look, Avner . . .' The line went dead.

For the rest of the day, Uzi was alone with his thoughts. He dwelled on how effectively the Office turned people from idealistic, open-minded recruits into cold-blooded, self-serving operatives. He remembered the sociometric sessions, where trainees were encouraged to rate each other's performances in front of their peers, brutally and openly, no holds barred. Several times people broke down, and fights sometimes erupted. At the time it seemed like just another challenge. It was only later that he realised how the Office was moulding his character, and the characters of those around him. The recruits responded to the pressure by forming allegiances and gangs. They started to double-cross each other. Any sense of trust was wiped permanently from their psyches; they had become different people, harder people, and there was no way back.

After the assassination of Anne-Marie, he had made an appointment to see Yigal. To share his burden of guilt. To seek reassurance that his first hit had been justified. Instead, he was ordered, in no uncertain terms, not to 'become a man who thinks too much', or he 'wouldn't be around very long'. This memory, which marked the first step on his journey to disillusionment, caused everything to come back to him in a rapid succession of images, voices, memories: the drug smuggling, the arms deals, the money laundering, the corruption, the sex, the assassinations, the double-deals, the disregard for life, the money, the coldness of the money. The advancement of Israel at all costs. As if awakening from a slumber, he had gradually become a man who thinks too much. And some years later, after Operation Cinnamon, he had finally made the decision to escape. Too late.

Ram Shalev. The picture of him in the garden, his wife, his two children. Trees, blue sky, button-down shirt. Uzi had known him a little, and he had always come across as a decent man. One of the few, perhaps, who had been drawn to politics for the right reasons – it wasn't impossible. Killed because he had found out that his government was scheming to bomb a fictional target in Iran, just to inject some patriotic vigour into the country before the election. Killed by Operation Cinnamon, killed – among others – by Uzi. Killed by his own countrymen; killed by the very people who were supposed to protect him.

At three thirty exactly, Gal knocked on the door of the shed. The felt-tip heart had been washed off; when Uzi asked her about it she pretended not to have heard him. She drove a purple Volkswagen Beetle. Her parents, she said, had bought it for her when she turned seventeen. They drove away, ignoring the stares of the crowd of girls clustered around the bus stop.

'So what are you doing in England?' she asked him, eyes on the road. Her hand was resting on the gear stick and he fought the urge to cup it with his own. He looked out of the window at the grey autumn sky, which stretched dismally above them.

'You know,' he said at length. 'I just needed to get out of Israel.'

'I never want to leave when I'm there,' she replied, 'I love it.'

'Why?'

'It's our land.' There was no irony in her voice. He looked at her; there was no irony in her expression either.

'What about England?' he said.

'England's my country, not my land.'

'What's the difference?'

'I don't need to tell you that. You were in the army, right?'

'I was.'

'So.' She stopped talking to concentrate on negotiating a roundabout. They were silent for a while. He wondered what she would say if she knew that the people who govern her land were going to attack Iran on false pretences, and would kill anyone who stood in their way, even fellow Israelis. That he was planning to stop them.

She turned on the radio. 'I'm joining the IDF once I finish school,' she said over the music.

'The army?'

'Like I said, it's our land,' she said. 'The only democracy in the Middle East. Our home. Our people.'

'Good for you,' he said darkly.

'Come on,' she said, giving him a brief, disgusted look. 'What were you fighting for?'

Uzi had no idea how to answer that question. He continued to look out of the window. She was from a different world, this girl, a different time. She reminded him, somehow, of the sea; of his parents, his sun-drenched childhood, the beach. With this girl he could have stayed up all night playing guitar, discussing which army unit they wanted to join. They could have drunk beer and gone to parties, swum naked in the ocean. She could have watched him fooling around with his friends in the Negev desert, doing stunts and jumps on dirt bikes. They could have hiked in the mountains, explored the ancient, biblical ravines, lain on their stomachs on the earth and fired M16s on target ranges. He looked at her again, silhouetted against the greyness of London, and was torn between an impulse to make love to her and extinguish her life with his hands.

'Can you imagine what it's like to kill?' he said.

She didn't take her eyes off the road. 'That would depend who you were killing and why.'

'There's only ever one victim, and only ever one motive.'

'What do you mean?'

'Think about it.'

She gave him a sidelong look. 'This is getting heavy,' she said suddenly.

'It was you who made it heavy.'

There was a pause.

'Have you heard of Esther Cailingold?' said Gal suddenly.

'Who?'

'Esther Cailingold. A British schoolteacher. She fought in the War of Independence in 1948. At the age of twenty-three she was killed in the defence of Jerusalem.'

'Your point is?'

'Isn't it obvious? I'm doing a project on her at school.'

'OK, OK. Turn right here. I live there on the corner.'

'Nice neighbourhood.'

'I've seen worse.'

Uzi instructed Gal to stop the car a block away from his flat, where a gang of hooded teenagers were eating out of cardboard boxes. A swirl of grimy leaves fluttered across the bonnet. 'I'm not getting out,' she said. 'I'll wait for you here. With the windows closed.'

'Have you heard of Arik?' said Uzi, opening the door.

'Who?'

'Ariel Sharon.'

'Of course I have. Think I'm stupid?'

'In 1982 he was found guilty of allowing thousands of Palestinian civilians to be massacred. A government report called for him to be dismissed from his post, that he should never hold public office again.'

'You mean Ariel Sharon who later became prime minister?'

'No, Ariel Sharon the peace activist,' he said drily.

'Look, Daniel. I don't know what you're trying to say to me.'

'Nor do I, kid. But I do know what you're trying to say to me.'

He went up to the apartment alone and got the dope. With the eighth in his fingers, he crouched on the floor, his eyes screwed tightly shut, dissolving himself into the blackness. Then he rose and stood in front of the bathroom mirror, examining the shadow of bristles across his chin, the lines etched around his mouth, across his forehead, the eyes that could devour the world. He ran the water and splashed his face again and again. Then he checked the cyst on his shoulder. It was sore today. I am starting to forget who I am, he thought. He dried himself with a towel and went downstairs to the street.

'What took you so long?' she said.

Without a word, Uzi got into the car and tossed the eighth on to the dashboard. Gal handed him a twenty-pound note and he pocketed it. But he didn't move.

'Er, hello?' said Gal. 'This is where we go our separate ways.'

'You said your parents are away in Israel, right?'

'Yes,' Gal said slowly.

'We'll go to your place, then. Watch a movie or something.'

Gal paused, then smiled, then laughed, then started the engine. 'You army guys are all the same,' she said casually. 'I love it.' She turned up the music loud.

16

'Drink?'

'What have you got?'

'My dad always has beer in the fridge. And there's wine in the rack, whisky, gin . . .'

'One of your dad's beers would be fine.'

'OK. Do you want a yellow one or a brown one?'

'A what?'

'Look, there are two colours.'

'Oh. A lager. The yellow one.'

The house, on the outskirts of Golders Green, was just as he had expected. Large, comfortable, lived-in: spacious garden overgrown around the edges, oversized television facing a well-used sofa; half-read magazines, Post-it notes on the mirrors, piles of paperwork and books. He followed Gal up several flights of stairs to the loft extension, which smelled of new carpets. As they walked up the stairs, his face was at the level of her hips.

'You're good at that,' she said as he rolled the spliff. 'A pro.'

'Practice,' he said, and lit up. She opened the skylight and turned on a desk lamp. Her phone rang, and she turned it off. Then she put on some music and lay sideways on the bed. He joined her; their legs touched. He sent smoke rings up to the ceiling.

'So you're seventeen,' he said.

'How old are you?'

'A little older.'

'Old enough to be my father?'

'A young father perhaps.'

'Wife?'

'If I had one, would I be here?'

'Come on, Daniel. I'm not stupid.'

'No wife. Not that you have to worry about it.'

They smoked.

'I think it's wonderful,' said Gal, breaking a comfortable silence.

'What is?'

'I can see you're hurting, Daniel. I can see you've been through a lot. That's a sacrifice, you know. You've given a part of yourself for your country. Your hurt is a gift to your people. It's wonderful. I mean it. It's heroic.'

'You don't know anything about me.'

'I don't need to. Our land depends on people like you accepting burdens that almost destroy you. I'll bet lots of your friends gave their lives, but you continue to give. You give till it hurts for your country. People like you are the real heroes, the quiet heroes of our people.'

Uzi tried to laugh but no sound would come. He looked over at the person beside him, her unlined face, her clear eyes looking into his, her lips which could smile forever without losing their joy. She didn't look real. She sucked on the spliff and little threads of smoke traced the contours of her face. He thought of a word. Then it passed from his mind without a trace. He got up.

In the bathroom, he looked out of the window at the sky. It was dark and starless above, and an orange light from the streetlamps was glowing. Of course he was married, technically at least. You had to be married to be a Katsa. This was one of the most glaring ironies of the organisation. Sex in the Office was free and rampant: secretaries, Katsas, wives of Katsas, agents, technicians, translators, audio specialists. The sexual connections went back and forth, web after web, trophy after trophy. But so long as you were married, it was all right. If you were married, you were less vulnerable to bribes. That was the official line.

He took out his Glock – he carried it everywhere now – and aimed it at the bathroom door. He imagined killing the girl, walking calmly into her room and shooting her the way he'd been taught, six times in the body followed by a single shot to the temple. He knew exactly what he would do then, how he would set up the murder scene, remove fingerprints, make a swift and anonymous escape, avoid witnesses, evade detection and capture. It would be easy – an easy thing to do. It would be simple.

'Uzi.'

'You again.'

'This is dangerous, Uzi. You're losing your grip.'

'Maybe I am. But a voice in my head isn't helping.'

'You're better than this.'

'Than what?'

'Stay focused. Remember who you are.'

Uzi opened up the Glock and emptied all the bullets into his hand. Then he placed them in the pocket of his jacket – he was still wearing his jacket – and concealed his gun again. Weird, he thought. Weird what things can do to a man.

He left the bathroom and saw Gal sitting on the end of her bed, her back to him, hunched over her computer. Facebook. Her neck – something about her neck. So tender. He suddenly felt as if a hole was opening in the centre of his chest, and he was filled with an overwhelming feeling of affection for the girl, love streaming out of him. She was only a little older than Noam, he guessed; Noam his son, Noam who he knew he would no longer be able to recognise. He walked quietly up behind her and stretched out his hand. It hovered just above her shoulder for a second, two seconds, three, four, and then dropped back down to his side. He sat down heavily on the bed, and she yelped with alarm.

'Shit, you scared me, Daniel.'

'What am I doing here?'

'What?'

'What the fuck am I doing here? What am I doing?'

'Take it easy.' She finished what she was doing, slid over next to him and put her arm across his shoulders. 'Like I said, you're hurting. I've seen it before. You're carrying a burden. Plus you're stoned.' She took his calloused hands in both of hers and began to kiss them, slowly, each finger, each joint, one by one. He stared at her, this girl, this child, kissing his hand. He stared at her and did not know what to feel.

His phone went off. He pulled his hand away and answered it. Gal drew back and lit a cigarette.

'Hello?' he said, moving out of earshot.

'Tommy?'

'Squeal? Is that you?'

'Tommy, listen to me.'

'Speak up, I can hardly hear you.'

'There are people in your apartment. I can hear them.'

'What? Which people?'

The line went dead.

17

Uzi stopped the taxi two blocks from his building and stepped into the clammy chill of the autumn darkness. It was a normal night, like any other. The buses groaning through the streets, the graffiti on the bus stops, the people, drunk, veering across pavements. He approached his apartment on foot, sticking to the shadows. From the outside, nothing looked out of the ordinary. No lights were on, there was no sign of disturbance. He phoned Squeal again, and still there was no answer. He cracked his knuckles and put an unlit cigarette between his lips. All his senses were alert.

The only way to approach his flat was up the main stairs and through the front door. That was why he had chosen it. It was easy to escape from the window, being only on the second floor, but difficult to break into from the outside. He walked up to the entrance of his building and slipped in as a neighbour went out. The foyer had a motion-sensitive light which cast a faltering neon glow over the stairwell. He found the fusebox under the stairs; when the lights went out, he disabled them so that his arrival would go unnoticed. Then, in the dark, he loaded his Glock and stowed it in his jacket pocket. As quietly as he could, he ascended, chewing his unlit cigarette.

Uzi's mind felt clear and alert, and his breathing was barely audible. A white-hot rage was brewing in him, streamlining his focus, giving him strength. On the first floor he could smell home cooking, and hear the clatter of pans, the alternating rhythm of voices. He was about to go up to the floor above when there was a noise from below. The click of a door. The wind? He took his

Glock out of his pocket and listened. For a few seconds, nothing. Then the sound of somebody creeping up the stairs towards him.

Uzi took up a position in a doorway and transferred his gun to his left hand, aiming it into the blackness above the stairs. The footsteps got louder, the sound of breathing, the jangle of keys. Then a man appeared and, unaware that a gun was aimed at his head, entered the door opposite. Uzi concealed his Glock in his pocket again and carried on up to the second floor.

Everything looked normal. The door of his flat was closed, a newspaper still on the mat, angled as he'd left it. He ran his finger along the door; his piece of chewing gum was still there, bridging the door and the frame. He relaxed slightly. He rang Squeal's bell, and rang it again; nobody answered. But the smell of dope was strong. Through the letterbox he could see him lying on the sofa in a stupor, a burnt-out spliff in his fingers, his mobile on the floor. He cursed under his breath. Squeal just smoked too much and got paranoid, he thought. There's no danger.

He broke the piece of gum and let himself into his apartment, still holding his Glock in his pocket. Nothing unusual, nothing out of place. His computer desk, his slick, his sofa and TV. His fridge. He turned the lights on. Everything exactly as he'd left it. He made his way through to the kitchen.

As he was opening the fridge, he heard a sound. He was unsure what it was; a click, an echo, the pipes maybe, or a mouse. But he was on edge, and ready for anything. He drew his gun and removed the safety-catch. Then he prowled through the flat, rehearsing what he would have done if there had really been an intruder, going through the procedure in his mind. He went from the sitting room to the bathroom, parted the shower curtain with his gun, then on into his bedroom. Bed, desk, wardrobe, chest of drawers. Nobody was there.

Just as he turned to leave the room, he became aware of somebody standing behind him. He half-turned and saw a figure almost within reach, and another directly behind. Time seemed to stand still. He shouted, tried to spin, to aim his gun, but it was too late. The men were there, arms outstretched. Their hands were on him. His arm was twisted and the Glock ripped from his grasp in a single expert move. As he fought he felt a scratch to his neck. Chemicals entered his bloodstream and suddenly his legs felt like rubber. He bellowed, stumbled, and crashed into the wardrobe. The rubberiness turned to numbness, spreading throughout his body. Within seconds he had fallen to the floor, feeling like he was open to the wind. He knew what had happened. He had been disarmed using a straightforward Krav Maga technique then given a neuromuscular blocker. He had done this countless times himself.

His vision blurred, then sharpened. Two men, nondescript, casually dressed. Neither had made any effort to disguise their identity: Shilo and Laufer, old hands from London Station, both with nasty reputations. One of them closed the curtains. He knew what would come next, and cursed himself for making it easy for them. Without speaking, they dragged him through to the sitting room, tied him to a chair, then opened his trousers and pulled out his penis. Standard procedure all the way.

'So, Feldman,' said Shilo, resting his foot on Uzi's chair, between his legs. 'It's been a long time. Are you glad to see us? No? That's disappointing. I thought you'd be filled with joy.'

Slowly, casually, he lit a cigarette. Then he weighed Uzi's Glock in his hands, exhaling thoughtfully. Inside, Uzi was screaming, trying to force himself to move, to struggle against the paralysis. But it was hopeless. He couldn't even speak. He was at their mercy.

'Thank you for taking such good care of weapons and equipment that belong to the Office,' Shilo continued. 'We thought we'd come and remind you that you've left the Office now. So we'd like our equipment back.'

Uzi drew on his training, tried to quell his mounting panic by accepting the situation, to build up a reservoir of strength, as he'd been taught. How strange, using the Office's own training against their interrogation techniques. He saw Laufer leaning against the wall, arms folded. As usual, he was letting Shilo do the talking. That was what how they worked.

'Thank you also for using our Sayanim,' Shilo went on, 'and promising them large sums of money on our behalf. Thank you for that.'

Laufer turned on the television and cranked up the volume. Shilo approached the coffee table and brought his heel smashing down on it, again and again, breaking through the false top until the slick was exposed. Then he plucked out Uzi's Beretta.

'You see, Adam? We know everything. We know about this little slick. We know about every piece of kit you have. We know how busy you've been.' He pressed both weapons hard into Uzi's temples. Drool was spilling from his mouth and down his shirt.

'I could kill you right here,' said Shilo in a low voice. 'I could blow out your brains and leave your body to rot. I could cut off your dick and feed it to you, then stick this Beretta up your arse and shoot your guts out. I could do anything. That is the power of the Office, remember? That is the power of the Office.'

He paced the room, wiping his forearm across his brow like an animal. Then he crossed to the door of Uzi's cannabis room and kicked it, smashing it with his heel, until it splintered and caved in. 'You see?' he said. 'We know about everything.'

He strode in, followed by Laufer, and began smashing up Uzi's plants, his equipment, his stash of dope, his livelihood. Before his eyes, his lamps went out, his cultivation tents collapsed on themselves, his pumps buckled and split. Rage whipped through him, but his body would not respond. He was entombed in it.

The two men swivelled Uzi round on his chair again, forcing him to watch as they attacked the rest of his apartment. The destruction was swift and total. In a matter of minutes, nothing was intact.

'Now, Adam, my brother,' said Shilo, advancing with a table leg in his hands, 'let's make sure you never forget what we have taught you tonight.' He raised the cudgel high above his head, stretching as if trying to hook down something from a shelf; then, making a noise that reminded Uzi of the wild dogs in the Negev at night, he brought it down with all his strength.

By the time Uzi regained consciousness, the room was dark. He was on his side, still tied to the chair, his penis lying in a pale curve across his thigh. His head was a fist of pain. He groaned softly; at least he could still make a sound. Around him in the half light were broken and jagged silhouettes, all that was left of his apartment. He was cold.

'Uzi. I'm sorry, Uzi. I couldn't do anything. I don't have any authority. I'm just a voice.' Smooth, neutral tones. Like rich milk.

'If you're just a voice,' muttered Uzi woozily, 'at least tell me what to do.'

'There's only one thing to do. Now's the time, Uzi.'

Uzi nodded as if the Kol could see him; the voice went quiet. It took Uzi several minutes to break free of the chair, and when he did so he collapsed to the floor. His neck was stiff and aching. He ran his hand across his face and felt a web of scabs and weals. It was impossible to tell what time it was; the face of his watch was smashed and his phone had been taken. Like a statue coming to life, he uncurled his back and massaged his limbs. He struggled to his feet – he could still stand – and put his penis gingerly back in his trousers. He tried the lights. Nothing. The light bulbs were smashed. He rummaged in his pockets and lit a cigarette.

In the flicker of the lighter, he hobbled from one room to the next, surveying the damage. Everything was smashed up, everything. The flame could bring nothing but destruction from the darkness. They had stolen his entire stash. His slick was empty. His guns were gone. He let the lighter go out and drew on his cigarette in the gloom. The ash glowed orange and the hiss of burning cigarette paper was loud as he smoked. They'd fucked him. He was still alive, but the Office had fucked him. He'd been goading them, he knew that, but this? He scanned through his memory of the attack, piecing together precisely what Shilo had said. He hadn't mentioned Uzi's meeting with Liberty, or his connection with Avner – still an Office employee – or Operation Regime Change. Any one of these things would have resulted in far more than a warning. So Uzi was still one step ahead. And the Office clearly hadn't known about all of his slicks.

Rage flowed suddenly through him. He kicked a door that was hanging haphazardly on its hinges, and kicked it again, and again. Then he crouched, head in hands, until the cigarette burned out in his fingers and a worm of ash fell, unseen, to the floor. He came to a decision. From now on there would be no holding back.

In the bedroom he opened the curtains. By the weak light of the moon, he searched in the wreckage of his wardrobe and found the hollow metal tube on which coat hangers used to be hung. He prodded inside it with a wire hanger and drew out roll after roll of fifty-pound notes and hundred-dollar bills, all wrapped in cellophane. Placing these in a rucksack, he changed his torn and bloodied clothes and went into the bathroom. The light there worked and he spent some time cleaning his face and wounds, rubbing the blood out of his hair in the sink. Then he dried himself off and, with the spoon that he used for scraping the shower head, prised some tiles from the wall. They came away with a dry cracking sound, followed by a cloud of dust. Behind, in a cobwebbed cavity, was a newspaper-wrapped package containing a pocket-sized pistol – a 9mm Rohrbough R9, designed for close-range combat – some ammunition, and a brand new mobile phone in several different parts. There was also a buff folder, the all-important folder. These went into his rucksack too. He took one final look around the devastated apartment. Then he left.

The motion-sensitive light came on as Uzi stepped into the foyer. Somebody must have fixed the fusebox. He blinked in the light. Before he had set foot on the staircase, Squeal appeared from his apartment, looking dazed.

'You OK?' said Uzi.

'Yeah. Yeah, I think so.'

Uzi hesitated for a moment, then helped him back into his flat and sat him on the sofa.

'What's going on with you?' said Uzi. 'Too much skunk?'

'Guilty as charged,' said Squeal.

'Do you remember calling me?'

'Oh yeah. I was just having a bit of a smoke when I heard people moving around in your gaff. It looked dodgy, the lights were off. So I called you, then my phone cut out.' He looked down at his phone. 'Looks all right now.'

'Then what happened?'

'Not sure. I think I was grabbed from behind or something, but that might have been a dream. I was pretty out of it. Something over my face. Then nothing until just now. Guess I fell asleep.' He laughed, once, loudly. 'Did you find out who it was?'

'Burglars,' said Uzi, 'but it's all right now.' A strange smell was clinging to Squeal's dreadlocks. Uzi leant closer and sniffed. He'd know that smell anywhere. Sickly sweet to the point of being nauseating. Desflurane ether gas.

'What's up?' said Squeal. 'I smell bad?'

'So what else is new?' said Uzi.

'Sorry, man,' said Squeal. 'I'm just freaked out about my mum. She's taken a turn for the worse.'

Uzi stopped. From his pocket he took a roll of bank notes and pressed it into Squeal's palm.

'What's this, dude?'

'I'm going to lie low for a while,' said Uzi. 'You know how it is. Go and see your mother, OK?'

Squeal looked at the money in disbelief. 'Are you sure?'

'Sure. Then when you get back I'm going to thrash you at pudding wars.'

Squeal broke into a grin. 'Never. I'm on a roll now. I'll pay you back, OK?'

Uzi gripped his hand with unusual tightness and held it for several seconds. Then he turned, left the apartment and made his way downstairs to the street.

18

From now on it's simple, Uzi told himself as he strode towards the tube station. It couldn't be simpler. Loyalty is dead. I'm afraid of nothing. I believe in myself, I know who I am. Outside the station, he put the mobile phone together and switched it on. Then he took from his inside pocket a business card and dialled the number. It rang.

'Yes?'

'OK. I'm in.'

Liberty paused for a moment. 'Adam, how nice to hear from you.'

'I'm in. Whatever it is, I'm in.'

'I'm so glad you've changed your mind.'

'Yeah, yeah. What's the first step?'

'Why don't we meet for dinner?'

'Where?'

'Kensington Roof Gardens? They do delightful seafood, and they have a superb wine list. Two hours' time. Ask for Eve Klugman. They'll show you to my private dining room.'

'I'll be there.' He hung up and looked around him. London buzzed like a hive, lights streaked by on the road. Overhead, a streetlight flickered. He lit a cigarette and, from memory, dialled Avner's number.

'Yes?'

'It's me.'

'What number are you calling from? I almost didn't pick up.'

'New phone.'

'Are you calling about the operation? If not, don't bother.'

'I'm going to do it.'

'When? You've been saying that for ages.'

'As soon as I can.'

'You've been saying that for ages too, my brother.'

'This time I mean it. Schedule the meeting, schedule the meeting. Fuck them.'

'You're definitely in?'

'Definitely.'

'Good.'

'What about the file I need?'

A pause. 'My contact says he's pulled it up from the archive,' said Avner. 'He's going to transmit as soon as it's safe.'

'What, wait till everyone's looking the other way?'

'More or less.'

'You're a hoot.'

'Just don't back out on me.'

'I won't.'

'I'll get you the file, don't worry.'

'Listen, don't hang up yet.'

'What?'

Suddenly Uzi found himself unable to speak. He held the phone against his chest and looked up at the tarry sky, breathing deeply. Then he sucked the last flicker of life from his cigarette, stubbed it out and put the phone to his ear again. He cleared his throat. 'Are you still there?'

'Still here.'

'Listen, I need you to do something for me.'

'What?'

Uzi took another deep breath. 'I've had a visit from the Office.'

'Shit. Oh, shit. Do they know about us?'

'No. They know nothing. I'll explain when we're in four eyes. But I need you to make me a slick. Nothing elaborate, just a grab bag.'

'What, passport? Money?'

'That's right.'

'You need a gun in there?'

'If you can.'

'Shit. Fucking shit. Shit.'

'Look, it's nothing. I just need an escape route. In case anything happens.'

'Fine. Remember this. 83 East End Road, London. The house is owned by a Sayan, a businessman. Outside is a green electricity box. The slick will be in there from midnight tonight. The passport – I've got a Canadian one ready for you already.'

'Thanks.'

'The electricity box will be locked. You need to lift the whole thing upwards and it will come away. Inside will be a double-locked suitcase. The codes are 9826 and 2034. OK?'

'OK,' said Uzi, committing the numbers to memory.

'And don't back out on me. Please. We're running out of time. The yellowcake operation . . .'

'I know, it's happening soon. Don't worry, I'm in.'

'When can we meet in four eyes?'

'I don't know. I'll call you.'

'Good luck.' The line went dead.

Uzi dismantled the phone to prevent it being traced, and put it back in his pocket. Then he took several more deep breaths, trying to settle his nerves. He was hungry. He needed a spliff. He went underground.

The tube was busy and he couldn't get a seat. His right knee was stiffening up, and his back was badly bruised. His head – well, his head. He caught sight of his reflection in the window as the train jolted along. At least the face was not too bad. Shilo and Laufer must have had specific orders to damage him only within certain limits. Otherwise, knowing them, he would barely be alive. Perhaps it was Moskovitz working for him behind the scenes. Or Rothem. Perhaps his old horses hadn't completely forgotten him.

He arrived at Sloane Square and made his way through the windswept streets, past the news stands and groups of well-heeled Londoners to a boutique at the top of the King's Road. There he bought a new set of clothes: grey suit, blue shirt, black shoes. Stylish and well fitting, the most expensive available, yet inconspicuous, at least in this part of town. After leaving the shop he went into a café and, in the toilet, fixed his lead weights into the corners of the jacket. Then the suit was his.

At another shop he purchased a black cashmere coat; a wallet; and a briefcase for his ammunition and cash. As an afterthought, he bought a silver-plated Zippo and cigarette case. He transferred his cash and cards to his new wallet and loaded the case with cigarettes. Then, in the privacy of the changing room, he put the mobile phone together, loaded his R9 and concealed it in his waistband. Back on the street, he gave his old clothes, bag and wallet to a tramp. There was a possibility they contained minute listening or tracking devices. He needed a clean start.

Uzi had reduced one of his cash-rolls significantly now, but his briefcase held many more. He couldn't even remember how many. He was clean – untracked and not followed – and filled with primal rage, a bull bleeding in a stadium. Feeling his old power seeping back, he hailed a black cab and instructed the driver to take him to Kensington Roof Gardens. Now he was ready for Liberty.

19

Uzi had been to Kensington Roof Gardens once before, when he was still a Katsa for the Office. He had been undercover as a Russian arms dealer, trying to sell a stash of old Israeli Galil assault rifles to a representative of the Georgian government. The Office had been training Georgia's special forces, and the Georgians were desperate to equip their troops with the same weapons they had used in training. The Office was withholding its supply so that Uzi, posing as a Russian, could come in through the back door and sell at an inflated price – the aim being to conceal the fact that the Office, to whom they were paying large sums of money for the training contract, was ripping them off.

The extra profit would be used, Uzi was told, to fund the Office's activities abroad. He hadn't contested the operation openly, but by that point, the rot had already set in. He had started to question Yigal about the missions he was being given and the methods he was being encouraged to employ. He had been ordered to kill three people in cold blood, and told to adopt an increasingly brutal approach. Yigal had warned him several times, in forceful terms, that he shouldn't question direct orders, that he was thinking too much, that he had to trust in the chain of command. Uzi knew he was endangering his own career but found himself unable to swallow his opinions. He lived in the hope that his horses, Moskovitz and Rothem, would be able to contain any damage that Yigal could do to him when his meagre stock of patience was exhausted.

He got into the lift behind two women in expensive coats and stood in the corner. Nobody noticed him. In his new clothes, he fitted in. The women got out; he travelled to the top floor alone. The doors slid open. Everything was as he remembered: the ornamental fish tanks, the quietly clinking cutlery, the black-clad waitresses, the spectacular views over London. He hoped that the escape routes he had memorised last time were also still intact.

At the mention of Eve Klugman, the waiter's eyebrows raised just a fraction and he took Uzi's coat with special care. Then he vanished. Uzi wandered over to the massive window and looked out over the city. Millions of individual lives lay under his gaze. Births, deaths, dreams and frustrations, love and cruelty. Normal lives. How had he ended up like this, orbiting society, dipping in and out of violence and horror? He could feel his R9 digging into his back like a magnet, like a curse.

The waiter beckoned Uzi to follow him through the restaurant and out on to a private balcony. Uzi ordered a vodka tonic and the waiter melted away, leaving him alone. It was cold, but gas heaters burned into the night overhead. It was deserted. In his mind were scenes of a riot near Duheisha refugee camp two decades in the past. He made his way along the balcony, the city spreading out on one side, sparkling and cold and beautiful. He kept one hand in his pocket, ready to draw his R9. The balcony curved around the corner of the building. He followed it; there, leaning against the railing, was a figure. For a moment he thought it was a woman in a hijab. Then he saw it was Liberty, a cashmere stole drawn around her shoulders against the chill. Diamonds glinted at her throat, a small handbag was tucked under her arm, and what could only have been a Pernod and water glowed blueish in her hand. Once again she was the picture of elegance, but this time she looked different. More powerful, more mythical, and more dangerous.

'Hello,' she said. 'Drink?'

'I've ordered one already,' he replied. 'A vodka tonic.'

'A vodka tonic,' Liberty repeated, and laughed.

Uzi smiled in return, trying to decipher her mood.

'You've had some trouble?' she asked, gesturing towards his wounds.

'I fell over in the shower.'

'Ah, that's a relief. I was worried it was domestic abuse.'

'If you knew my wife, you wouldn't say that.'

'Why not? Is she very sweet?'

'No, she's a bitch.'

'I bet she's not a patch on me.'

'You could be right.'

Liberty gave him an ambiguous look and beckoned him through a door on the far side of the building. Inside was a private dining room with a single table. Waiters emerged from the shadows and pulled out the chairs for them. A sommelier presented Uzi with a leather-bound wine list.

'Any preferences?' said Uzi.

'Red,' Liberty replied. 'Let's start with a red then go to white with the meal.'

'South African?'

'No. Something rich, fruity. Something deep.'

Uzi cast his eye down the list, ignoring the cheaper vintages. 'How about a Primitivo?' he said. '2005?'

With a nod, Liberty dismissed the sommelier and they were left alone. 'You know your wines,' she said, 'and presumably your food as well. I've always been impressed by Israeli spies.'

'We practise at the PM's dining table.'

'I know. I know all about the Mossad.'

She leaned closer, smiling at the expression that flicked across his face at her open use of the word. 'Don't worry,' she said. 'This room is completely clean. The waiters will only come when I call them. We can say whatever we want. Total privacy. It's what we need – it's what I can guarantee – if we're going to work together.'

'How do I know what your guarantees are worth?'

'It's clean. That's all you need to know.'

'I'm beyond caring, anyway.'

'Of course.' She sat back.

'I was expecting you to have security,' said Uzi.

'Oh they're here,' said Liberty casually. 'You just can't see them.'

Uzi watched her face and still could not discern whether she was telling the truth. 'Well,' he said, 'since we can talk openly here, I might as well say this. You seem to know all about me. But I also know about you.' He had seized the initiative. He watched her face, looking for any telltale signs. There were none.

'Am I supposed to be alarmed?' she said.

'Good,' he said, pressing his advantage. 'Then before we talk about working together, why don't you tell me why a nice Jewish girl like you left the CIA?'

'You know all about me, but you don't know that?'

'I asked you a question,' said Uzi. 'I want to hear the reply.'

'What really happened to your face? These are nasty bruises.'

'Never mind my bruises. Why did you leave the CIA?'

She sighed. 'The same reason you left the Mossad.'

He shook his head. 'You can do better than that.'

There was a pause.

'Do you want the real reason, or the one I gave the Agency?'

'Which do you think?'

'Fine, I don't mind playing kiss-and-tell.'

'You approached me,' said Uzi, blowing smoke into the air. 'Remember?'

'Of course.' She nodded to the corner of the room. Instantly a waiter appeared, holding a bottle of wine like a baby. The bloody liquid slipped into the glass. Uzi considered the colour, the body; he smelled it, tasted it, aerated it in his mouth. He nodded. The waiter filled their glasses. They were alone again.

'What do you make of it?' said Liberty.

'What?'

'The wine.'

'Lots of secondary flavours but still coherent. Typical of the region. Not bad at all.'

Liberty smiled. 'Sometimes I think men are like robots. Especially spies.'

Uzi felt his temper rising. Then he realised that was precisely what Liberty was trying to achieve. 'Remind me,' he said evenly, 'what were we talking about again? Before we were interrupted?'

'You're good,' said Liberty, taking a sip of wine. 'You're good.'

They drank for a few moments. Then she began to speak.

'OK. The reasons I left. Number one: Iraq. Is that not a good enough reason in itself? Oil, arms and drugs. Do you know how much American arms companies made out of the war? And American mercenaries? Do you? Billions of tax dollars going straight to private contractors. I gathered the intel, for Christ's sake. Blackwater. I'd gladly shoot anybody who worked for Blackwater.'

'Xe.'

'Whatever. Different name, same evil. When I first joined, the CIA was the CIA. These days, the Agency recruits people from Blackwater, and vice versa. It goes both ways; there's no difference between fighting for your country and fighting for a buck.'

'OK. What else?'

'Don't dismiss what I'm saying, Adam.'

'Uzi. Call me Uzi.'

'OK, OK. But don't dismiss what I'm saying. I'm serious. I worked in Iraq. I worked in Afghanistan. I know what's happening on the ground. The more fighting we do, the more money is made by special interest groups. The more drone strikes we carry out, the more terrorists we create. A few hundred thousand people die – so what? It's worth it to generate the cash. But al-Qaeda isn't broken, even post-Bin Laden. It's just moving its centre of gravity.'

'Africa? Southeast Asia?'

'Obvious, isn't it? Obvious to everyone but the US fucking government. Or so it seems. In reality they know it only too well. For the people who count, war is much more lucrative than peace.'

A hardness was emerging in her, a coldness that he knew only too well. She broke off and took another sip of wine. 'I knew it was a dirty job from the beginning, but I was idealistic when I started out. I was naive. I still thought there was something noble about it all – land of the free, home of the brave. National security, protecting our way of life. But America is the biggest bastard of them all, Uzi. We're the bullies of the world. My eyes were opened, and what I saw left a bad taste in my mouth.' She sipped her wine.

'So you left.'

'So I left.'

'You got yourself pregnant, and you left.'

'That was the official reason. Maternity leave.'

'And you didn't go back because your family were killed.'

Liberty lowered her eyes for the briefest of moments before replying. 'I'd never intended to go back. I'd had enough of being the bully of the world.'

Uzi regarded her carefully. She sat, straight-backed, composed, not giving anything away. Her hand rested near her handbag. He consulted his instincts, his logic, his powers of observation. None of these were sending him any warning signs. The woman was telling the truth.

'Almighty dollar,' he said.

There was a note of bitterness in her laugh. 'Shall we eat?' She waved for the waiter and he appeared with the menu. Uzi ordered for both of them: a variety of seafood and a 1999 Chenin Blanc. The waiter brought them the wine and disappeared again. Uzi looked out at the vastness of the city. He thought about war, that moment in a battle when suddenly you find yourself no longer part of a mighty force. When you've achieved your objective, and you look round and find you've lost sight of your comrades. When the enemy fire, previously so random and ineffective, now unifies against you like something elemental. When you can no longer see your helicopters overhead, and you realise that you're a nothing but a man, a solitary human being who could be killed as easily as a rat.

'So,' said Liberty at last, 'what about you? Did you abandon your country or did your country abandon you?'

'I've never told anyone that.'

'Not even Avner Golan?'

'What do you know about Avner Golan?'

'I've read your files, remember? I couldn't avoid your old comrade-in-arms. He was all over the place.'

'Avner and I both fell from grace, in our different ways. He's lucky he was only demoted.'

'You call falling from Katsa to Bodel lucky?'

'You really do know everything, don't you?'

'The CIA keep me happy. I've seen a lot of sensitive things and they don't want me spilling my guts to WikiLeaks. So they help me with my business from time to time. Of course, I hate those bastards, but it doesn't mean I can't use them now and again.'

'So you used your CIA connections to put me under surveillance?'

'Come on, Uzi. You've been under surveillance anyway.'

'Fuck.'

'You didn't know?'

'I knew. I just didn't want to be told.'

'Don't worry,' she said gently, patting the back of his hand. 'You're not being watched any more. Nobody knows where you are. Even the Mossad don't know where you are. You're with me now.'

The food arrived and they began to eat, sliding oysters off shells, cracking lobster claws, washing their fingers in fingerbowls. Uzi tasted the ocean on his tongue, and marvelled at the passage of time, how things had changed.

'My organisation didn't expel me,' he said suddenly. 'I left. I'd had enough, so I upped and left. It was after . . . a difficult operation.'

Liberty looked up. 'Difficult?'

'I'm not going to talk about it.'

'Good for you,' she said.

'I probably would have been kicked out anyway. If I'd stayed any longer.'

'Why?'

'Simple. I challenged the chain of command. I was a free thinker. I thought the unthinkable. And once – just once – I spoke the unspeakable. I was bugged in the privacy of my own home. But I was thinking aloud, nothing more.'

'So you said something controversial?'

'That's right.'

'What did you say?'

'I'll tell you from the beginning,' Uzi said, and stopped. He collected his thoughts. Could he really do this? He took a breath and let it out. Then he took another. And let it out. Then a third. 'Have you heard of Nahal Sorek?' he asked. There. It was done. His blood ran hot, then cold, then hot again.

'I'm not sure I have,' said Liberty.

'You've heard of Dimona?'

'The Israeli nuclear facility. Of course.'

'But you haven't heard of Nahal Sorek,' said Uzi.

'No.'

'Exactly.'

A pause.

'So?'

'The truth is that Israel has twice as many nuclear weapons as you think we do. At two different locations.'

Liberty swayed back, very slightly, in her seat. But her face remained inscrutable. 'What has this information got to do with anything?' she said.

'Call it a gesture of goodwill,' said Uzi. 'You could use it as a bargaining chip when you want to get something out of the CIA. For example.'

'It's worth a lot, that information.'

'Use it. I don't owe my organisation anything. They owe me. During my last year at the Office . . .'

'The Office?'

'That's the code word for the organisation.' He swallowed, took a breath. 'The Mossad.' Hot, cold, hot again. His mouth was

134

dry. 'I made a lot of enemies at the Office. Well, not enemies. Not on a personal level. But there were people – people higher than me – who disapproved of my views.'

'Sounds familiar,' said Liberty, taking a sip of wine.

'When I was recruited, my ideology was the same as everyone else's. But over the years, when the new director came in . . .'

'ROM? He's pretty tough.'

'That's right. When ROM came in, when I saw how he wanted us to operate, and what his decisions were based on, and what sort of methods he expected us to use – and how little it resembled the dream we all shared since childhood – I began to feel differently.'

'Go on.'

'Look, I'm a free thinker. That's what made me good at my job. I wouldn't take anyone else's word for anything. I would judge things for myself and come up with strategies that nobody else would have thought of. Exactly what is needed in a commando.'

'And a Mossad Katsa.'

'And a Mossad Katsa.' He heard himself sigh. 'War,' he said suddenly. 'It does things to a man. You know? It changes you forever.'

A pause.

'What did it do to you?' said Liberty.

'It opened my fucking eyes.' Without really intending to, Uzi got to his feet and crossed to the window. He looked out at the city, seeing nothing, lost in the past.

'You were telling me about Nahal Sorek,' said Liberty. At the sound of her voice, Uzi's attention returned to the room. Typical spy, he thought. Hears a name once and never forgets it. Even in a foreign language. He returned to the table and sat down.

'KAMG, heard of it?' he said brusquely.

'Of course. Israel's nuclear programme, Kure Garni leMachar.'

'You speak Hebrew?'

'Not really. I went to Sunday school for a few years as a kid. I can pronounce it OK, nothing more. We were pretty irreligious, I guess. Jewish only by name.'

He laughed once, short, harsh. Then, prompted by Liberty's silence, he continued. 'Towards the end of my career at the Office, Avner and I were assigned to counter-espionage operations in Iran. There had been a leak within KAMG, and the Office was worried that the Iranians had found out about Nahal Sorek. We were deployed to go undercover in Tehran and find out what they knew. As it turned out, they knew nothing. But in preparation, we were shown around the Nahal Sorek nuclear facility.' He leaned forward. 'It blew my mind,' he said in a faraway voice. 'I already knew it existed, of course. But when you see these things with your own eyes, it's a different matter. The scale of it. The potential. I could stretch out my hand and touch a missile, a single weapon that alone could destroy the human race. One of many. I was in a temple of destruction, face-to-face with a terrible god.' He lowered his eyes. 'Nothing was the same after that.'

'So what happened?'

She's trying to keep up the momentum, thought Uzi, not giving me time to think. The more I talk, the more I talk, and she knows it. It's textbook stuff.

'Avner came round for a drink that evening,' he continued. 'It was forbidden to discuss work at home, but we all did.'

'We were the same,' said Liberty, with a little too much enthusiasm.

'We drank and talked for hours,' said Uzi, 'decompressing. My guard was down and I shared an idea with him. He changed the subject, and we forgot all about it. But we had been bugged. The Office had been listening.'

'What was the idea?'

Uzi poured himself another glass of wine. Having started down the road of disclosing classified information, he was feeling strangely calm. It was as if he had been carrying inside him a Gordian knot of secrets, which now was starting to unravel. He felt lighter, intoxicated almost. He drained his glass and poured himself another.

'We were going over the old debate about whether nuclear weapons are a force for good or evil,' he continued. 'On the one hand they have the capacity to kill billions. On the other, they are the ultimate deterrent against war. The world has never known such peace as it has since the dawn of the nuclear age.'

'So?'

'Avner's not interested in that stuff. He's just in the game for the money, the sex, the excitement. But me – I'm different. It means something to me, you know? So I started talking about politics. I was disillusioned. The Office knew I wasn't toeing the line, and they'd overlooked me for promotion. I was angry. We drank a bottle of Scotch and I got carried away. I talked about how Israel is isolating the international community for the sake of protecting a handful of illegal settlers. How Israel puts the Arabs in a pressure cooker, cooks them until they explode, then punishes them mercilessly. How with every act of brutality we create an enemy for ourselves, and then force ourselves into a position where our only option is more brutality. How for more than half a century we've been dominating an entire people, expelling them, starving them, disrupting their lives on every level, taking away their freedom. How it's a perpetual cycle. And how difficult it was to be part of that.'

'You were brave,' said Liberty, swirling the wine gently in her glass. 'We have a lot in common, you know.'

Uzi didn't hear her. He paused, took a breath, drank wine. 'For most people, none of this would be controversial. But in the Office, such views are seen as treason.'

'Was that all you said?'

'No. That was bad enough, but it wasn't what really caused the damage.' He got to his feet again and crossed over to the window. 'You don't understand what it means to oppress people. Families. What it does to you as a young soldier, at the age of eighteen . . . To see the nation we've become.'

'So what did they hear you say?' said Liberty gently.

He sat down, feeling more awkward this time. 'I said ... I speculated that the conflict stems from the power imbalance.

That's what allows Israel to throw its weight around. I said that what Israel needs is an existential threat. Something real, something serious. If we weren't the only regional power to have nuclear weapons it would make us think twice before continuing this oppression. We would go to war less readily. Our neighbours would have less reason to retaliate. Over time it could open the door to peace.'

'You mean Iran?'

'Yes, Iran. Or Syria. Though there's not much chance of that after we bombed their facilities in 2007.'

'You realise this is crazy, don't you?'

'Why?'

'For Iran, nuclear weapons would be more than a deterrent. They'd try and wipe you off the face of the earth. And the USA would be next.'

'Typical American answer,' Uzi retorted, sitting back in an explosion of energy. 'Typical ignorance. You haven't worked in Iran, I take it?'

'I haven't. Afghanistan, but not Iran.'

'If you had, you wouldn't have such a simplistic view of the country. Persia is a proud and ancient civilisation. For centuries they were a dominant force in the world, at the forefront of science, mathematics and culture. Their leader is nothing but a figurehead, a public face. He's not really pulling the strings. They wouldn't instigate a nuclear holocaust any more than we would.'

'But . . .'

'If they launched a nuclear attack they would bring instant death and destruction on themselves, and they know it. Not even the Iranian leadership would be that stupid. However fanatical they are, they cannot erase their instinct for self-preservation. They want a nuclear weapon because they want a deterrent. They want to be respected by the West. They want to give the Muslim world back its dignity. They want to stand up to the bullies, the USA and Israel. They want to give us a reason to stop and think next time we're about to launch a drone, or invade a weakling nation, or meddle in Iranian internal affairs. That's what I told Avner and that's what the Office heard. I even gave it a name: the Doctrine of the Status Quo. Perhaps unconsciously I knew I was being bugged, I don't know. Perhaps I wanted them to know what I really thought.'

There was a silence. Liberty waved for the waiters and they glided in with cheese and a bottle of port. They disappeared again. Neither Uzi nor Liberty moved.

'Like I said, I'm a free thinker,' said Uzi suddenly. 'I don't take anything as a given. I look at things that nobody questions and work them through for myself.'

'So Avner didn't report you?'

'No, he didn't. He's a bastard, but he's only interested in making life better for himself, not making life worse for anyone else.'

'Do you believe in your Doctrine of the Status Quo now?'

'No.'

'The way you were talking, it sounded like you did.'

'I always talk like that.'

'Not in my experience.'

'You don't have much experience.'

'OK, then. So why don't you believe it now?'

'It's too much of a risk. Deep down I'm certain that a nuclear deterrent in the Arab Middle East would be a good thing. But on paper, it's just too risky.'

'So you believe it with your heart, but not your head.'

'You could say that.'

Liberty shook her head and finished her port. 'So the Mossad didn't kick you out right away when they heard that drunken speech of yours? I'd have expected them to get rid of you immediately. Or worse.'

'No. I was lucky enough to have horses in the right place at the right time.'

'Horses?'

'It's a word we use. Powerful allies. Everyone in the Office has at least two: one to look out for your general interests, and the other to get you out of the shit in an emergency.'

'So this was an emergency.'

'Too right. I called in a few favours. My horses gave me a hard time, but they contained the damage and I kept my job.'

'Your horses are still looking after you now?'

'To some extent,' Uzi said. 'When I decided to leave, my horses persuaded the decision makers that I wasn't a threat. They said I'd gone off the rails – suffering from combat stress but still loyal. So the Office let me run. They stamp me down occasionally and think that's enough of a deterrent. Anyway, they know they can always pick me up whenever they like.' He gestured wearily to his bruised face.

'Let's step out on to the balcony,' said Liberty, picking up her drink and handbag. 'Get some fresh air.'

He followed her out into the night. Side-by-side, they looked over the city. The flame heaters blasted into the vast, empty sky above them. She doesn't know about Operation Regime Change, or even Operation Cinnamon, thought Uzi. I know in my gut that she doesn't.

'What I don't understand,' said Liberty, 'is that if you're so upset to have left them, why did you join up in the first place?'

Uzi sighed into the blackness. 'Being Jewish and being Israeli are two different things. Diaspora Jews might talk about Israel a lot, but they can't understand what it means to live there. In Israel, there's nowhere to go. If you drive far enough in one direction, you'll reach a border and be turned back. In another direction you'll be shot, or stabbed, or lynched. You can't disappear. You can't hide. If there was a war and the enemy pushed several miles into Israel, we would be fighting on our doorsteps with our kitchen knives. In Israel everything must be defended, and you know that right down to your core. You have no choice but to fight to protect your mother, your father, your brothers and sisters, your house, your school, your neighbours. I came to hate the Office, but I could never abandon my people.' He paused to collect his thoughts before continuing. 'Every man in Israel would have traded places with me when I was a Katsa. I was part of a legend. However flawed the Office is, without it the country would be finished. Do you know how many Katsas are operational worldwide at any one time? A hundred and fifty. A hundred and fifty people strike terror into the hearts of every regime in the world. That's what I was part of, and even today I'm still proud.'

'It doesn't make sense,' said Liberty. 'You're being inconsistent.'

'I never said it made sense,' Uzi replied. 'I never claimed to be consistent.' In the distance, the blinking lights of a plane moved in a slow arc above London. Uzi had talked more in the past hour than he had ever intended. It was a wholly new experience. It was reckless, and he knew it couldn't last.

'So,' he said, 'we haven't spoken about business.'

'Oh that,' said Liberty. 'I'd almost forgotten.' She turned her back to the city and rested her elbows on the railing. Uzi continued to stare into the darkness. 'It's simple,' she said. 'Since my husband died, I've been running his organisation. Russians, all of them. It suits me; I can speak their language, I know their mindset. I keep them at arm's length – it's safer that way. The power is in my hands alone. We supply the best stuff wholesale, to the top end of the market. Then we cut it with caffeine and so on, and sell it a bit cheaper to the main pushers on the estates.'

'What's your percentage of the market?'

'Sixty, maybe sixty-five per cent.'

'Sixty-five per cent?'

'About that.'

'Fuck.'

Uzi drained his glass. He was feeling a little drunk. It was difficult to imagine that this sophisticated woman had the ruthlessness to run such a major drugs cartel. But he knew from experience that this only indicated how dangerous a person really was.

'My sources are ones I picked up while I was working in Afghanistan,' Liberty went on. 'I made my husband's business into an empire. Nobody else has such a good supply line as me. I import the highest-quality substances on the market, by a long way. My problem is, I've heard a rumour that some of my employees have been trying to discover the source so they can siphon off the business themselves. I need to know how loyal my people are. That's what I want you to help me with.'

'So it's a one-off thing?'

'No, no. At the moment, it's just me at the top. But I could make use of someone like yourself – with your skills – up there with me. Another member of the tribe, you know? This is just to get you started.'

'What's the pay?'

'Four thousand pounds a month.'

'That's it?'

'What did you expect?'

'I want somewhere to live as well.'

'Done.'

'I want to move in tonight.'

'Not a problem.'

'And I can quit at any time, with a ten thousand-pound bonus.'

'Sure.'

Uzi paused. He had been expecting her to drive a harder bargain. 'And I want eight thousand pounds a month.'

'Six,' said Liberty.

'Seven.'

'OK,' she said. 'Seven a month, somewhere to stay. Quit and you get a ten grand golden handshake. Do we have a deal?'

He turned to face her. He reminded himself of who he was. He was Uzi, and this was his chance to fight back against the Office – to change the course of history, as Avner put it. Through filtering sensitive information to the CIA through Liberty, he could put the Office on the back foot, give them something to worry about, soften them up for Operation Regime Change. In the end, of course, they would catch up with him; at best, he would be shot. But until that day, he would fight them. For a moment he became aware of himself and Liberty: their two weapons, his R9 pressing into his side, her Taurus revolver like a dark secret in her bag. Both fully loaded, both accessible in seconds. The night hung cold around them. He stretched out his hand, and she gripped it. Her palm was as cold as the night. They shook and the deal was done.

20

'You did well,' said the Kol quietly. 'You're believing in yourself.'

'Thanks,' said Uzi grudgingly.

'And that jumbo you gave her won't harm the Holy Land. It will just serve to instill fear into the hearts of the enemies of Israel.'

'If you say so. I feel like I don't know any more.'

'Believe. Never stop believing. Believe.'

Despite everything, there was a lot Uzi had been proud of about the Office. One mission in particular he had always kept locked away in his memory as a resource, something to draw strength from when times were hard. Even now, as he mobilised himself against the organisation, he found himself returning to the memory; even now it was able to give him strength, despite his treachery.

The operation had been conceived when the Office received intel that the head of the Syrian Mukhabarat – the Syrian secret service – was on his way to Paris for a secret meeting with his French opposite number from the Direction Générale de la Sécurité Extérieure, the DGSE. As ever, the key was in the detail. The Office had learned that while he was there, he planned to indulge in some shopping; in particular, he intended to purchase a Bohemian glass chandelier for his underground headquarters in Damascus. Everyone at the Paris Station was busy gaining intel on the substance of the meeting itself, but to Tel Aviv the shopping spree was an opportunity too good to miss. So the chandelier mission was given to Uzi, to carry out quietly while everyone was looking elsewhere.

Uzi, at the time, was positioned as a 'hopper'. This meant that he was based in Tel Aviv and could be dispatched at short notice anywhere in the world to carry out swift, one-off operations. Being a hopper was not a popular role, and Uzi loathed it. He wanted to be outside Israel; he wanted to forget. Everything about the place reminded him of his parents, everything reminded him of Nehama, whom he hadn't seen for two years. And everything reminded him of his son – his faceless son. So when the opportunity came to leave the country and go undercover again, he jumped at it.

Under the alias of David Moreau, a French businessman, Uzi departed Tel Aviv on an Air France flight and landed in Paris in the early morning. He spent the flight reading a file about luxury chandeliers that had been prepared for him by the research department. Nobody met him at the airport; contact with operatives from the Paris Station would be minimal, as they couldn't risk being directly linked to an operation as audacious as Uzi's. So he made his way, alone, to Le Meurice hotel on the rue de Rivoli in the centre of the city.

The Office planners in Tel Aviv had identified two key personnel who would prove vital to the success of Uzi's mission. The first was Reem Al-Zou'bi, an aide to the Syrian Mukhabarat chief, whose responsibility it was to oversee the purchase of the chandelier. According to his Office file, he was a dedicated family man who, unusually, was faithful to his wife: no leverage there. But there was a glimmer of hope. Al-Zou'bi was sending his children to private schools, and his mother required expensive medical treatment. As a consequence, he had fallen badly into debt. To the Office psychologists, this presented an obvious weak point: avarice.

The second person was a man by the name of Pierre Tannenbaum, a red-headed interior designer who lived and worked in the trendy La Madeleine quartier of Paris. Tannenbaum was a dyed-in-the-wool Zionist and a trusted Sayan, who had proven his mettle several times in providing loans to Katsas at short notice.

According to the Office psychologists, Tannenbaum would relish the opportunity to become more involved in an operation. Uzi invited him to the hotel, where together, over coffee, they devised a plan.

Within twenty-four hours Uzi and Tannenbaum had set up Lüp, a front company specialising in luxury interior lighting. The Office designers in Tel Aviv created a brochure and business cards, and Tannenbaum organised business premises with a young female Sayan posing as a secretary to answer enquiries. The stage was set. The Syrian delegation landed in Paris, and the eyes of the entire intelligence community in France, from all nationalities, turned towards the meeting. Uzi and Tannenbaum, meanwhile, focused their attention on Al-Zou'bi and his task of procuring a chandelier.

After twelve hours of surveillance, the time had come to make their move. Through tapping his phone line, they learned that Al-Zou'bi had an appointment at Perrin Antiques on the rue du Faubourg Saint-Honoré, not far from Tannenbaum's penthouse. They also discovered that he had been given a budget of €35,000 for the purchase; that was the crack in which Uzi planned to insert his lever. He followed Al-Zou'bi to the antiques shop and sat in the window of a nearby brasserie, sipping black coffee; Tannenbaum, who knew the owner of the antiques shop, Monsieur Perrin, was sitting in his car around the corner, waiting for Uzi's signal. Uzi watched as Al-Zou'bi got into conversation with Perrin and they went from chandelier to chandelier. After several minutes, when Al-Zou'bi seemed to be focusing on one chandelier in particular, Uzi dialled Tannenbaum's number, allowed it to ring twice, and hung up.

He didn't have to wait long. Within seconds Tannenbaum could be seen sauntering down the street and entering the antique shop. Uzi turned on his earpiece and listened as Tannenbaum greeted Perrin and fell easily into a conversation. They talked business for a while, and out of politeness Perrin introduced him to Al-Zou'bi. Tannenbaum made some general conversation about chandeliers and ascertained that Al-Zou'bi had developed an interest in a particularly fine Rococo revival piece. He then excused himself and left the shop, crossing the road to the brasserie and taking a seat at the table behind Uzi. So far, everything had gone according to plan.

When Al-Zou'bi left the shop, Uzi and Tannenbaum hailed a cab to a restaurant near the Place de la Concorde. They knew that the Syrian had made a reservation there for lunch, and Uzi had reserved the table opposite. Again, they didn't have long to wait. When Al-Zou'bi entered, Tannenbaum caught his eye, greeted him, remarked on the coincidence, and asked him how the shopping was going. Then, seamlessly, Uzi commented that Perrin's profit margins were exceptionally high and congratulated Al-Zou'bi for his good judgement in not having yet made a purchase. The Syrian visibly rallied at the compliment, and Tannenbaum chose that moment to invite him to join them for lunch. Al-Zou'bi accepted. The die was cast.

By the time the main course was concluded, Uzi and Tannenbaum had struck a deal with Al-Zou'bi. They presented him with a Lüp brochure, which showed some unusually cheap prices. All chandeliers were sourced directly, they said, avoiding retail overheads. Uzi waited for his moment, then offered to procure exactly the same Rococo chandelier that Al-Zou'bi had been admiring at a price that was some €10,000 lower. Then, delicately, he offered to provide a receipt for the full €35,000. There was a pause. Al-Zou'bi's mind could almost be seen working through the possibilities: he could deliver a €35,000 chandelier to his boss, spend only €25,000, and pocket the difference. It was a no-brainer. The men shook on the deal, Al-Zou'bi wearing the expression of a man who believes himself to be very clever – and very lucky – indeed. He paid a deposit there and then, and went away happy.

Later that day, Uzi returned to Perrin Antiques and bought the chandelier on the Office account. Overnight it was shipped to Israel and fitted with tiny fibre-optic cameras and microphones.

Thus, hours before the Syrian delegation was due to leave the country, Uzi and Tannenbaum delivered the chandelier to a delighted Al-Zou'bi. Before the week was out, it had been installed directly above the desk of the chief of the Syrian secret service, the most secure place in the country, from where it transmitted a continuous stream of footage to Tel Aviv. It had been a perfect operation: no blood spilt, no death, no torture. Just a little ingenuity combined with good old-fashioned chutzpah. It didn't get any better than that.

21

'Check this out,' said Avner, holding up his iPhone. He tapped the screen and put it down on the ornate coffee table. 'All bugging devices within a five-metre radius are hereby disabled.'

'I've never seen that before,' said Uzi.

'Modified iPhone,' Avner replied. 'Standard issue.'

'Technology moves fast.'

'Faster than you, that's for sure,' said Avner, running his hand over a gilt griffin bedpost and looking around the room. 'This is a nice place. A little tacky, but nice.'

'What do you mean, a little tacky?' said Uzi, lying back on the four-poster bed with his hands laced behind his neck. 'This is luxury, my friend. Neoclassical luxury.'

'Neoclassical?'

'Yes, Neoclassical. Weren't you concentrating during our British Culture lectures?'

'That was a load of shit.'

'You're a load of shit.'

'What's with the aggression?'

Uzi smiled. He was in a good mood. The night before he had slept well, then spent the morning shopping for clothes using an advance on his first month's salary from Liberty. Lunch had been brought to him by room service, and the afternoon had slipped away in a combination of spliffs, movies and naps. Now evening had fallen, and the adrenaline was flowing pleasantly. The WikiLeaks men would be arriving soon.

This was Home House, a private members' club in Portman Square: Uzi's new home. Liberty had chosen well. The major hotels were crawling with operatives from the Office and count-less other agencies, so something more out of the way had been required. Home House, set behind the polished black doors of three Georgian townhouses, was perfect. The interior was opu-lent and the exterior discreet; it was outside the high-pressure world of diplomatic London, the sort of place where a man could hide away in comfort. Above all, it was the last place the Office would look.

'You can't be getting all this for nothing,' said Avner. 'This place is pricey. Has the woman asked you to do anything yet?'

'Not yet. But it's only been a day.'

'Something isn't right about this, my brother. I hope you know what you're doing.'

'You forget how much money there is in heroin, Avner. You underestimate the power of having exclusive suppliers. I know exactly what I'm doing.'

'I hope so, my brother. I hope so.' Avner parted the curtains and looked down at the rain-swept street. 'They're late.'

'Only by a couple of minutes.'

'It makes me jumpy when people are late.'

'Relax. Have a drink.'

'This woman is using you,' said Avner. 'I feel it in my gut.'

'She's using me; I'm using her,' said Uzi. 'It's a working rela-tionship. You should thank me.'

'What for?'

Uzi took a breath. 'I'm giving her jumbo.'

'Jumbo?'

'Why not? It'll confuse the Office. Distract them. Make Oper-ation Regime Change more effective.'

'OK, but jumbo? Actual jumbo? You'll get yourself killed.'

'This is all or nothing, Avner. Total war. You know that.'

Avner studied his friend's face. 'Not KAMG?' he said. Uzi didn't reply. 'You've told her about KAMG, haven't you? Shit, my brother, shit.'

'Look, are you serious about Operation Regime Change or not?' said Uzi, irritated that Avner – as an old friend – had been able to read his mind.

'You've just taken this to a whole new level,' said Avner. 'A whole new level.'

Uzi sat up and lit a cigarette. For once he felt strong, confident, comfortable in his own skin. The Office had no idea where he was, he was sure of that. Finally he was fighting back. And this time, with Liberty on his side, he had some protection. This was still reckless, of course; the whole thing was based on recklessness. But sometimes – just sometimes – recklessness can bring strength.

'Get serious, Avner,' he said through a curtain of cigarette smoke. 'If we're going to do this, we should do it properly.'

'You're allowed to smoke in this place?'

'I'm with Liberty. I can do whatever the fuck I want.'

'A match made in heaven.'

There was a knock at the door. They exchanged glances. Avner opened it, his hand hovering above his sidearm. Two men slouched in the doorway; one was holding a computer bag.

'Who are you?' said Avner.

'We're here for a data-gathering appointment,' said one.

'Where's J?'

'J doesn't do these meetings himself.'

'I thought he'd be here.'

'It doesn't work like that. J doesn't have time to waste on every joker with a tale to tell and half a stolen document.'

Avner scowled. 'Show me some ID,' he said, 'I'm not taking any chances.'

'With pleasure.'

Avner took the ID and disappeared into the adjoining room of the suite to call J. Uzi flashed his R9, took the computer bag and shut the door, leaving the WikiLeaks men outside. He examined the bag, tossed it on the bed and began removing the equipment: a laptop, specialist cameras and recording devices. Sophisticated stuff, but no weapons. He could hear Avner raising his voice on the phone.

When the bag was empty, Uzi turned it upside down and shook it. Nothing came out at first; then a small grey object bounced on to the bed. He leaned over and picked it up. An encrypted USB drive. The sort that would wipe itself if the pass code were entered incorrectly. Uzi had used them countless times for the Office.

Avner came in from the next room, slightly flushed. 'OK, J's not coming. Lazy bastard. But he has vouched for these guys,' he said. 'Says they're sharp as fuck. Let's see if they are.'

'So what do you think?'

'I think we do it anyway. But it's your call.'

'OK. Let's do it.'

While Uzi shoved the equipment back in the bag – keeping the USB – Avner ushered the two men in. Keeping an eye on Uzi and his pistol, they sat awkwardly, side by side, on the bed. Uzi scrutinised them. The first looked surprisingly young, barely out of his teens, and was dressed in a crumpled tracksuit and baseball cap. His skin had a sallow complexion, as if he rarely saw the sunlight. The other was older – thirties, perhaps – but no less scruffy. His body was embedded in folds of material, a baggy hoodie and jeans, like a fat man trying to disguise his weight, or a petty pusher concealing a weapon. His face was sharp and unshaven; a mischievous smile played around his lips.

'I'm Johnson, from WikiLeaks Comms,' he said. 'This is Skid, one of our techies.' The sallow-faced man nodded without smiling.

'Johnson?' said Uzi doubtfully.

'What about it? It's a common name.'

Uzi held up the USB. 'Recognise this, Johnson?'

'Shit,' said Johnson, turning to Skid. 'You kept that in your bag?'

'Where else?' Skid replied in a nasal voice. 'Up my arse?'

'That wouldn't be a bad idea,' said Johnson, 'but your finger is taking up all the space.'

'Children, children,' Uzi interrupted, raising his gun. The two men fell quiet. 'Just tell me what's on here. And where you got it from.'

'It's intel,' said Johnson cagily. 'If you're nice, we'll tell you what it is.'

Uzi walked towards him until the gun was several inches from his nose. 'I don't need to be nice.'

'OK, OK. Whatever, right? I was going to tell you anyway. It's a list of all the active assassins in the Office.'

'The Kidonim?' said Uzi. 'How did you get that?'

'We never discuss our sources,' said Johnson loftily, 'but we'll need your help to break the encryption. J says the intel will add another, like, dimension to your story.'

'It's not a story,' said Uzi.

'Whatever. Testimony.'

Avner placed the USB carefully on the table. There was a pause. These men were clearly not spies; they were relying too much on posturing, and buckled under the slightest pressure. Yet they knew their stuff, J had vouched for them. Uzi holstered his weapon and lit a cigarette.

'So,' he said, 'I suppose you two will be wanting a drink?'

22

'OK,' said Uzi once they were settled with beers and the sound equipment had been set up. 'Roll the tape. I'll tell you the story first, as it happened, and then show you the evidence.'

'Roll the tape,' chuckled Skid. 'I haven't heard that in a while.'

'From now on, everything is on record,' said Johnson. 'OK?' Uzi shrugged his acquiescence.

Skid turned on the table mic and spoke into it, stating the date, time and Uzi's name – his real name. Then he gestured for Uzi to begin and put on a pair of headphones. Uzi cleared his throat, glanced at Avner, who was sitting beside the door cradling his gun. The microphone seemed ridiculously large. Uzi began to speak.

'I'm going to give an account of Operation Cinnamon,' he said, 'the joint Mossad–Shabak operation to murder the interior minister, Ram Shalev.'

Johnson was taking notes on the laptop, his hands tapping away as if they had a life of their own. 'Describe your involvement,' he said, without looking up.

'My role was to liaise with the Shabak and the Kidon, and to contribute towards the accomplishment of the objective,' said Uzi. 'From the start, it didn't feel like a regular operation.'

'Hang on a minute,' said Johnson. 'For the record: by "Shabak" you mean the Shin Bet, Israel's domestic secret service. The Israeli MI5, so to speak. And by "Kidon" you mean a Mossad assassin.'

'Right. Normally we would receive our orders in briefing sessions with the section commander. This time, I was called for a

154

meeting with ROM himself – the director of the Mossad – on behalf of the PM.'

'Hold on,' said Johnson. 'I just want to be absolutely clear about this. You're saying that you were called into a meeting with the director of the Mossad on behalf of the Israeli prime minister?'

'Yes, that's what I said.'

'How did you know it was on behalf of the prime minister? Did ROM say so explicitly?'

'Yes.'

'What were his exact words?'

'He said, "I'm calling you into this meeting on behalf of the prime minister."'

From across the room, Avner sniggered.

Johnson flushed. 'Fine.'

'Thanks,' said Uzi drily. His throat was sore from the cigarettes and his lungs were tightening. 'From the start, all orders were issued verbally. No documentation whatsoever.'

'And that was unusual?' said Johnson.

'Yes, it was unusual. Now just shut up and listen. You're driving me crazy.' Johnson made no response. 'The whole thing was very strange. It didn't feel right. Operation Cinnamon was to be carried out within Israel's borders. Ordinarily the Mossad only works abroad.'

'The Mossad being the Israeli MI6.'

'If you must make that comparison, yes.'

'Why do you think the Mossad was being used domestically in this operation?'

'Because ROM and the PM go back a long way. They are both kibbutzniks, both of the same political stripe. The PM knows he can trust the Mossad more than the Shabak or any other intelligence unit; they're like his own family. And, of course, he chose us because of our expertise. In assassination.' There was a silence. That word, with all its ugly sibilance, hung in the air horribly. 'But I had been taught not to ask any questions. So I agreed to take on the operation.'

'Did it bother you that the target of the assassination was an Israeli minister?'

'Of course it bothered me, but I could only assume he was an enemy agent of some sort.'

'ROM gave you no reason for the hit?'

'None whatsoever. I found out later.'

'I see.'

'Look, by that point my career was unstable. I had been asking too many tricky questions, and was relying on my horses – powerful allies on the inside – to limit the damage. But I knew they couldn't protect me forever. Cinnamon was a Priority One operation, and I was flattered that they offered it to me. You just don't refuse a Priority One operation. I knew that I needed to carry it off in style if I was going to survive in the organisation.'

'Why do you think ROM chose you?'

'My horses had set it up that way. I'd promised them that I'd stop challenging authority, that I'd toe the line no matter what, and they wanted to give me a chance to get my career back on track.'

'OK.'

'So Operation Cinnamon began. The Shabak's undercover Arabists had already infiltrated a cell of suicide bombers in Gaza. Myself and a Kidon were assigned to the Shabak unit. Our plan was to pose as Hamas terrorists, instruct one of the suicide bombers to kill Ram Shalev, and pass it off as a terrorist attack. This suited the government, by the way. Whenever there is an attack in Israel, public opinion swings to the right. Just the thing with an election coming up.'

'Did you know the identity of the Kidon?' said Johnson.

'No,' said Uzi coldly. 'They're the most secretive unit in existence. I did meet with him several times to discuss the operation but he only ever called himself K20.' He lit another cigarette. Through the smoke that was leaking from his mouth, fogging his eyes, the world looked dream-like, mystical.

'Everything went smoothly. The undercover Shabak operative made contact with a prospective suicide bomber, and we set up a meeting in Gaza. I posed as a high-ranking terrorist in Hamas who had arrived to give him a personal mission. He was a young boy, not more than sixteen, whose parents had been killed during Operation Cast Lead. Nadim Sam Qaaqour was his name. A lanky kid, wiry. He'd been brainwashed – totally brainwashed – as if somebody had removed everything inside him and filled him with . . . I don't know . . . a sort of gas.'

'Gas?'

'Some kind of spirit, I don't know. Anyway, we told him that Ram Shalev had been one of the main architects of Operation Cast Lead and that he was planning another offensive against the people of Gaza. The boy didn't need any more than that. He agreed to do it there and then. We left it a week, then scheduled another meeting. Nadim was as keen as before, keener in fact. So we provided him with a suicide vest and instructions. The Kidon – K20 – arranged a meeting with Ram Shalev in the private garden of a hotel in downtown Jerusalem. The plan was to smuggle Nadim out of Gaza and drop him off in Jerusalem. Then he would make his way into the hotel garden via a side entrance. When K20 saw him coming, he would excuse himself and walk into the hotel, leaving Shalev alone in the garden. As soon as K20 was inside, Nadim was to run over and detonate the bomb. K20 would then return to the scene to make sure that both Shalev and the boy were dead. If not, he would finish them off with a miniature explosive charge to the head, made of the same substances as the suicide vest.

'It was the sort of plan that only the Mossad could have come up with. The Shabak, well, they're sophisticated operators but they don't have the same flair.'

Uzi paused, got to his feet and walked over to the window. He parted the curtains. Outside it was dark and the rain was coming down in great flapping sheets. He saw his face reflected in the glass.

'Do you want to stop the recording?' said Johnson.

'No, leave it. I'm fine,' said Uzi. He returned to his seat, passed a hand over his brow, and resumed the narrative. 'I was uncomfortable with the whole operation. I felt there was no doubt that Nadim would blow himself up sooner or later. In his mind, he'd already crossed to the other side. But using him as an instrument of assassination?' He shook his head. 'There was something I couldn't put my finger on, something that wasn't right.'

'Do you normally trust your instincts?'

'This operation was far from normal. Anyway, what really bothered me was the target: Ram Shalev. It didn't add up. He just didn't seem like the type to be an enemy agent; my gut was telling me it was all wrong. But I convinced myself that since it was a Priority One operation, it wouldn't have been approved without good reason, especially at such a high level. Call me naive, but that's what I wanted to believe. It's what I wanted to be true; this operation was going to be very good for my career.'

'So what happened?'

'Well, K20 had instructed me to get Nadim to hand over all the money he possessed the week before the attack. This amounted to three thousand dollars; his parents had left it to him to be used as a dowry for his sister. K20 said that it was standard practice to take money off suicide bombers, as it made them more committed. If they didn't have any money, it made them more determined to blow themselves up; they'd have nothing to go back to.'

'Where did the money go?'

'I remember K20's face when I handed over the cash. There was a very slight change of expression, greed, I guess. And then I knew exactly where the money was going. I knew I was being played. But I let it slide.'

'So the operation went according to plan?'

'It did. It was the strangest thing, taking a suicide bomber to his target. That was Nadim's last journey, and he seemed so calm, so otherworldly. I picked him up in Gaza, smuggled him out and drove him into Jerusalem. There was something eerie about the boy. He was praying constantly. I waited outside the hotel until the bomb went off. Then I drove away. Later I found out that Nadim had been killed instantly, but Ram Shalev had only been injured. K20 had finished him off.'

'With the explosive charge to the head.'

'With the explosive charge to the head. Then he disappeared.'

Uzi sat back, running his hands through his hair. He glanced at Avner, who gave him the slightest of nods.

'So what made you investigate further?' said Johnson.

Uzi sighed. 'That night, I couldn't sleep. I kept seeing the faces of Ram Shalev, of Nadim. When the objective had been achieved and they were both dead, it really hit me. I didn't know why, but the whole thing stank. The following morning, the PM called me personally to congratulate me and thank me for my dedication. It was when I put the phone down that I knew I had to find out what lay behind the operation. I needed to know what I'd done.'

'So what did you do?'

'I was sure that K20 knew the truth. The Kidonim are the highest-ranking intelligence operatives in Israel; he had to know the full story. I managed to make contact with him by making a formal request for a one-to-one, intelligence-sharing session. Surprisingly enough, the authorities agreed. We met in downtown Tel Aviv, and I threatened to inform his superiors that he had extorted three thousand dollars from Nadim. This freaked him out. Don't get me wrong, corruption is rife in the regular Mossad, but the Kidonim are held to a different standard. They're not meant to be players like the rest of us. And if they break the rules, the penalties are high.'

'How did K20 respond?'

'He started to threaten me, but I told him that I'd left a letter containing this information with a friend, to be opened if I were killed or injured. I said I just wanted to know the nature of my crimes, that I had no intention of leaking any intelligence. That it wouldn't be worth risking my life over. I distinctly remember telling him that I wasn't that stupid.' Uzi smiled to himself bitterly.

'So K20 gave you the information?'

'He did. We met the following week and he handed over a file of documents. I had them for only five minutes. I used a clamper – you're familiar with a clamper?'

'Yeah, that's our stock in trade.'

'OK, so using a clamper I photographed all of the documents. I read them through that evening. And what I saw shocked me.'

'Do tell.'

Uzi took a deep breath. 'Ram Shalev was assassinated on the orders of the PM because he had some information that he was going to make public. The information was this. The government was planning – is still planning – to carry out lightning air strikes on Iranian nuclear facilities, in an operation called Desert Rain. They say that the Iranians have enriched uranium and produced yellowcake. This yellowcake represents an existential threat to Israel, so if it existed, the attacks would be justified. But, in reality, according to Ram Shalev, the yellowcake is a paper tiger. It doesn't exist. Operation Desert Rain is simply a publicity stunt to drum up some patriotic fervour in Israel, and swing the country in the run-up to the election.'

'Talk about playing with fire,' said Johnson. 'If Iran were to retaliate, this would mean war.'

'I know,' Uzi replied. 'This government is nothing if not arrogant.'

A silence fell, a tangible silence broken only by the tapping of keys as Johnson made feverish notes.

'So let me just run through this again, for purposes of clarity,' Johnson said, trying to keep his voice matter-of-fact. 'The prime minister has authorised an attack on a bogus target in Iran in order to get the public on his side before the election.'

'Right,' said Uzi. 'Operation Desert Rain.'

'Ram Shalev, one of his own ministers, found out about the plan and intended to make it public.'

'Correct.'

'So the prime minister used the Mossad to assassinate him. He killed his own interior minister, and he used the Mossad to do it.'

'That's right.'

'And you personally were involved in this operation. Operation Cinnamon.'

'Absolutely.'

'And this testimony is all completely true. Everything happened exactly as you said it.'

'That's right.'

'Fuck,' said Skid from the corner of the room. He stopped the recording and removed his headphones. 'This is massive.'

Uzi reached into his inside pocket and drew out the buff envelope he had taken from the slick in his old apartment. He tossed it over to Johnson. 'Here are copies of all the documents I photographed with the clamper. They confirm everything I've told you.' Johnson took the envelope, with a forced casualness. 'Leak them, Johnson, whatever your name is. Let the world know about Operation Cinnamon, Operation Desert Rain. Once the information is out there, the government can't bomb Iran.'

'That's your motivation? To avert war?' said Johnson.

'That and the money,' said Avner from beside the door.

'What money?'

'J didn't tell you? Political donations,' said Avner. 'And speaking of money, we have agreed with J that you won't make this information public until we've received a cash deposit in our accounts. Do you understand that?'

'Whatever,' said Johnson, slowly closing his laptop.

'No, not whatever,' said Avner, getting to his feet. 'Put it like this. If my colleague's testimony leaks before we get our money, we will hunt you down and kill you. Not J, not anybody else, just you. Understand now?'

Johnson nodded, avoiding eye contact. The two WikiLeaks men hurriedly packed up their equipment and prepared to leave. Uzi took out Avner's MacBook and turned it on. Skid came and watched over his shoulder as he inserted the Office's USB and ran the de-encryption software. Then he opened the file.

The four men huddled around the glowing screen. Within seconds there appeared a gallery of head-and-shoulder photographs of the Mossad's forty-eight Kidonim, all of whom looked young and serious, and six of whom were female. Uzi breathed in sharply. Just setting eyes on these pictures meant an instant death sentence.

'Present from J,' murmured Johnson.

'Him,' said Uzi, pointing to one of the images. 'That's K20.' The picture showed a baby-faced man with longish black hair, pale green eyes and a high-bridged nose. Uzi opened his file, read his name. 'There you are. Yakov Ben Zion. Aged twenty-six.' He turned to Johnson. 'You make this guy's name public as well. Make sure of it.'

After the men had left, Uzi and Avner sat in silence for many minutes, lost in their thoughts. The rain could be heard pounding on the window with a renewed ferocity, heightening the stillness in the room. Then Avner took out his phone and dialled a number.

'It's Michael here,' he said. 'Yes, it's done. All went according to plan. We're waiting for our money. When we receive it, we'll give J the green light.' And he hung up.

There was a pause.

'Well,' said Uzi, 'that's it. It's done.'

'It's done,' Avner repeated. 'Doesn't that feel good? We're fucking the Office, preventing war with Iran, and making more money than we can spend in a lifetime. All at once.'

'Yeah,' said Uzi impassively, 'feels good.'

'I'm going to go home, have a hot bath, and start making the arrangements for my new life,' said Avner, getting to his feet. 'I suggest you do the same. When the story breaks, we both want to be far away.'

'I've told you, I'm staying right here,' said Uzi. 'I've got a good thing going here with Liberty. Good work, well paid. And I have protection.'

Avner looked at him as if he were about to say something. Then he changed his mind. He walked over and rested his hand on Uzi's shoulder. Then he turned and left the room.

23

In a backstreet between Soho and Covent Garden, beneath a constantly flickering streetlight, lay an underground vodka dive. It had no official name, but was known to the people who knew about it as Pogreb – the Cellar. The place was subterranean; to enter you had to descend a flight of slippery stone steps, pass through a steel door – which was always closed, and manned by an armed bouncer – and go down a spiral staircase into a converted wine cellar. Its customers were pushers, pimps, money launderers, even the occasional arms dealer. All Russian.

In a shadowy corner, hunched over a bottle of flavoured vodka, cupping shot glasses in their hands, sat two men. One, an Afghan named Aasif Hamidi, was swarthy and sullen, with a black moustache and a jacket collar turned up in a low fan behind his neck. His companion, Alexey Mikhailovich Abelev, had tightly curled blond hair, thick white eyelashes and eyes that looked like marbles.

'So,' said Abelev, 'this is your first time in London?'

'Yes.'

'How do you like it?'

'I was sent from Afghanistan to check on how the woman is selling our product,' he said; his Russian was thick with an accent from the Afghan borderlands. 'That is all.'

'Your boss is losing confidence in her? That's what I am hearing.'

Hamidi shrugged. 'Business is business. We have to make sure we get the best price.'

At this, Abelev smiled in a crafty sort of way and sat back in his chair. Hamidi took a Mild-7 cigarette from his pocket and lit it with a Zippo. Then he offered one to Abelev, who declined.

'I'm a serious man,' said Abelev in a surprisingly soft voice. 'I want you to know that before we talk any further.' He took the vodka bottle and refilled their glasses.

'That's good,' Hamidi said. 'Then we're both serious men. That's a good start.' He emptied his glass of vodka down his throat and winced.

'In that case, I'll get straight to the point,' said Abelev. 'I want to know what your boss's terms are with the woman.'

'Liberty?'

At the mention of her name, Abelev glanced around nervously. 'Of course,' he said in a hushed voice. 'Who else?'

'Don't piss your pants. We're talking about a woman, not a goddess,' said Hamidi drily.

'You obviously don't know her.'

'Come on. You think Afghanistan is a playground?' Hamidi refilled their glasses, exhaling a jet of smoke.

'Do you have to puff on that thing? I'm allergic to smoke,' said Abelev, coughing.

'I'm allergic to lack of smoke,' Hamidi responded.

There was a pause. Somebody at the bar dropped a glass, and everyone bristled for a fight. The barmaid cleared it up and things returned to normal.

'So, you want to know the terms my boss has agreed with your boss,' said Hamidi after a time. 'That's what you're telling me?'

'That's what I'm telling you.'

'Let me try to understand. Liberty protects you, right? She pays you well. She looks after you. So why are you asking me a thing like that?'

'It's obvious, isn't it?'

'Not to me it isn't.'

Abelev took a swig of vodka and sighed. 'You're right, Liberty pays me. And she looks after me. But she keeps me on the street. I don't want to be on the street. I want to be pulling the strings.'

'Why don't you just be patient? Be a good boy? Work your way up like everyone else?'

'It's impossible with her. Since her husband died she's held all the power herself, made all the decisions. We don't even know what decisions she's making, it's that bad. A lot of guys who work for her don't even know each other. There's a guy who's been with her for years, and he's still working the same estate. I can't stand it any longer. I've got plans.'

'But she pays well.'

'Yes, but I'm ambitious.'

'So what are these plans?'

'I have . . . other contacts.'

'Who?'

'Never mind who. An organisation just as big as Liberty's. An organisation that wants a piece of your product. There's no reason you should only sell to Liberty. No reason at all.'

'So you're planning to offer my boss better terms than the bitch. Right?'

'That's right.'

'And you're planning to become the number one dealer.'

'Eventually, yes. The other lot have promised to make me a partner if I can get you to sell to them.'

'That's your ticket off the streets.'

'Yes.'

'And you're planning to avoid getting killed by Liberty.'

'I know what I'm doing. Don't worry about me.'

'You look worried, if I may say so.'

'This is business, Hamidi. Business.'

'OK, then tell me something,' said Hamidi in a hard voice. 'Why aren't you worried that I'll go straight back to the bitch? Tell her you're trying to stab her in the back?'

Abelev blanched. 'You wouldn't do that.'

'I wouldn't?'

'This is money we're talking about. I know the rules of the game, Hamidi. Sell to me and your boss'll be far richer. Liberty would be ancient history.'

'The bitch won't go out without a fight. You'll have a battle on your hands, make no mistake.'

'I'll sort it. All you need to know is volume will be high, and it'll increase by increments as time goes on. And we'll pay you fifteen per cent more than Liberty.'

'Fifteen?'

'That's what I said,' said Abelev, holding the other man's gaze.

The swarthy man smiled. 'I like you, Abelev. You're a straightforward man. A serious, straightforward man.'

'I want to do business, to make money,' the blond man said. 'That's all.'

Hamidi leaned forward in a cloud of cigarette smoke, his collar casting a shadow across his cheeks. 'Let me tell you something, my friend. The goods we provide – they are the best quality. The very best quality. Direct from Afghanistan, one hundred per cent pure, mixed with absolutely nothing. Pure, potent and powerful. You won't find better anywhere in London, anywhere in the world, my friend. The whole world. Our goods are –' he kissed his fingers softly '– out of this world.'

'I know,' said Abelev. 'That's why I'm approaching you and no one else. Real money depends on a good reputation. And a good reputation depends on a high-quality product.'

'Not just high quality. The best quality, Abelev. The best.'

'The best. I know. The best.'

'We don't trust just anyone. So far, we've only trusted the bitch.'

'But now your boss no longer trusts her. That's why you're here.'

'Why should we trust you any more than her?'

'Because I'm offering you a better price. It's as simple as that.'

'What is the name of this organisation you're talking with?'

'You wouldn't know them. Only people in London know them.'

'I need to know. It's a matter of trust.'

'They'd kill me.'

'And I wouldn't? It's a matter of trust.'

'I can't tell you. That's also a matter of trust.'

Hamidi sat back, musing.

'It makes sense,' said Abelev quickly. 'Business is business. Whichever way you look at it, it makes sense.'

'So,' said Hamidi, sucking on his cigarette, 'how well do you know the goods? Do you know them in your brain, in your heart, in your veins? Do you know them from your own experience?'

'I don't take smack, if that's what you mean.'

'What about crack? Cocaine?'

'No.'

'What's your poison, then? Cannabis?' He wrapped his lips lethargically, mockingly, around the word.

'No. I never sample the goods I sell.'

'Don't tell me: you're a serious man.'

'Don't mock me, sir. I came here to do business. Not to drink vodka and be mocked.'

'Tell me something,' said Hamidi, stubbing his cigarette out with a square forefinger. 'What would the bitch do to you if she found out about this conversation? What would she do to you?'

Abelev cringed, shifted in his chair, almost got to his feet. 'She will not find out. The question is not a question.'

'Of course,' said Hamidi, 'of course.' He drained his glass and grabbed the bottle by the neck. 'If you're really serious about doing some business, we should get to know each other a little first.'

'What do you mean?'

'You might not like drugs, but you like pussy.'

'Well, who doesn't?'

'You like Polish slave girls?'

'What do you want me to say?'

'I want you to say you'll fuck two little Polish girls at once.'

'Who wouldn't?'

'Then we'll discuss terms, OK? When you're a little more relaxed.'

For the first time that night, Abelev smiled.

'Come on,' said Hamidi. 'Let's drive.'

The two men made their way upstairs to the street. Beneath the streetlight lay a sleek, glistening car, a capsule of power. As Hamidi approached, the doors unlocked with a clunk.

'Get in,' said Hamidi, 'and don't make anything dirty.'

'Is this one of the new Porsches?'

'Of course. I chose white – you like white?'

'White's OK.'

'And tinted windows.'

'Not bad.'

'Not bad,' repeated Hamidi, turning the key. The car awoke instantly with a perfectly controlled growl. 'You're a funny man, Abelev, you know that? A funny, serious man.' He steered out into the traffic and lit another cigarette. This time, Abelev did not protest.

'What's the music?' said Abelev, swigging from the vodka bottle.

'You don't recognise it?' said Hamidi, surprised. 'It's the most Russian of all Russian composers.'

'Tolstoy?'

'You fucking idiot. This is Mily Balakirev,' Hamidi said, reaching into his inside pocket. 'Remember that: Mily Balakirev.'

Without taking his eyes off the road, he raised his fist. For an instant, a hypodermic needle flashed; then he brought it down in an arc into Abelev's leg. The man moaned once, slumped against the window. Hamidi reached over, shoved him down in the seat and opened the glove compartment. It illuminated automatically; inside was a packet of cigarettes, a Rohrbough R9 pistol, and a fresh roll of brown packing tape. He turned off the main road and headed towards a quiet alleyway, into the heart of the night.

24

The car had come as a complete surprise. Uzi had been at Home House for two days, and in that time he had replaced his wardrobe and personal effects, bought a laptop – a PC – and recuperated following the beating he had received at the hands of his own kind. He recovered quickly; he always did. His body had grown used to regenerating in the few hours permitted to it. Like a survivor making do with the limited resources available, he healed in the smallest windows of downtime.

It wasn't until the evening of the second day, when Avner had left and the countdown to the maelstrom in Israel had begun, that Liberty first made an appearance. It was early evening, and Uzi had just extinguished a spliff. He was sitting in front of the television in a pair of Armani jeans, watching the Discovery channel. Automatically his mind was dwelling on his memories – while a documentary droned on unnoticed before his eyes, they were playing out in his head. The Lebanon war. The cry of the infantry as they mounted an attack, almost drowned out by shell bursts and gunfire. A fearsome noise, but also melancholy. As it drifted up to Uzi – he was holding a position on a rocky outcrop – it became the sound of souls calling to everything they loved, calling on their families to raise their heads from their pillows, to hear for the last time the voice of a father, a husband, a son, a brother. It was drowned out by the bombardment, and Uzi adjusted the sights on his weapon. Soon it would be time to move off behind enemy lines again, and his stomach was churning. So he sat between his memories and the Discovery channel, numb.

There was a knock at the door. He climbed awkwardly to his feet, racked his pistol and removed the safety catch. It was Liberty.

'I see you've settled in,' she said, easing her way into the room. 'Can't you open a window or something?'

Uzi obliged. A stream of cold air surrounded him as if trying to suck him out into the night. Liberty sat in an armchair.

'Aren't you going to offer me a drink?' she said.

'Pernod, isn't it?'

'And water.'

Uzi was surprised – then not surprised – to find a bottle of Pernod in the minibar. He opened a lager and sat opposite her on the bed.

'What's your favourite colour?' said Liberty.

Uzi looked up woozily. 'My favourite colour?'

'That's what I asked.'

'I don't know. Depends on the situation. Depends what you're talking about.'

'I'm talking about a car.'

'What sort of car?'

'A Porsche. The new Turbo S.'

'Oh. Well, white. It's got to be white.'

Liberty laughed. 'Why white?'

'Red is too much like a cock. Black is too much like a dealer.'

'Too much like a dealer? You're hilarious, Uzi, you know that?'

'So have you come to give me a job?' said Uzi.

'I haven't finished talking about the car.'

'The car?'

'Your white Porsche.'

'My white Porsche?'

Liberty smiled. 'That intel you gave me over dinner – the KAMG intel?'

'What about it?'

'It's about to make me a lot of money. I wanted to say thank you.'

'My pleasure.'

'I'll order the car tomorrow. Compliments of Liberty Inc.'

'Thanks,' said Uzi, listening to his own voice and finding it hollow.

'We're going to be good together, you and I,' said Liberty. 'I can tell.'

Uzi had always been bad at accepting gifts, particularly extravagant ones. Ever since he was a child, the bigger the present, the more depressed he became; he felt like he was being taken advantage of, lured into debt against his will. And this time, with the car, it was more complicated. He was forgetting who he was; his allegiance was shifting. Even the Kol didn't understand. Liberty was winding him closer into her web, and it was dangerous. He wasn't her victim, he was a victim of his own recklessness. That made him feel sick.

He pulled his Porsche into the wasteland around the back of a derelict pub within reach of the river. The wheels bounced uncomfortably over the uneven ground. Liberty's Maybach was parked on the far side, next to a BMW saloon. He steered into the shadows and killed the engine. A strange part of London, he thought. Old gangland meets Docklands. Around him were abandoned building sites, burnt-out cars, buildings with boarded-up windows and doors covered in galvanised steel; in the distance towered the gleaming skyscrapers of Canary Wharf. A helicopter buzzed overhead.

He sat for a while in the shadows. No noise was coming from the boot; the drugs wouldn't wear off for another half an hour. He peeled the moustache from his upper lip, wincing, and cursed under his breath. Normally he had no problem with the latex adhesive, but it was starting to itch. He pulled out his phone and called Liberty.

'Have you got him?' she said. There was a coldness in her voice that he hadn't heard before.

'In storage,' he replied.

'I'm in the building behind you, on the first floor. Bring him up.'

'He's heavy. I'm going to need some help.'

'You haven't killed him, have you?'

'No.'

'Then bring him up yourself. I need my men here.' The line went dead.

Uzi thumped the steering wheel with his fist and cursed. He had been expecting this; deep down, he had sensed that Liberty was a ruthless woman, and now she thought he owed her something. Well, he didn't. He wasn't one of her pawns. He wasn't under her command. He called back.

'What?' she said.

'Send me someone to help carry him. Or I'm leaving him here.'

'You won't leave him there. You'll bring him up here to me.'

'He's too heavy. Send me help or I'll leave him here.'

'You do that and it's over. I mean it. It's over.'

'You've got five minutes, Liberty.'

He hung up and got out of the car. This was petty, but he knew he was doing the right thing. He cleared his head and listened to his gut. This was a test, he thought. She was testing him, trying to see how deeply she had come to possess him. He had to admit, butterflies were in his stomach. She almost had him. Almost. But nobody would ever have him completely. Fuck her luxury, her money. He had his slick on the East End Road, he had an escape route, and he was prepared to use it. His freedom would never be bought. He drew his gun, racked it, held it inside his jacket. The wasteland was deserted, long shadows clustered around broken walls and buildings. A pile of car tyres, overgrown with ivy, lay several feet away. His upper lip itched and his palms were clammy. He looked at his watch. Three minutes. The sky was overcast and he could hear the hum of the traffic, the sound of the city. Far off, a siren. Two minutes. He pressed the button on his car key and the boot hissed open, exposing the unconscious Abelev. The stakes were high: Liberty knew a lot about him that the Office would like to know. But he was gambling on the fact that he was too valuable to throw away. One minute. He reached into the glove compartment, took out his cigarettes, his Zippo. He thought about the children in Arab villages, how they run after foreigners in the street, hassling them for money. How they'll never stop unless you stand up to them. Never. You had to beat them. Thirty seconds. Perhaps Liberty was planning to call his bluff. But there was no bluff. He tightened his grip on his pistol. He was ready to go.

Then, without warning, there was a grinding noise, and the metal door of the building behind him opened. Two burly Russians stepped out and approached the Porsche.

'Aasif Hamidi?' one said.

'Yes,' replied Uzi in Russian.

'Liberty said you need some assistance.'

Uzi smiled to himself and gestured towards the boot, not removing his gun from his jacket.

'That package needs to be delivered to her room,' he said. 'It's fragile.'

The Russians, concealing their surprise at the glistening, mummified man-fish, hauled it out on to the gravel. Then, between them, they dragged Abelev into the building. Uzi followed them, buoyed by a sense of triumph. Fuck Liberty, he thought. He had called her bluff. Now they could work together.

'Throw him in the bath and get out of here,' said Liberty, flicking her revolver towards the broken bathroom door. Without a word, the two Russians heaved Abelev into the dilapidated apartment and rolled him into the rusty tub. Uzi had cut a hole in the packing tape around his nose; as he breathed, a little flap moved back and forth.

'This is becoming your signature,' said Liberty when the Russians had left, 'this packing tape.'

Uzi scowled in response. 'That little game you played just now. Don't think you can fuck with me.'

'Oh don't be so uptight,' said Liberty, brushing his arm with her hand.

'I don't like being fucked with,' said Uzi. 'I've been fucked with enough in my life.'

'People like getting fucked,' said Liberty, looking at him like a girl.

Uzi shook his head and bent over the bath. Abelev was starting to squirm more vigorously; the drugs had all but worn off.

'For a professional, you're not very professional,' he said over his shoulder.

Liberty, inexplicably, laughed. Then she approached the tub. 'Sit him up and uncover his face. Let's see what he has to say.'

Uzi did as she asked, hauling Abelev to a sitting position and peeling the tape back from his face. He screamed, thrashed and fell on to his back; Uzi slapped him hard and propped him up again, a fat caterpillar in the gloom.

'Where am I?' he said, his voice breaking, his eyes swivelling in their sockets.

'Tell me something, Alexey Mikhailovich Abelev,' said Liberty in soft Russian. 'Do you think you are a clever bastard? Do you have a fucking PhD in cleverness or something?'

The Russian said nothing. His marble eyes slid from side to side in his head, flicked all around. His breathing was shallow and sharp and sweat stippled his moon-like face. Liberty raised her revolver and struck him a resounding blow, startlingly powerful for her size. Abelev's head bounced off the broken tiles behind him and an X-shaped incision appeared on his forehead, then immediately started to bleed. Within seconds, half his face was black with blood. He moaned, a high-pitched whine, like a cat.

'Tell me who you're working for,' she hissed.

The man evidently knew his end had come and that nothing could be gained from holding out. 'The Oswald Street Crew.'

'The Oswald Street Crew,' said Liberty. 'You fucking double-crossing turncoat.' She gripped him by the shoulder and his whine became a full-throated, animal scream.

'Just don't hurt me. Please,' he moaned.

'Get the fucker up,' said Liberty. Uzi complied, dragging the man awkwardly to his feet. She grabbed a broken ladder that was leaning against the wall and together they strapped Abelev to it.

'What I want to know,' said Liberty as they leaned the ladder against the bathtub, 'is who else in my organisation is a fucking grass like you.'

'Nobody,' he said. 'I promise. Nobody. It's just me.'

Liberty brought her face close to his. 'You're lying,' she said. His blond eyelashes fluttered, twin moths. 'I can smell it. Can you taste your own blood? Can you taste it? And now you're lying to me?'

She tied a towel around his face and Uzi knew what she was going to do. There was a single muffled shriek. The packing tape crackled horribly, like snapping twigs, as Abelev struggled. Liberty filled a jug with water from the stuttering tap; Uzi tilted Abelev backwards until his head was below the level of his feet. Then Liberty poured water into the towel – once, twice, three times. There was a choking, coughing sound from beneath it, followed by a strangled cry. Liberty repeated it again, and again, until a stream of muffled words started. She gave Uzi a signal and he tilted the Russian back upright.

Liberty tore the towel from his face. The man was weeping. 'I'm telling the truth,' he said, 'I'm working alone. I'm working alone. I'm working alone.'

'Liar!' screamed Liberty, suddenly all-powerful and terrifying, and struck him again with her gun. Blood filled his mouth, spilled over his jaw. Despite himself, Uzi shuddered. She tied the towel back around his face, and at her signal Uzi tilted the man back again, an old feeling of discomfort twisting his gut.

More water. More. And more. Liberty was smiling – was she smiling? Abelev was coughing, choking, spluttering. A gargling moan, then silence. Uzi heaved the man back upright and removed the bloodstained towel. His skin was pale, clammy; his eyes were closed. Vomit threaded in a web across his face. But he was breathing. Liberty paced the room like an animal.

'I've never seen anybody hold out against that before,' said Uzi. 'Maybe he really is working alone.'

'He isn't,' Liberty replied. 'He's part of a network, I know it. He's just a stubborn fuck. Pity he didn't stay on my side. I can always use stubborn fucks. As you know.'

'But he told you about the Oswald Street Crew. Why would he lie?'

Without warning she raised her gun and fired. Abelev's head was thrown backwards then he nodded enthusiastically, like a doll. A dark cloud appeared across the mildewed tiles behind him. Fragments of brick and cement spiralled into the air and pattered around their feet, followed by a cloud of dust. There was a silence.

'Fuck,' said Uzi wearily. 'Fuck.'

'He wasn't going to break, the bastard,' said Liberty, checking the chamber of her weapon.

'It doesn't matter now.'

'Everything matters, Uzi.'

'You didn't tell me you were going to kill him.'

'You didn't tell me he was a stubborn bastard.'

Liberty turned away and took out her phone. Uzi watched the corpse. The mangled head. How easily a man becomes a body. How easy it is to make a ghost. He was doomed, he knew that; he could never again be clean.

'Business is business,' said Liberty over her shoulder, as if she had read his mind. 'We had to do it. Are you going to tear your fucking clothes and cover yourself in ashes?'

'What you mean "we"? You did it.'

She gestured for him to be quiet and spoke into her phone: 'Get in here. Mr Abelev needs to be disposed of . . . I don't know, the river. The old Kingsway tram tunnel. I couldn't give a shit. Just get in here.' She hung up, shaking her head.

For a while, they stood side by side in silence. Then the two Russians appeared at the door. Liberty nodded to the corpse and left the room; Uzi followed her into the night air.

'He wasn't working alone,' she said without looking at him. 'Nobody ever works alone. Not even you. Not even me.'

'Then how did he resist?'

'Some people are just made that way. Weak, but stubborn.'

'No. He was telling the truth. Anyway, what's done is done. He won't tell us anything now. Do you have any other leads?'

'I have six names, all from one informant.'

'That's easy, then.'

'What do you mean?'

Uzi looked up at the silhouettes of Canary Wharf sparkling against the night sky. Israel was so far away. 'Let me tell you a story I heard from a friend in the Shabak,' he said, without looking at Liberty. 'Once upon a time, when Hamas still roamed freely in Bethlehem, three terrorists arrived in the Duheisha refugee camp carrying a stash of explosives. They were planning to carry out simultaneous suicide attacks in Jerusalem. The Shabak had a stinker – an informant – in Hamas, and he alerted them.'

Liberty was looking around as if she wasn't listening; Uzi could tell she was.

'The problem was, the stinker was high-level Hamas, and he was the only person on the West Bank who knew about these attacks. If the Shabak were to arrest the terrorists, the identity of the stinker would have been obvious. Yet at the same time, they couldn't let the attacks go ahead.'

'So what did they do?'

'Easy. They arrested the three bombers, locked up two and sent the third home with a thousand dollars. Everyone assumed he was the stinker. He was lynched.'

'You Israelis,' said Liberty, shaking her head, 'you fucking Israelis.'

'You could do something similar,' said Uzi, his breath forming clouds of condensation in the blackness. 'You bring in your six suspects. Then you release one with a big bonus. A car perhaps – I know you like cars. Then you place him under surveillance. As soon as he is threatened, or beaten up, you hunt down his attackers. Then you have your network.'

Liberty smiled. 'I like the way you think,' she said. 'You're one clever bastard.'

The metal door scraped open. They turned to watch the two Russians carrying Abelev's body to the BMW saloon. A funeral cortege.

'What took those guys so long?' said Uzi.

'They were cleaning up.'

'You have them well trained.'

'Of course.'

Uzi turned, but Liberty pulled him back.

'Look,' she said, suddenly earnest, 'do you know what it means to be a woman in this game? A woman at the top? It means you have to be strong. Stronger than any man, more ruthless. As soon as you show any weakness, you're done for. It's all about the signals you send. It's not just your business that depends on it, it's your life.'

Uzi curled his lip and turned away. This time she didn't pull him back. He headed to his car and unlocked it; Liberty walked over to her Maybach. 'Let's have a drink,' she called as she climbed in. 'Decompress. Back at Home House.'

'Is that an order?' he asked.

'It's a request.'

He slid into his Porsche, slammed the door and drove out on to the street. The engine hummed as if it had never been asleep, ebbing and flowing with the pulse of the city.

25

'You know we're doing the right thing, don't you?' said Avner, his words slurred. 'I mean, you know we're on the side of the righteous.' He looked at his watch, struggling to read it. The bar was dark, the music battling with his words. 'Now, right now. There's been a delay with the transfer of funds, but it's got to be only a matter of days until we get our money and all hell breaks loose in the Holy Land. It might even happen tomorrow.' He laughed, drained his glass, smacked his lips.

Uzi sat brooding. Fragmented – he felt fragmented. Since he had taken up with Liberty, his life had become nocturnal. He would get up in the early evening and go to bed at dawn. His plan had worked like a dream; Liberty had uprooted a network of twelve men now, and that seemed to be the last of them. Now she was giving him only the occasional job, saving him for 'something big'. In the meantime he was doing nothing but smoking, watching television and going for aimless drives in his car – he knew the Porsche was a magnet for attention, but he couldn't stop himself. The voice in his head was becoming bolder, appearing when he least expected it, criticising his relationship with Liberty as if it were jealous. He was constantly on edge. Public places had taken on a sinister nature. Who knew where his enemies may be lurking? Who knew who might see him, by chance, and report him? And who knew how careful Liberty was in protecting her sources? At any moment, he knew, the shadows could become flesh and he would be done for. The CIA must have bought the information from Liberty by now. It was only a matter of time before the leak was traced to him.

The strain was beginning to have an effect; the cushioning effect of his recklessness was starting to wear thin.

'What?' he said. Avner had been saying something.

'The Avenue of the Righteous. You know, at the Holocaust Centre, Yad Vashem. It'll be like that. You'll be a true hero. Like, like Yitzhak Rabin. Enough of blood and tears. You know? You'll have prevented a war with Iran. You want another drink?'

Uzi nodded and returned to his thoughts. He knew all about spy syndrome, of course he did. The Office had trained him thoroughly in psychology. He knew that to get someone to do what you wanted, you needed a lever, a hook. You had to identify their weak point, be it sex, money, the desire for revenge or the desire to escape. And he knew how to read his own psychology, too. He knew how to listen both to his mind and to his gut, how to cut through the white noise of panic and grip the hard facts. He knew how to keep the Kol in check, how to hold on to his sanity even when hearing voices in his head. But now it was all becoming hazy. Of course, from one point of view, he had never had it so good. He had no financial concerns. He lived rent-free in luxury. He had the sort of car men would kill for, and a lifestyle of leisure and ease. But it was in his head that the storm was brewing. The little bone bowl of his skull contained an entire universe of paranoia. He continuously tried to dispel it with rational thought, but that was as useless as fighting off darkness with a knife.

'What about you? Aren't you concerned?' he said as Avner returned with their drinks.

'Concerned about what?'

'You still work for the Office, for fuck's sake. If they knew you were meeting me – planning what we're planning – you'd be fucked.'

'Sure, I work for the Office. For the moment. That's why I can meet you. I know what our operatives are doing, where the eyes and ears are.' He leaned closer, his breath whisky-hot. 'And they're not here.' He threw his head back and laughed. Then he was talking about something else.

As Avner came out with strings of words he could barely hear, let alone understand, Uzi scanned the drinkers around them, as surreptitiously as he could, looking for some sign, some giveaway, something to make him kick over the table and swing draw. Nothing; so far, nothing. He drank whisky, thought about the words 'fire water'. Avner was still talking, his long arms draped across the back of the sofa. Avner, who he had known for so many years, who he had seen mature, fill out, grow a little fat. Compulsively Uzi slid his hand on to the butt of his R9, pretending to be looking for his phone; for the sake of form he took it out, checked for messages, put it back in his pocket.

'You've got to start following the news in Israel,' Avner was saying. For some reason, he was speaking in French. 'The polls are in favour of the government, but only by half a percentage point. People are getting sick of being held hostage to the settlers. When our story breaks, it will be game over. I have some big contacts in politics . . .'

'Oh you do?'

'I do. And they're keeping Ram Shalev's death on the media's agenda, ready for our entrance to the stage.' He laughed, coughed, laughed again. 'One week, no more than that. They promised me. One week and we'll be out of here. We'll be whipping up a storm in Israel without even lifting a finger. We'll be sipping piña coladas somewhere watching a beautiful sunset while peace explodes at home and the Office is shaken by an earthquake.'

Uzi drank. He needed a cigarette. 'This plan of yours had better work, or I'm fucked.'

'Just run,' said Avner. 'Disappear. You can come with me if you want. Anywhere you want: South America, Thailand, Africa – there's money to be made in Africa.'

'You know what?' said Uzi. 'Maybe I will.'

He saw Avner laugh, felt his hand on his shoulder, raised his glass for Avner to clink. He remembered the clink of a glass in his hand following the birth of his son at the Hadassah Hospital in Jerusalem. But it had not been Avner holding the drink up in congratulations that time. It had been his father. He remembered now the way the glass sat dwarfed in his father's palm, the tips of his fingers like pebbles. He remembered the heat of the alcohol filling his mouth, tracing a line down into his belly, burning in his throat. He remembered the smiles they exchanged. He remembered the words: *L'Chaim*. To life. Yes, Abba, to life. He remembered looking down at Nehama lying smiling in the bed, Noam feeding at her breast. He remembered his father saying *Mazal tov* both of you – you have brought into the world a boy, another soldier to defend our people. Yes, he remembered all this. But he could not remember the face of his son.

'What?' said Uzi. Avner had asked him a question and was sitting there, a silly smile on his face, awaiting a response.

'I said have you fucked her yet?' said Avner.

'Who?'

'Who do you think? Your boss.'

'No, if you must know,' said Uzi.

Avner shook his head. 'I could tell she was going to be trouble. I've never laid eyes on her but I always knew she was going to be trouble. And now you've fallen for her.'

'Fuck you.'

'Look, my brother. Let's go and get some girl. How about it?' He was speaking Hebrew now. Some girl, get some girl, get some girl. Uzi got to his feet and Avner grinned broadly. 'I knew you couldn't say no, my brother. It's exactly what you need to unwind. To forget about things a little. That American woman is turning you into even more of a psycho than you were already.'

The two men walked out into the cold night air, their ears ringing from the music.

'Come on,' said Avner, 'we can take a taxi and pick up our cars later.' He stepped into the street, waving at a black cab, pedestrians streaming around him. All at once, Uzi was overcome with a

26

As the Porsche cut through London, and the city swept past its windows like a pageant, Uzi settled in the womb-like seat and his mind reduced itself to a single Hebrew word, appearing in black spray paint: *nekama*. Revenge. For years this had been his personal barometer, the way he judged the political climate of his country. But *nekama*, that ugly word, was a failsafe indicator. Every so often, the Old City of Jerusalem would awake to find that during the night the word had been scrawled many times across the ancient cream-coloured stone, on doorways, on walls, even on the time-smoothed paving slabs. Nobody knew who was responsible for it. Uzi used to imagine it was a ghost informing the city of impending doom. Revenge. When he had first noticed the graffiti, almost two decades ago, it had never lasted long. The local people would clean it off within the hour. As the country lurched to the right, however, they lost their enthusiasm to erase it; these days, it was a permanent fixture.

Uzi waited for the Kol to speak up, but it did not make an appearance. Suddenly he knew who he was going to call. His fingers hovered over the phone in its cradle on the dashboard – hovered but did not dial. They found their way back to the steering wheel, then to the butt of his R9, then to the packet of cigarettes in his inside pocket. He lit one, inhaled hungrily. Then he moved his fingers again, and this time they were successful.

'Hello?' came a voice – a girl's voice.

Uzi hesitated. 'It's Daniel.'

'Daniel?'

'Yes, you know. From – from school.'

'The security guy?'

'That's right.'

A pause, a hesitant intake of breath. 'Where have you been?'

'I . . . you know, I have a different job now. I moved to a different part of town.'

'You've got a new number, too.'

'Yeah, new number.'

'You could have called, you know.'

'I want to see you. Tonight.'

'I'm studying. I have exams.'

'I'm going to see you.'

'You should have thought about me before. You should have called.'

'Are you at home?'

'I've told you. I'm studying.'

'And I told you. Fuck studying.'

Another pause, another breath. But she didn't hang up. Uzi felt a rush of energy. 'Tonight,' he said.

'If I fail, my parents will kill me.'

'I'll be with you in half an hour.' He hung up, swung his car around and switched the sound system on loud. Hadag Nahash began to boom through the speakers: *people, you don't really have an excuse, you know the suits don't give a damn, you lean on them like a broken wicker chair, they know this is the countdown to the explosion . . .* He nodded to the beat, trying to lose himself in the music, that aggressive groove. The tune went round and round, churning up the conflict in his head. The dissonance was too much. He turned the music off and drove on in silence.

Twenty minutes later he parked outside Gal's house and killed the engine. It was a quiet night; the house looked comfortable and secure, a little nest of warmth in the darkness. He dialled her number. It rang off. He cursed and dialled again; again, no answer. A prickling irritation rose within him, spreading its ten-drils across his scalp. He started to compose a text message but he couldn't concentrate. There's nothing for it, he thought; parents or no parents, I'm going in.

Just as he was about to get out of the car, the door of the house opened. For a moment there was only a slim rectangle of light. Then a silhouette appeared and slipped out. The door closed. The irritation in Uzi's body transmuted into something else, something equally potent. Gal looked young, sexy, reckless. Her hair was still raven-black, slightly longer now. She glanced up and down the street without seeing him. He opened the car door and caught her eye. She approached.

'I can't be long,' she said in Hebrew. 'I've got a lot to do.'

'So have I. Get in.'

'Is this a real sports car?'

'No, kid, it's a camper van. Get in.'

She walked slowly through the parallel beams of the head-lights. Then she was in the front seat, half an arm's length away, her legs stretching out in two sleek lines to her trainers. The worried face of Gal's mother appeared in the upstairs win-dow. Uzi started the engine and started to drive. He turned the corner.

'Where are you taking me?' said the girl.

'Out. I don't know. I wanted to see you.'

'Why?'

'I felt like it.'

'Is this your car?'

'No, I stole it.'

'It's nice. You must be making money now.'

'I must be.'

'What's your new job? Anything to do with Israel?'

'You ask a lot of questions, you know that?'

'So?' she said testily.

A pause.

'Did you tell your parents about me?' he said.

'What's to tell? That this random security guard came round for a smoke and left without saying goodbye?'

'I thought you said I was an Israeli hero.'

She laughed. He took a spliff from the glove compartment and tossed it on to her lap. She lit it and inhaled noisily. He was starting to realise why he had wanted to see her, and it was making him feel uncomfortable. Something about what she had said was creeping under his skin. But still he felt warm, energised.

'Look,' said Gal after a time, 'enough with the bullshit. I can't stand bullshit. If you want to fuck me just say so.'

Uzi hesitated. 'And if I did, what would you say?'

'Who knows?' said Gal. 'I'd see what I felt like.'

'You're just a kid,' said Uzi.

Gal rolled her eyes. 'I've got to be back in an hour.'

The Porsche had found its way to Hangar Lane, and Uzi steered it on to the A40 towards Oxford. The traffic thinned and the car picked up pace, the speedometer ticking higher and higher. The engine settled into a comfortable purr. Gal smoked, looking out the window. Finally Uzi broke the silence.

'OK,' he said, 'start by sucking me off.'

'What, now?'

He pressed the car to go faster. She looked at him through a roll of smoke, lights streaking past behind her, then she shrugged moodily and leaned into his lap, releasing her seatbelt as she did so. She was clumsy in loosening his trousers. He saw a little crescent of skin where her shirt pulled away from her skirt. Unblemished, pure skin. What a shame, he thought, what a shame. The motorway tunnelled past in chains of red lights, white lights, traffic cones, darkness. She found his penis and took it into her mouth; he felt lava welling within him, slipping down to his groin. The speed slipped past ninety. His fingers tightened on the wheel.

Gal's head was moving up and down now. Who knows what secrets her little skull contained? She had asked about his new job. She had asked whether it was anything to do with Israel. He adjusted his shoulders in the seat as she found her rhythm, the steering wheel behind her like a halo. Anything to do with Israel. Why would she have asked that? This wasn't spy syndrome, he thought. This was real. The fact that she was sucking his cock so readily only confirmed his fears. After all, he had been at her house when the Office broke into his flat. And by the time he got home, they had been waiting for him.

He reached into the glove compartment and took out a hypodermic needle. The Office might be watching, but there was always going to be that risk. The speedometer crept past a hundred. She moaned but didn't break her rhythm. He raised the syringe then hesitated. The lava was pooling in his groin, starting to overtake his thoughts. How old was this girl? Seventeen? Would the Office really recruit a girl of seventeen? Perhaps she was older, posing as a schoolgirl. But age was very difficult to disguise. What if she were innocent? An image of Anne-Marie flicked into his mind, followed by the other Office assassinations, followed by Nadim Sam Qaaqour and Ram Shalev, followed by the battered death mask of the Russian, Abelev, a bullet hole gaping in his forehead. What if he were wrong about Gal – was it worth taking her life just to make his own safer by several degrees? His mission was more important than hers could ever be, and she was getting in the way. But did she really deserve this?

He paused for what seemed like an age, caught between two worlds; then he put the needle back in the glove compartment. The Porsche was cruising at a hundred. I've saved her life, he thought. I've saved her life. His whole body was tingling now, the pressure becoming unbearable. Gal was making little noises in the back of her throat and for some reason this aroused him

27

'Adam? Adam?'

Suzi Feldman rested her hand gently on her son's shoulder, expecting him to react at once. But he continued to stare into the bowl of ice cream in front of him. Then, as if experiencing a delayed reaction, he gave a small start and looked up at her.

'Darling, you're miles away,' she said. She was about to say something else but stopped herself. 'Eat your ice cream, before it melts.'

Adam mustered a smile, dipped his spoon into the snowy peaks and ate. His tongue tingled with cold, awakening his senses, as if life itself were being infused into his system. He swallowed another spoonful, and another, imagining that each one was transporting him step by step into the past; when the bowl was empty, he would be fully awake, a child again.

'Well,' said his father, breaking the silence that had crept into the room, 'needless to say, we are both very proud of you. We are all very proud of you, the whole family. But we didn't want to make a song and dance about it. It's classified, right? We thought it best to celebrate quietly, just us.'

'Yes,' said his mother, 'we wanted to celebrate since you first got the news, but you've just been so busy.'

The glass doors on to the balcony were open and a cool breeze was blowing in from the Mediterranean. The floor tiles, too, were cool against Adam's bare feet. But the air itself was hot and still and humid. He wiped a glassy layer of sweat from his brow and moved uncomfortably in his chair. Then he ate another spoonful of ice cream.

'What I don't understand,' his mother continued, 'is why they don't give you more leave. Every military unit is supposed to give proper leave. We haven't seen you since you started at Shayetet 13. It's been months.'

'The boy's been training,' said his father in a gravelly voice. 'The Navy does what it needs to do.'

'That's right,' said Adam. 'Training, then my first operation. They don't give you leave until you've completed your first operation.'

'You're doing a wonderful thing for us, for your people, for the land,' said his mother. 'I just wish we could see more of you. It can't be good for you, to work every day for weeks on end. Coffee?'

Adam looked out the window, out to sea. It all looked so beautiful from this distance. By the time he turned back, his ice cream had melted; he hadn't managed to finish it in time. He turned a spoon in the painty sweetness. His mother disappeared into the kitchen and returned with a pot of coffee. Then she went back for the cups; then, as if remembering for the first time, went back for the spoons and sugar. Beside the open window was an easel displaying her latest painting, a seascape in luminous turquoises.

'You look tired,' she said as she poured the coffee. 'Look at the colour of that. A perfect brown. A shame to spoil it with milk.'

'Of course he's tired, Suzi,' said his father, 'he's just got back from operations.'

'I know,' his mother retorted sharply, 'I was just saying. A woman can say things, can't she?'

Haim shook his head and slurped up the dregs of his coffee. 'Come, my boy, let's talk in the garden. I want to hear all about it.'

'But I want to spend time with my Adam,' said Suzi.

'You have something to say about soldiering?' said Haim.

'What do you think the housework is?' she replied. 'The cleaning, the cooking, the washing? It's worse than any battle.'

'A war of attrition,' said Haim.

'Exactly,' said his wife, 'a war of attrition. I'm an artist. I'm a slave.'

'Come,' said Haim, ushering his son to his feet. 'There's still an hour of sunlight left. Mother will leave you the washing-up. You can do it later.'

'My son is not doing the washing-up tonight. He's exhausted. Haim?'

He beckoned his son out of the apartment and closed the door behind them.

It had been only three days since the completion of Adam's latest mission, off the coast of Libya. The objective had been simple enough: to blow up a ship carrying a cache of weapons. He had not been told where the shipment had originated from, or where it was headed. He did not need to know. The Office lay several years in the future; now he was nothing but a fresh-faced commando, and his only responsibility was his missions. Intelligence was not yet his concern.

This was Adam's virgin operation for Shayetet 13, and he was anxious to prove himself. He set off as part of a team of four at dusk, in a SAAR-5 missile vessel, wearing diving gear and night-vision equipment, and armed with limpet-mines. The sun sank into a bloody pool on the Mediterranean horizon, and before long they were cutting through the darkness, through the water, in silence, each man concentrating on the job in hand as the regular crew worked the ship around them. They had all been fully briefed before setting sail. Now they needed to go through the plan in their minds, repeatedly, so that when the time came to act, they would do so as second nature.

The black Egyptian shoreline melted into the rocky coast of Libya, and the tension on board increased. All the lights were killed, then the engine, and the vessel drifted the last few miles with the current. Finally they reached the drop-off point, several miles perpendicular to the small port of Darna in eastern Libya.

Through a pair of binoculars, Adam could see strings of lights twinkling in the hills beyond. The harbour itself was quiet, as it was only open during the hours of daylight. Nevertheless, patrol boats could be seen churning through the black waves, their cockpits illuminated in a yellow light. A disproportionate number of patrol boats. For a moment he caught sight of an unshaven, tired-looking Libyan soldier at a helm, smoking a cigarette. He could see the acne scars on his cheeks.

They waited, drifting, bobbing, for what seemed like an age, hoping they would not be spotted. Listening. Finally a succession of explosions could be heard, and the boat bucked in the shockwaves in the ocean. That was the signal. The Libyan forces had thrown hand grenades into the water to mitigate the risk of hostile frogmen; according to the intel, they did this at two-hourly intervals. Now the grenades had exploded, and the clock was ticking. It was time for the commandos to act.

Adam and his 'buddy' pulled down their masks, pressed the regulators into their mouths and slipped into the shadowy water, followed by the other pair. As the new world pressed in on him, and a liquid chill crept across his skin, Adam began to feel safe. The water had always had that effect, ever since he was a child. His feet dragged pleasantly in their fins against the salty weight of the ocean. A torpedo-shaped object plunged over the side of the boat, bejewelled with bubbles and strings of foam. The frogmen swam after it, took hold of it, strapped themselves on. Then the engine fired, the propeller spun and the 'wet sub', with its saboteurs, bored through the murky water in the direction of the Libyan port.

To begin with, all went according to plan. It took forty-three minutes to reach the whale-like hulls of the ships, and the target vessel was located in another nineteen. From time to time patrol boats appeared overhead; the Israeli frogmen were using 'rebreathers', which recycled the air they exhaled, meaning no giveaway trails of bubbles. So the patrol boats didn't spot them. Periodically searchlights cut into the water, but still they remained unseen. Luck was on their side tonight. So far.

The plan had been so ingrained into their minds that the frog-men didn't hesitate for a moment. They spread out along the hull, each pair fitting a limpet-mine: two muffled clunks. Then they regrouped, mounted their wet sub once more, and set about making their escape. As they hummed through the water towards their rendezvous point, Adam was filled with a sense of jubilation. It had all been so easy, so straightforward. He breathed deeply, the sucking sound loud in his ears. Mission accomplished, he thought.

The first sign of trouble was when the pitch of the wet sub's engine dropped to a throaty groan, and it began to lose speed. Then it cut out altogether. Adam investigated: inexplicably the battery had failed. The sub would have to be abandoned. But it would take over an hour to swim out to the rendezvous point, and they had only thirty minutes of submergence time left. There was no way they could make it to safety before their oxygen ran out.

They sent out a coded distress signal, tied the wet sub to a buoy – another team would retrieve it later – and swam at top speed away from the harbour. Their first priority was to get out of range of the Libyan grenades. The operation was collapsing around him, but Adam's emotions were under control. His survival instinct had been activated and was being channelled in the most efficient direction. His heartbeat was slowing, not speeding up; his breathing was more regular, not erratic; his senses were heightened but had lost none of their accuracy. He was determined to survive, to win. This was what he had been trained for.

And then the explosions started. Far away at first, they crept closer and closer, and the shock waves spread towards the frog-men, causing them to pitch and roll in the water. The Libyans had started bombing early. Then, suddenly, a grenade exploded nearby and Adam spun over and over, losing all sense of orientation, his regulator ripped from his mouth. Desperately he groped after it, blinded by the sediment that had been kicked up in great clouds around him. His mask was full of water; his eyes were stinging. The night vision, what had happened to the delicate night vision? Breathe out, he had to keep breathing out, or the pressure would destroy his lungs. He forced himself to be disciplined. Thirty seconds was all he had – thirty seconds between him and unconsciousness. He stopped flailing, lay still on his side, allowed himself to be buffeted by the ocean until it began to calm. Ten seconds. The regulator, he hoped, would soon be dangling below him so that he could retrieve it with a sweep of his arm. Unless it had been ripped clean off the tank. Don't panic, he thought, keep calm. Panic would mean certain death. He waited, waited, breathing out, then arced his arm – and there was the regulator. He gathered it up, activated the 'purge' button to clean it, and pressed it into his mouth. The air was sweet. He couldn't see a thing. He pulled his mask away from his face, blew into it through his nose, clearing it. The night vision flickered, then awoke. He looked around. Where was he? The explosions had stopped but the water was still cloudy. He waited for the sediment to settle, making his breaths as shallow as possible, knowing that his air was in limited supply. Eventually some shadowy silhouettes appeared through the watery gloom; his comrades. The relief was palpable. There was no time to waste. Together they swam out to sea.

Their air ran out just as they were leaving the harbour, and they agreed – through sign language – to perform the 'sunflower' manoeuvre. At the press of a button their buoyancy control devices inflated and their wetsuits ballooned, providing buoyancy and thermal retention. They floated to the surface, removed their regulators, breathed deeply the cool night air. The SAAR could be anywhere by now; it was in stealth mode and they had missed the rendezvous. This was dangerous. They were visible above water, and could be spotted at any moment. But there was nothing for it. The most important thing was to keep as still as possible. They tied themselves to a length of rope and slept, changing lookouts every fifteen minutes, trying to conserve their energy for whatever lay ahead, hoping that they would be rescued before the limpet-mines went off and all hell, inevitably, broke loose.

'It's always like that on your first operation, my son. The first ones never go smoothly.' Haim Feldman took a bottle from under his seat and twisted it open. 'It's when they go smoothly that you have something to worry about. Arak?'

Adam nodded. He hated the stuff, but always accepted it when his father offered. Haim handed him a cigarette and they sat in the shade of a lemon tree, watching the sun go down over the distant Mediterranean, smoking and sipping on the aniseed liquor.

'It bothers me,' Adam replied. 'That was the first time I lost a comrade.'

'Lost a comrade? But I thought you all escaped?'

'That's what I told Mother.'

'What happened?'

'We waited in the water for ninety minutes. Then a dinghy came to pick us up. Just as it arrived, the limpet-mines went off and the weapons boat exploded. The Libyans started firing indiscriminately in all directions, and Avi was caught by a stray bullet. It went in behind his ear, came out of his forehead. His face opened like a fruit.'

'Did you know him well?'

'We were minutes away from safety. Minutes. We weren't killing anybody. We were just blowing up illegal weapons.'

Adam sipped his Arak, smoked his cigarette, and gazed into the branches of the lemon tree. An expression of concern clouded his father's face. He took his son's hand for a moment then, awkwardly, released it.

'It reminds me of my first commando operation,' he said. Adam came out of his reverie immediately. His father rarely talked about his own combat experience.

'When was that?' said Adam.

'1973, during the Yom Kippur War. I had just been assigned to Arik's unit.'

'You mean Sharon? Ariel Sharon?'

'Who else?'

'You served under Arik? And you never told me?'

'There is a time and a place to talk about such things. I think now is the time. And here, beneath this lemon tree, is the place.'

'You should have told me earlier.'

'I'm telling you now.'

'What was Arik like?'

'Different to how you might imagine. A very learned person. He studied for many years at Hebrew University. And his courage – I'd never before seen such courage in a man. And never since.'

Adam shifted uncomfortably in his chair, suddenly doubting the extent of his own bravery. 'Were you part of the operation that split the Egyptian forces?'

'I was. By that point in the war, Israel was at breaking-point. We had been caught completely unawares on the holiest day in the Jewish calendar. Many of us had been fasting when war broke out, and within hours we were fighting for our lives, and the lives of our families. Arik was called out of retirement. He begged to be allowed to charge the Egyptian forces, guns blazing. David against Goliath.'

'He was refused?'

'The commanders had a better use for him, something more covert. Only a man of his courage could have pulled it off. I was privileged to join him. Under cover of darkness, we left our own army behind and crossed the Suez Canal with bridging equipment. Then we mounted a surprise attack through the Tasa corridor, pierced the Egyptian frontline at the weak point between two of their armies, and came around behind them. The fighting – I'd never known such fighting. The casualties were great. When the route was cleared, Bren Adan's division followed us over the bridgehead and encircled the whole of Suez, trapping the entire Egyptian Third Army. Then we pressed deep into Egypt. By the end of the war, our forces were only a hundred kilometres from Cairo.'

'And in the north, Israeli paratroopers were only sixty kilometres from Damascus.'

'That's right.'

'You were part of a legend. I never knew,' said Adam.

'If it hadn't been for Arik, Israel would have fallen,' Haim continued, as if he hadn't heard. 'There would have been a genocide. Another genocide.' He drained his glass and leaned towards his son. 'I still have nightmares about that war, even today. The bodies, the flames, the screaming faces. But to me, that is part of my sacrifice. The moment the guns fall silent is only the beginning of the battle.'

'But it was all so much simpler in your day. Our unit lost a comrade, father. For what? This was an operation to blow up a ship, not a war like yours. We weren't defending our homes, our families.'

Haim looked his son in the eye. 'Yes, you were, Adam,' he said. 'Yes, you were.'

They fell silent for a while. The breeze cooled as night approached, and insects could be heard buzzing around them.

'You need to understand something,' said Haim at last. 'We Jews have a right to be here, a right to live in peace. But the Arab countries around us are hungry for our blood. During the war they supported Hitler, and drew up plans to bring the Final Solution to Palestine. Then, the moment Israel was formed, they attacked us in overwhelming numbers. This was before our victories, before the settlements, before anybody here had even heard the word "occupation". We had to beat them back in 1948, and 1967, and again in 1973, all completely unprovoked. We were faced with an enemy determined to put us all to the sword – men, women and children. Now we need to keep the lessons of the early wars alive. We need to achieve dominance and maintain that dominance. The Arab world is still baying for our blood. If we weaken, even for a moment, the hordes would come pouring through.'

Adam nodded. He had heard this lecture many times before. But now, for the first time, despite his feeling of unease, it seemed to make sense.

'In some ways things are more complicated now, but in other ways they are simpler,' his father continued, stubbing out his cigarette. 'The wars of my day demonstrated to your generation that we cannot talk our way to peace. Fuck what the rest of the world thinks. They are not the ones who would be wiped out if their concessions backfired. We can't afford to let go of anything. We need the settlements as a buffer zone against Israel proper. We need the mountains of the Golan Heights, or the Syrians would overrun us in a matter of hours.'

He opened the bottle of Arak again and filled their glasses to the brim. 'To you, my son,' he said, raising his glass a fraction, 'and to all your future operations. Everything you do is protecting our people. It makes us all very proud.'

28

Another night, and Uzi hadn't slept. The money still hadn't been deposited. His head had hit the pillow at half past four in the morning, and the darkness had haunted him, hazy figures emerging and disappearing before his eyes. The Kol had a lot to say, most of which he ignored. At eight he got up, red-eyed, and smoked a spliff. All around him he could hear the sounds of the club, the city, awakening. The clink of room service, the breakfast trays in the corridor. The sound of buses outside. Voices. Danger.

The spliff mellowed him, and he tried again to sleep. By now, light was filtering through the curtains and he felt at odds with the world. His mind kept churning, churning; a strong electric current was coursing through him. The usual gallery of images arose, reconfigured, combined, gave way to each other like a tag team: the Office, Liberty, Cinnamon, the people he'd killed; Operation Regime Change, Avner, Gal. Nadim Sam Qaaqour, Ram Shalev. Then, further back, his son, Nehama, his parents. The sun rose in the sky and the sheets wound themselves around his body as he struggled to find release.

And then it was lunchtime. Uzi hauled himself out of bed, ordered room service. Would today be the day? Would Liberty turn up and give him another job? He needed some action, anything to keep his mind off this self-defeating cycle. He ate his lunch while surfing Israeli news sites on his laptop, scratching the back of his neck. Today there was a report on a failed assassination attempt on an Iranian scientist three months before – a scientist who, the newspaper contended, was conducting research in the biological sciences, not the nuclear project. As Avner had said, the death of Ram Shalev was still in the news. There was more analysis of the suicide attack – even more – with animated maps of the Jerusalem hotel and amateur footage of the explosion. There were more tributes – even more – to Shalev. His picture, pictures of his funeral. The stage was set, but where was the money? Not long now, Avner kept saying, not long now. If we don't have the money in a week, we'll start being less polite.

After lunch he turned on the television, toyed with the idea of phoning Gal, did not pick up the phone. Action, he really needed some action. He smoked another spliff and slept for an hour. Then he woke up. Two films on cable, back-to-back; a packet of cigarettes. Room service. By the time he had turned off the television, and the room had become silent in a way he had almost forgotten, it was growing dark outside. Days seemed to slip by while his life remained frozen. Too nervous to go out, too tired to sleep, he sat in his room while the days rolled past; one after the other, never stopping, everything advancing around him. This is the sort of life he had been willing to accept when he joined the Office all those years ago. A life of commitment to an ideal, of waiting for the opportunity to act, no matter how long it took. A life of intelligence. But those days were gone. In reality, this half-existence, this half-life in which nobody knew the truth any longer – in which he himself had almost forgotten how to discriminate the truth from lies – was bleaker, more meaningless, lonelier than he could ever have imagined.

It must have been around six in the evening when there was a knock at the door. Uzi sat motionless for a few seconds, then got to his feet, gripped his R9 and turned out the light. He racked his weapon, the metallic double-crunch loud in the room. Through the peephole, nobody could be seen. His forehead clammy with sweat, he opened the door.

'Hey,' said Liberty, breezing past him into the room, 'take it easy. Turn the light on. Why did you turn it off, anyway?'

'What is this, an interrogation?'

'I saw the light going out. Is that what the Mossad taught you? How to give yourself away?'

'I wanted the advantage of being in the dark. I wasn't going to pretend.'

'Oh look at this,' said Liberty, taking his gun in her hands. 'Cocked and ready to rock.' She ejected the bullet from the chamber. 'What's up, Uzi? You're way too jumpy.'

'Do you blame me?'

Uzi checked the corridor; so far as he could tell, she was alone. He closed the door behind her. Liberty sat on the bed. It was only then that he noticed how different she looked. Gone were the elegant clothes, the jewellery. Tonight she was wearing jeans, trainers, a hoodie. She looked younger, normal almost. And, curiously, more attractive.

'Don't look at me like that,' said Liberty. 'Come and sit down.'

'You look different,' said Uzi, aware that he was stating the obvious. In the back of his mind, he wondered if she had come to shoot him.

'I'm off duty tonight. This is a social call.'

'Social?'

'Look, I told you. Sit down. Actually, before you do that, get dressed.'

Uzi, who had been wearing nothing but his underwear, pulled on jeans and a sweatshirt. Then he sat down, scowling.

'Finally.' Liberty pushed back her hood, shook out her hair. 'Look, there's something big coming up for you. Something nice on the horizon. Interesting job, fat bonus. So tonight, I figured we'd go out. Get away from it all. Forget our woes, you know? Then we can hit the ground running.'

'What kind of job?'

'I'm not going to discuss it tonight. Tonight is for relaxing. Clearing out the system.'

Uzi made no response. What did this mean? Was it a trap? She may have come to execute him, but that didn't feel right. Why would she do it herself? Liberty laughed, her dark eyes flashing.

'Come on, man, relax,' she said, as if reading his mind. 'Stop being so suspicious, all right? I'm just a fun-loving girl. All work and no play . . .' Her words faded as she read a text on her phone. Then, once again, he had her full attention. 'All work and no play,' she repeated, and smiled.

'Where are we going? Tonight?'

She leaned closer. 'It's a surprise.'

'I hate surprises.'

'Come on, Uzi, chill out. You're not a spy any more. You're your own man.'

'Stop playing around, Liberty. Just tell me where we're going. I can't afford to take any risks.'

'Look,' said Liberty. 'I'm worried about you, you know? I don't want you freaking out on me. I need you.'

'Freaking out?'

'Yeah. Spy syndrome. I mean, just look at the way you answered the door. And look at the state of this place.'

'My life expectancy's not great,' said Uzi, anger rising quickly through him. 'You know that.'

Liberty shook her head dismissively. 'We've got to get you out for a while, change of scenery. Get your energy back. Come on.' She took his arm – her grip was surprisingly strong – and pulled him to his feet. For a moment they were close, half an arm's length away, looking at each other. He pressed his gun into his waistband. And then they were out in the corridor, and she was leading him towards the lift.

29

Outside the air was black and crisp. Uzi's lungs felt different, felt good. None of Liberty's bodyguards could be seen, but Uzi doubted she was without some protection. She was good at blending in; they left Home House and nobody seemed to notice. He would have expected nothing else. Old habits kicked in, and Uzi too became grey, anonymous. She took his arm again and led him down the street, ghosting away from the underground car park.

'We're not walking, are we?' he said.

'Are you kidding? It's much too far.'

They stopped in front of a long line of municipal bicycles, known as 'Boris Bikes' – after the city's mayor.

'You're not serious?' said Uzi as Liberty inserted her key fob into the docking station.

'No, I'm not,' she said, 'and I'm trying to make you less so.'

The bicycles were released from the docking station, Liberty adjusted her seat, and suddenly Uzi was pedalling, struggling to keep up. Liberty wound ahead through the rush-hour traffic, exhaust rising in plumes around her.

'Come on,' she called, looking over her shoulder, 'you can do better than that.'

'I haven't ridden a bike for years,' he shouted in response, and coughed. He stood on the pedals and the distance closed between them; he found that he was laughing. The bike was heavy, cumbersome, with a string of flashing white lights on the front. For a moment he saw himself on a donkey.

The ride was longer than he had expected, and with each rotation of the pedals a burden seemed to lift, something constrictive loosened, and his mind seemed to clear. He was still coughing. He had left his cigarettes in his room but he didn't seem to care. Liberty jinked through the traffic and he was impressed by her agility; from time to time she glanced back over her shoulder and grinned. They climbed a hill, his lungs ballooning, and freewheeled down the other side. Still she was ahead. Other people on Boris Bikes occasionally caught their eyes, acknowledging a bond of solidarity: us against the traffic, us against the world. Us and our ugly grey machines, our flashing headlights. Uzi liked that. Still he could see nobody following him or Liberty, no bodyguards. And then – for the first time in a long while – he stopped assessing everything for danger.

Eventually Liberty swung her leg over the bike, bounced it up on to the kerb and slotted it into a rack. Uzi followed, looking about him, trying to catch his breath. This part of the city was vibrant, dirty, teeming with life. East London. Brick Lane.

'Do you like curry?' said Liberty as they strolled through the hubbub like tourists.

'Doesn't everybody like curry.'

'Spoken like a true curry lover.'

Uzi smiled. He felt as if he had stepped into a dream, become a brand new person. He could be walking to his death, he knew that. Liberty took his arm and they wound their way along the pavements, ignoring the suggestions from men in doorways to step inside their restaurants. Liberty was huddling up against his shoulder like a teenager on a date. He could feel the swell of her breast against his biceps, and occasionally the jab of the gun in her pocket.

'You've got nobody protecting you, do you?' he said.

'I have you,' Liberty replied. A tingling sensation passed across his scalp as he felt the weight of her breast against his arm. His R9 felt hard and hot against his lower back. His mind had begun to send him warnings: stay strong, stay centred. There has to be more to this than meets the eye. There must be. Don't get drawn in. Stay ready. But his gut was telling him something different. This was exactly what he wanted. Something in him had wanted it for a long time.

Liberty drew him into a doorway and he followed her up a narrow flight of stairs. There was a strong smell of spices. And then they were in a restaurant, being seated. Pink napkins perched like origami birds in uniform patterns on the tables. Uzi was reminded of something he'd read once about origami – something about a paper bird foretelling a violent death.

'Why here?' said Uzi as they sat down.

'It's quiet, out of the way,' Liberty replied. 'Nobody would expect us to come here. No prying eyes. And they do a great Lamb Biryani.' She ran her fingers through her hair. Uzi glanced, as casually as he could, around the room. Only one entrance; only one exit. The windows might be used in an emergency, but they were fairly high up. Risky. The waiting staff looked lethargic, unmotivated. He didn't think they were hiding anything. Nevertheless, Liberty had led him into a situation known in the Office as a 'bottle'.

They drank Cobra and ordered food. Uzi was beginning to need a cigarette. He drank deeply instead. Liberty settled herself in her chair like a cat.

'So,' she said, half serious, half in parody, 'tell me about you.'

'There are things you don't know?'

'Sure.'

'Like what?'

'Love life?'

'That's usually the first thing the CIA finds out.'

'I'm not with the Agency any more, remember?'

'You read their file.'

'Tell me in your own words.'

Uzi drained his bottle and waved to the waiter for another. 'I fuck girls from Hungary. Among others.'

Liberty smiled. 'Fuck buddies, eh? For some reason I knew I'd get a cliché from you.'

'It's the truth. I don't lie any more. I don't have to.'

'But it's all bullshit, isn't it? Just layers of stories with nothing underneath.'

Uzi shrugged. She cleared her throat. 'I can't do love either.' She paused. 'It shows too much . . . weakness. Nothing since my husband died.'

'Killed?'

'Careless. He was a man with a lot of enemies. But let's not talk about him.'

'What do you want to talk about?' said Uzi.

'Your wife's Hungarian?'

'Please. I'm a nice Jewish boy.'

Liberty laughed. 'They don't have Jews in Hungary?'

'Not any more.'

Uzi's second beer arrived and he took a long draught. He had known every detail about Nehama: the sound she made when she rolled over in the night, the expression she wore when she was concentrating, the way that her left heel always wore down quicker than her right, the voice she used when she was trying to impress people, her way of laughing – and crying – when you least expected it. How, although she was insecure about her strength of mind, she would fight like a lioness to protect the people she loved. The time she was angry with him and stormed out the house, only to find she had nowhere to go.

Liberty ordered a glass of house red.

'No Pernod tonight?' Uzi asked.

'I hate that shit. It's just for appearance's sake. Mystique.'

'You've got to be joking.'

'I'm not. It's the little things, Uzi. They make a difference. The Maybach, the Pernod, the restaurants, the clothes.'

'The murders.'

'Like I said, it's the little things. Actually I hate being called Liberty.'

'What do you prefer?'

'My name, for fuck's sake. My name. Eve Klugman.'

Her wine arrived with the poppadoms, served by an unnecessary number of waiters. She leant over and broke one into quarters. For some reason, the cracking sound made him wince. He spooned some mango chutney on to his plate, tapping the end of the spoon on the china.

'You see?' said Liberty, biting into a poppadom. 'We're normal people really. Just out for a curry. Just normal.'

'But we're not,' said Uzi. 'We're not, are we?'

'Come on,' said Liberty, frowning, 'we can pretend. Just for tonight.'

'Sure,' he replied.

There was a pause as the main course arrived.

'Do you ever wonder,' said Liberty, 'what you'd be doing if your life had gone a different way?'

'A parallel universe?'

'I guess.'

'No.'

'I thought you wouldn't. I do. I know what I'd be doing. I'd be an attorney or something, living in Manhattan. With kids. Sometimes I wonder what I'd say if I met myself in the street.'

'Nice thought,' said Uzi. His curry was good.

'You'd be a businessman. Travelling the world. The Mile High Club. All that.'

'I'm already a member,' said Uzi. 'Everyone was, in the Office.'

'Fucking Israelis,' said Liberty, shaking her head.

They finished their meal and went in search of a local pub. Liberty was casting a pleasant spell over him, and he wanted to leak some more intel, something that would really hurt the government. He had a piece of jumbo connected to the Washington Station in mind, but he knew it wasn't safe, not out here. It could wait. They found a dimly lit pub on the Whitechapel Road and sat in a secluded corner in a pair of ancient leather armchairs. There they got steadily more drunk; with the alcohol they talked more naturally, more effusively, like old friends. They all but forgot about their guns. From the outside, they began to look like lovers.

'In our game,' said Liberty, leaning back into the creaking seat, 'you know you're going to be lonely. That's the nature of the job, right? The secrets. All that.'

Uzi shrugged in agreement and took a single gulp from his pint.

'But what they don't tell you,' Liberty went on, 'is that this is a life sentence. You can't escape. Even when you quit the service, you can't get away. You're branded. For life.'

'You didn't think about that in the beginning?' asked Uzi. 'You did?'

'That was the reason I joined,' said Uzi wryly.

A man walked past them in the direction of the toilet; they fell silent until he had passed.

'But don't you get tired?' said Liberty in an undertone, once they were alone again. 'Isn't it exhausting being alone? Just you against everyone else?'

'I don't know what it means to be tired. I've never known what it means to sleep.'

'Oh come on, Uzi. You can't have been always like this.'

'As far back as I can remember.'

'Well, I haven't. I remember the person I used to be.'

'And what would you say to her now?'

Liberty paused. 'I would say I was sorry.' She looked down at the table, tracing a small circle with a fingertip. Uzi watched his hand moving across the table and cupping hers. The spell was working. Two hands, so much blood. Their eyes met, their fingers tightened. Uzi hesitated, tried to pull his hand away, but she held on to it. She smiled, and his fingers relaxed. 'Have another drink,' she said. He shrugged, then nodded.

At closing time, they got a cab back to Home House. He still didn't know where she lived. Liberty walked him to the door of his room, holding his arm, her breasts still touching his biceps; now he wanted to press her against the wall and fuck her. She thanked him, and he thought it was genuine. She said it had been the most normal evening she had had in a long time. Nobody was around. Both of them were light-headed, happy. Below them, music pounded. He wanted to give her the intel he had been mulling over all day; the words kept bubbling in his head to ask her into his room. But he didn't trust himself. He was drunk. There was something seductive about her, in her hoodie and trainers. He had to protect himself. But on the other hand – there they were, they had had a normal evening, perhaps they should end it the way normal people would. Anyway, he was losing his self-control. His body was a Frankenstein's monster, and this woman seemed suddenly vulnerable. He was drunk, he was happy. She had him.

30

The curtains were drawn against the day. A watery light filtered through a tiny chink in the curtains. The people in the bed didn't care. Neither of them was asleep. Uzi, who had just had a hushed conversation with the Kol in the bathroom, lay with his arm behind his head, smoking a cigarette as if it were a golden hookah. The orange point of light glowed as he inhaled. Liberty was standing by the minibar, in a pair of black briefs.

'Come on,' she said, 'I feel like we've got something to celebrate.' She held up a bottle of Moët, condensation beading on its dark green skin.

'Bring it here,' said Uzi. 'I have something to tell you before you suck my dick again.'

Liberty laughed and slipped into bed beside him, scooping her hair over one shoulder, exposing the side of her neck as if she were offering herself as a sacrifice. Uzi popped the cork and dropped it, spinning, on top of the coffee table. He drank from the steaming bottle, then she did. Then he drank again.

'So?' she said. 'Are you going to propose to me?'

'I'm going to propose we do some business.'

Liberty sighed. 'No work. That's for tomorrow. We're on holiday today. We agreed.'

'Fine. I just wanted to give you some more intel, that's all. Make you some money.'

Liberty raised herself on her elbows and the sheets fell away from her breasts. 'You've persuaded me,' she said. 'Give it here. Then no more work.'

Uzi felt a frisson of excitement. When he gave her jumbo, saw the expression of admiration and excitement on her face, he felt like the most powerful man in the world. He leaned over to the bedside table, pulled out the top drawer and turned it upside down. Underneath was a pad of brown tape; he peeled it away to reveal a USB stick.

'What's this?' she said.

'You can't wait?' said Uzi playfully.

'Just tell me.'

'It's a list of the Office's secret unit in the Playground. I haven't encrypted it so you can read it at your leisure.'

'The Playground?'

'Mossad's codename for Washington.'

'What?'

'Washington. The Playground. You didn't know?'

'Fuck,' said Liberty, 'that says it all.'

'The unit,' said Uzi, 'is called the Neshek – the weapon. It's top secret. Most of the guys at the Washington Station don't even know it exists.'

'Dare I ask what it does?'

'It focuses on the Dog.'

'The who?'

'The President.'

'You call him the Dog?'

'That's right. And his inner circle is monitored too. The Lizard, the Rat, the Chameleon.'

'The Chameleon?'

'Secretary of State.'

'Come on. This is just hocus-pocus. This isn't serious intel.'

'You think so? Take a look at the list. You'll be surprised who is working for us. We reach right into the Oval Office.'

'I refuse to believe that.'

'Take a look at the list, and open the file called Scenarios.'

'Scenarios?'

'Assassination plans. All up-to-date, all fully operational. Any one of them could be executed in a matter of minutes by the Neshek. Depending on the President's movements, of course.'

'Don't tell me . . .'

'The whole inner sanctum has been provided for. On a contingency basis.'

Liberty searched his face and saw that he meant what he was saying. Gradually her face clouded over. 'This – this is worth a fortune,' she said at last. 'But it would seriously fuck the Mossad. And Israel. Diplomatically speaking.'

'Be my guest.'

'Why don't you just sell it to the Agency yourself? Keep the money?'

'Too dangerous. I'm a marked man. I'm happy to get a bonus from you. We're together now.'

Liberty sat up in bed and gathered the sheets around her. A chink of light from between the curtains fell across her face.

'Uzi,' she said girlishly, 'there's something you're not telling me.'

'What do you mean?' he replied, drinking from the bottle of champagne.

'The damage you're doing to the Mossad. I mean, I don't care or anything. But what is going on in your head? You're making yourself into Israel's public enemy number one. You're doing everything you can to fuck your own country.'

'No, I'm not,' said Uzi. 'I'm doing everything I can to fuck the Mossad, this government. There's a difference.'

'Is there?'

'I don't have to tell you. You know what the current regime is doing to the peace process. To the region. The Israeli political elite is dominated by people hell-bent on setting the Middle East alight.'

'How so?'

'How so? What sort of a question is that? Isn't it obvious?'

'No. Not to me. Not to the Agency, either.'

'Put it this way. The Palestinians have quietly been offering us concessions for years. East Jerusalem, the Settlements, the Right of Return. They've been offering to sell their grandmothers, and we're still no closer to peace. This fucking government is quite happy with war. Like you said, war equals money. I've got the intel on that too. Thousands of documents.'

'Conclusive? Genuine?'

Uzi didn't reply. Instead, he began to roll a spliff.

'So, what you're trying to tell me is that your only motivation is your principles? That you're some sort of whistle-blowing white knight? A Jewish Robin Hood? Come on, Uzi.'

'Look, I'm not going to pretend this isn't personal. I gave my life for the Office, my family, everything. My son – I haven't seen him in years. And my parents were taken from me by a suicide bomber. The way I see it, the bomb wasn't created by Hamas. It was created by our government's obsession with fucking the Palestinians. My parents, you know? My parents. Nobody should die like that.'

Liberty looked at him for a moment.

'I started by believing in the Office,' Uzi replied wearily, 'and was disillusioned again and again until I couldn't take it any more. Like I told you, I had it coming. I was the only one in the Office who actually cared about peace. Or at least I was the only one who had the balls to say so. My views would have been my downfall, if I hadn't decided to leave before they could fuck me.'

'The Doctrine of the Status Quo?'

'It would work. An extreme problem demands an extreme solution. Israel's nuclear deterrent balanced by Iran, or Syria, gaining an equal deterrent. Israel will start behaving itself, and there you have it. Nuke-imposed peace. Look at Russia and the US. There's a precedent there.'

'Now you sound like you believe it.'

'Of course I fucking believe it.' Uzi got to his feet, lit the spliff, paced over to the window. 'I'm not going to pretend any more. Fuck it. I've already laid down my life for my country. It's just a matter of time until they come and collect their dues. But it'll be worth it. Explode the Office, explode the government, and peace will enter the vacuum. It's as simple as that.'

Liberty got to her feet and stood behind him, slipping her arms around his waist. Almost imperceptibly, his body softened. 'Nothing's going to happen to you,' she said, 'to us.' She traced a line with her lips across his shoulders. 'It's only been a short time, I know, but things have changed. I'm tired of all this. Neither of us needs the money. I just want to be . . . let's get out of this business. One more job, then away. Start again. Let's just be normal.'

Uzi turned to face her but found himself afraid to look her in the eyes. 'I've told you. We could play at being normal for a while, for a week or two even, but it would all be a lie.'

'What are our lives anyway, if not lies?' said Liberty. 'Let's just exchange one lie for another, Adam Feldman.'

Cannabis smoke swirled around them from the spliff smouldering in his fingers. They kissed, their bodies intertwining. All at once, something began to gush through Uzi and didn't stop. They kissed again and again, bound together as if by a spell; then they rolled back on to the bed. Although neither of them knew it, they were both filled with an identical rage at the unfairness of life. For even as their barriers collapsed, they – like all people – were doomed to separation in the end.

31

Uzi woke up in the late afternoon, smelling of sex and cannabis. The cyst on his shoulder ached. He remembered something Liberty had said during the hazy, half-asleep time after they had made love. Something about how he should get it checked out. The sun was slanting into the room. His head was foggy. Liberty was no longer there, but he hadn't heard her leave. He was surprised, at first, that he was still breathing, that she hadn't killed him, and that he had no memory of giving away any secrets, or at least none that he had wanted to keep. His defences had been dissolved; she could have reached in and taken anything she wanted. But she had taken nothing. In fact, he felt like he had been given something.

He got up, had a shower, went out, sat in the womb of his Porsche with the engine running. The Kol was silent; it had spoken its mind already, told him to watch himself, remember who he was. On his phone was a text message: 'last night. dream?' Impulsively he tried to call her; she didn't pick up. He read the text again. Maybe his world wasn't completely submerged after all. Hers too, perhaps. He gripped the steering wheel and noticed, as if for the first time, that he felt alive. The world around him was teeming. He was not alone; at last he had a reason to hope.

He pulled out into the traffic. The paranoia that had plagued him until yesterday had subsided. He was still wary, still on his guard, but no longer jumping at shadows. The spy syndrome had passed. Suddenly it seemed so beautiful, the way it all fitted together. He had given his secrets to WikiLeaks, set the wheels in motion, and soon the genie would be out of the bottle. The government would begin to crack, and he would have his money; and countless people would be gunning for him. And now this comes along, this woman. One job, she had said. One final big job, and then they would cut loose. Together they would be formidable. Two people who needed to escape.

He drove north on the Finchley Road with no destination in mind. He considered going to see Avner, but he knew there would be no fooling his old comrade, and he wasn't ready to talk about Liberty, not yet. So he forgot about everything and drove, just drove, relishing the throb, the ebb and flow of the traffic, the greyness of the world outside his window. His thoughts, for the first time in a long while, drifted to his son. To Noam. How strange to love somebody you had met only a handful of times, to miss someone you would never recognise. Because he did love him; he did miss him. Even when he wasn't thinking about him, even when he didn't enter his mind from one week to the next, Noam was still there, somehow, somewhere in his heart. He was still present; he was still absent. How did the boy look now? How much did he resemble his mother, how much his father? Had Nehama even told the boy about him? Or had she remarried – replaced Uzi seamlessly with another man? Not that it mattered. Uzi had known what he was getting into, that joining the Office would spell the end of his family life, such as it was. The secrets, the long operations away from home, the dedication the job required. He had wanted that. But his son – his son. The innocent victim. Might he have ended up with Uzi's hair? His broad, square-ended thumbs? His quick eyes, his forehead, his temperament? And was there a gap in the boy's life, too? Did Noam feel the absence of his father as keenly as Uzi felt the absence of his son?

Suddenly he knew who to visit. It was too dangerous to call the man on the phone. He knew how the Office worked. They would be tapping every phone line connected to Uzi. But they wouldn't be expecting Uzi to return to his old flat, to put his head into the mouth of the lion. It was reckless, perhaps, foolhardy even. But before he disappeared to his new life with Liberty, something in Uzi – this newly emotional man – needed to find out if Squeal had been to see his mother in Ghana. He needed to know that either she had made a recovery, or that Squeal had been at her bedside for her death. This was the reason he gave himself as he directed his Porsche towards Kilburn. But something else, some unfathomable instinct, was also driving him on.

When he arrived he parked around the corner and contemplated lighting a spliff. But he talked himself out of it; the most dangerous part would be entering the flat, and for that he would need his wits about him. He consoled himself with the thought that once he was inside, and had established that all was safe, he could share a joint with Squeal and play a round of pudding wars. One more round, for old time's sake, before he vanished. Before he became somebody else for the rest of his days.

He approached the apartment building on foot, blending into the street, allowing his hands to hang casually by his sides, in easy reach of his R9. The street was quiet, and no different to how he remembered; the graffiti, the litter, the oversized buses roaring past. Fate seemed to be smiling upon him. As he approached the door a woman with a baby was making her way out, and he held it open for her as she manoeuvred the buggy down the steps. She didn't seem to notice as he slipped inside.

Uzi padded silently up the stairs, his hand straying to his weapon. First floor, second floor. And then he arrived – his old flat. Or was it? Gone was the worn door with peeling paint and a bell that didn't work. In its place was a gleaming white door of a plastic/metal composite, the brass numbers shining in the half-light. Of course, the landlady may have taken the opportunity to carry out some renovations. But something didn't feel right. He went to the peephole and peered through. Even with the warping effect of the lens, he could see that the whole interior had been replaced. No trace remained of the flat he used to live in. Everything was immaculately tidy, like a show flat, but somebody had been there recently. There was a newspaper open on the table, and through the half-open bathroom door a fresh towel could be seen on the rack. It didn't feel right. It was as if his old flat had been extracted like a tooth, and a new one implanted in its place. What did it mean? His mind began to grip the situation, piecing together theories, scraps of information, possibilities. Then he heard a noise behind him.

Squeal had caught sight of his old friend and stopped completely still, half in and half out of his apartment, a pile of letters in his hands. It took Uzi a few seconds to recognise him. The dreadlocks were gone; in their place was a neat crew cut. Gone also were the scruffy clothes; the man was dressed in a way that could only be described as smart but casual. He looked at Uzi blankly, and Uzi stared blankly at him.

'Tommy,' he said at last. 'Tommy, I thought you were . . .'

'You thought I was what?'

Squeal said nothing.

'You look different,' said Uzi.

'Yeah. Different.'

A bad feeling crept up Uzi's body like a rash. His unconscious was connecting the pieces of the puzzle; something uncomfortable was emerging.

'What happened to the hair, man?' he said.

'The hair? Oh you know. Time for a change.'

'Your mum?'

'Ah, she's fine.'

'Fine?'

'Full recovery.'

'Seriously?'

'Yeah.'

'That's great.'

Squeal attempted an awkward smile.

'You did go to see her,' said Uzi.

'Sure. Yeah, thanks for that. The money and stuff.'

'Aren't you going to invite me in?'

Squeal pursed his lips. 'I'm not living here any more, Tommy. I moved out. I just came back to pick up my post.'

His front door swung open behind him. He caught it with his heel and pulled it closed, but not before Uzi had caught sight of the interior. It was new, brand spanking new. Neat, untouched, anonymous. And identical to Uzi's old flat, even down to the furniture. Squeal closed the door and began to say something, but Uzi was no longer listening. Instead he was looking at the envelopes he was holding: gas bills, phone bills, circulars, and a single unmarked envelope. Without a word, Uzi snatched it, opened it, knowing what he would find. Squeal tried to grab it back, but Uzi shoved him away and pulled out the contents of the envelope. A bundle of notes held together with a blue rubber band. But it wasn't pounds, or euros, or dollars. It was Israeli currency.

Uzi looked up and saw Squeal edging towards the top of the stairs; in his hand was his mobile phone, glowing with an orange light. He had just finished writing a text message. Before Uzi could stop him, he pressed 'send'. Uzi lunged forward but he spun away and leaped down the stairs. He drew his gun, had him for a moment in his sights, but didn't pull the trigger. Squeal disappeared from view; for a few seconds his footsteps could be heard spiralling down the stairs. The downstairs door slammed and he was gone.

So the Office had Squeal. They had been keeping tabs on him all along. They had even been taking his rent money! He had stumbled into a trap, and now, just as a shred of hope had entered his life, he had walked straight back into their clutches. He slammed his fist against the wall, cursing his stupidity. Then he tried to collect his thoughts. Squeal's text message. They knew where he was. He needed to get out of there, fast. This building had no other exit. He had no choice. Aiming his gun in front of him, he hurried down the stairs, feeling once more that death could be close.

32

Uzi knew how quickly the Office could move, and when he left the apartment building, tucking his gun-hand inside his jacket, he was expecting them to be waiting. But the streets were deserted; Squeal was nowhere to be seen. He slipped down the road and back to his Porsche. Behind the wheel, he felt better. He steered towards the High Road.

Three minutes passed before he saw it for the first time: a dark blue Audi, expensive but not flashy, high-performance but not a car that would attract attention. He didn't know why it caught his eye. It had been instinctive. He couldn't see the occupants clearly, but there were two of them, and the driver was wearing a hooded top.

He turned down a side-road, intending to loop back on himself. There was a queue of cars, and the blue Audi passed him. As it did so, for the briefest of moments, the driver's eyes flicked up, allowing Uzi to see straight into his soul. And he knew.

His heart began to beat faster as he turned down the side-road at a normal speed and tried to cut through to the High Road. Speed bumps. Again and again the undercarriage of the Porsche crunched against the tarmac as he sped over them, faster and faster each time. His chances of escape – of survival, perhaps – were slim. The blue Audi was nowhere to be seen, but the Office were on to him now; he knew it. With the amount of technology at their disposal, they could be observing him at this moment, even in this deserted street. But what were his options? Should he get out of the car and lie down on the road, his hands behind his head, and wait for them to pick him up? No. He was going to fight them all the way. Maybe, even with all their gadgets, their superior numbers and their firepower, he could find a way to out-wit them.

Heading for home was out of the question. He couldn't risk giving his safe house away. So Uzi wound his way through London, plotting figure-of-eights and diamonds, doubling back on himself, speeding up and slowing down, waiting for the Office to make their move. He would have to confront them today, out-manoeuvre them, outwit them and leave them behind. Otherwise they would lock on to him with their surveillance and call in their dues. There was no doubt: in the language of the Office, this was a 'no zero' moment.

He drove around for an hour, cursing under his breath, taunting the Office in his mind, daring them to break their cover. Where were they, damn it, where were they? They had to be out there. And then, as he turned on to the A41 at Padding-ton, he saw the blue Audi again. He was sure it was the same one; years of memorisation and observation training had made Uzi infallible. It was cruising seven cars behind, close enough to maintain a visual, far enough away not to cause him to panic. Then a black van overtook him and settled in five cars in front, and an old grey Mercedes took up a position in the lane to his left. Finally a Ford 4×4 – a white one – completed the diamond formation on the right. This was all classic Office strategy. The vehicles were all different but all the same, all clean but not too clean, all dirty but not too dirty, all being driven carefully, precisely, in a manner that would not attract attention. Uzi had been 'boxed'. He knew the procedure, he had done it himself, many times. He was surprised the Office hadn't come up with something less obvious. They stopped at one traffic light after another, picking up speed when they hit open road, slowing down when they encountered congestion. The Office vehicles didn't make a move, and neither did Uzi. This wasn't the time. Not on this single road with no exits, with congestion and traffic lights and speed cameras. Uzi knew it, and the Office knew it.

But the stage was set. They would wait for him to make a mistake then tighten the box and force him to stop. If he tried to break the formation and race away, they would either speed after him or call in other operatives, depending on the assets they had in the field. Alternatively this could all just be a ploy. They knew that Uzi was familiar with their tactics. They could be planning something special.

He did nothing for thirty minutes as he drove away from the city at a steady pace, trying to dull his pursuers' concentration, perhaps frustrate them a little, cause them to lose their focus. His ear itched and the Kol – the older Kol this time – started speaking in its smooth tones, apologising for only being a voice, telling him there was nothing it could do to help. Telling him to be careful, to believe. Uzi ignored the voice as best he could. He considered calling Avner, but that would just make things more dangerous. This was something he had to deal with alone. And then he knew it was time. He floored the accelerator, chinked past the white Ford and slipped into the fast lane, allowing his speedometer to tip 100mph. The Ford was forced to join the grey Mercedes to his left. Uzi's Porsche hit its stride, and in a matter of seconds he had overtaken the black van. Now he had them all behind him. He accelerated again, pressing towards 120mph, trying to string them out. The Porsche was singing with happiness. His pursuers lagged behind but kept him in sight and waited to see what he would do. Perhaps they were calling in reinforcements. They wouldn't shoot, he knew that. The risk to civilian drivers was too great, and the Office was too clever; these things always got messy if the police got involved. He edged towards 130mph.

Then, suddenly, Uzi pulled the wheel to the left, cut across three lanes and veered on to an exit. The black van and Ford 4×4 were slow to react and disappeared off along the motorway, but the Audi and Mercedes managed to swerve off after him. He circled the roundabout, tyres smoking, without turning off; his pursuers followed him and for a moment it was unclear whether they were chasing him or the other way round. He saw his opportunity, drew his R9, leaned out the window and fired; the front tyre of the Mercedes exploded. The car rotated a quarter-turn and skidded to a halt on the grassy bank beside the roundabout. Then he wrenched the steering wheel to the right and, with a whine of tyres, the Porsche howled across the roundabout and down a two-lane side-road. The blue Audi appeared in his rear-view mirror, but not too close. To his surprise, no shots were fired in return; they were playing it cool. This was more worrying than comforting. Perhaps they were under orders to bring him in alive. He couldn't get a clear shot at the Audi behind him, and the drivers knew it. They sat on his tail. In the distance, police sirens could be heard. Making a decision, Uzi swung the car across the hard shoulder, off the road, through a gap in the barrier and on to a dirt track that led into a wood.

The Porsche growled bad-temperedly as he pressed it along the bumpy track, mud spraying from the wheels. In his mirror he saw the Audi pulling over to the side of the road, and two men casually getting out. He remembered his training: there was no reason for him to stay in the vehicle. A foot pursuit may be more to his advantage. He forced the Porsche on as far as he could until the track became too uneven and the trees were good and thick. Then he killed the engine, grabbed his gun and his cigarettes and jumped out. Liberty had told him that the vehicle had been cleaned of identifying marks, and he could only hope she had done a good job. From the glove compartment he took a spray can, and turned it on the number plates; instantly the letters and numbers dissolved. Then he sprayed the steering wheel, the dashboard, the seats, eroding them with acid and destroying his fingerprints. A hurried job, but better than nothing. Setting the car alight would attract attention, and he couldn't risk that. But at least now the police would have nothing to go on. Breathing hard, he slipped off into the trees.

The sun was setting, and the trees were cast in bronze highlights and ochre shadows. The clouds sat low and heavy in the sky. The noise of the traffic was incessant, masking the sound of his movements, and those of any pursuers. He jogged along in parallel to the road, weaving between the trees, then began to double back.

He made his way to the brow of a small hill, then climbed into the branches of a tree and surveyed the wood around him. It was still; empty. A cloud of rooks flew into the air to his left, and a spider crept down the gnarled bark beside him. In the distance police lights were flashing at the roundabout. If they found the bullet hole there would be trouble; a manhunt would make things difficult for him but the implications would be far worse for the Office. He smiled. Whatever happened to him, it would be worth it.

He tried to predict the actions of the men who were hunting him. If he had been the driver of the Audi, what would he be doing? There were two of them. They would have got out of the car and entered the wood, then split up, number one following the tracks of the Porsche, number two looping around. If number two had chosen to plot his course to the east, Uzi would be a safe distance away. But if he had gone to the west . . .

There was a noise. Uzi raised his R9 and scanned the woodland below. Another noise. Cracking twigs, rustling leaves, sounds that didn't fit. Not the unthinking movement of an animal through the undergrowth, but the stop-start progress of a human being trying to remain undetected. It had to be number two: he had to have gone west. Uzi strained his eyes, peering into the wood, trying to catch a sign of movement, opening his ears to all sounds. There it was again, that same cracking noise. And then: there was the man.

He was wearing a pair of Oakleys with golden lenses. His movements were stiff, almost mechanical, and in the dying sunlight he looked as though he were made of bronze. His hand was tucked inside his jacket, and even from this distance Uzi could see the flush on his face. He remained squatting, motionless, in the tree, as the man's eyes flicked from side to side. At one point Uzi thought he was looking straight at him, but then his eyes moved away, still searching. The first thing the human eye looks for is movement. If you remain utterly still, a person can look straight at you without really seeing you. The man blew his nose in his hand, flicked it into the undergrowth. Then he continued his path through the trees, twigs and branches cracking beneath his feet, and disappeared back into the wood.

Uzi waited for ninety seconds, then slid down the tree to the ground. The blue lights were still flashing at the roundabout, but the police did not seem to be searching the area. Now was a good time to escape. The Porsche, however, was a write-off – and without a car, he wouldn't make it. A crazy plan began to form in his mind. The two Office operatives would be deep in the wood by now. From their perspective, he was on the run and they were the predators. They were the deadly ones; he was running scared. No huntsmen in their right minds expect their prey to act with audacity, even if they know he used to be one of them. They wouldn't be expecting him to steal their car.

He ducked through the undergrowth and found his way on to a footpath heading towards the bank leading up to the road. The top of the Audi was visible above the barrier. The driver's door was hanging half-open. Only a junior Katsa would make such a mistake, he thought. Or a complacent old hand.

As he approached the edge of the wood he saw, out of the corner of his eye, the flicker of a shadow that didn't belong. He spun, jabbing his R9 towards it; nothing. Perhaps it had been his imagination. But his gut told him it was real. He stood in silence, scanning the wood to the east, moving his gun in a slow arc. And then, from perhaps ten feet behind him, he heard the crunch of a pistol being racked.

'Adam Feldman. It's been a long time. Put your sidearm on the ground and turn around slowly.'

The Audi was close, but not that close; if he tried to run, he would be dead. He turned around, but did not put down his weapon.

'I said put your sidearm on the ground,' came the voice, wavering this time, then rising at the end in an effort to sound authoritative.

Sensing weakness, Uzi faced him. 'Kahane?' said Uzi. 'Shimon Kahane?'

The man shifted his weight awkwardly from one foot to the other. He was big, well over six feet tall, with burly shoulders and a grizzly beard. A streak of orange light from the setting sun slashed in a diagonal across his body; his Beretta glinted.

'I'm sorry, Feldman,' said Kahane, looking as if he had stumbled across his quarry by accident. 'Put your weapon on the ground.'

'You still working at London Station?' said Uzi. 'What happened, they run out of decent Katsas? They had to get in the amateurs? You left your fucking car door open.'

Despite himself, Kahane smiled. 'Never mind me,' he said, 'look at you, eh?'

'I was thinking about you just the other day,' said Uzi.

'You keep those thoughts to yourself,' Kahane replied.

'Yeah, yeah. No, I was just thinking about the time in Brussels when you ate ten burgers in a row. You remember? How much did you win again?'

'Five hundred dollars.'

'Five hundred, that's right. I couldn't remember if it was five hundred or five thousand.'

Kahane stiffened and raised his pistol.

'Look,' said Uzi, before Kahane could say anything, 'you know I'm not going to shoot you. And you know I'm not going to surrender. I'm going to put my gun in my pocket and walk up to the road. Then I'm going to disappear. So I suggest you disappear in the other direction. Just go back into the wood and pretend this didn't happen.'

Kahane did not move. He made no sound.

'*Shalom, chaver*,' said Uzi. Goodbye, friend. Slowly, fighting his instincts, he lowered his R9 and slipped it into his pocket.

Then he turned his back on Kahane, and Kahane's Beretta, and walked slowly out of the wood and up the grassy bank. It seemed to last for an age; every second that passed Uzi heard gunshots in his ears, saw in his mind's eye the bullet ripping through the back of his head, throwing him, lifeless, to the earth. But the shot never came; there was nothing but the noise of the birds, the traffic, Uzi's feet pushing through the grass. Finally he reached the road. When he looked back over his shoulder, Kahane was gone.

Uzi approached the Audi, running through in his mind the procedure for hot-wiring the car and disabling the GPRS device that kept London Station alert to the vehicle's movements. He had one foot inside when he caught sight of a vehicle approaching. A black Maybach, followed by a BMW. It drew to a halt behind the Audi, and through the rear window Uzi caught a glimpse of the driver.

Liberty stepped out of the car and walked towards him, her hand resting by her hip where her Taurus must have been concealed, looking around for danger.

'What's going on?' she said.

'How the fuck did you find me? What are you doing here?'

'Tracking device in your car. We picked up erratic movements, followed your trail out here, and now we find you in the middle of a wood. Where's the Porsche?'

'You've been tracking me all this time?'

Liberty shook her hair away from her face. 'Of course,' she said, looking him in the eye. 'I want to make sure I don't lose you.'

Uzi's fury dissipated like dust in the wind. 'It's the Office. I had to abandon the car.'

Liberty froze. 'Come on,' she said. 'Let's get out of here.'

They climbed into the Maybach and the small convoy roared away. After they had travelled in silence for a few minutes, Liberty leaned over and kissed him hard on the mouth. 'Soon we'll be out of this game,' she whispered. 'Soon it'll just be you and me.'

33

Uzi's trainers slapped against the pavement. He was out of condition. Gone were the days he could jog through the night, weighed down by a stretcher, weapon and full kit. His breath was rasping unhealthily as he exhaled. Fighting the irrational urge to stop for a cigarette, he made his way along New Oxford Street, trying to plot a clear course through clumps of pedestrians. It was evening now, and the crowds of the day had thinned, but the streets were far from empty. His black woollen hat was pulled low, and sweat was seeping down his forehead. He clenched his fists and, panting, forced himself on, a deep oval stain spreading down from his neck towards his belly.

Two factors had led to Uzi's renewed commitment to fitness. The first was his performance in the operations he had been carrying out for Liberty. When all went according to plan, of course, his speed and agility made no difference; he had the advantage of many years in the field, and that counted for a lot. But when the unexpected happened – unavoidable, even in the best-planned operations – he found himself reacting a split second later, moving a split second slower, and he knew that if the wrong set of circumstances came together, that split second could cost him his life. Especially now.

In addition, there was Liberty herself. Uzi had never been overly concerned about his appearance, but when he lay beside her in bed, his hand resting on her taut stomach or slipping down her sculpted legs, he found himself becoming self-conscious about his own body, which looked and felt like a melting version of the one from several years before. Liberty was committed to her fitness; she knew how important it was. Every day she worked out in the gym, every day without fail; even when they had been awake for most of the night fucking and drinking, even when they had been smoking dope. Many times Uzi would wake up, hungover and groggy, to find Liberty returning from her workout, her hair slicked back from the shower, purged of all toxins, fresh-faced and ready for the day. And if they were going to spend the rest of their lives together, he would need to keep up.

Struggling to remind his body of what it meant to run, he cut across a car park and wound his way towards Exmouth Market, his feet pounding on the black pavement, his heart pounding faster. A helicopter throbbed in the air overhead; automatically Uzi stuck to the shadows, not behaving erratically but not making himself a visible target, until it passed. Believe in yourself. Spy syndrome.

The market dozed in an evening stagnancy. Outside a dingy-looking doorway he stopped, rested his hands on his knees and tried to catch his breath. He knew he was bright red, he could feel the heat in his face and his eyes were itchy and bloodshot. His R9 was digging uncomfortably into his back. He took out a cigarette – it would be silly, after all, to give up overnight – and lit up, inhaling greedily. This calmed his nerves and he slid to the ground, resting against the wall, watching the cars passing by. When the cigarette was finished he smoked another, then got awkwardly to his feet. He took off his hat and wiped his face and head on his T-shirt, stretching it up from his belly. Then he passed a hand over his face, composed himself, and rang the third-floor bell.

'Yeah?' came a tinny voice.

'It's me.'

The door buzzed and Uzi entered, making sure it closed properly behind him. It was quiet in the stairwell, and it smelled of old carpets and piss. He climbed the stairs with heavy feet; when he got to the third floor, the door of the flat was open and the sound of a television could be heard. He went in.

'Uzi, my brother. What the fuck happened to you?' said Avner, approaching him with twin bottles of beer. Uzi made no reply but grabbed one and took a long draught. 'Has there been trouble?' said Avner, and it was unclear whether or not he was joking.

Uzi checked the curtains were closed, pulled his R9 out of his waistband and laid it on the table. Then he collapsed into an armchair and drank the rest of his beer. The flat was completely bare; no personal belongings whatsoever, just furniture. Avner got him a glass of water but he waved it away.

'Thanks for coming,' said Avner, smiling as if it were his birthday. 'I didn't want to tell you over the phone. I've got some news.'

'Go on.'

'It's arrived.'

'What?'

'The money, my brother. It's arrived.'

Uzi felt a wave of coolness come over him, then heat, then the world seemed to constrict then expand. 'All of it?'

'Every last dollar. Check your account online when you get back. We're rich men, my brother. Rich men.'

Uzi got to his feet, suddenly lightheaded, and before he knew it he and Avner were embracing. Then he was back in his chair. The whole world felt like a different place. Don't forget who you are. Believe.

'The important thing,' said Avner, 'is to keep it together. We've got the money. So far, so good, but we need to get the fuck out of here. As soon as the information appears online, the Office will be after us.'

'When will it break?'

'Tonight.'

'That soon?'

'Our sponsors didn't want to wait. The election is getting close.'

Uzi looked around. 'That would explain this.'

Avner grinned. 'I've cleared everything out. I was going to suggest meeting in a bar, but I think we should play it safe. My plane leaves in six hours.'

There was a pause. Gradually Uzi's emotions stopped cart-wheeling and settled into a gentle buzz.

'So,' he said at last, 'this is your last night. You're really ready to go?'

Avner nodded towards the door, where a shoulder-bag lay under a coat. 'Take a look at this,' he said, tossing a small green passport casually on the table. Uzi picked it up. 'German?' he said.

'Jawohl, mein Herr. Where I'm headed Germans are always welcome.'

'Don't tell me where you're headed.'

'I wasn't about to.'

'This is good work,' said Uzi, examining the photograph closely. 'Top-level document, no?'

'One of the perks of being an Office jobsworth. When you want to disappear, you can.'

'So this is it,' said Uzi, giving the passport back. 'The death of Avner Golan. The end of a chapter. Any final words?'

'Money,' said Avner, 'that's my final word.'

'Profound.'

'You're now looking at Franz Gruber,' said Avner. 'I think it has a nice ring to it, don't you? Franz Gruber.'

'I like it,' Uzi replied. 'It sticks in the throat.'

'WikiLeaks are gearing up for the big splash in Israel,' said Avner. 'Everything's in place. Tomorrow you'll be front-page news, coming out against the PM, spilling the beans on Cinna-mon. This is it, this is really it.' He took a swig of beer then leaned closer. 'Uzi, my brother, there's still time. Nothing's set in stone. Why don't you consider . . .'

'Forget it,' said Uzi abruptly. 'I've got a good thing going in London and I'm not going to leave it behind. The Office hasn't managed to find me so far, and I've been leaking enough jumbo to make me a prime target. If they could have got to me, they would have done it already. Trust me, I'm under the radar.'

'You can't live the rest of your life like this.'

'I'm not afraid. If anything should happen to me, Liberty will spread the word to the CIA and the media. Overnight, Israel will find themselves with another embarrassing crisis on their hands. It will only make things worse for them.'

'Unless they silence Liberty.'

'They wouldn't silence Liberty. They couldn't.'

Something in Uzi's tone of voice made Avner recoil.

'You're fucking her, aren't you?' he said.

Uzi shrugged.

'Just tell me you're not in love,' sighed Avner. 'Tell me you haven't completely lost it.'

'You know what?' said Uzi, draining his bottle of beer. 'I think I am in love. I think I am, and it feels fucking great. You should try it some time, you know?'

'What's wrong with you? Have you lost your mind? You sound like a teenage girl,' said Avner. 'Liberty's one of the biggest players in the city.'

'She wants to get out of this business. We both do.'

'Get out?'

'Yeah, cash in and go somewhere quiet. Start again.'

'Bonnie and Clyde, huh.'

'Liberty wants to do one final job. I don't know what it is, but it seems important to her. Then we walk away.'

Avner shook his head in disbelief. 'Who are you trying to kid? Drug dealers don't just walk away. No quitting, no retiring, no escape. They're in it till the end.'

'You don't know,' said Uzi, 'you just don't know.'

'Oh I know,' said Avner ambiguously. 'I know very well.' He paused. 'I just want you to be careful, that's all. Lie low, very low, OK?'

'Yeah, I know.'

There was an uncharacteristic weight to Avner's words, and Uzi's emotions were moved in a way he didn't understand. They drank.

'The things you have to do when you're an Israeli,' said Avner drily. 'Ignore the situation and you're political. Try to do something about it and you're political. Either way, you're in danger. There's no escape.'

'That's the nation of Israel for you. After thousands of years we have our own country, but the water is bitter. It's in the babies' milk. We've all accepted it. Another suicide bomb, *bang*. Another war, *bang*. Assassination, *bang*. Kidnapped soldier, *bang*. The PM using the Office to kill his own minister, *bang*. We have no hope – all we can do is keep going, keep going, keep going. I always hoped that peace would be like that. One day, completely out of the blue, nothing to do with us. *Bang*, and that's it. Peace. Millennia of struggle, all over at once.'

Avner laughed and took a swig of beer. 'If only. I've only ever been in this for the money. From here on, I'm living a life of luxury. An easy life.'

Uzi sucked his teeth. 'The way I see it, even if I am killed, it will have been worth it. If nobody stops Operation Desert Rain, it would be total war.'

'Just what the Office wants,' said Avner.

Uzi groaned.

'Thing is,' said Avner after a time, 'the Office has never understood the meaning of trust. We've never trusted other intelligence services, with even the most basic intel. Things haven't changed, you know. They've got worse.'

'Remember the British SIS?' said Uzi suddenly. 'The locks they asked us to test?'

'Yeah, I was the one who drafted the report telling them the locks were impregnable.' They both laughed, and Avner opened two fresh bottles of beer. Then their smiles faded.

'The Office is only working for their own interests,' Anver continued. 'They're not interested in anyone else. They're not even interested in their own country. Just in war, money and sex.'

'We were bastards,' said Uzi, still thinking about the locks. 'Bastards like the rest of them. And some of us are still bastards. Just in a different way.'

'I'll drink to that,' said Avner. 'But soon you'll be a hero bastard.'

'A hero bastard,' Uzi repeated. 'Old school Mossad, eh?'

'Old school Mossad.'

'Cheers.'

By the time Uzi got up to go, twelve empty beer bottles sat on the floor. They weren't drunk, but they weren't entirely sober, either. Uzi felt a little unstable on his fee and he was already dehydrated. He slipped his R9 back into his waistband, and in the doorway the two men embraced for the last time.

'Remember this,' said Avner. 'I'm not going to write it down. Fgruber4367@yahoo.com. Six months, then you can reach me there. We'll see how things have panned out.'

'Sure,' said Uzi. He descended a few stairs, then looked back. 'Here's hoping this fucking plan works.'

Avner walked down after him and took him by the elbow. 'I know you won't listen to me but I've got to say this one last time. If you must stick with that Liberty woman, at least persuade her to give up the business now. You have the money. Get the fuck out of the country. You have a passport in the slick I made you, you have plenty of money, you have everything you need. Take it, take her, and get out of here. Before it's too late.'

Uzi grinned. 'It's never too late, Herr Gruber,' he said. He turned his back, went down the stairs and jogged off unsteadily into the darkness.

34

By the time Uzi got back to Home House, it was late and the night staff was on duty. A party was taking place in the downstairs bar, and crowds of revellers were milling about in the foyer. Uzi, out of breath and sweaty, in running gear, attracted some glances, but the staff knew he was with Liberty. He was untouchable. He went up the ornate staircase to his room, finding that the jog had sobered him up.

In his room, he closed the door and stood listening to the muffled sounds of the party below. He was Uzi. He was Uzi, and he was rich. Just like that, he was rich. He had been calling on all his discipline to stop himself thinking about how he might spend the money, the sort of lifestyle he could buy. All that could wait. He didn't want to get carried away, he didn't want to lose himself; his life was in danger, and it would remain that way until his final breath.

His chest was still heaving from the exertion of the run, and he waited for his breathing to settle. He felt meditative, peaceful, perhaps on account of the endorphins. Tiredness was nowhere near him; these days he rarely went to bed before three. He logged on to the Internet and checked his balance; it was there. The money was there. It felt like a dream. On a whim, he decided to have a soak in the jacuzzi. He had never used one before but knew they were supposed to be beneficial after exercise. Normally he would have turned on the television as a matter of habit, but tonight he didn't feel like it. He put his R9 in a drawer, peeled off his sodden clothes and flexed his muscles, stretching. He was already starting to stiffen up. In the bathroom he started to run the water, letting the steam float up around his face. When the bath was full he lowered himself in – it was almost too hot to bear – and turned on the jets. The bubbles reminded him of countless diving operations. He lay back in the near-scalding heat.

You got so lost in the struggle, he thought, you got so lost in the fight. In Israel everyone was struggling: this faction against that, this ideology against the other, races and peoples, tribes and brothers. Everything was enflamed by religion. He had never been inclined towards the spiritual himself, had never been able to understand how people could take superstitious claptrap seriously. But they did; and where he came from, it mattered. The influence of religious groups on the country was deep-seated, with little separation between church and state. The rabbis even gave pep talks before troops went into battle; Uzi had always resented that. They who had no knowledge of sacrifice; they who – on account of their 'beliefs' – were exempt from service themselves.

It was all connected, wasn't it? The Holocaust, his parents, himself, all the operations he had ever done, the son he had never known. The religion. The winds of history had swept through his land, his people, for years, and he had been drawn into it as inevitably as everyone else. His time, of course, would pass, and history would continue, a relentless juggernaut, raising other people to take his place; this was a war of attrition, a life of no escape, a dead-end hell. He knew that Operation Regime Change would make no real difference. Even if it succeeded in its objectives, it wouldn't be long before history interfered, sucked up all hope and kick-started the chaos. He was under no illusions. Yet at the same time he knew he could not do nothing; as an Israeli, even doing nothing meant doing something.

Pink-skinned and warm, Uzi raised himself from the bath and put on a dressing gown, his hair glistening with moisture like steel wool. In the bedroom, he poured himself a large rum cocktail and lay on his bed. He opened his laptop again. Nothing on the Israeli news sites; the story hadn't broken yet. He was rich. Suddenly he had a feeling that was familiar from his Navy days, the sense that he was sailing in the direction of rough weather, that storm clouds were gathering on the horizon. He put down the laptop and lay on his back for a few minutes. He felt drained and warm, like a freshly bled carcass. He considered rolling a spliff, but changed his mind and sipped his rum cocktail. Then, although he rarely received anything, he decided to check his email.

There was one new message, from 'ORC4367' – Avner. ORC stood for Operation Regime Change; 4367 was his combatant number backwards, and multiplied by two. It had been sent just twenty minutes earlier. Uzi hesitated, then opened it. It read: *See attached. It turned up in the end. A bit late, I know. You don't need to thank me. See you in another life. ORC4367.*

There was an attachment. Uzi ran it through his de-encryption software, and opened it. His heart missed a beat. It was Liberty's file. But there was something wrong. As soon as Uzi saw it, his eyes widened and his rum cocktail slipped through his fingers to the floor, spreading and seeping into the carpet. He gripped the laptop with both hands, hoping that his eyes were deceiving him, feeling like he was going to be sick.

At the top, as usual, was Liberty's background information: date of birth, nationality, place of residence, physical description, languages spoken, threat category, known aliases, immediate family. Then there was the intel itself, compiled from various cables; at the end was a list of sources and the operatives who had provided it.

If Uzi had read through the document, he would have found that everything corroborated what he already knew. It was all there: her upbringing, her CIA career, her disaffection, the deaths of her family, her marriage to a Russian drug dealer, her relocation to the UK and reinvention as a dealer herself. But he read none of this. He didn't need to. His eyes had travelled no further than the photograph. It was a simple head-and-shoulders shot in black and white, like a passport photo, certified as authentic by a Mossad stamp. The woman in it was dressed in American military uniform, and half-smiling in a pleasant sort of way; her face was a clean oval, with an aquiline nose and widely spaced eyes. Uzi stared at the photo, unable to breathe, feeling as if the air had been sucked out of his lungs by some elemental force. He did not recognise this person. At first glance she looked similar to the Liberty he knew; but the bone structure, the composition of the face, was different. And you couldn't alter the composition of a face. If this woman was Liberty, the person he had fallen in love with – the person who had saved his life – was an imposter.

'Kol,' said Uzi. 'Kol.'

There was a pause. Uzi could hear his own breath loud in his ears.

'Uzi,' came the voice in his head.

'This can't be happening.'

'What can't be happening, Uzi?'

'The photograph on the file. It isn't Liberty. The Office hasn't updated their intel. They've missed it.'

'Are you sure?'

'No mistake.'

'Mistake in London Station, perhaps. These things happen, even in the Office.'

'And Liberty surely has spyware on my Internet connection. Before long she'll know I have this file. If she doesn't already.'

'Don't panic.'

'I think this is the time, Kol. Everything rests on now . . .'

'Just believe. Just believe.'

The door bleeped. He hadn't called room service, and only one other person had a key card. Uzi sprang to his feet; before he could reach his R9, the door had opened. Liberty closed it carefully behind her and stood in front of him, holding a cigar. She leaned forward and kissed him on the lips. He smelled expensive perfume.

'Uzi,' she said playfully, 'I'm glad I caught you.'

35

Uzi felt himself pause for what felt like an age. The party was still going on downstairs; he could hear the muffled bass, the occasional bellow, burst of laughter. Anger was beginning to well up inside him, bitterness and fear and confusion. Liberty noticed the change in his manner at once.

'Darling,' she said, 'what's wrong?' But instead of moving towards him, she began to back away. She was good – her intuition was very good. 'What's happened? Has something happened?'

'What's with the cigar?' asked Uzi, playing for time.

'Oh this? I just thought we could have a small celebration.'

'Celebration of what?'

'I just sold some more of your intel.'

'Rewarding?'

'Yes, very. And I – I bought you some new wheels. The keys are waiting for you downstairs at reception.'

The words hung in the air like a bad punchline. Uzi felt himself growing dark with rage. Liberty took another two steps back. He had no idea what should be done, but in a flash he knew how he should start. He lunged at Liberty and within seconds had pinned her to the floor, rolled her on to her stomach and twisted her arms behind her back. All the while she uttered not a single sound, and this made Uzi's skin crawl. He took off his dressing-gown cord and used it to tie her hands; then he frisked her, found her revolver and lifted her on to the bed. Finally he sat on the armchair, panting, cradling her gun. Still neither of them had said a word.

A different expression had come over her face, one that he had seen only once before. Her eyes hardened, flicked around the room as if noting every detail. Her mouth was taut, her chin raised in a display of haughtiness. A tendril of hair hung loosely down her cheek.

Uzi broke the silence. 'Simple question: who are you?' His voice sounded too loud for the room.

'What do you mean, who am I?' she said carefully.

'Come on, Liberty. We both know all the tricks, so save us both the hassle and tell me straight. How long did you think you could get away with it? Have you just been lying all this time?'

'I don't know what you mean,' she said.

Uzi, making an effort to restrain himself, turned the laptop to face her and pointed to the picture with the barrel of her gun.

'Here we have exhibit one: the real Eve Klugman. AKA Liberty. This is a Mossad file. They don't get these things wrong. But it's not you, is it? It's not you. So I return to my simple question: who the fuck are you?'

Liberty continued to stare impassively at the screen.

Uzi got to his feet. 'I want answers, Liberty, or whatever your name is. I trusted you, I was falling in love with you. I need an answer.'

Liberty answered with a ferocity that took him aback, her black eyes flashing. 'I loved you too. And, believe me, I still love you. I love you more than life itself.'

'Stop! Who are you? Tell me. Tell me the truth.'

'I am telling you the truth and I will tell you the truth. But first untie me. Untie me now. Now.'

'Not until you tell me who you are.'

'Nobody is who they seem, Adam Feldman. Untie me.'

'Don't call me that.'

'Untie me.'

'So you can alert your goons?'

'So I can have a conversation without feeling like a hostage. If I'd wanted to destroy you I could have done so before now. Untie me. You've got my weapon, haven't you? Untie me. Untie me. Untie me.'

Her insistence swayed him; I have her weapon, he told himself, I am stronger than her, there is nothing to fear. As if hypnotised, he untied the dressing-gown cord and set her free. She sat there like a child, rubbing her wrists.

'Now,' said Uzi, raising the gun. 'You have your freedom. So talk.' He lit a cigarette; his fingers were trembling.

'I am not Eve Klugman – not Liberty,' she said. 'I took the woman's identity several years ago when she was killed, along with her family.' The ghost of a smile flickered across her face and was gone. 'My real name is Leila – Leila Shirazi. I am a Persian Jew.'

'You weren't in the CIA?'

'No. I was never in the CIA.'

For the first time, Uzi thought he could hear the trace of an accent in her voice. He got to his feet and paced to the window and back again, rubbing his thumb along the side of the gun. Believe in yourself. Believe.

'Who are you working for?'

The woman's voice suddenly softened. 'Uzi, I will tell you everything. Everything, I promise. But first I think we need a drink. Come on, there's nothing to fear. We're on the same side. We share the same principles. You know me well enough to know that.'

Uzi hesitated and took a long drag on his cigarette. Then he poured two gin and tonics at the drinks cabinet, handed her one and sat down, resting the gun on his lap. His anger was fading and a strange new feeling was emerging – a sense, almost, of triumph.

'Leila Shirazi,' he said in Persian, 'a pleasure to meet you.'

'You speak excellent Persian.'

'I worked there.'

'I know.'

There was a pause.

'Leila Shirazi. Not bad as a cover identity,' said Uzi.

'It's my real name.'

'I'll reserve judgement on that. OK, we have our drinks. Now tell me your story.'

She took from her pocket a small envelope and tossed it across to him. Inside were pictures of herself as a girl, as a teenager, as a young woman, all clearly in Iran. There was also a copy of her birth certificate. 'You see?' she said. 'I came prepared. I was going to tell you this evening.'

Uzi laid out all the photographs and documents in a long line across the desk, casting an eye over them for signs of forgery. They were genuine.

'So,' he said, 'Leila Shirazi. It will take some getting used to.'

'Me too. I haven't used the name in years.'

'Who do you work for?'

'I'll tell you. Give me a moment and I'll tell you. You tied me up pretty tight, you know.'

She massaged her wrists and sipped her gin and tonic. All at once, the music downstairs stopped. Somebody was laughing drunkenly, and someone else could be heard trying to move them on. The party was over.

'I was born and brought up in Shiraz,' said the woman he would learn to call Leila, 'in a small community of Persian Jews. We're protected by the constitution, you know; we have synagogues, kosher food, Jewish hospitals. As you know, Iran is not as it is often portrayed in the West.'

Uzi nodded, smoked, said nothing.

'My father was a war hero,' she continued, 'a colonel in the army, one of the founders of the Quds Force, the highest-ranking Jew in the Iranian military. He had no sons – only me. All his hopes and ambitions rested on my shoulders, from when I was a little girl. I went to university in Tehran to study political science, and that made him proud. But what he really wanted was for me to stand up for my country.'

'What was the name of your first tutor at University?' Uzi interjected.

'Doctor Amir Arshan,' she replied smoothly. 'You can verify that yourself. See, I'm telling the truth, Uzi. No more, no less.'

He nodded and gestured for her to continue.

'After university, my father arranged an interview for me with the intelligence services.'

'The MOIS?'

'Yes, but it's not what you think.'

'So you're MOIS,' said Uzi, a note of finality in his voice. He walked to the window and peered through the curtains, as if merely uttering the word would bring danger. Portman Square was all but deserted. He passed his hand over his face, sat down. It all began to slot together in his mind. 'Played by the MOIS,' he said. 'I can't believe I didn't see this coming. Played by the fucking MOIS. I'm a dead man.'

'No,' said Leila, 'you weren't played. And you didn't see it coming because you're a good man. We share our principles, so what else matters? MOIS, Mossad – they're just names. We are the same, you and I. We have the same heart.'

Uzi sighed. 'So your father arranged everything for you. And you accepted.'

Leila sipped her drink and continued. 'Sure I accepted. Of course I did. I've always been my father's daughter. Look, I'm not a blind patriot. I object to the President's rhetoric as much as you. I'm no supporter of the religious fanatics threatening to choke our country. My father and I were no supporters of the Shah, but we stand for old Persia, the proud civilisation that still exists beneath the layer of madness, the posturing, the sabre-rattling. That's all bullshit. Iran is bigger than that. I wanted to make a difference. For the sake of my father.'

'Israel didn't worry you?'

'Israel worries everybody.'

Uzi laughed bitterly. 'Where did you serve?'

'My first tour was deep cover in America.'

'Straight to deep cover? You must have been good.'

'It was my father,' she said, without any hesitation. 'Anyway, I got top marks all the way. I loved the work. I was a sleeper in the States for ten years – until Eve Klugman was assassinated. That was when I found that my time had come.'

'She was killed by you, I assume. Your organisation.'

'She deserved to die, Uzi.'

'You killed her?'

'Not personally.'

'Plausible deniability – that's the CIA term, isn't it? Not that you would know.'

'It wasn't me who killed her.'

'You assassinated her family, too. Her children.'

'That wasn't my decision. The MOIS is much bigger than just me. But you have to understand: Klugman was cruel, Uzi. Some of the things she did . . .'

'Let's leave the dead in their graves. To cut a long story short, you took her place.'

'I did. We shared many of the same physical characteristics. I learned how to dress like her, speak like her, act like her. I broke with all her old contacts and set myself up in a new place, using her identity. It was risky, but it worked.'

'So what I'm hearing,' said Uzi, 'is that I've been groomed. You're nothing but a honey-pot.'

'Come on,' Leila replied, 'we both know it's not as simple as that. I'm in love with you. That was never a pretence before, and it isn't a pretence now.' For an instant she looked like she might come over, embrace him, kiss him, as if the last few minutes hadn't happened. He could almost smell her hair, feel her lips, the softness of her skin. But neither of them moved.

'The MOIS have had you under close surveillance since you first arrived in England,' she said. 'Twenty-four-hour surveillance. Our people within the Mossad – yes, there are a few – have been following your career for a long time. We've seen you stand up for your principles, particularly over the killing of Ram Shalev. The Mossad tried to break you, but you couldn't be broken. You're a good man, Uzi. A brave man. Like I said, we share the same principles. And,' she shifted closer towards him on the bed, 'we know about you and Avner. We know about Operation Desert Rain. We know about Operation Regime Change. And we are full of admiration.'

247

Uzi stubbed his cigarette out, not knowing what to think, far less what to say, unable to look her in the eye.

'I've wanted to say this for a long time,' she went on. 'You and Avner are heroes. Operation Regime Change is a courageous plan. You two are the only people in the entire Mossad actually concerned with peace. You're even willing to sacrifice yourself for it. The entire MOIS is looking on in awe . . .'

Uzi looked up. Their eyes met, and he knew – at least, he thought he did – that she was telling the truth. 'Yeah,' he said awkwardly, 'thanks.'

They finished their drinks and Uzi poured them each another. Neither spoke until they were settled again; this was the space where only small talk would fit, and this was no time for small talk.

'I have the money,' said Uzi at last. 'Twenty million dollars. In my account right now. Tonight my testimony and documents go live on WikiLeaks. Then the shit will start.'

'I know,' said Leila, 'but I have some intel for you.'

'Intel?'

'About Operation Regime Change.'

'OK . . .'

'It will never work.'

'Why?'

'Sure, it will damage the Mossad, it will compromise the government, it will probably lose them the election, but it will never stop Operation Desert Rain. It will never stop them bombing our yellowcake.'

'Why not? When the world finds out that it's a false target . . .'

'It's not a false target, Uzi.'

A pause.

'What?'

'The Israelis are not planning the attack as a trumped-up PR exercise. No. Avner and his friends got it wrong. The Islamic Republic's yellowcake is real. It exists.'

'Real?'

'That's right. Our nuclear programme has been making good progress. We've reached the yellowcake stage. I've seen it with my own eyes.'

Leila passed him her mobile phone, on which was a photograph of a line of white barrels, filled with a startlingly bright yellow powder. Yellowcake; it was unmistakably yellowcake. The barrels were in a warehouse with a distinctive pattern of interlocking girders across the roof. Uzi recognised it instantly from previous operations: the secret Iranian enrichment plant at Natanz.

'That must be a doctored image,' said Uzi, handing the phone back.

'It isn't. The Mossad's intel was wrong. Our yellowcake is real.'

'So Ram Shalev was wrong? There's a genuine threat? Operation Desert Rain is not just a ploy to win the election?'

'That's right. Shalev was convinced the yellowcake was a paper tiger, and he was about to leak the details of Desert Rain. So he had to be killed. The yellowcake represents an existential threat to Israel. Destroying it is more important to your government than the life of one man.'

'Fuck. This means I'm fucked too. When my testimony goes live, I'll be fucked. Even more than I thought.'

'You won't be. You'll be with me. Together we'll be safe.'

'If you knew all along, why didn't you tell me?'

'I couldn't be sure you wouldn't turn on me if I revealed my identity. Anyway, Operation Regime Change wasn't a waste of time. It will still topple the government. With a different government in power, there will be a greater chance of peace. But it won't stop them bombing the yellowcake. Nothing will. That's why I need your help.'

'What do you mean?'

'Only someone from inside the Mossad – someone like you – can protect our yellowcake from the Israeli air strikes. That's been the reason for my whole operation. That's why the MOIS has sent me to make contact with you. You're a man of principle. We need your help.'

'I see,' said Uzi slowly. 'Now it's starting to make sense.'

'Help us, and you'll be guaranteed protection for life. I'm not going to explain the details now – this is not the place – but think about it,' said Leila. 'The Mossad will hunt you; we can protect you.' She paused before continuing. 'And don't forget your Doctrine of the Status Quo. You said yourself that a nuclear Iran would be in the interests of world peace. You know better than anyone that without a nuclear deterrent coming from the Arab world the Israelis and Americans will have no interest in negotiation or compromise. You've seen it from the inside. You know the game. If you really want to protect our yellowcake – if you want to stand up for a nuclear Persia – then join us. Help us to avoid the Israeli air strikes.'

Uzi stared at Leila, speechless.

'We'll smuggle you out of the UK and take you to a secure location where we'll do the job together. Nothing dangerous, no loss of life or bloodshed. Just remote intel work, decoding intercepted messages. Child's play. You've done far more difficult jobs than that for me already. And when Operation Desert Rain has failed and our yellowcake is safe, you and I can leave the business once and for all. We'll be given new identities, and guaranteed protection. We'll get more money than we could spend in a lifetime. You have twenty million dollars already – we'll be able to make a fresh start somewhere together. Leave everything behind.'

'Where could we go?'

'We'll work it out. Somewhere nobody will find us, not the Mossad, not the MOIS, nobody. Meeting you has caused me to think about my life, Uzi. It's a terrible way to live, isn't it? All these secrets, all this danger, all this isolation. I've realised that for all these years, I've just been trying to please my father. My love for my country is really my love for him, which I've never been able to express.' Uzi opened his mouth, but found he had nothing to say. 'And now,' continued Leila, 'I've found somebody I love more than my country.'

'You'll give it all up for me?'

'I'll do anything you want. I'd give up everything for you. Let's leave the whole mess behind.'

Suddenly Uzi understood. 'So this is the last big job you talked about.'

'Of course. This is the last big job,' said Leila. Tentatively she stretched out her hand and rested it on his knee. Uzi didn't move away. 'Take your time,' she said gently. 'Think about it.'

36

When the woman – Leila – had gone, Uzi poured himself a whisky and sat brooding. The Kol was silent. Outside the night was thick and black with no stars. The streetlights spread an orange wash over the cars whispering through Portman Square. Uzi thrust his hand into his pocket and pulled out his mobile phone. Almost without thinking – it had been drummed into him relentlessly during training – he typed the secret emergency protocol number for the Office. His thumb hovered over the 'send' button. But he left it too long and the screen went dark. He laid the phone on the desk.

Minutes passed. Then Uzi remembered the cigar that Leila had brought with her earlier. There it was, lying forgotten on the bed. He lit it, inhaled, coughed. The smoke was coarse and pungent, but it was an expensive cigar and better than nothing. Then he picked up his phone and dialled a number.

'Franz Gruber.'

'You answered. Thank fuck.'

'I'm at the airport.'

'I have to speak to you,' said Uzi.

'What's up?'

'I have to speak to you. Have you checked in?'

'I'm in the queue.'

'Then wait. I'll meet you. What terminal are you at?'

'My flight leaves in two hours.'

'What terminal?'

'Four.'

'I'll meet you at Café Rouge on the mezzanine level. Thirty minutes.'

'This had better be important.'

'Be there.' Uzi hung up.

He put on his jacket, checked that his R9 was loaded and pushed it into his waistband. Then, wondering whether this night would be his last, he stepped out into the corridor.

It was late, and Home House was quiet. He padded along the deep-pile carpet and made his way down the staircase. The night porter was on duty, looking bleary-eyed and bored, but he made an effort to brighten himself up as Uzi approached.

'Mr Hamidi,' he said with a courteous nod, 'good evening.'

'Do you have any cigarettes?' said Uzi, cigar between his teeth.

'I do, sir. Marlboro Reds. Do you want one?'

'Give me the packet. I'll pay you for it.'

'But, sir . . .'

'Just give it to me.'

Uzi took the cigarettes and thrust a ten-pound note into the porter's top pocket. Then he turned to go.

'Sir? The lady left something for you,' the man called after him.

He rummaged on his desk and placed a white envelope on the counter. Uzi took it, thanked him, and left the building. Out on the street he glanced about, exchanged the cigar for a cigarette, and seeing that there was nobody around, opened the envelope. Inside was a set of keys, to which was attached a plastic tag with a registration number on it. He examined the tag closer: the make of the vehicle was nowhere to be seen. What was going on? He had expected a decent ride, but maybe Liberty – Leila – had thought it was better for him to be less conspicuous. Perhaps she'd learned her lesson after what happened to the Porsche. Either way, at least he had wheels. Accompanying the keys was a brief note: 'Underground car park – L'. That was all.

For a moment Uzi reflected. The car was bound to be fitted with a tracking device, and he didn't have the time to disable it. But did it matter now? The MOIS knew his every move anyway; they knew all about Operation Regime Change and they surely knew Avner's plans for fleeing the country. What difference could it make? And now, time was of the essence. He came to a decision and jogged down into the car park where he was greeted by the smell of petrol and exhaust fumes. A gleaming Mercedes slid past him and out on to the street. He held the keys in front of him, searching for a car with a number plate that matched the fob. Down aisle after aisle he strode, past Mercedes, Porsches, BMWs, the occasional TVR and Maserati, but nothing matched his registration number. Where was this damn car?

And then he saw it, and stopped in surprise. The number plate matched. He shook his head in bewilderment, approached the vehicle in a state of something resembling awe. It was unique: sleek, black, dull and mean, made of lightweight carbon, titanium, aluminium and aircraft steel. He had read about yesterday while browsing the Internet aimlessly and had mentioned it to Liberty. She had remembered. This was 'The One', a one-off motorcycle developed by H. R. Erbacher. It looked like a cross between a Chopper, a Harley, a 1930s classic and a top-of-the-range Superbike. It was powered by a 110-horsepower modified Harley engine and could reach speeds of over 200mph. This was pure power, pure muscle, pure grace. He took the helmet off the handlebars, put it on, and pulled down the black visor. Then he slipped in the key, turned it: the beast sprang to life. He smiled: if he was going to be dancing with danger, he might as well do it in style. No mistake: the MOIS didn't do things by halves.

The motorbike snarled through London like a panther, the reflected streetlights streaking along Uzi's helmet. The heart-stopping speed purified him; he felt a sense of release that he hadn't experienced since his Navy days, the feeling of cutting through the elements like an animal, at once deadly and scared, at once hunter and prey. He accelerated away from the city and cut west in the direction of Heathrow. Few vehicles were on the road; the night was entering its darkest hour.

He arrived at Terminal 4 and left the bike in a shadowy corner of the car park. Then he approached the terminal building on foot, his helmet under his arm. Perhaps due to the stress – or lack of sleep – he was taken by the impression that this was the last place on earth, that there had been a nuclear apocalypse. Here, he thought, were the last glowing remnants of civilisation, contained within this bleached-out, grimy terminal. He slipped up the stairs to the mezzanine level. He couldn't see Avner at first but he hadn't been expecting to. He knew that he would have sought out an out-of-the-way corner somewhere in the back. After a little searching, he found him.

Avner looked different, older. He was wearing a pair of rimless glasses, his hair was flecked with grey, and he was sporting a wispy moustache. He had altered the shape of his face by inserting cotton wads in his cheeks; his back was hunched slightly, as well. Uzi was impressed – a nice touch.

'Mr Gruber?' said Uzi in English.

Avner looked up. 'Take a seat,' he said, in a slight German accent. 'You are alone?'

Uzi sat down, took out a cigarette and tapped it nervously on the table, waiting for the waitress to approach.

'Why don't you just step outside and smoke that fucking thing?' said Avner in a low voice. 'You're really annoying when you're like this.'

Uzi didn't respond. The waitress came over and he ordered a Peroni; they sat in silence until it arrived. Avner eyed Uzi's motorcycle helmet but said nothing. Then, when all seemed clear, Uzi leaned forward and began to speak quickly. 'Things have changed.'

'Stop,' said Avner in German, 'let's switch languages. A small thing, but you never know.'

Uzi scowled. 'Things have changed,' he began again, in German. 'It's Liberty. She's working for the MOIS.'

Avner's expression didn't falter; he had come prepared for something big. 'The MOIS? I should have seen that coming. I told you that bitch was bad news. What did she want with you?'

'She gave me the inside story,' hissed Uzi urgently. 'Listen, the yellowcake is real.'

'What?'

'Your intel is wrong. The yellowcake is no paper tiger. This is real. Operation Desert Rain will go ahead no matter what we do.'

This time Avner couldn't control his reaction. He took off his glasses, sat back in his chair, and scratched at his face as if it were covered in insects. Then he replaced his glasses and made an effort to compose himself. 'She's lying.'

'Why would she be lying?'

'I don't know. But this contradicts all my intel sources.'

'She showed me a photograph. She showed me a fucking photo. I recognised it. Natanz.'

'Could it have been a composite image?'

'You never know. But it didn't look like it. And my instinct . . .'

'Fuck your instinct.'

They sat in silence for a moment, each man searching his thoughts, his feelings, his intuition, as the world shifted around them.

'So Shalev was killed because he was about to compromise a genuine operation on a genuine threat?'

'Right.'

'Fuck,' said Avner again, and pulled his iPad out of his briefcase. Uzi watched as he connected to the Ha'aretz website. 'Fuck,' he said once more, handing the iPad to Uzi. 'Fuck, fuck, fuck.'

The headline read: 'Exclusive: Ram Shalev Killed By Mossad'. The reporter had done a good job. The whole story was there. All around it were links to analysis, related features, comments, editorial, opinion columns. Already the article had over three hundred comments; according to the website, it had been published just twenty minutes before.

'Big splash,' said Uzi pointlessly.

'The ball is rolling now,' said Avner, 'and there's nothing we can do to stop it. We've got to think this through. We've got to work out how it's going to affect things.'

'For one thing, they're going to be coming at us with a vengeance,' said Uzi. 'Especially me.'

'You've got to run,' said Avner. 'You've got to leave the country. We've got in over our heads. Who knows how much damage we could be causing? The yellowcake's real . . . fuck.'

'Nobody escapes Israeli justice, as we know.'

'Fuck.'

'We'll never stop them bombing the yellowcake now,' said Uzi.

Avner glanced up and caught Uzi's eye. In that moment, with the insight of an old friend and the astuteness of a veteran spy, he knew exactly what his friend was thinking. 'She's got you, hasn't she? You've agreed to help the MOIS. You've agreed to help them stop the air strikes.'

'I haven't agreed to anything.'

Avner clasped a hand to his forehead. 'So that's what all this has been about. She's been targeting you all along. God, we've been so blind. It all makes perfect sense.'

'I haven't agreed to anything, I'm telling you,' said Uzi again. 'I haven't committed to anything. I can still refuse.'

'Do you really think the MOIS will let you walk away? After this? Come on, Uzi.'

'It's not the MOIS I'm dealing with. It's Liberty.'

'I thought she worked for the MOIS?'

'She does. But – we also have a personal connection.'

'You're not going to tell me that you're still in love with her?'

'Look, all I'm saying is . . .'

'Fuck, she's got you good. She's got you really good.'

Uzi felt his temper rising. 'Shut up and listen to me,' he said, making an effort to control his voice. 'We might be spies, but it doesn't mean we're not human beings. There's always room for human emotions, even in a game like this.'

'My god, she's completely turned your head. The woman has turned your head. What's wrong with you?'

'Are you telling me that people from different cultures can't . . .'

'Listen to yourself, my brother. Just fucking listen to yourself. Listen to what you're saying.'

They fell into a morose silence.

'My plane is leaving in an hour and a half,' said Avner after a time. 'I have to go.'

Uzi didn't answer.

'Look,' said Avner, 'neither of us knew what we were getting ourselves into. So you want my advice? Cut loose. Find the slick I made you, take on a new identity, and fuck off out of the country. Run and keep running, my brother.'

'But . . .'

'If the MOIS are involved, who knows what's going on behind the scenes? One wrong move and we could both be dead. You're being played like a two-dollar whore. So just cut loose and run. We've done enough.'

'But what about our principles?' Uzi burst out. 'We've come this far. We've got to see it through. If Iran went nuclear, there would finally be a deterrent. Israel and the US would be forced to stop throwing their weight around . . .'

'Keep your voice down.'

'What about Russia? If they didn't have a nuclear deterrent, fuck knows what would have happened.'

Avner opened his palms and laid them in parallel on the table. 'I know this is your pet theory,' he said in a strained voice, 'but what we're dealing with now is reality. Real life. Real fucking life.'

'Look, I believe in my convictions. I stand by my beliefs. I kept quiet for years in the Office, kept my head down, and look where it got me. I'm not going to waver again.'

'But how do you know your precious Doctrine of the Status Quo is right? If you're wrong, you could be personally responsible for a nuclear war.'

'You didn't work in Iran like I did. You don't know the language, the culture. If you did, you would understand that a nuclear Iran is the region's only hope. For as long as Iran is the underdog, the fighting will never end. Peace can only be made between equals. Everyone knows that.'

'And if you're wrong? Iran will use their yellowcake to start a nuclear war. Millions will die. And it will be your fault.'

Uzi took an aggressive swig of his beer as if trying to extinguish something inside him. 'I'm not responsible for the choices I'm given. I didn't ask for this; it found me. I have to stand by my beliefs one way or the other – either help Iran go nuclear, or allow their yellowcake to be destroyed. There's no third option, is there?'

'Just walk away, my brother. Walk away.'

'I can't walk away from what I know is right. You don't understand – Mossad and MOIS are just words. Liberty and I might be on different sides, but we share the same vision. We share the same heart. I have more in common with her than with many Israelis. This is the way of the future. The way of peace.'

Avner sighed deeply and sat back in his chair, collecting his thoughts. Then he pulled himself together, took Uzi's arm and looked him full in the face. 'I've wanted to say this to you for a long time. Maybe I should've said it before. You've been a different man since your parents died. I'm no psychologist but I've seen the change. This thing with Liberty – she's managed to get under your skin. The MOIS are clever bastards. They have psychologists working for them, just the same as we do. She's found your weak point, and she's got herself in there. That's your Achilles' heel, my brother – the death of your parents. You need love more than you know. This Iranian agent has exploited that, and now she's taken over your thoughts.' He got to his feet, picked up his briefcase and overcoat. 'Trust me, you're not in your right mind. Find the slick. Pick up your new identity. Walk away from Liberty and get the fuck out of the UK, before it's really too late. Work all this stuff out in your own time. Never mind the future of the fucking world.'

Uzi felt as if he'd been punched in the stomach. As he watched Avner disappear into the bustle of the airport, a knot of emotion butted up into his throat. He left a ten-pound note on the table, hurried from the café and rushed into the nearest bathroom. Locking the cubicle door behind him, he flung his motorcycle helmet on the floor and slammed the walls with his fists. Then he crouched down, head in hands, moaning. The Kol started babbling in his head, all the usual things, making his ear itch unbearably. He let it wash over him, did not reply. For several minutes he stayed there, waiting for somebody to come; surely somebody had heard the racket, surely the airport police would come and pick him up. But nobody came. He remained like this, crouching in an anonymous toilet cubicle, for a long time.

By the time Uzi rode away from the airport, his rage had eased and a coolness of mood had taken its place; the storm had blown itself out, and even though the future was uncertain, he somehow had a new clarity of mind. He rode back towards the city, not allowing his bike to climb above sixty, not giving the machine its head even as it strained at the bit.

Before long he was in East Finchley, driving up towards East End Road. The sky had taken on the colour of his old uniform; dark grey with a hint of blue. The dawn was about to break. On the horizon, a pale yellow light was beginning to appear. He stopped the bike across the street from number 83. Avner hadn't told him precisely who owned the property; Uzi assumed it was a safe house of some sort, but that didn't mean it was safe for him. The first few birds were beginning to sing, and a solitary bus rumbled past in the distance. Uzi put the bike on its stand and dismounted, then made his way quickly to the electricity box. He knelt down, examined it. There was no sign that it had been tampered with. It was a little stiff but the cover came away upwards, just as Avner had said. Inside was a suitcase fastened with a padlock. It was surprisingly heavy. Uzi strapped it to the back of his bike and rode away in the direction of Muswell Hill, looking for somewhere inconspicuous.

In an alleyway by the edge of a small park, Uzi killed the engine and dismounted. A fox trotted from bin to bin in the shadows. He searched his memory for the code – 9826 – and opened the padlock on the suitcase. Inside was a small safe with a combination lock. He looked around. Nobody. He entered the number 2034. The lock clicked and the safe popped open.

Inside, just as Avner had promised, was the Canadian passport and driving licence, both under the name of Jay Maxwell Taylor. Alongside it was a bundle of hundred-dollar notes wrapped in clingfilm. Uzi estimated forty or fifty thousand dollars. Beneath these were three credit cards, also in the name of Mr J. M. Taylor, with their PIN numbers written on stickers on the back. Uzi memorised them, then peeled the stickers off and discarded them. Finally there was an Austrian-made 9mm Steyr M9 self-loading pistol. But this was no ordinary gun. Being made entirely of plastic, it could be carried undetected through metal detectors. This was every Office operative's favourite toy; small enough to conceal comfortably on an aeroplane, yet large enough to pack some serious stopping power. There was a box of bullets, as well – plastic yet deadly. Uzi loaded the weapon. Then he pressed it into his waistband, dropped the rest of the slick into the cavity beneath his motorcycle seat, and disposed of the suitcase and safe. Then he gunned the engine and rode off into the heart of London.

37

Morning was breaking. The revellers of central London had gone home, and street sweepers shuffled along the gutters. On Portman Square, in the car park beneath Home House, all was still. The dawn light was moving from orange to grey outside, and the occasional sound of traffic could be heard.

A steel door at the back of the car park opened and a figure emerged, cradling a motorcycle helmet under his arm. He threaded his way through the gleaming luxury cars, ignoring his reflection that stretched and contracted across the highly polished contours. He arrived at his vehicle, mounted and put the helmet on his head, muffling the world. His mouth tasted of strong coffee and cigarettes – he had not slept last night – and his mind was gripped by a combination of adrenaline and concentration that for years had pre-empted 'no zero' operations. This was it. Before lowering his visor and starting the engine, he checked that his R9 was fully loaded and ready to go, and he secreted in his inside pocket the plastic Steyr M9. Then he rolled the bike off its stand, twisted the throttle and moved out into the first light.

London had a different character in the early morning, before the tsunami of the rush hour broke; on the roads distances shortened, journeys that would normally take the best part of an hour could be accomplished in mere minutes. As Uzi drove north, limiting his speed, he observed his surroundings carefully, making a mental note of everything that might have a bearing on what was to come: roadworks, lorries parked in the street, delivery vans unloading, pedestrian crossings, skips. In his mind he was constructing a map of what he saw: an obstacle here, a short cut there, an opportunity to double-back around that corner. Preparation was of the essence: he was approaching the race of his life.

Uzi turned on to the Edgware Road in the direction of Maida Vale. The traffic was denser here, and as each minute passed and the rush hour approached, the traffic got denser still. When he arrived at Little Venice, he slowed, swung the monstrous bike round and killed the engine. The buildings were low and the pavements broad, and the trees were losing their leaves. The sky spread like a great grey canopy above, gathering the light of day. He slipped his hand into his pocket and turned his comms device on.

'OK, I'm in place,' he said. 'Do you copy? Over.'

There was a pause. Then a voice in his earpiece: 'Copy that. Stand by. Leaking your location now.'

He sat back in the saddle and lit a cigarette. He had minutes, only minutes. His mind felt fresh, focused, ready for danger. A woman walked past with a dog on a lead, mumbling incomprehensibly to herself. Across the road, a man slept on a bench. A bus rumbled past, sending little tremors up Uzi's legs. He smoked.

'OK,' came the voice in his earpiece, 'location leaked. Prepare for interception. Good luck. Over.'

Instinctively he glanced at the circular mirror attached to one of the handlebars. Nothing, of course. Even the Office couldn't mobilise that quickly. Nevertheless, he lowered his visor, leaned forward and started the engine. It throbbed beneath him. He was ready.

Two minutes passed. He swung the bike at a right angle to the road to maximise manoeuvrability; there was no telling whether the Office would come from the north or the south. Uzi knew they would try to box him in, so in all likelihood they would approach from both directions at once. As soon as they came into view, he would need to decide on his move instantly and execute it with precision. There could be no hesitation. He was already gambling that they would try to take him alive rather than shoot him on sight. The margin for error was zero.

The woman with the dog disappeared around the corner; the man on the bench still snored. Another bus groaned by, half-full with half-asleep Londoners. Uzi looked up and down the road, north, then south, then north again, looking for signs of the Office. They would come on motorbikes, he knew that. It would be stupid to try to chase down a bike with cars in a built-up area like this. But they didn't know what he was riding; the only information that had been leaked was his location and the fact that he was on a motorbike. This high-performance machine would come as a surprise, and – at least, this was the plan – give him the edge he needed.

The first sign of his hunters was invisible. The buzz of engines, perhaps three or four, in the distance, growing in volume. Behind his visor, Uzi gritted his teeth and blinked hard to clear his vision.

And there they were. On both horizons at once, north and south, as he had expected, the morning light glinting off their helmets. They were approaching fast, but at this distance he was unable to see what sort of machines they were riding. He rocked his bike off its stand and drove slowly into the middle of the road, trying to judge distances. Yes, the two bikes coming from the city would reach him first. He waited. A single drop of sweat trickled down the side of his face like a spider. This was it. He was confident of the preparations he had made, and the machine he was riding. So long as they didn't open fire at him, this had a good chance of success.

Just as the motorbikes were almost upon him, he twisted his throttle aggressively and his bike sprang into life like a beast. He swung it round and accelerated towards them, the front wheel lifting off the ground as he gained speed. The two riders in front of him swerved in surprise, and Uzi jinked between them and roared off down the Edgware Road. In his wing mirror he saw them looping their motorcycles around and joining their comrades who had been approaching from the other direction. Then all four sped after him in pursuit. Uzi let out a whoop, deafeningly loud inside his helmet. He was alive – he was alive. The first phase of the operation had gone according to plan. His timing had been perfect, and the Office could not box him in now; his pursuers were strung out behind him, and he was the one leading the way. They had taken the bait. The chase was on.

There was no real contest. Uzi's motorbike was superior in every way, and it ate up the tarmac hungrily. The gap between him and his pursuers widened as bus stops, cars, trees, traffic islands flashed by. His comms device crackled and a voice came through into his ear: 'I can see they've found you, over.'

'Too right,' said Uzi excitedly, 'the fuckers don't stand a chance against this thing. Over.'

'Try not to lose them. We want them to keep you in sight, over.'

'Copy that.'

Uzi turned left, and his pursuers were out of sight for a few long seconds. He was home and dry, he thought. He should kill his speed, allow them back in the game. But just as his motorbike was screaming through the network of flyovers and slip-roads on the Marylebone Road, something unexpected happened. Another two motorcycles shot down the slip-road from the flyover, swerved in parallel across the intersection, and fell in directly behind him. Where had they come from? They were close, too close; their bikes were chunkier, faster than the others. He opened the throttle, the huge back tyre squealed, and even at this speed the front wheel of his bike sprang into the air as it accelerated. But the two riders behind him accelerated too, and their front wheels rose as well; he was not going to lose them so easily. He heard a dull pop and something grazed his helmet, throwing his head to the side and making his bike swerve then right itself. He glanced in the rear-view mirror: one of the riders was aiming a gun at him. From the sound of the shot, and the fact that his helmet was still intact, he guessed he was using rubber bullets. He hoped.

Instantly Uzi pulled his bike off the road and on to the pavement, narrowly missing a cluster of pedestrians, and took a sharp left on to Lisson Grove. This gained him some advantage; his two pursuers overshot the turning slightly, and lost speed as they veered from one side of the road to the other, trying to keep up. As he approached the zebra crossing he made another unexpected turning and sped down Harewood Row. This was a narrow street, and the howl of Uzi's engine echoed deafeningly off the flat-faced apartment blocks on either side. But the Office riders could not be fooled twice, and they lost no time in turning after him. There was about twenty metres between them; that was all.

At the end of the road he swerved left, then right, and screamed along the road that led past Marylebone Station, front wheel lifting off the ground. Just as he approached the wrought-iron canopy that stretched across the street at the entrance to the station, a black taxi pulled out in front of him. Uzi pulled the handlebars to the right; for a moment his leg dragged against the flank of the taxi, and then he was away amid a volley of honks and shouts. He glanced in the mirror, just in time to see one of his pursuers swerving around the taxi, mounting the pavement and colliding with the pillars at the station entrance. The man rose in the air as the bike somersaulted beneath him, then he spun like a dancer against the wall, landed hard on the pavement, and skidded several metres before coming to a halt. Believe.

The chase was still on. The Office had its prey fully in its jaws, and Uzi's ploy suddenly looked about to collapse. Perhaps he had gone too far this time. Perhaps he had been too audacious. But it was too late; all he could do now was ride for all he was worth. The remaining Office rider was pushing his machine hard, staying close to Uzi and looking for the opportunity for a clear shot. In the mirror Uzi could see that he was riding a red Kawasaki, a Ninja he thought, and wearing a red helmet. He raised his gun and Uzi ducked; there was a succession of pops, but nothing hit. Uzi wove erratically, mounting the pavement and then back into the road, turning corners without warning, keeping his speed as high as he could.

'Everything all right?' came the voice on his comms device. 'You've taken a couple of detours, over.'

266

'I'm handling it, over,' said Uzi, surprised at the volume and pitch of his voice.

'Are they shooting? Over.'

'Rubber bullets, I think, over.'

'Don't shoot back. We need them to follow you all the way. But for fuck's sake don't get shot, either. Over.'

'Copy that.'

The rush hour was approaching now, and the traffic was beginning to thicken. Uzi turned down Great Central Street and back on to the Marylebone Road, speeding past the idling rows of cars, buses, vans. In his mirror he could see the original four pursuers trying to catch them up – so they were still in the race. Uzi shot through a red light and careered across the intersection, avoiding a white van by inches. Then he headed down Baker Street, the red rider still uncomfortably close. More popping sounds came from behind. He needed to put some space between them; it was only a matter of time before one of those shots hit home. In the distance he heard some police sirens start up – the chase had evidently been reported. But it didn't matter now. He was almost there.

Halfway down Baker Street, the way was blocked. A skip was protruding into the street and two buses were trying to negotiate their way past it. Uzi's fingers hovered over the brake – he was going too fast to stop and he would have to mount the pavement. There were lots of commuters about now, it would be difficult not to hit anybody. Then, in a flash, it came to him. Those endless afternoons as a teenager, messing around in the Negev desert with dirt bikes, racing them, jumping them, doing tricks, impressing the girls. The old stunts, the old knack, were just a memory away.

Propped up against the lip of the skip was a plank of wood, used as a ramp by the builders. Already they had started work; a shop was being gutted by a gang of four or five men in high visibility jackets, who were ferrying rubble in wheelbarrows up the plank and into the skip. Years ago, Uzi had used ramps like this thousands of times. He knew he could still do it. Praying that the plank would hold his weight, he accelerated.

In the mirror he saw the red rider hanging back, obviously confused; Uzi's riding seemed suicidal. Hunching over the motorcycle, Uzi sped towards the skip. All at once his wheels were on the plank and it was carrying him upwards, upwards; then the bike was in the air, wheels spinning furiously, borne by nothing but its own momentum. For a moment, the world fell silent. The feeling of the Negev came back: the dust, the heat, the bottles of beer, the pre-Army freedom, the girls. The bikes. The plank fell away from the skip behind him, bouncing softly on to the road. On the street below, Uzi saw the workmen gazing upwards; office workers with cardboard coffee cups turning to stare; faces gaping in windows; people pointing. Then the ground approached, too fast, and the sound of the world returned all at once, dominated by the shriek of tyres on asphalt. This was London. The bike skidded on landing, snaked but didn't fall. The impact sent a shock wave whipping through Uzi's body and then he was in control again, speeding in the direction of Portman Square, scattering a cloud of pigeons that had been pecking along the gutters. In his mirror he saw the red rider on the pavement, negotiating his way round the skip and accelerating towards him. But Uzi had gained some all-important ground. Now all that remained was to lure the Office back to Home House, where everything was set up for the next phase of the plan.

38

In the car park beneath Home House, life was stirring. Dawn had given way to a greyish morning, and from time to time gleaming luxury cars moved in or out, their velvety engines echoing against the concrete. Well-dressed men strode purposefully to and from their vehicles. A dark figure, adjusting the collar on his black leather jacket, wound his way through the vehicles, stopping on occasion to let them pass. He made his way up to the street and waited. In his earpiece, a comms device crackled.

'Get ready,' came a voice, 'he's almost here, over.'

'Copy that,' the man said in a thick accent. He pulled his helmet on, flexed his fingers and waited. He was unarmed, and this always made him jumpy. But that was the nature of this assignment; and he was being paid handsomely.

Seconds later, he heard the roar of an engine and then a low-slung, black motorbike snarled around the corner. Its handlebars were evocative of a Harley but it was longer, more compact, with an oversized back wheel that seemed to be straining to break free. The rider was wearing a black helmet, black leather jacket, jeans and leather gloves; they were, in fact, identical.

The motorbike skidded to a halt and the rider dismounted hastily, exchanging places with the other man. For a moment they looked at each other as if in the mirror. They were indistinguishable: the same helmet, the same clothes, the same build. A chorus of engines could be heard several streets away, getting louder by the second. The new rider glanced over his shoulder, gunned the engine and sped off.

In the shadows of the car park, Uzi removed his helmet and slipped behind a pillar. In seconds, he saw the Office hunters speeding past after his imposter: the red rider first, followed by the others. His heart was thumping, and a cold layer of sweat lay on his brow. It had been a close thing – closer than he had intended. The noise of the engines faded. He hurried back towards the steel door. Before he could reach the handle, it opened.

'Uzi,' said Leila, removing her comms headset. 'Thank god.' They fell into a brief embrace. 'All OK?'

'More or less,' said Uzi. 'The main thing is they fell for it.'

'The Mossad is about to be led a merry dance,' said Leila. 'I wouldn't like to be Stefan when they catch up with him, but then again, I'm paying him enough.' She steeled herself. 'OK, are you ready to get out of here?'

'Let's do it.'

They hurried up the spiral staircase at the back of the building and made their way to Uzi's room, locking the door behind them. On the bed, two sets of clothes were laid out. For Leila there was a navy-blue suit and blouse, with a blue-and-white neckerchief; for Uzi a matching navy-blue uniform with brass buttons and gold trim around the sleeves, and a cap with a gold-edged peak. This was who they were now; these were their new identities. He was a commercial pilot; she was a senior flight attendant. The uniforms belonged to Turkish Airlines; ever since the flotilla debacle, the Turkish Intelligence Services had been more than willing to cooperate with the Iranians.

Without a word, they dressed. Uzi transferred his plastic M9 into the pocket of his uniform. Leila took her time applying heavy make-up and pinning up her hair.

'Before we go,' said Leila, 'I'm going to have to ask for your weapon. I'm sorry.'

Uzi, his eyes cast into shadow by the peak of his pilot's cap, regarded her for a moment. Reluctantly, he reached into his waistband and pulled out his R9.

'Thank you,' said Leila, slipping it into her handbag. 'I'm glad you trust me.'

'I don't trust you,' said Uzi. 'I love you.' They kissed once, briefly, on the lips. Then they took their suitcases and left the room for the last time.

On the journey to Heathrow they barely spoke. Both stepped effortlessly into the shoes of their characters: Uzi, secretly wondering whether the Office had caught up with his doppelganger, read the Metro, checked his phone, gave up his seat for the elderly; Leila kept her eyes downcast, absorbed – it seemed – in a paperback, shyly acknowledging the lascivious glances she received from occasional men.

They arrived at the airport in good time, and instantly blended in. Like all the other cabin crew, their passage through check-in and customs was cursory and without incident. They even found time for a little duty-free shopping; Leila bought herself a small bottle of perfume, and Uzi contemplated – but did not purchase – a box of expensive cigars. They made little eye contact, not wanting to give away the fact that they were romantically involved. They were colleagues, nothing more than that. In the quiet minutes, as they sat in the departure lounge sipping last-minute coffees, Leila apparently still absorbed in her book, Uzi found himself imagining the final stages of planning that would have been underway in Tel Aviv at that very moment. He knew the level of care and attention to detail that preceded an operation like Operation Desert Rain. This was a 'no zero' operation if ever there was one. If a pinpoint attack on the Iranian nuclear facilities went wrong, the repercussions would be instant – and dire. Not only would there be a political maelstrom both at home and abroad, but it would give the Islamic Republic an indisputable casus belli. Should they choose to take it, it would mean regional – even worldwide – conflagration. So at that moment the Tel Aviv planners would be hunched over their planning tables, referring to overhead computerised maps and running endless simulations, looking at contingency plan after contingency plan. The atmosphere would be tense, charged with the importance of the mission, and the participants would be wired on caffeine, smoking endless cigarettes. Representatives from the different intelligence agencies would be vying with each other to have an influence on the operation and to catch the attention of the PM, who would be seated, brooding, at the head of the table, in his high-backed leather swivel chair, making occasional cutting remarks and drinking carbonated water. All available resources would be focused on Operation Desert Rain; after all, if the MOIS sources were accurate – and he had no reason to believe they weren't – there were only eighteen hours until the attack commenced.

Departure time arrived, and they boarded along with the rest of the crew. While Leila took care of her duties with the passengers, Uzi strapped himself into his seat alongside the pilot – an undercover operative from the MIT, the Turkish secret service – and went through the final checks. The aircraft was a Boeing 737, relatively straightforward to handle, and even though Uzi had not revisited his Mossad flight training for several years, he felt comfortable enough as co-pilot. Leila made the announcements in Turkish and English over the intercom, then she joined them in the cockpit. They taxied to the runway, exchanging good-natured remarks over the roar of the engine, and lined themselves up for take-off. Then the jet engines fired, the plane leapt forwards, the runway shortened rapidly in front of them, the nose of the plane lifted as if on a thermal current, and they were airborne, one metre, two metres, ten, fifteen. Clean air between them and the strife-ridden earth. London diminished below them, turning into a map before their eyes; the pilot banked then steered into the open blueness. They had done it. They had evaded the clutches of the Mossad.

39

When the 737 reached its cruising altitude on automatic pilot, Uzi and Leila said they wanted to speak in confidence. The Turkish operative nodded and left the cockpit. The comms were off, the door was locked, and there was no way they could be overheard. This was perhaps the most secure place they could ever be, ten thousand miles in the air in the cockpit of a commercial aeroplane.

For a moment they looked at each other in silence, both adjusting to the fact that it was safe to drop their cover. It was almost a physical experience; the pilot falling away from Uzi, the flight attendant from Leila, peeling off like the skin of a snake.

'Well,' said Leila, 'that was easy.'

'It had to be,' said Uzi, 'after that motorcycle chase. There were a couple of times where I thought I was taking my last breath.'

'But it worked, didn't it?'

'Sure, it worked. We've made it.'

'Poor Stefan,' said Leila with a laugh, 'I hope the Mossad don't rough him up too much.'

Uzi looked out of the window at the endless blueness, at the carpet of cloud below them. There they were, just the two of them, thousands of miles up, the dashboard, with its hundreds of buttons, lights and switches, curved in a semi-circle around them.

'You make a great flight attendant, by the way,' said Uzi.

'You think?' she replied, piqued. 'Well, you make a great co-pilot.'

'Can I smoke in here?'

'Of course not.'

'Even as the man who is about to bring peace to the Middle East?'

Leila shrugged. 'Even for the Messiah himself.'

'There's something I wanted to ask you. Why are we heading to Syria? Why not Iran?'

'If the Mossad were to pick up our trail, a destination in Iran would give us away. So we're heading to Syria. Iran and Syria support each other's nuclear weapons programmes. So if you help us protect our yellowcake, you'll be helping the Syrians as well.'

Uzi nodded and looked out of the window again. All he could see was clouds and empty space. It was as if the world didn't exist.

'So,' he said, 'this is where you give me the briefing?' He removed his headset and placed it on the dashboard.

'This is where I give you the briefing,' Leila confirmed, untying her neckerchief. She paused to gather her thoughts. 'As you know, after a stopover in Istanbul, we'll land in Damascus. There we'll liaise with two Syrian agents who will drive us to the port town of Al Lādhiqīyah. There's a villa complex on the coast which the President of Syria gave to the MOIS as their base of operations in his country. We call it "Little Tehran". It's low-profile, completely secure, and offers a delightful view of the ocean.'

'We might as well do this in style,' said Uzi.

'And this is only the beginning. When it's over, we'll be able to leave it all behind and live in luxury for the rest of our lives. Together.' Uzi had a sudden impulse to reach over and kiss her, but Leila was totally focused on the mission; even their relationship was being factored in like an operational concern. 'The intel we have is as follows. We have an agent codenamed Omid sitting right in the heart of the Tel Aviv regime. He has been delivering an uninterrupted stream of intel about Operation Desert Rain, mainly Mossad cables. It is all highly encrypted; a decoding team based at Little Tehran has been working on the intel round the clock. So far, they have ascertained exactly when – and how – the air strikes are going to take place. At midnight Iranian time, three

Israeli fighters will fly in from the north-east, violating Iranian air space. That will be a decoy to draw our attention away from the real target. As soon as the Iranian Air Force has engaged, five Israeli jets armed with American-made GBU bunker-busters will come in under the radar from across the Caspian Sea, hit the target and run. Simple but effective. Or so the Israelis hope.'

'Sounds clear enough. So what is the target?'

'That's where we need your help. As you know, there are five different nuclear sites in Iran.'

'Yes,' said Uzi. 'There's the heavy water plant at Arak, the secret enrichment plant at Qum, the uranium enrichment centre at Natanz, the uranium conversion centre at Isfahan, and the nuclear power station at Bushehr.'

'Full marks. With your background, I would have expected nothing less,' said Leila ironically. 'Now, two of these – Qum and Natanz – have underground bunkers deep enough to store the yellowcake. The problem is that the decoding team at Little Tehran have been unable to figure out which the Israelis are targeting.'

'I'm not surprised.'

'Oh?'

'For the last eighteen months, the Mossad has been using a code that has an entirely different system for targets.'

'That would explain it.'

'The MOIS hasn't worked that out until now?'

Leila flushed.

'Where is the yellowcake really stored? Natanz or Qum?' said Uzi directly.

'I can't tell you that. Not now. The point is, the Israelis might be planning to bomb the wrong place – after all, we've gone to some lengths to feed them false intel. On the other hand, they might have the right target.'

'So you need to know which site they're going to strike.'

'Exactly. Look at it this way. When the Israelis decide to hit a target, they'll hit it – nothing and nobody will stop them. So if they have the right target, we'll have to move the yellowcake elsewhere. But transporting it is a dangerous business. For a start, the Israelis will have the target under surveillance – we'd need to get the yellowcake out without arousing their suspicion. Then there's the question of safety. At the moment it's stored deep underground, and it will be difficult for the Israelis to destroy it. But once the material is above ground and on the move, in the back of a truck or whatever, it's much more vulnerable. If the Israelis spotted it, they wouldn't need bunker-buster bombs – they could just fire a missile and boom. No more yellowcake. Or it could be hijacked by bandits or tribesmen. Or the truck could have an accident. Anything could happen.'

'So what you're saying is, you don't want to move it unless you have to.'

'Absolutely.'

'So you want me to decode the intel and tell you where the Israelis are going to drop their bunker-busters.'

'That's right. The intel is from a Mossad source, so the encryption methods should be familiar to you.'

'You don't think the Israelis might be planning to bomb both?'

'All of our intel points to only one attack.' She paused, searching his face. 'Iran needs you, Uzi. I know you've got what it takes. I know you've got the strength to see this through.'

Uzi's face hardened. 'Peace can only be made between equals. That's my guiding principle.' He sat back, looked out of the window. 'Maybe it's the altitude. Everything seems simpler from up here.'

There was a pause.

'There's something special about this operation,' said Leila. 'We're changing the lives of millions of people. We're like a force of nature, a tsunami – that kind of power. I'm filled with . . . I don't know. It fills me with energy.' Her voice changed, became softer, lower, almost hypnotic. 'This is what we were born for,' she continued. 'I've never been one for religion. But this? This is our time.' She moved closer and Uzi sat forward to meet her. 'We're like gods.'

For a moment neither of them moved; the sound of the engine filled the space between them. Then Leila grabbed him and pulled his mouth to hers, as if his soul were buried somewhere deep inside him and she was trying to devour it.

40

The stopover in Istanbul went smoothly and they were on the final leg of the flight. Everything was quiet. Lulled by the hum of the engine, Uzi tipped back his chair and tried to get some sleep. He was only hours away from the crescendo, yet he felt strangely at peace here at the tip of the aeroplane, with nothing but air and cloud for miles in every direction. The temperature in the cockpit was cool; the air felt fresh and pure. His mind drifted and settled, but did not succumb to sleep completely. Through the haze of semi-consciousness, he found himself winding back through his memories and arriving twenty years before, in the blackness of the pre-dawn night on the eastern edge of the Judean Desert, overlooking the Dead Sea, the lowest point on earth. He was eighteen years old, and had just completed his Tironut, basic training. His unit had formed into single file, and each man carried a loaded weapon and backpack with full kit, and held a flaming torch aloft. He glanced up and saw his bolus of flame blazing into the eternity of the night above him, a single point in a chain of thirty torches; thirty soldiers trained and willing to die for their country. Through the darkness they marched hard up the impossibly steep Snake Path, sweat blooming on their foreheads; they were at the peak of physical fitness, both mental and physical, and their minds were set on reaching the top.

The string of flaming torches wound its way higher and higher up the mountain, every step filled with grinding determination. They were climbing the vast rock plateau of Masada, a place of potent symbolism for Israel. In 72 AD, during the first

Jewish–Roman war, a community of Jewish warriors known as the 'Dagger Men' had taken refuge in the fortress at the summit. Flavius Silva's army laid siege, and by constructing a vast ramp of earth and stone they were able to march up to the fortress walls and penetrate them with a battering ram. But they found nothing but dead bodies. The Jews – 960 of them – had put themselves to the sword rather than fall prey to the enemy. Now every unit in the Israeli Army held a night-time passing-out ceremony in the ancient Masada fortress.

It was a long march, but Uzi and his comrades were so focused it seemed to pass in no time at all. This was their moment. Chests heaving, they formed into a square; the blue and white flag was raised; and the ceremony began.

Uzi would never forget the feeling of standing there in the orange flicker of the torches, shoulder-to-shoulder with his fellow men. Now, in the cockpit of the plane, he felt light, unfettered, free. Nothing was pulling him down, nothing was restricting him; his body felt almost translucent, as if it were formed of some sort of rainbow. But that night on the summit of Masada, with his boots on the ground where those Jewish warriors spilled their own blood centuries before, he had felt wholly rooted in the earth. No, not just rooted in the earth – more than that. He felt part of the earth. As if the great boulders and dust and silt of the Holy Land had thrown out a man-shaped Golem; as if the bloodstained earth of his forefathers had come alive in him. His skeleton was made of holy rock, packed over with Dead Sea mud; his eyeballs were crystallised globes of salt, and within the grooves of his veins flowed the lava of Jewish pride. For this was the land of his birthright, this was the substance of his inheritance, in equal parts cursed and blessed. And when the ceremony drew to its final, rousing conclusion, and he opened his mouth alongside all his brothers, their teeth glinting like chips of marble in the gloom, the sound that came out was the thunder of a thousand earthquakes: *Masada shall never fall again! Masada shall never fall again!*

Uzi slipped towards the surface of consciousness, and found that the Kol was speaking to him. It was saying something about Qum and Natanz, something about Leila. It was telling him not to stop believing, not to forget who he was. Then he awoke, and found that he had been speaking aloud, saying I wish you would get out of my head, I can't wait to get you out of my head. He glanced over at the pilot, who was avoiding his eyes, pretending not to have heard.

The engine was rumbling louder now; the plane was making its descent. The pilot, without looking at him, handed over his headset. 'Look,' he said in halting Arabic. 'Look down there. Syria.'

Uzi looked. He was surprised to feel a pang of homecoming. This was, after all, the Middle East; Tel Aviv was only 130 miles south of Damascus. And yet he didn't feel this sentimental when he flew into Tel Aviv. When he landed in Israel, his feelings were far more ambivalent. Especially on El Al flights, when groups of youngsters erupted in traditional songs, he would find himself not knowing how to feel. Syria was easier, somehow. Less complicated. For here he was free of the burden of loyalty, and could relate to who he really was.

The MIT operative landed smoothly, and Uzi and Leila disembarked with the cabin crew. As soon as the Mediterranean sun touched his skin, as soon as he breathed in the clean, spiced fug of the air and heard the energetic voices of the people, Uzi could feel his system adjusting to its default settings. The last time he was in Damascus, he had been undercover for the Mossad. But despite this, it was good to be back. Uzi and Leila went through customs without a hitch, and made the rendezvous point in good time.

The Syrian agents looked exactly as he had expected: black suits, dark glasses, no hint of subtlety. But in a strange way their overtness helped them to blend in. In a country like Syria, which was sustained and controlled by the secret police, men like these were not unusual. Uzi and Leila were ushered into the back seat of a saloon car and driven out into the afternoon Damascus traffic. Everywhere there were yellow taxi cabs, people jostling for position, women in hijabs and the occasional niqab, men carrying baskets of fruit. And everywhere there were placards displaying the faces of the president and other political figures. It was a good idea, in Syria, to demonstrate one's loyalty to the regime, and the best way of doing this was to display a prominent image of one of its stalwarts.

The car, playing Al Medina FM loudly, made its way through the outskirts of the city and headed north. Nowhere could be seen any sign of unrest. The rough desert stretched out in great caramel plains on either side, and the road ahead shimmered in the late summer heat. Before long there were no billboards, no crash barriers, no road markings even. Just a long snake of tarmac flanked by endless desert. As the radio blared on, and Arabic jingles followed advertisements and sanitised discussions on politics, Uzi and Leila fell quiet, each looking out of their own window, absorbed in their private thoughts. To begin with, the agents in the front seats checked on them regularly, surreptitiously, in the rear-view mirror. Then Uzi gave them each a cigarette, and the three men smoked out the windows. This put them at ease, and before long they all settled down. An air of bored acceptance gradually filled the vehicle.

The light was bronzing as they drove down towards the coastal city of Al Lādhiqīyah. They threaded through the narrow streets and made their way down towards the fresher air that was coming from the sea. Before long, the ocean appeared on the horizon, revealing itself in the spaces between buildings and disappearing again. And then, there it was – the Mediterranean in all its splendour. The car turned north on the coastal road, past beaches, strips of hotels and restaurants, and cafés serving coffee and seafood. The sea stretched out to their left like a vast tongue. After a time they began to climb a ridge, and they arrived at a military checkpoint. There was only one way to play it, and Uzi and Leila played it the same way: with practised insouciance. The agents showed the soldiers their papers, and the soldiers waved them through.

The road broadened as it wound along the ridge, and the view of the ocean was spectacular. Nestling in the foliage of the road were luxury villas, built like marshmallow palaces into the rock. The car slowed; the radio was switched off as they turned off the main road and down a winding driveway towards an impressive villa complex surrounded by discreet yet formidable electric fences. A pair of plain-clothed men with sunglasses and AK-47s stood guard at the gates. The car stopped. With the muzzles of their guns, the men indicated that Uzi and Leila should leave the vehicle. They did so, stretching their legs and loosening their necks in the late afternoon sunshine. The two Syrian agents took their luggage from the boot and left it by the side of the track. Then, without a word of farewell, they reversed the saloon back along the driveway and disappeared.

'Let me see your papers,' said one of the men in Farsi. Leila handed over some documents – Uzi assumed they confirmed her identity as a MOIS operative. Upon inspecting them, the mood of the guards changed. '*Salaam alaykum*,' he said. 'Welcome to Syria. We have been expecting you. Does the man speak Farsi?'

'I do,' said Uzi, 'and I thank you for your hospitality.'

'We are poor hosts,' the guard replied, following the elaborate *taarof* etiquette of Persia. 'I am sure you are accustomed to far more extravagant surroundings.'

'Not at all,' said Uzi, replying in kind. 'It is more than I deserve.'

One of the guards walked out of earshot and spoke into a walkie-talkie. Then he returned. 'Come with me, please,' he said, hitching his gun back over his shoulder. 'Allow me to take your bags.'

The villa complex turned out to be larger than Uzi had expected. It wrapped around the coastal road in a network of interlocking buildings and walkways, all painted pale ochre, and capped with rust-coloured roofs. Balconies protruded like shelves, and people could be seen resting on them in their shirtsleeves, smoking and looking out to sea. Discretion seemed to be the watchword. Apart from the two guards Uzi and Leila had encountered at the fence, no other display of force was visible; the place might have been mistaken for a hotel hosting a conference. Rows of cars nosed up to the walls, and people walked briskly in business suits, carrying folders and briefcases. But when Uzi looked closer, he could see disguised dugouts and sentry posts stippling the area, nestling in the trees, standing discreetly in the shadows and corners. He noticed two soldiers in heavy camouflage disappearing around the side of a building. There was no lack of security here.

'Little Tehran, eh?' said Uzi as they were shown through the main doors. 'This is a big set-up.'

'It's not usually so busy,' Leila replied. 'At the moment, this whole place is dedicated to countering Operation Desert Rain. Extra staff have been drafted from all over.'

The guard led them through a maze of corridors with whitewashed walls and terracotta paving. On the breeze from the round-topped windows came occasional bursts of mint and eucalyptus. Eventually Uzi was shown into a simple room with bars across the windows, containing nothing but a table and four chairs. Leila hung back, and with a salvo of apologies from the guard, he was left alone with his luggage. The door was locked.

Uzi walked to the window and almost took off his jacket. But then he remembered the plastic pistol in the inside pocket and stopped himself. They hadn't searched him yet. It was hot, and the trousers of his uniform were tight around the crotch. He squirmed uncomfortably and rearranged them.

'You're nearly there,' said the Kol suddenly. 'Just hold your nerve, Uzi. Don't forget who you are. Believe.'

The door opened and two men entered. One, a bodyguard, stood beside the door. The other sat down opposite Uzi. Leila was nowhere to be seen.

'Welcome to Syria,' said the man in eloquent Farsi. 'It is a pleasure to make your acquaintance. I'm sorry we do not meet in my own country, today. But I hope that next time we may welcome you there as an honoured guest.'

'I wouldn't dream of imposing.'

'No, no. You shall stay in my personal home. My home will be like your home. My name is Abdel Ghasem.'

'A pleasure. I am Uzi, but of course you know that. Where is Leila?'

'She is doing some paperwork, which is required when an operative brings in a prisoner. Technically, of course, you are our prisoner. But, in spirit, you are our guest.'

Insouciantly, instinctively, Uzi observed every detail of the man sitting opposite him. He was burly, and carried himself as if a great deal of weight was resting on his shoulders. He had bulging, fleshy lips – the lips, Uzi thought, of a liar – and hair that was coiffed and sleek. The sleeves of his shirt came to a stop some inches before his meaty hands, and from his left wrist dangled a loose-fitting Rolex watch that rattled as he moved. From his shoulder holster protruded the butt of a Walther P99 pistol.

'Your Farsi is excellent, my friend,' said Ghasem, in honeyed tones.

'I am sure it cannot compare to your English.'

Ghasem waved the compliment away. 'Can I offer you some tea?'

'No, thank you. I'm fine.'

'Please, I insist. Have some tea.'

'Really, I'm OK. I'm not thirsty.'

'Our tea is not worthy of you, but please do have some.' The taarof etiquette done with, the bodyguard opened the door a crack and motioned to somebody waiting outside. A silver tray of tea was brought in and placed on the table, together with a heavy bowl of fruit. There being no women present, the tea duties fell to Ghasem. He poured a little dark liquid into a glass and raised it to the light, assessing its colour and strength. Then he poured some into two small glasses rimmed with silver, diluting it with boiling water from a samovar. Following Persian custom, Uzi put a piece of sugar in his mouth and sipped the tea around it.

'I know Leila has made this clear to you already,' said Ghasem, exhaling through his nose, 'but let me reiterate that we are all filled with admiration at your courage and principles. There are very few like you in the Zionist regime, very few. During the course of our surveillance you have shown yourself to be a man of great moral fibre. So for all this, I would like to salute you. The Islamic Republic of Iran is about to owe you a great debt.' He raised his glass and Uzi inclined his own in acknowledgement. 'It goes without saying,' Ghasem continued, 'that when this operation is complete you will not have to worry for the rest of your life. You will not develop even a single white hair. We guarantee that. You will have as much money as you could possibly desire, as well as constant protection from the MOIS. Anything you want we will provide, until your dying day.' He raised his glass again, and Uzi raised his own in return.

'Has Leila explained,' said Uzi, 'that she wishes to leave the MOIS once this is over? That we are going to find some corner of the world to make a life together, and leave this business behind? Start over as ordinary people?'

Ghasem paused for a moment. 'Of course,' he said. 'My pledge applies to both of you. Leila Shirazi is a brilliant operative, and a fine woman. Congratulations.' For the first time since arriving at Little Tehran, something didn't feel right to Uzi. It was something about the way Ghasem had hesitated before replying; the way his face had frozen, like a seasoned spy disguising his emotions. Uzi sipped his tea through the last of the sugar in his mouth and picked up another piece.

'Fruit?' said Ghasem. 'Please have some fruit. We have all sorts, but I can recommend the oranges. They are extremely succulent this time of year.'

'No, thank you,' said Uzi, 'I'm not hungry.'

'Please, I insist. Have an orange. At least have an orange.'

'No, thank you. Really, I'm fine.'

Ghasem placed an orange on a side plate and passed it to Uzi, along with a knife. His Rolex rattled as he moved. Uzi thanked him obligingly, and began to peel the fruit. A delicious citrus smell sifted into the air.

'Now,' said Ghasem, 'you'll forgive my rudeness if I get straight to the point; as you appreciate, time is of the essence. The Israeli air strikes are planned for just three hours from now.' He sat back in his chair and rested one fist on each knee. 'All we are going to need from you, my friend, is one word. In return for all the riches and protection I just described: one word. The name of the target that the Israelis are going to strike. We know everything else, but not that. We need to know whether they're targeting Qum or Natanz.'

'What intel do you have? Audio? Cable?'

'Both. Whatever you want.'

'Just one word?'

'That's right.'

Uzi did not hesitate. 'I'm ready.'

'Good,' said Ghasem, stretching his lips into a smile. 'But first, if you don't mind, there is a formality we must attend to. Regulations.'

He gestured to his bodyguard who in turn opened the door and nodded to someone outside. A white-coated man with a neat beard came in, placed a handheld machine on the table. It looked like the sort of device that a courier would use to take a customer's signature when delivering a package, but with an assortment of wires and clips dangling from one end.

'Nothing but a formality, you understand,' Ghasem repeated.

Uzi looked from the device to Ghasem and back again. 'What's this?' he said carefully.

'You haven't seen one before?'

'No.'

'I hadn't realised the Mossad was so behind the times,' said Ghasem cheerfully. 'This is an American made PCASS – a

Preliminary Credibility Assessment Screening System. The newest generation of lie detectors, my friend. State of the art.'

'You still believe in this polygraph stuff? It seems to me that the MOIS might be the ones who are behind the times.'

Ghasem smiled. 'The PCASS has its limitations, of course, but we do not have enough time for a proper interview. I hope you'll forgive us for that.'

Uzi shrugged. 'Seems unnecessary to me,' he said, 'but like I said, I'm ready. I've been ready for a long time.'

41

'Keep calm,' said the Kol gently. 'Forget about everything. Clear your mind. Just believe in yourself, remember who you are. Count backwards from a thousand in the back of your head. That will prevent your measurements from fluctuating.'

With some difficulty, Uzi stifled his reply. The man in the white coat approached and rolled his left sleeve up to the elbow. A black box the shape of a bar of soap was strapped to his wrist with Velcro, two electrodes were adhered to his palm with sticky pads, and a pulse sensor was attached to his middle fingertip by way of a clip. With a grunt of satisfaction, the man sat back and booted up the handset; it made a quiet whining noise that gradually rose in pitch until it could no longer be heard.

'This is an unrivalled lie-detection device,' said the man, rubbing his fuzzy chin. 'It is far more advanced than the traditional polygraph machines you may have seen before. This machine will register any increase in stress that you feel in response to our questions. The electrodes on your palm gauge the changes in the electrical conductivity of your skin; the pulse oximeter on your middle finger observes any changes in your cardiovascular activity. This data is processed through a complex algorithm that leads to a simple diagnosis: either you are lying, or you are telling the truth. The margin of error is very small indeed.'

'I have nothing to hide,' said Uzi.

The man in the white coat looked at him noncommittally. 'So let us begin. I will ask some routine questions, then I will hand you over to my colleague. First of all, I would like you to tell me a lie. Are you a Mexican?'

'Excuse me?'

'Are you a Mexican? Lie, please.'

'Oh I see. Yes, I am a Mexican.' The device beeped softly.

'Are you bald?'

'You want me to lie again?'

'Yes, please.'

'Yes, I am bald.' Another beep.

'Now,' said the man in the white coat, 'please answer the following test questions truthfully. Were you ever a member of the Mossad?'

'Yes.'

'As a Katsa?'

'Yes.'

'Very good. I can confirm that we are getting accurate readings. I'll now hand over to my colleague.'

Ghasem roused himself as if his thoughts had been far away. He smoothed his hand across his swell of hair and sat forward, clasping his hands in front of him.

'Now, my friend,' he said, 'you are about to betray your country. Do you feel comfortable about this?'

'I am not betraying my country. Not the way I see it.'

'No?'

'No, I am taking this action in pursuit of peace. It is in the best interests of my country, in my opinion.'

The PCASS device was bleeping crazily. 'If we can stay with yes or no answers, if you please,' interjected the man in the white coat.

There was a pause. Uzi and Ghasem regarded each other like gladiators. Finally Ghasem spoke again. 'OK. Do you realise that once you have given us our information, you will never again be able to set foot in Israel?'

'Yes, I realise that.'

'Does it worry you?'

'No.'

'You will never be able to see your family or friends again. Are you telling me that doesn't worry you?'

'I don't mind. My parents are dead. I will have Leila. She is my world now.' *999, 998, 997 . . .*

'Of course. Now, as I explained before, the MOIS will offer lifetime protection as well as financial rewards. Nevertheless, you will be top of the Mossad hit list until the day you die. Does this worry you?'

'No. I am used to living with danger.' *992, 991, 990 . . .*

'Even that sort of danger?'

'What other sort is there?'

'Please,' interrupted the man in the white coat, 'yes or no questions only.'

'Very well,' said Ghasem, 'I'll get down to business. Are you doing this in all sincerity?'

'Yes, I am.'

'Do you have any ulterior motive?'

'No.'

'Are you secretly working for the Mossad, the CIA, SIS or any other intelligence agency?'

'No, my only agency is my own conscience.'

'When we give you the encrypted intel, will you provide us with the correct interpretation?'

'I will.'

'Let me ask that a second time. Will you decode this intel accurately, and to the best of your ability?'

'Yes.'

'And a third time. Will you be completely honest when you decode the intel?'

'Yes. As I've said I want to obstruct the Israeli air strikes as much as you do.'

'I doubt that, my friend, but I thank you. That will be all.'

Ghasem gestured to the man in the white coat to remove the machine from Uzi. Then both men left the room, taking the PCASS device with them. The bodyguard followed, locking the door.

Uzi's right hand strayed casually across his ribcage and inside his jacket. The plastic gun bulged reassuringly against his knuckles; it was as if he was protecting it, like a baby bird. He got up and went to the window. A few slowly swaying trees obscured the lower third of the rectangle, but beyond that he could see the distant sea, the sky. Boats no bigger than fruit flies were drifting lazily offshore. He turned away and sat down again, just in time for the door to open. In silence, Ghasem, the man in the white coat, and the bodyguard took up their previous positions. Then the door was locked again. Ghasem was holding the PCASS device.

'You're lying to us,' he said softly.

'I'm not.'

'The machine indicates that you have been lying,' said Ghasem.

'It must be malfunctioning,' Uzi replied.

Ghasem's face clouded over. 'Do you realise that you are only a hair's width away from death here? You are in Syria. You are in Little Tehran. Every man in this country, every man in this building – in this room – hates the Zionist regime more than you could ever imagine. Every man would gladly take you down to the basement and spend a long time bringing about your death. A long time. And now you are lying to us.'

The Kol was saying something, but Uzi wasn't listening. He leaned forward suddenly, slamming his palms on the table. 'Don't talk to me like that,' he hissed. 'How dare you trust that machine more than me? You know what I have given up to be here. You know what I have gone through. My death would be of no consequence to me any more, quick or slow. My only motivation is to bring peace to our countries. I have no other agenda. So do not accuse me of lying. Throw away that machine. You decide: trust me and let me help you, or do not trust me and kill me now. But do not allow my fate to rest in the hands of a machine.'

He sat back, fuming. To his surprise, Ghasem broke into a grin. 'Well done, my friend,' he said, 'you have passed the lie detector test. The device indicated that you have been telling the truth all along. And now I have challenged you, and you have remained true. You are an impressive man, my friend. A man of honour. Welcome to our family.' He got to his feet and offered Uzi his hand; Uzi hesitated then shook it vigorously, rising to his feet.

There was a knock at the door and the bodyguard opened it. Uzi's heart skipped a beat. There was Leila. She had changed her clothes; now she was wearing a flowing skirt and a light embroidered blouse, together with a peach-coloured headscarf loosely framing her face. She looked more Persian than he could have imagined, and also more beautiful.

'My sister,' said Ghasem warmly, 'the time has arrived at long last. After all of your toils. Come and sit down. Come and witness the fruit of your labours.'

For a moment Uzi and Leila caught eyes, and something wordless and powerful was exchanged between them. Then they all sat down, and the bearded man set about attaching the PCASS machine to Uzi once more. The bodyguard left the room and came in with another silver tray of tea; Leila began to brew it.

'Now,' said Ghasem magnanimously, 'I apologise for subjecting you to the machine again when you have already passed all the tests. But you know how it is.' He shrugged. 'The bosses are paranoid.' He opened a laptop on the table and began to boot it up.

'First a lie, as before, please,' said the man in the white coat. 'Are you now in Syria?'

'No,' said Uzi, watching Leila make the tea, inwardly begging her to look up at him. The machine beeped.

'Very good. And now please tell the truth. Are you an Israeli national?'

'Yes,' said Uzi, aware of the brief expression of triumph that flitted across the face of everyone in the room – even, he thought, Leila.

'Very good,' said the man again. Then he nodded to Ghasem, who turned the laptop slowly around to face Uzi. On the screen was a cable – an intercepted Mossad cable. Uzi could tell it was written in top-level code. Alongside it was the translation that the MOIS code breakers had produced. Uzi had to admit: they had done a very good job.

'Look through the translation, please,' said Ghasem quietly. 'Take your time. You will see a recurring code word, each time in capitals, which we have been unable to break. This is the target of Operation Desert Rain. When you are ready, please tell us the real name of this target.'

'A computer would usually do this,' said Uzi. 'Luckily I've been trained to do it manually as well.'

He pored over the document, drawing it close to his face, his movements made awkward by the wires connecting his hand to the PCASS device. Meditatively he lit a cigarette. The smoke rose in a lazy double helix towards the ceiling. An almost religious silence fell in the room as he concentrated. Even the Kol fell silent. Uzi noticed that a silver-lipped glass of tea had appeared by his elbow, together with two pieces of sugar. He glanced up at Leila and saw that she was gazing at him now, her eyes aflame.

'Take your time, please,' said Ghasem again.

The PCASS device was humming almost imperceptibly. A tiny fruit fly that nobody had noticed before crawled at a diagonal across the screen of the laptop, then spiralled up into the air. The man with the beard swatted his palm at it automatically. The soft scent of orange still hung gently in the air. Uzi took a long drag on his cigarette and concentrated.

'Can I have a pencil and paper?' he said. In an instant, one appeared beside him. He began to sketch out some tables, filling each cell with a syllable – scores of them – from memory. 'The Mossad uses a phonetic, syllable-by-syllable code,' he said, almost to himself, 'and they wrap that within a sleeve code which is numeric.' He didn't look up from his work but was aware of his companions exchanging glances. 'In the special case of target names, the sleeve code is encased once again within a phonetic code, and this is once again rendered into figures.' He jotted down a column of numbers. 'Has anybody got a calculator?' Again, one appeared instantly. He noticed Ghasem sneaking a look at his watch. The air strikes were hours away; but if the yellowcake needed to be moved, there wouldn't be very much time.

Uzi punched numbers into the calculator, his cigarette clamped between his teeth, eyes slitted against the stinging smoke. Then, slowly, he copied down the digits that were glowing on the screen and ran his finger down the table of syllables. A puzzled expression came over his face and he went through the calculations again, and again. Then he sat back, frowning. The atmosphere tightened. He stubbed out his half-smoked cigarette, placed a piece of sugar on his tongue, and sipped from the small glass of tea, not removing his eyes from the piece of paper in front of him.

'No,' he said softly, 'this isn't working. This isn't right. I've made a mistake somewhere.' For what seemed like an age he sat there without moving, like a chess player examining a complicated board. He hunched over, crossed out a few figures, scribbled some more, shook his head.

Following a sip of tea, he pressed his palm to his forehead and exclaimed, 'Of course, of course. They've put it in three sleeves. Three sleeves.' Feverishly he hunched over the pad of paper, making notes and punching digits into the calculator with a single hooked finger. Around the room, people shifted in their chairs. Uzi continued to write, continued to scrawl, relating his figures repeatedly to the table of syllables like a mad scientist. Finally – finally – he breathed a profound sigh and smiled. He flipped the pad on to a new page and wrote out a single word in block capitals. Then he turned the pad around, and the Iranians saw what was on it. A single word: NATANZ.

There was a pause; everybody seemed to be holding their breath. Ghasem exchanged glances with the man in the white coat, who nodded.

'This is the target?' said Ghasem.

'Yes,' Uzi replied.

'You have been completely honest with us?'

'Yes.'

Ghasem looked at the man in the white coat again and saw that he was grinning broadly. All at once, a ripple of relief flowed through the room, and then the Iranians were all on their feet, embracing each other and smiling. Uzi knew that there could only be one reason for this display of jubilation: the yellowcake wouldn't need to be moved. The Israelis had the wrong target.

He sat there in a daze until Leila walked deliberately around the table and raised him to his feet. They were both gripped by an impulse to fall into each other's arms, but in the present company they had to resist. They held hands; Leila's was trembling. When she raised her face to him, he thought that her eyes were filling with tears. But he couldn't be sure.

'Thank you,' she whispered, 'thank you.'

Ghasem strode over and clasped him heartily by the hand as the bearded man removed the PCASS device.

'This should be a day of national celebration,' he said, 'in honour of you, my friend.'

'I am flattered,' Uzi replied. 'Really I have not done much.'

Ghasem waved his protestations away, Rolex rattling. 'You have saved our nuclear weapons programme,' he said. 'That is not something to dismiss.' He rubbed his hands together like a salesman. 'Now you two go and relax,' he said, addressing Uzi and Leila together. 'You deserve to – what do they call it? – decompress. We will take care of everything. We will move our forces into position and await the Israeli jets. And, finally, may I add this: congratulations on your engagement.'

Uzi looked quizzically at Leila, who smiled up at him. Instantly he understood that marriage was the only way they could be together. A smile spread across his face like the rising sun. But then he glanced over at Ghasem – and something didn't fit. For a brief moment he saw the Iranian exchanging a glance with a bodyguard, giving him the smallest of nods. It was a businesslike nod, one that was obviously intended for the bodyguard only. But something in Ghasem's steely expression – and in the bodyguard's barely perceptible acknowledgement – made Uzi's blood run cold.

Then, before he knew it, they were being bustled out of the room arm-in-arm, and Leila was clinging to him as if she would never let go. The bodyguard was carrying their luggage behind them; someone else was leading them on at a brisk pace down corridor after airy corridor. All at once they were outside, in the evening light, amid long shadows, being steered across a flagstoned courtyard lined with lemon trees, in the direction of a white-washed cottage in the grounds of the villa. Leila was whispering in his ear: I'll do anything you want, my love, I'll do anything you want. And then they were inside, and their luggage was stacked neatly in the corner. The doors were closed, and the bodyguard took up a position outside. Laughing with sudden abandon, Leila flung herself on to the scented bed. Uzi joined her. They had done it. Operation Desert Rain was doomed. The yellowcake would lie undisturbed many miles beneath the earth at Qum, while the fury of Israel fell on Natanz, many kilometres away. And in a matter of months – only months – a nuclear Iran would be a reality, bringing balance to the Middle East, to the world. Uzi removed his jacket and hung it carefully in the wardrobe, leaving the M9 in the pocket. Then he returned to the bed and received kisses that were more passionate and uninhibited than he had ever received before. The bodyguard – the one who had received the nod from Ghasem – was still outside.

42

When Uzi awoke, night had fallen. He snaked his arm from under Leila's head and looked at his watch. But the luminous hands were not glowing brightly enough; he couldn't read the time in the darkness. His ear began to itch.

'Uzi,' said the Kol firmly. It was the older voice.

'What time is it?'

'Air strikes will commence in sixty minutes. Sixty minutes. You need to move.'

Fuzzy-headed, Uzi slipped out of the bed and crossed to the window. Outside there was the silhouette of the bodyguard, who now had an AK-47 slung over his shoulder. Silently Uzi opened the shutters, allowing the moonlight to fall into the room. Then, in the half-light, he made his way to the wardrobe and put his jacket on. He slipped his hand into the inside pocket, gripped the butt of his M9.

From the bed, Leila moaned and propped herself up on her elbows, rubbing her eyes.

'My love,' she said sleepily, 'come back to bed.'

He had to think fast. 'Not now,' he said. 'I can't sleep. The air strikes are coming soon. I need to be out on the beach, under the stars. Anyway, I need a cigarette. I don't want to smoke here while you're sleeping. And it's a beautiful night. Look.'

Smoothing her hair, Leila got to her feet and crossed to the window, opening the shutters wide. 'You're right, it is beautiful. Just look at that moon. You would never get a moon that size in the West.' She took him by the hand and drew him to her.

'Uzi,' said the Kol quietly in his ear. 'Fifty-eight minutes.'

He rested his hands on Leila's hips and traced a line of kisses down her neck. 'Come on, then. Let's see if we can persuade that bodyguard to let us go for a stroll in private.'

Leila took a shawl from her luggage and draped it around her shoulders, then wrapped her headscarf loosely over her hair. They put on their shoes and went out, holding hands.

'Good evening,' said the bodyguard politely, turning towards them and tightening his hold on his gun. 'Is there something I can do for you?'

'We want to go for a walk on the beach,' said Leila. 'Would that be possible? We have just got engaged.'

The bodyguard thought for a moment. 'Wait here,' he said. He walked a few paces away, not taking his eyes off them, and spoke softly into a two-way radio. Then he came back. 'It would be possible,' he said, 'but I would need to accompany you.'

'Why?'

'Those are my orders. Please forgive me, but you and the Zionist need to be under constant guard.' He glanced sidelong at Uzi. 'And Ghasem said he might need to speak to you at short notice.'

'Look,' said Leila, standing a little closer to him. 'I am an operative, you see? A MOIS operative.' She took her ID card from her bag and showed it to him. 'Why don't you just give me the rifle and I'll guard this Zionist.'

'Not Zionist,' added Uzi in perfect Farsi, 'Israeli.'

The guard dismissed them both with a wave of his hand. 'It's my job to look after you,' he said, and smiled. His gaze was firm and opaque. Once again, Uzi felt his blood run cold.

'But I am a MOIS operative.'

'I'm sorry, sister. Orders are orders.' This time his face remained stony.

'No problem,' said Leila, smiling charmingly to disguise her annoyance. Then she and Uzi walked down the path hand-in-hand, briskly, with the bodyguard several paces behind. Uzi could hear him slipping a magazine quietly into his gun. He didn't turn around.

They crossed the courtyard again – the moonlight bathed everything in a ghostly light – and skirted the main villa. All the lights were on inside, and from time to time they encountered armed men on patrol. Leila flashed her ID card again and again, and the bodyguard nodded to his comrades. Through a window Uzi saw a room full of men wearing headsets, typing. And then they were at the front entrance, weaving their way through several rows of cars, heading in the direction of the perimeter fence.

'It's a breathtaking night,' said Leila, looking up at the stars. 'Just breathtaking.'

'It's a historic night,' Uzi replied softly. 'Let's get down to the beach to appreciate it.'

'Uzi,' said the Kol. 'Forty-seven minutes.'

The moon sat low and yellow above them as they approached the fence. Two different guards were on duty this time; when they saw the bodyguard, they waved them through. Leila was beguiling in the moonlight, and dignified despite the bodyguard.

'Sorry about our gun-toting babysitter,' she whispered. 'Tehran is bound to be jumpy until it's all over. But once the Israelis have made their move, and the yellowcake is safe, people will relax. We'll be free to do as we please.'

They made their way down the winding, tree-lined driveway and out on to the road on the spine of the ridge. Night sounds were all around them: nocturnal birds, animals in the undergrowth, the wind. Uzi thought he could hear the bodyguard breathing; now that they had passed through the perimeter fence, he was walking much closer behind them. Leila drew her shawl tighter around her. 'Where shall we go?' she asked.

Uzi's ear began to itch. 'Head over the road,' said the Kol. 'There's a track that leads down to the waterfront.'

Uzi turned to the bodyguard. 'We're going down to the ocean,' he said casually.

'For a short time,' said the bodyguard.

'Can't you give us a bit of space? Some privacy?'

The bodyguard made no response, remaining behind them as close as before. Uzi noticed that he had the safety-catch off. Leading Leila by the hand, Uzi crossed across the road and there, just as the Kol had said, was a rough dirt track winding down the side of the ridge. The rough grass and sand was monochrome in the moonlight.

'How did you know about this?' said Leila. 'Have you been here before?'

'I noticed it on the way here,' Uzi replied. 'Come on.'

They scrambled down the track, supporting themselves on smooth-faced boulders and desiccated trees. Twice the bodyguard ordered them to slow down. But each time Uzi, prompted by the Kol, said that he needed to get down to the ocean.

'So once this is all over, where shall we go to live?' said Leila breathlessly as they neared the foot of the ridge. Only a few rows of houses, still warm from the heat of the day, lay between them and the sea. 'Money will be no object.'

'It would need to be somewhere obscure,' said Uzi. 'How about somewhere in Latin America? Do you speak Spanish?'

'No,' said Leila, 'do you?'

'No,' said Uzi. Leila burst out laughing. 'What?' Uzi protested. 'We can learn.'

'I was thinking more of Jakarta, Bali, somewhere like that,' said Leila. 'It's remote enough, and beautiful enough, for our purposes. And there are elements there loyal to Iran.'

'I like that,' said Uzi. 'We could have a wooden villa on the ocean with hammocks. And a maid to make us Nasi Campur.'

'Nasi Campur?'

'An Indonesian national dish – rice with peanuts, vegetables, meat, eggs and shrimp flakes.'

'How do you know that?'

'I just know.'

They weaved their way through the narrow streets approaching the seafront. Leila was pressing close to him, he could feel the weight of her against his arm, could smell the scent of her perfume on the night breeze, and an intense wave of love broke through him. And with it, an intense wave of uncertainty.

'Uzi,' said the Kol. 'Forty minutes.'

Finally they broke free of the houses, hurried across the road and stepped on to the soft sand. The beach was deserted. Far off, lights twinkled. Leila paused to remove her shoes, and Uzi went on ahead; she ran to catch him up and swung into his arms. Uzi took her hand and led her down to the sea. Now that there was nowhere for them to run, and nowhere for them to hide, the bodyguard hung back a little, his AK-47 cradled loosely in his arms.

'Hurry,' said the Kol suddenly. 'There is a cove about a hundred metres down, over that outcrop of rock. Hurry.'

'Why don't we head for that cove?' said Uzi. 'There might be more privacy there.'

'I can't see a cove.'

'Just down there. Look.'

'There's no privacy anyway,' said Leila, 'not with our friend here. Let's just sit down here and watch the waves.'

'No, come on.'

'What's going on?'

'Nothing. Trust me.'

Leading her by the hand, Uzi strode through the sand towards the cove. The bodyguard called out but Uzi didn't stop. He heard the man cursing, scrambling after them, his weapon scraping against the rocks. The moon was clear and vivid, and the world was enchanted with shadow. The ocean could be heard breaking on the shore, each wave releasing secrets that had been locked up in the depths for centuries. Leila fell silent.

Before long, they scrambled down into the cove. Here the sand was softer than before, the waves were less energetic, and tiny shells were scattered in their thousands. A crab scuttled across their path, taking refuge in a crack in the rock; a starfish lay pulsating in the darkness by the edge of the water. The bodyguard, seeing that they had come to a halt, swore loudly and took up a position in the rocks. Uzi made a calming gesture to him and looked out to sea, catching his breath. He was sweating. Leila stood beside him, holding his hand, but not pressing against him any more. A streak of lunar light lay across the waves in front of them. On the horizon, tiny ships passed.

Uzi's ear itched. 'Now is the time,' urged the Kol gently. 'Be subtle.'

Uzi turned to Leila and drew her to him.

'I need to talk to you,' he said. 'There are things I need to say.'

'Let's talk later,' said Leila, gesturing subtly towards the bodyguard who was sitting just out of earshot, watching them closely. 'You've been through a lot. This operation must have taken its toll. But it's almost over now.'

Uzi drew breath sharply. Then, gently, he pulled away from Leila and looked into her eyes. 'Fate is strange,' he said. 'A strange thing. Like an ocean. You can be carried along in the waves for years, but then suddenly you need to swim against the current. Or die.'

'What are you saying?' said Leila uncertainly.

'I'm saying,' Uzi gathered his strength, 'I'm saying that sometimes you need to decide your own fate. Like the tree of life – sometimes you must choose to follow a different branch. And now that time has come.' He flicked his eyes, almost imperceptibly, in the direction of the bodyguard. 'Can you feel the danger?' he said.

'What do you mean?'

'Are you wondering why he's watching us so closely?'

'He's only there as a precaution . . .'

'Come on, Leila,' said Uzi, lowering his voice to an urgent whisper. 'What does your intuition tell you? Did you see the look in Ghasem's eyes? Do you really think the MOIS will allow us to live happily ever after?' A cloud passed across Leila's face, and Uzi knew that something inside her was responding to his words. 'Listen to your instinct,' he continued. 'They don't trust us. They're keeping us alive until the Israelis have made their move, then they'll kill us both. And can you blame them? I'm a Katsa – there is nobody on the face of the earth that they hate more. And you're in love with me.

They'll never let us live. They only let us come down to the beach so we don't suspect anything.'

She opened her mouth to deny it, but at first no sound came out. 'You're being too cynical,' she said at last, her voice suddenly weak. 'I'm their top operative. And you've helped them avoid . . .'

'Don't. There's no time,' said Uzi. 'Don't kid yourself. You know what I'm saying is true. We're expendable to the MOIS. They have no reason to keep us alive. Once this is over, they'll torture us to death. Now is the time to make our move. We're only going to get one opportunity to be free.'

'What could we possibly do?' she said. 'We're surrounded on all sides. This place is swarming with MOIS. We can't just swim across the Mediterranean. If we tried to escape, we'd be dead for certain.'

'No,' said Uzi with an intensity that made her draw breath, 'we wouldn't. I have a plan.' He pulled away from her and took a cigarette from his pocket. Then he patted down his pockets and waved to the bodyguard.

'A light. Do you have a light?' he called. He could feel Leila's body going tense. She began to say something, then fell silent.

For a long moment, the bodyguard didn't move. Then, reluctantly, he walked towards them rummaging in his pocket. As soon as he was within range Uzi seized the barrel of his gun and struck him a vicious blow to the throat. The man made a gurgling, wheezing noise and staggered. Uzi tried to pull the gun from his grasp but the man was strong and well trained; he twisted around, dropped to his knees and swung the barrel in an arc towards Uzi. Leila screamed and moved in to help, but then there was the sound of a gunshot – not loud – half the volume of a regular shot. The bodyguard lay dead in the sand.

'You have a weapon?' said Leila in disbelief. Uzi lowered his plastic M9, watching the bodyguard for any sign of movement. There was none. There were no longer three living people in the cove. Swing draw.

'What have you done?' said Leila. 'What have you done?' She began to pace back and forth in the moonlight, clasping her hands to her head. 'You've signed death warrants for us both. They'll come for us wherever we are. We won't survive the night.' He could see her visibly calming herself, drawing on her training.

'They were going to kill us anyway,' said Uzi. 'You know it's true.' He went over to the bodyguard. The life had left him. His skin was white in the moonlight; a perfectly round, perfectly black hole was above his right eyebrow. It looked like a fly, as if you could brush it away with your hand. A dark halo was spreading into the sand beneath his head. Uzi picked up the AK-47. Had he been a split second slower, this would have been the weapon that killed him.

'Nobody has ever escaped from Little Tehran,' said Leila, her voice more controlled now. 'I know what the security here is like.'

'Don't worry,' said Uzi. 'Listen to me. I'm just like you. You joined the MOIS because of your father. I joined the Mossad because of my family, the way I was raised. But we are our own people, Leila. We can go somewhere together. We can be free.'

Leila's eyes flicked from his face to the ocean and back again. 'I don't know what you're trying to tell me,' she said. 'You're making no sense.'

'Leila, Leila. I have to tell you something. I need to come clean . . .'

Suddenly the woman's expression changed. Her eye had caught a disturbance on the face of the water, far out in the strip of moonlight. 'What's that? I saw something. Seventy-five metres out.'

Uzi took her arms and held her firm. 'Look at me,' he said. 'I'm saying – god, I'm saying I want to be with you. I'm saying . . . I'm saying this has all been a mission for the Mossad.'

A pause.

'The Mossad?'

'Yes. I'm still a Mossad operative. I'm just under cover. Deep cover.' The secret was out. Time seemed to stand still. For the first time, Uzi saw Leila at a loss. Her mouth worked, but no words came; it was as if he had just shown her a conjuring trick. 'There's no time to explain,' he said, his voice hoarse. 'I've sworn that this is my last operation. I want to escape, to be with you. We can leave all this behind.'

The Kol's voice appeared softly in his ear. 'Be subtle. We want her alive for interrogation.'

'I – I don't understand,' said Leila. 'You fucked the Mossad. You gave me all that intel. You helped us avoid an air strike. You've saved our nuclear weapons programme. It doesn't make sense.'

'Look, there's no time to explain,' Uzi repeated. 'Anyway, it doesn't matter any more. None of it matters. It doesn't matter whether Iran wins this battle, or Israel wins – the war will be endless. The Mossad has been exploiting me, and the MOIS has been exploiting you. We're both pawns, don't you see? They both use operatives until they're killed, then recruit more to fill their shoes. They don't see us as human beings. They're using us, just like they used that young boy to kill Ram Shalev. We need to get out of the whole game. Both of us.'

He glanced over his shoulder. Two dark objects had broken the surface of the ocean thirty metres from the shore, a pair of black round domes bobbing side by side, trailing wisps of surf behind them. For a moment they disappeared as a wave swelled in front, then they reappeared again. Now more could be seen: the heads of two frogmen, their masks reflecting silver in the moonlight, their regulators like jewels in their mouths.

'Gently,' said the Kol. 'Gently.'

'I love you,' said Uzi desperately. 'I'd give up everything for you. I love you more than my country. Remember? Think – you said the same to me. I know you understand me, I know it. You've been made into a weapon in an endless war. We both have. Now the Mossad is coming to take me to safety. Come with me.'

Suddenly Leila broke from his grasp and tried to run back towards the rocks. Uzi chased her, grabbed her in a bear hug. 'If you go back to the MOIS, they'll kill you. They'll kill us both. Come with me. Come with me, and I'll protect you.'

'Then I will be a martyr for my country!' said Leila. 'My life is a price worth paying for a nuclear Iran!'

'You don't think that. I refuse to believe you think that.'

'I'd rather be killed by MOIS than the Mossad,' she replied. 'Let my own people kill me, if that's what I deserve.'

'No – you deserve life! I told you, I have a plan. We'll use the Mossad to get out of here. Then we'll escape, I promise.'

'You promise?' she laughed bitterly. 'I'm supposed to believe you because you promise?'

She spun round and, in a seamless movement, tripped Uzi into the sand. He rolled onto his side and saw that in a flash she had grabbed the AK-47. 'Leila,' he said, 'think. Who cares whether we escape from the MOIS or the Israelis? The important thing is that we stay alive. We can make a life together. We can go where no one will find us, and live a normal life.' She didn't respond. Slowly she raised the barrel until it pointed directly at his heart.

There was a long pause. The sea whispered harshly into the silence. Out of the corner of his eye, Uzi saw the frogmen's heads breaking the water. They weren't far off now. He took his M9 carefully from his pocket and tossed it down in the sand.

'Look,' he said, 'I'm at your mercy. This is your moment to decide. Kill me and kill yourself. Or take the chance of life – and trust me.'

'I won't allow the Mossad to interrogate me.'

'Trust me.'

'I can't betray my country. I can't betray my father.' The barrel of the gun was perfectly steady.

'Trust me, Leila. Together, we can do anything. Your country is using you, just as my country has been using me. We'll piggyback out of here with the Mossad, then escape and disappear. We'll start a new life. A normal life. To go back to the MOIS will mean certain death. Come with me, and there will at least be a chance.'

306

Leila lowered the gun, first by an inch, then two; then it dropped to the sand.

'Well done,' said the Kol quietly.

The frogmen arrived. Like mythological creatures, they rose to a standing position, removed their fins and jogged into the cove, the sand clogging on their feet. Each was armed with an APS Special Underwater Assault Rifle, and their suits were studded with equipment.

'We can do this,' whispered Uzi. 'I promise.' He raised a hand; the frogmen raised theirs in return, and jogged over to him. They lowered their masks, revealing quick, intense eyes. Their wetsuits glistened like dolphin skin. When they caught sight of Leila, they lifted their weapons and eyed her suspiciously.

Uzi joined the frogmen, who were starting to unpack equipment: wetsuits, masks, BCDs, weighted belts, air cylinders. He passed a set to Leila, and began to put one on himself. She hesitated, picked up the wetsuit, put it down again. Then she turned and took a few steps back towards the rocks, the eyes of Uzi and the two frogmen following her. Her body language revealed great distress. One hand was on her forehead, the other wrapped around her stomach; she was shaking her head and shifting her feet in the sand. This was a woman being torn, in body, mind and spirit, between two different worlds.

She turned back to face them, and for the first time Uzi saw her face purely, without the layers of different masks that normally concealed it. She took one step closer, then another; then she stooped towards the AK-47 that was lying on the sand. Instantly the frogmen raised their weapons. Her hand hovered in the air above the gun. Then she straightened up, and Uzi could see that her eyes were moist with tears.

'Come on,' he said softly. 'I'm with you. I'm offering you a life. Come on.'

She took a deep breath, filling her lungs as if for the last time with the fragrant air of Syria. Then she came over to join them, picked up the wetsuit, and, without looking at any of them, began to take off her clothes.

'We should disable her,' mumbled one of the frogmen in Hebrew. 'Bring her in unconscious.'

'What,' said Uzi, 'and have her drown on the way?'

'We'll hold her regulator in her mouth. She's too dangerous. We can't take any chances.' The frogman opened a pouch on his belt and Uzi saw the head of a syringe glinting in the moonlight. He stepped in front of the frogman, screening it from Leila.

'It's too risky to transport a high-value prisoner unconscious under water,' he hissed. 'The regulator might slip out of her mouth. Her tongue might block it. She could choke. Look, I've persuaded her to come of her own accord. Leave her be. I'll take full responsibility.'

'I'm not going to compromise our mission,' said the frogman, stepping forward.

'This woman is a senior MOIS operative,' Uzi replied. 'Interrogating her could save many lives. Jewish lives. I'm not going to risk bringing her in dead.' The man hesitated. 'I'm not asking for your opinion,' said Uzi. 'The prisoner is not going under water unconscious. I'm the senior officer here, and that's an order.'

Reluctantly the frogman conceded. Uzi, seeing that Leila had put on her full equipment, beckoned her over. Then, with her permission, he handcuffed her to his wrist. The hatred between her and the frogmen was palpable, and Uzi tried to stop her glancing at them. For what seemed like eternity, he looked into her eyes. The whole universe was reflected in those two silent globes; the ancient struggle of humanity against itself. Uzi and Leila did not kiss. They pulled their masks over their eyes.

When the four of them reached the waterline, they put on their fins, placed their regulators in their mouths and slipped into the water like turtles. Uzi began to swim out after the frogmen, pulling Leila after him. Just before he went under, he looked at her. She was floating on the surface, bobbing gently; water was lapping at her face. What could be seen of her skin was marble in the moonlight, and the mask was reflecting the stars. Behind her, on the beach, he could just make out the dead bodyguard, the AK-47, and two crumpled piles of clothes. The time had come. He dived, pulling Leila behind him into the depths, without even the slightest splash.

43

The four divers clung to the wet sub, tunnelling like an eel through the black depths of the Syrian Mediterranean. In this watery alter ego of the world, the conflicts between men and countries seemed irrelevant. From time to time Uzi looked at Leila, but he couldn't see her eyes behind her mask, in the murky water, in the darkness. They rode the wet sub for what seemed like hours. Then, several miles off the coast, they cut the engine and guided the machine towards the surface. From beneath the shimmering face of the water they could see the hull of a large yacht, silhouetted against the moonlit sky. The wet sub gradually rose through the water until it was directly below the vessel. They activated its electro-magnets and, with a dull clang, the sub adhered to the hull; they finned around the side of the boat before silently breaking the surface.

The ship towered above them into the star-speckled sky. Its engine was idling quietly and all the curtains were drawn across the windows; here and there some dim light could be seen spilling through the cracks. This was more than just a ship. Uzi recognised it at once. This was the *Minerva*, a 377-foot vision of luxury, a billionaire's plaything, with a helipad, a luxury spa, a swimming pool and a miniature escape-submarine. To the casual observer, it would seem as if a powerful oligarch was taking a discreet pleasure cruise in the warm waters between Cyprus and Syria. To the coastguard, this was the sort of ship that should be left well alone. But to Uzi it meant something else. It meant he was free, and that sent a frisson of emotion through him like a sudden storm. One of the frogmen made a radio transmission and within seconds a rope ladder was flung over the side and landed with a splash in the water. It was impossible for Uzi and Leila to climb the ladder while still cuffed together; Uzi opened the handcuffs and went ahead, while the frogmen kept a close eye on Leila. At the top, friendly hands helped him over the railing and into the yacht itself. Then they hauled the prisoner up and into the vessel.

Suddenly there was the sound of a scuffle on the deck. Uzi turned to see Leila struggling with the frogmen; with a yell she gave one a stinging blow, and he almost toppled over the side of the ship. Dozens of men, all dressed in black, appeared as if from nowhere; Uzi lost sight of her as she was surrounded. He tried to shove his way through the crush. She's biting, someone was shouting, she's biting! Neutralise her! The mass of bodies parted for a moment and Uzi saw one of the frogmen thrusting something into Leila's back; she let out a wild scream, which became a moan, which became a sigh, and crumpled lifelessly to the deck. Uzi fell to his knees beside her.

'What did you do?' he shouted.

'She was resisting,' said one of the frogmen, catching his breath. 'She didn't like me grabbing her. Fought like a fucking vixen.'

Uzi ran his hand along her back and brought his hand to his face; he could see no blood. He felt her pulse: she was alive. 'What did you do to her?' he said, trying – and failing – to keep the emotion out of his voice. 'Was it a knife?'

'She'll be fine,' said the frogman, laughing nervously and holding up a syringe. 'I gave her a shot of Haloperidol, that's all. In two hours' time, she'll be as good as new. We should have disabled her in the first place.'

Uzi breathed a sigh of relief. Then, trying to disguise his feelings, he stood up briskly. 'We need this woman alive. She's a high-value target. If anything happens to her, I'll shoot you. Personally. Got it?'

Gradually order was restored. The frogmen were directed below decks while Uzi was wrapped in an anti-hypothermia blanket. Leila's mask was removed and she was placed on a stretcher, soaked and shivering, unconscious but alive. She was whisked away below decks; Uzi felt a tug as she disappeared from view, as if he were losing part of himself. He looked around and did not recognise any of the black-clad crew that were fussing on deck, removing his mask and scuba tank, patting him on the back, taking his temperature and blood pressure. He was ushered along the gangway and through a steel door into the ship. Framed aerial photographs of Israel were on the walls, up-lit. Somebody was saying congratulations, Colonel Feldman, congratulations, let me be the first to congratulate you. Someone else was whispering how Colonel Feldman had not only completed the mission, he had brought in a MOIS operative – alive – for interrogation. He was a hero. And then he was standing in front of a pair of heavy wooden doors, the largest he had ever seen, like two colossal slabs of halva. Someone knocked twice and the doors swung open, revealing a long, low-ceilinged room decorated in soft colours. The place was filled with the scent of luxury. There were about ten people in the room. And all eyes were on him.

Dreamlike, he stepped through the double doors, his wetsuit trailing drops of water on the deep-pile carpet. The doors swung closed noiselessly. He blinked, tried to take stock. To the left and right of him were six people, four men and two women, standing to attention in their uniforms. They were looking at him and smiling, without breaking their discipline. He recognised them like characters from a dream. Of course: these were his colleagues. These were the other members of the Tehorim, 'The Pure', the unit so elite that the rest of the Mossad didn't even know it existed. The ultra-secret operatives that specialised in high-risk, deep cover operations. Nobody at London Station knew about the Tehorim; they had had no idea that Uzi, the man they had been pursuing, was risking his life for the State of Israel. Even his friend, Avner, hadn't known. But Uzi was one of The Pure; and these were his colleagues.

Ahead of him were four people standing side by side, their hands clasped in front of them. On the left, smiling in a grandfatherly way, was the unassuming figure of ROM – the director of the Mossad. On the right were two women that he did not recognise. One was older, the other younger. And in the middle, dressed as always in an immaculate suit and tie, was the most imposing figure of all: the prime minister of Israel.

'Your timing is excellent,' said the prime minister. 'You are just in time to watch the show with us.' From the ceiling behind him a projector screen slid down. The lights were dimmed and somebody placed a chair behind each of them. They sat.

The screen flickered into life. A hazy black-and-white image appeared: an aerial view of an industrial installation on the outskirts of a city. At the bottom of the screen was a clock counting the split seconds as they passed. Alongside this were the words 'live cockpit camera' in Hebrew, along with the location: 'Qum, Iran.'

The prime minister looked at his watch. 'I have just given the order to fire at will.'

For several minutes nothing happened. The image of the city revolved and magnified as the pilot homed in on his target. A circle appeared on the screen, capturing a precise point on the installation. The pilot moved closer. Cars could be seen moving on the roads at the edge of the screen. Then, without warning, a chain of dark objects could be seen falling down towards the circle; seconds later a fireball spiralled upwards, devouring the image in a white light. Then it cleared. Flames could be seen blazing all around the installation, in the centre of which gaped a jagged, fiery crater.

Words appeared across the screen: 'awaiting confirmation'. They remained there, blinking, for what felt like a long time. Then, finally, they were replaced with two more words: 'target destroyed'. The room erupted in applause. The lights came on; the prime minister leaned over and shook Uzi heartily by the hand.

'A good job, Colonel Feldman, an excellent job,' he said. 'You should see the satellite images of Natanz. The Iranians put so much firepower there, you'd have thought we were sending in our entire Air Force. The whole Revolutionary Guard, as well as the Artesh, turned out.' He chuckled. 'But now there is no longer any such thing as Iranian yellowcake. Their nuclear programme is over. At least for another ten years.'

Uzi – no, Uzi was dead now, Adam, Adam Feldman – smiled and turned away, but the prime minister hadn't finished. 'If it hadn't been for your excellent work,' he said, 'within months Israel might have been facing a nuclear attack.'

The chairs were removed and everybody got to their feet, returning to their original formation with a sense of great ceremony. Adam was starting to recognise his colleagues better now. There was Hannah, who had buddied with him in the early stages of training. There was Yoav, the ballistics expert. There was Eli, who could speak more languages than anyone he had ever met. Adam, understanding what was expected of him, clutched his blanket closer and walked towards ROM, the prime minister, the two women, flanked by his appreciative colleagues and surrounded by the sound of applause.

ROM was the first to clasp him by the hand.

'Well done, brother,' he said. 'An absolutely perfect operation. Absolutely perfect. And you brought back the MOIS operative, too! You even made her fall hopelessly in love with you. Flawless.'

'Nice boat you've got here,' Adam heard himself saying.

'We borrowed it from a Sayan,' ROM replied. 'He doesn't use it much these days. His new one is much bigger and fancier.' He leaned closer. 'It has a helipad. And a miniature submarine.' ROM pumped his hand again and directed Adam to the two women.

'You did it,' said the older one happily. 'You believed in yourself. You believed.'

'You,' said Adam. 'You're the one who's been fucking with my head for months.' Good-natured laughter rippled throughout the gathering as, despite the water still clinging to Adam's wetsuit, they embraced.

'You don't have to say it,' said the younger woman. 'We know. You couldn't have done it without us.'

'Well,' said Adam, 'it's good to put a face to a voice.'

An aide stepped forward and handed the prime minister a glass display case. He shook Adam's hand again, and presented the case to him. In the centre, on a backdrop of black velvet, was a stiletto dagger, the kind traditionally used by the Mossad. On the blade was engraved a passage from Psalms 121:4: *'Behold, the guardian of Israel neither slumbers nor sleeps.'* Adam felt dizzy, and shook his head to clear it. Beaming, the prime minister pulled him into a bear hug.

'You've done your country proud,' he said, 'you've done us all proud.'

'Careful,' said Adam, 'your suit is getting wet.'

'Fuck the suit,' replied the prime minister. 'Under this suit beats the heart of a soldier, same as you.'

'Look,' said Adam, 'Operation Regime Change . . .'

'Don't mention it,' said the prime minister magnanimously. 'I completely understand. You had to go along with that bastard Avner and the WikiLeaks scenario. You had no choice – the MOIS were watching you day and night. To refuse would have made them doubt your animosity towards the Mossad. Your first duty was to your operation, to maintain your cover. That is the nature of the Tehorim. I know that.'

'Yes, but I mean Avner. Don't hunt him down. He's just a piss artist.'

'I won't be concerning myself with that fool. We'll contain him, but we'll let him keep his freedom. He has his money, so what the hell. He won't be causing any more trouble.'

'Did it make things difficult for you? Politically?'

'WikiLeaks? Put it this way. For the last few days the whole world has been accusing me of assassinating my political opponents.

It hasn't been comfortable, to say the least. But the headlines tomorrow will be about the air strikes. We have arranged for an independent observer to confirm that the yellowcake existed, so it is clear that we had no choice but to strike preemptively. By tomorrow, your leak will discredited. We will win the election – for genuine reasons – and all will be well. And you will receive a new identity, as well as a generous reward for your troubles.'

Adam felt dazed, as if he had just awoken from a long sleep. But at the same time, the pain hadn't gone away; his bond with Leila had been violated. So far he had been reacting automatically, allowing platitudes to slip from his mouth without thinking. But now he thought he should try to verbalise the truth of his inner life. He opened his mouth to speak but no words came. There was nothing he could say; no way he could make anybody understand. So instead he simply said: 'This was my last operation. That was the arrangement.'

'Come now,' said ROM, taking his arm, 'there will be lots of time to discuss these things.'

'Can I get this thing out of my ear now,' said Adam, 'and out of my shoulder? It's been driving me crazy.'

The prime minister looked at ROM, who called to an aide. 'Take Colonel Feldman to freshen up,' he said. 'Then take him to the sick bay to have the mic and receiver removed.' He turned to Adam. 'Brother,' he said, 'you did well. Very well. I am indebted to you.'

'Thank you, sir, but with respect,' said Adam, 'this was my last mission. It really was my last mission.'

'Of course,' said ROM, giving him a packet of Noblesse cigarettes and a lighter from his inside pocket. 'Of course it was. Have a smoke, relax. We have time.'

Adam pocketed the cigarettes gratefully and found himself being shepherded out of the room and into the bowels of the yacht. The powerful engines were running now, he could hear them, he could feel their vibrations beneath his feet. The vessel was pulling away from hostile waters, he thought. Heading home.

After he had showered – vigorously, as if trying to cleanse his soul – and changed into a dry set of clothes, Adam sat on the bed and waited for someone to escort him to the sick bay. His ear, the cyst in his shoulder, felt heavy and hot. Instinctively he expected the Kol to appear in his head, to encourage him to stay strong, to believe in himself. But he knew that would never happen again. It was over. He closed his eyes, tried to collect his thoughts. Then he took ROM's cigarettes and left his cabin, carrying with him the dagger in its display case.

The deck was deserted. It was a warm night, but a cool breeze was blowing across the face of the ocean. Adam leaned over the stern, listening to the hum of the engines, watching the tail of foam fade in the sea. The ocean was inky and so was the sky; stars spread out above his head like a canopy of luminous insects, frozen in time. He smoked one Noblesse after another, allowing the wind to tear the smoke from his mouth and disperse it in all directions. The tobacco was rough, potent, stronger than cigarettes outside Israel. It burned his throat and brought back light bulb flashes of memories.

He wondered where Avner – Franz Gruber – was now. Avner, who always believed he was one step ahead. Avner, who would never have guessed, even for an instant, that Adam was really on an operation for a unit that he didn't even know existed. This mission had pitted Adam against the Office many times; many times the Office had tried to capture him, kill him even, under the impression that he was a loose cannon at best, and working for the enemy at worst. But Adam had given as good as he'd got. He'd survived. There had been no alternative: to blow his cover, even to the Office, would have damaged Israel far more profoundly than the odd skirmish with them in London. After all, the Office had been infiltrated by the MOIS; there was no telling how deeply their roots were embedded.

He turned to see the Kol, the older woman, leaning over the railing beside him. How long had she been there?

'Are you OK?' she said.

'I don't know how to answer that question,' he said.

There was a pause. Adam offered her a cigarette. The flame from the lighter lit her face up for a second, then all was dark again.

'Sometimes it can be dangerous to believe,' she said.

'Nice of you to say so,' Adam replied bitterly. 'But those were my instructions, right? To forget about my old identity, to bury myself, to allow Uzi to come alive. To become only Uzi, nothing but Uzi; to be the bait, to let the MOIS come to me. Not to allow Adam Feldman to draw a single breath. To think like Uzi, feel like Uzi, behave like Uzi, believe in him. Shit, I even passed a lie detector test.'

'I didn't say you were wrong. I just said to believe is dangerous. But in the end, it was only a mission. In time, with the help of our psychologists, you will readjust.'

'But it's not that simple, is it?' said Adam. 'Uzi was more than just a mask. That's why I was chosen.'

'That's true,' said the Kol. 'You have always been a troublemaker. We knew that you made controversial statements and thought too much for yourself. Ram Shalev even advised his MOIS controllers that you were the most likely operative to be turned. We knew all that. But this is the philosophy of the Tehorim: to take a seed from inside the operative's psyche and nurture it to create a watertight cover, to grow a new person, and for the duration of the mission, to have the operative inhabit him. To believe in him.'

'You never worried that I would go off the rails? That I would become Uzi and never return?'

'No.'

'Why?'

The Kol sighed. 'Your psychological profile. We understand the depth of Israel's hold on her children. For someone like you – the son of a war hero, the grandson of Zionist pioneers – to betray your country would be physically impossible, however politics sways you, whatever trauma you suffer. When Israel is in mortal danger, people like you are cleansed of any hesitation and fall four-square behind the State. This is the alchemy of a bloody history, the alchemy of nationhood. This is the alchemy of the Holy Land.'

'Ram Shalev,' said Adam dreamily. 'Fucking Ram Shalev. I can see his face now.'

'Don't worry about Ram Shalev. The man was a traitor of the worst kind. Ex-Mossad operative – and MOIS agent. For years, he was the lynchpin in a network of Iranian spies that had been grafted into the Office's power structure.'

'I know that.'

'But?'

'I didn't say but.'

'The man deserved to die, Adam. By the time we discovered his identity, he had already given the Iranians intelligence on the whole of Operation Desert Rain. Apart from the target, that is. And he was trying like hell to find that out.'

'I know.'

'He had planned to tell WikiLeaks that the prime minister was going to bomb Iran's nuclear facilities to gain pre-election popularity points. He wanted to put us on the back foot, use the media to force us to postpone Operation Desert Rain, to allow the Iranians a little more time – just a little more time – in which they would try to develop the bomb. Ram Shalev was a hair's breadth away from causing Israel's destruction. The only thing he didn't know was the target of Operation Desert Rain. And thanks to you, we fooled them.'

'What makes a man turn like that against his own people?' said Adam broodingly. 'What's the trigger?'

'Come on, Adam, don't be naive. You know what motivates people. With Shalev it was mainly money. Money and sex. And revenge, too, we think. Like everyone else.'

'I killed him. I played a part in killing him. I've killed so many people.'

'You should be proud – proud of the difficult tasks you've carried out for our homeland, and proud of the fact that you're a moral enough man to worry about it.' She leaned closer, and Adam saw her face half illuminated by the moonlight. 'You're not Uzi,' she said softly. 'You're Colonel Adam Feldman. You were always were Colonel Adam Feldman. You're a red-blooded Zionist. That's the truth.'

He flicked another cigarette over the side of the yacht and watched it disappear in the blackness. His throat hurt, and his ear and shoulder were aching as if the microphone and receiver were coming alive inside him. He opened the glass case and took the dagger in his hands, holding it up in the moonlight. *Behold, the guardian of Israel neither slumbers nor sleeps.* The engraving was detailed and elegant, and the dagger itself was solid, well weighted, with a leather-bound handle. He rested on the railing again, weighing the knife in his hands. The Kol was saying something, but he was no longer listening. He wanted Leila. He had been trained for this, of course. He had been taught how to construct an alternative persona and then, when the mission was over, to allow the character's psychology, fears, hopes, dreams, memories, to melt off him like a coating. But when he was Uzi, he had felt more genuinely himself. The Doctrine of the Status Quo – that had been his. It had only taken the creation of Uzi to bring it to fruition. Everything had been his, everything deep down had been his. He could not get rid of Uzi like a snake shedding its skin. Sometimes, he thought, a man has to act another role to find out his true identity.

He turned to the Kol. She was still speaking, gazing out into the blackness of the night.

'We need to discuss your friend,' she was saying. 'The woman. It would be best if you could join in the interrogation. We could do a lot if you were involved.'

'Where's the sick bay?' Adam interrupted.

'Why?'

'I just want to get rid of this mic, that's all. Somebody was supposed to escort me down . . .'

'I'm sorry, I wasn't thinking. Follow me.'

She led him down into the heart of the ship. He was feeling dizzy, despite the gentleness of the ocean beneath them. He rested on the handrail for support, and as he did so, with a single fluid movement, slipped the dagger into his pocket.

44

When Adam and the Kol approached the sick bay, he saw that a guard was posted outside the door. She's still in there, thought Adam. Leila must be still in there. To his surprise, the Kol left him with the guard and disappeared down the corridor; with a courteous nod, he was allowed inside.

The medic who greeted him was a man in his early thirties, with rimless glasses that glinted in the light. Leila was nowhere to be seen; the medic shook Adam's hand, murmured his congratulations and got on with the job without the need for instructions. They did not speak as he injected a local anaesthetic into Adam's shoulder, made an incision with a scalpel, and pressed a pair of tweezers into the 'cyst'. After a couple of attempts, he slid out a plastic chip about the size of a postage stamp. For months it had been sending audio information to Israel; everything that Adam heard, everything he said, had been transmitted directly to the Mossad in Tel Aviv. He stared at the bloodied chip lying on a surgical swab, like an amputated tongue. The medic sealed the wound.

'Now the mic in my ear,' said Adam.

'Are you sure, Colonel? Perhaps it would be better to wait until we reach Israel.'

'Why?'

'It's a more sensitive area, and a more complicated procedure. At sea, with the unpredictable movement of the ship . . .'

'Just get it out of me. I want it out of me now.'

'You've had it in there for months. What difference does a few more hours . . .'

'It makes a difference to me. I almost became schizophrenic with this thing inside me.'

The medic hesitated. Then he sighed and began to fill a new hypodermic needle. 'As you wish, Colonel.'

It took longer than Adam had expected, but with some effort he held himself firm. Finally the ear-mic, the mouthpiece of the Kol, lay on the swab as well. He had bandages on his ear as well as his shoulder, and both felt numb and fat.

'The prisoner,' Adam said, 'the woman. Is she awake yet?'

'Not yet,' the medic replied. 'She could be out for another half an hour or so.'

'I'm part of the interrogation team. I'd like to examine her briefly before I go.'

'Of course, Colonel.'

With no further questions Adam was led to a door, which the medic unlocked by passing his ID badge across a sensor. Inside, the lighting was dim. There, in a low bunk, lay Leila, lying on her back with her arms outstretched. She had been stripped of her wet clothes and – from what he could see under the blankets – dressed in military greens. Her left wrist was handcuffed to the bunk, and a drip-line snaked into her right arm.

Adam, his heart beating like a time bomb, leaned over her and, with gentle fingertips, lifted one eyelid, then the other. For a moment, he felt her breath brushing his hand.

'You're right,' he said. 'She's still under. You've treated her for hypothermia, I suppose?'

'Her notes are here,' said the medic, passing Adam a buff folder. 'We've warmed her up and put her on a high-energy drip. She's responding well.'

'How soon until we can start interrogating her?' said Adam, flicking through the notes.

'As soon as she wakes up. She'll be woozy, but not in danger. Not in terms of her health, anyway.' He smiled slightly.

Adam handed back the file, nodded, turned to go; but then, in one fluid movement, snatched the dagger from his pocket and shoved the medic against the wall, holding the blade to his throat, clamping his hand over his mouth. The man's breath bulged against his palm.

'One word,' snarled Adam, 'and I open your veins. Understand?'

The medic, wide-eyed, nodded. Adam released his hand from his mouth and grabbed his collar. 'Now,' he said, 'you're going to unlock those handcuffs. Do it now.'

'No,' said the medic, 'I can't open it. I don't have the key.'

Adam, noticing the man's eyes darting up and to the left – the classic sign of deception – pressed the dagger into his neck until it broke the skin. The man winced and made a noise like a startled animal. A thread of his blood slipped on to the blade and wound into the letters of the engraving: *The guardian of Israel neither slumbers nor sleeps.* Adam pulled back the dagger.

'I'm serious,' he said, 'release the handcuffs or I'll bleed you like a pig.' Panting, the medic stooped over Leila and freed her. Adam rolled the woman gently to the floor, handcuffed the medic to the bed in her place, and stuffed a handful of surgical swabs into his mouth. Then he freed Leila from the drip and dragged her into the other room. He knew that he didn't have long.

Gritting his teeth, Adam stood behind the door and collected his thoughts. The dagger gleamed in the lights of the sick bay. He took three deep breaths then opened the door; in an instant he was behind the guard, holding the knife to his neck. He disarmed him, struck him three times with the handle of the dagger until he lay still. Then he pulled him into the sick bay, and bound and gagged him tightly. Rolling him over, he searched his pockets and found an electronic entry card, like that used in a hotel, but with the addition of a high-security digital chip. Fate was on his side, he thought; finally, fate was on his side. He pocketed the card, took the man's gun and, with some effort on account of the numbness in his shoulder, hoisted Leila on to his shoulder. Then he padded quietly down the corridor, trying to regulate the rhythm of his breath.

Adam knew that the odds were stacked against him. He was on a vessel commanded by the Mossad, in waters dominated by the Syrians, with a lover who – until tonight – had worked for the MOIS. Even if he could get off the yacht, even if he could escape the clutches of the Mossad, MOIS and the Mukhabarat, even if he could find somewhere to hole up, he would still need to win Leila over to his position. She had chosen to take a chance with him rather than go to her death. She was brave; but that didn't mean he had won her trust. Was her love for him strong enough to endure all this? He couldn't be certain. He was surrounded by a universe of darkness, like a nightmare he had had once as a child – impenetrable darkness without end, stretching to the borders of imagination. The nightmare of death itself. Yet he knew this: now he was his own master, and from this moment on, for however long he had left on this earth, he would never again be enslaved.

With Leila over his shoulder, he climbed a shallow staircase and turned left along a corridor that he had noted on his way down to the sick bay. Three doors down was a door made of reinforced metal; through a porthole he could see an assortment of electronic equipment. Hoping against hope, he took the entry card from his pocket and slipped it into the slot. He held his breath. Nothing happened. Then, without warning, there was a low clunk and the door swung open. He entered and locked it behind him.

Machinery hummed all around. Adam set Leila down gently in a padded leather chair and set to work on the buttons and dials, bringing multiple screens to life, powering up complicated systems and preparing the equipment for action. He hadn't seen such sophisticated maritime computers for a long time – not since his Navy days.

All was set. He took Leila in his arms, an unconscious Cordelia, and carried her down the passageway and into the air-tight submarine launch chamber. The vessel lay in its docking bay, perfectly clean and in a state of constant preparedness. It was beautiful: dark grey in colour, as sleek as a bullet or a dolphin, as powerful and discreet a craft as he could have wished for.

With some effort, he struggled up the ladder and strapped Leila into the passenger seat. She looked so perfect there, unconscious, peaceful, oblivious to the world, her mind resting in inaccessible spheres.

The world was closing in. Adam climbed into the cockpit, strapped himself in and sealed the sub. Then he punched in the commands and, with a sound like a hundred waterfalls, the chamber began to fill with water. This is it, he thought. This is it. Within minutes the waterline crept up the walls of the sub and over the top of the cockpit, sealing them in an underwater realm. Finally a hole opened before them, a dark circle leading out of the yacht and into the boundless depths. Adam glanced at Leila – still no sign of consciousness – and activated the engine. The submarine dislodged from its moorings and moved towards the circular hole, spraying a cloud of bubbles in its wake.

No doubt: he was in more danger now than he had ever been before. But as the sub fell from the yacht like a bomb and disappeared into the tarry ocean, Adam was filled with the sense that everything he needed – everything in the world – was contained within the walls of this little vessel. The noise of the engine filled the craft, making it feel peaceful somehow, riding the currents of the sea. It was quiet. Outside a shoal of glittering fish floated past like a cloud. He was in the eye of the storm; he was at peace. He took the dagger out of his pocket and placed it on the dashboard.

Suddenly Leila stirred and shifted in her seat. She opened her eyes woozily and looked around. Then her eyes widened and she looked across at Adam, as if trying to place him.

'Uzi,' she said, 'where are we? I'm so tired.'

'Don't worry,' he said, 'you've been drugged. But you're safe now.'

'My vision is blurry.'

'That's OK. It'll pass.'

'Last thing I remember, I was fighting a guy in a wetsuit.'

'He won't forget you, that's for sure.'

'God, my eyes.'

'Just close them and relax. Give it time.'

'Have we left that awful ship?'

'We have. We've escaped, just like I promised.'

'We're in a sub, right?'

'Yes.'

'You won't get away with this, you know. As soon as I get my vision back I'm going to slap you hard.'

'I wouldn't expect anything less.'

A pause. The sound of the engine, of the water rushing by outside.

'Where are we going?'

'Somewhere they'll never find us. Somewhere we can be ourselves.'

'I don't think I know what that means any more,' said Leila.

'Nor do I,' said Adam, 'but together we're going to find out.'

Acknowledgements

Many years ago, I found myself going through the recruitment process for the Secret Intelligence Service. I passed the first couple of stages, but before long I was rejected. Presumably MI6 decided that a creative type like me, with an unusually small hippocampus and a dislike for anything practical, might not be of great benefit to our national security. So with the world of espionage closed to me, I thought I'd write a novel about it.

Not much has been written about the Mossad, so the brunt of my research focused on two compelling books: *By Way of Deception: The Making and Unmaking of a Mossad Officer* by Victor Ovsrovsky (which inspired many of the details and operations mentioned in this novel), and Gordon Thomas's *Gideon's Spies: The Secret History of the Mossad*. I am most grateful to both of these authors.

As ever, Danny Angel – to whom *The Pure* is dedicated – helped enormously by reading the book and offering his impressions. David Del Monté helped in a similar way, and Homa Rastegar Driver gave some invaluable advice about portraying Iranian culture. Toby Wallis consulted on scuba diving matters. Only my dedicated and excellent agent, Andrew Gordon, who spent many hours poring over the manuscript and whose advice is never less than sterling, surpassed their efforts. And the team at Polygon – Hugh, Neville, Alison, Sarah, Kenny – did an admirable job in editing, producing and distributing this book, and in believing in me once again. Thanks also to Caroline Oakley and Mark Ecob for their editorial and design input.

While writing *The Pure* I tweeted about it (@JakeWSimons). The following people joined the conversation and gave me their ideas: @icod, @belledechocolat, @badaude, @stupidgirl45, @Only WantsOne and others. They have my thanks.

I would like to mention by name a certain British diplomat, as well as the various intelligence and Special Forces officers, both British and Israeli, who gave me their views on the plot. For obvious reasons, I cannot. Nevertheless, they have my thanks.

Thanks also to Sha'anan Streett, Yaniv Davidson and Hadag Nahash, the best hip-hopsters in Israel, for allowing Uzi to listen to their music.

Finally I must acknowledge my family, particularly my wife Isobel and my three beautiful children. I'm lucky to have them.